Praise for Lilith Saintcrow

"Darkly compelling, fascinatingly unique. Lilith Saintcrow offers a breathtaking, fantastic ride."

—*NYT bestselling author Gena Showalter*

"Wow! This is a fast read. Mainly because I couldn't put it down."

—*Cheryl B, NetGalley reviewer on* Damage

"From cover to cover, I could not put this book down. So happy to be reading a new and exciting fast-paced series from Lilith Saintcrow."

—*Neal Bravin, NetGalley reviewer on* Sons of Ymre: Erik

"In the *Watchers* series, Saintcrow writes stories that are almost always nonstop action from beginning to end. Her women are kick-ass strong, her men ruggedly handsome and dedicated to the women they serve. It isn't a bad combination at all."

—*CJReading*

"I read *Dark Watcher* with growing delight. As chapter followed chapter, I never quite knew what was around the corner."

—*Ebook Reviews*

Of Dante Valentine. . . .

"Dark fantasy has a new heroine. . . ."

—SFX *magazine*

"Saintcrow snares readers with an amazing alternate reality that is gritty, hip and dangerously mesmerizing."

—Romantic Times *magazine*

"She's a brave, charismatic protagonist with a smart mouth and a suicidal streak. What's not to love?"

—Publishers Weekly

"This mind-blowing series remains a must-read for all urban fantasy lovers."

—*bittenbybooks.com*

Books by Lilith Saintcrow

The Watchers

Dark Watcher

Storm Watcher

Fire Watcher

Cloud Watcher

Mindhealer

Finder

The Sons of Ymre

The Sons of Ymre: Erik

Ghost Squad

Damage

Duty

The Society Series

The Society

Hunter-Healer

Other

The Demon's Librarian

Duty

by

Lilith Saintcrow

ImaJinn Books

IMAJINN

ImaJinn Books
PO BOX 300921
Memphis, TN 38130
Print ISBN: 978-1-61026-184-5

ImaJinn Books is an Imprint of BelleBooks, Inc.

ImaJinn Books was founded by Linda Kichline.

We at ImaJinn Books enjoy hearing from readers. Visit our websites
ImaJinnBooks.com
BelleBooks.com
BellBridgeBooks.com

10 9 8 7 6 5 4 3 2 1

Cover design: Debra Dixon
Interior design: Hank Smith
Photo/Art credits:
Background (manipulated) © Serge Novitsky | Dreamstime.com
Man (manipulated) © Romance Photos | Dreamstime.com

:Ldsf:01:

Dedication

For Brenda Chin, a true survivor.

Epigraph

Don't it make you want to go home?

—Joe South

Note

The reader is warned that some locations in this book do not exist. Others have been altered out of all recognition, and no similarity to persons living or dead is intended.

Good Luck

WHOEVER SAID *YOU can't go home again* was more expressing a fond wish than an actuality, Paul Klemperer thought, and wished the kid behind him would stop kicking the seat. Not that he blamed the tyke; everyone had to find whatever amusement they could in the world.

It was a daily struggle, that was for damn sure.

The only thing more terrifying than being sardine-packed into an aluminum tube hurtling through the atmosphere was how *normal* everyone around him considered it. He'd prefer a slick dropping him in-country—except he wouldn't, because that would mean a high chance of flying lead, and he'd caught enough of that to last him a lifetime. The chunk taken out of his left leg, close enough to the femoral artery to make it a miracle he was still breathing, left behind a scar full of relentless ache and a strange unsteady sensation when he thought about it too deeply.

He couldn't even shift uncomfortably in his too-small seat, because the elderly lady in the middle was miserably squeezed between his window seat and a beefy businessman on the aisle. It was enough to make him wish he'd paid for first class.

The lady had a cap of fluffy white perm-curls, a tartan purse clutched with thin liver-spotted hands to her chest through takeoff and the entirety of the flight, and a faint powdery smell of some grandma cologne. She was just a bitty thing, too, and each time the businessman burped, farted, or complained she flinched.

It was enough to make Klemp want to reach over her and thwap the suit-wearing idiot on the back of his expensively oiled head, but they frowned on that sort of thing while flying commercial. The alternative was to get up, force himself past Grandma's spindly knees, and punch the asshole into the aisle, then pick him up and toss him out of one of the emergency exits at thirty thousand feet—which might have been therapeutic for a soldier with anger-management issues, but would cause more problems than it solved. Or so Dez would say, and the good CO would probably show up to bail Klemp out of stockade with that faintly disappointed expression he wore when Boom got his hands on chemicals he shouldn't or Jackson started talking about "exact application of force."

The plane rattled; the old lady stiffened. A pair of bifocals dangled from an obviously handmade beaded pink-and-white holder onto her thin chest, and if her feet had reached the floor she might have pushed them down hard, like a green grunt on his first drop or a high school driving instructor trapped in the passenger seat while some enthusiastic child learned how to pilot a car.

"It's all right," Klemp said. "Just a little turbulence, ma'am."

She gave him an agonized look and a tight smile, her faded blue eyes bright with fear. It was enough to make a man feel like a Boy Scout.

The businessman loosened his tie, and his elbow whapped the lady from the other side with a jolt. Klemp swallowed a bright scarlet burst of anger, scrunching himself further against the window and looking out. It gave him the willies to see the curvature of the earth in the distance, but the trees crowding the swiftly rising terrain below meant they were close to their destination.

If this was a combat drop Tax and Grey would be compulsively checking gear one last time, Boom stretching his legs out but keeping his arms folded like a genie preparing to grant a wish, Dez listening to the squawk box, and Jackson would probably be asleep—or faking it; the fucker even pretended to be out cold while Klemp was driving, and *that* was almost a personal insult. Klemp's job, of course, would be to crack a few dirty jokes to keep everyone distracted and on an even keel, and Dez might even give faint evidence of a smile once or twice if he hit a good one.

If you had to go rappelling or 'chuting into hostile territory to do some hush-hush murder or mayhem for good ol' Uncle Sam, they were the crew to do it with. Nobody would ever know—that was what *black book* and *classified* meant—but Klemp had finally decided it was a blessing. Let the civilians have their illusions and the journalists their protests; he'd settle for a few good buddies who knew the cost of "freedom."

The kid behind him kicked the seat again, someone coughed like they had the plague, and the little old lady was finally moving, digging in her purse. The intercom crackled, the pilot's voice like God in an old Charlton Heston movie.

"Ladies and gentlemen, we are about to begin our descent to Portland International Airport. Please make sure all seat backs and tray tables are in the

upright and locked position. . . ."

Yeah, he should have paid for first class, and flown into Eugene instead. At least then he could've been mildly drunk and itching instead of stone-cold sober and attempting to think of a way to give the suit in the aisle seat a manners lesson.

"Stick of gum?" a dry cricket-whisper said to his right, and Klemp almost twitched.

The old lady had extracted an anemic pack of Juicy Fruit from her purse and blinked up at him hopefully, her tentative smile exposing strong teeth only faintly yellowed with age. Looked like Grandma believed in flossing.

"For the pressure," she continued, and her hand shook slightly. "Easier on your ears, young man."

"Sure." He extracted a stiff, dry rectangle from the package, hoping he wouldn't break her—those frail fingers bore a suspicious resemblance to dry sticks, and had the painful flipper-curve of rheumatism besides. "Thank you, ma'am."

"Military?" Though she was tiny and probably scared out of her wits, no moss grew on this dame; the hesitant half-smile tiptoeing through a forest of dry wrinkles said she'd seen it all and was mostly amused by every blessed part. "Reason I ask is, you're real polite."

"Try to be, ma'am. The Army insists." The plane bounced again as he unwrapped the gum; attendants were coming down the aisle once more, making sure everything was stowed. "You ever been to Oregon before?"

"Visiting grandchildren." She attempted to extract another stick, but the businessman shifted on her other side. The super-sized suit shoved his elbow into the aisle just in time to brush against a female attendant's hip—a redhead, cute and perky in uniform, with wide hazel eyes and a snub nose—and the plane jolted again.

God damn it. Klemp's hand blurred out; he caught the pack of gum as it attempted a leaping escape from the old lady's tentative grip. "Careful, ma'am. Here, let me."

"Oh, my stars." She sucked in her bottom lip, those blue eyes widening, and the flash of what she must have looked like when young was gone in a moment, like lightning over the hills back home. "You're quick."

"Just like playing baseball." He extracted another stick, and in short order they were both chewing nasty-ass dried sugar full of preservatives as the plane began to descend.

She pointed her toes, clad in sensible nurse shoes with thick soles, and leaned into his shoulder to get away from the suit. Klemp watched the ground get closer and closer, taking its sweet time. *I'd go with you,* Dez had said, *but Cara and Eddie—*

Don't, Klemp had answered. Cara was a doll, as ol' Footy Lenz would have said, and the little boy obviously thought Vincent Desmarais hung the moon. They needed him at home, and Paul Klemperer was a goddamn grownup. It was only a family reunion after a life-threatening wound putting him out to pasture, not a trip into hell requiring covering fire. Besides, he was the jokester of the Squad. This would all make a good story once he was back with the guys.

Except Dez was retired now, or so close it made no difference. Boom was getting married in a month and change, not to mention jumping through the paperwork hoops to retire as well, Tax and Grey were both on mandated medical leave for combat stress, and who the hell knew what Jackson was doing? Klemp wasn't about to go back into another round of duck-for-cover-and-kiss-your-ass-goodbye with a commander who *wasn't* Dez and guys he didn't know, and there was no use bitching over it.

The squad was scattered, no rendezvous set. All good things came to an end, and here he was falling to earth at high speed in a tin can while a lady old enough to be his dead grandmother closed her eyes, her thin dry lips moving as she prayed.

He was trying like hell to find the funny side, but it was a losing game like everything else. Klemp made his shoulder a rock for the poor lady and kept chewing.

REACHING THE ground without turning into a fireball was always good luck, but the suit in the aisle seat was a jackass all the way through taxiing to the gate, not to mention disembarking. Klemp got his elderly neighbor's wheelie-bag down from the overhead bin he'd stashed it in when they loaded up in Las Cruces, and even winked at the seat-kicking little bastard in the row behind them. His own carry-on was a ditty, familiar as his own limbs, and his leg wasn't hurting too badly.

Getting off the damn plane was a relief. He spotted the suit hurrying away, obviously intent on baggage claim and inconveniencing someone else, not necessarily in that order. For a bare second Klemp thought about it—trailing the fellow, finding a good spot to get the jump, a quick shot to the kidneys, get the skull cradled just right and *twist*, and *voila*. The asshole wouldn't be elbowing old ladies or pawing young ones ever again, thank you and goodnight.

But the grandma and her tartan purse were greeted by a heavyset man with her blue eyes and proud nose, who almost lifted her out of her sensible shoes as he hugged. His wife, beaming while she dandled a five-year-old little bit in a flowery pink dress on her hip, crowded close for an embrace while an older kid in blue Converse, denim overalls, and a red shirt stuffed some kind of electronic game in his pocket and threw his arms around Grandma, worming in and burying his face in her ribcage. They made a solid unit, and half of Klemp's mouth twisted up in a grudging smile.

"Paulie!" someone yelled, the crowd of meet-and-greet parted, and there was his Aunt Helena, tall and spare, her greying hair pulled back in a tight thin ponytail and her well-worn cowboy boots ready to sink into someone's backside if they gave her any sass. "Took your damn time, dintcha?"

She threw her lean, iron-strong arms around him, and because going to the airport was an Occasion she'd put on a dab of White Shoulders. The familiar scent enfolded Paul, mixed with a breath of cut grass, fresh air because she'd been driving with the windows down, harsh fabric softener on her red plaid flannel shirt, the Head & Shoulders she used religiously though she'd never had a flake in her life, and the ever-present dry rasp of cigarette smoke—Paul inhaled gratefully, and relief he'd never admit to was a fragburst in his belly.

He'd been sure nobody would bother to come pick him up, even if it was his first trip home since leaving for basic. Getting shot up and almost bleeding out on a slick's metal deck made a man think about family; it was inevitable as gravity or a noncom getting his tighty-whities in a bunch.

"Hey, auntie." Klemp wrapped an arm around her waist and lifted, hoping his leg wouldn't buckle; she made a short, hoarse, delighted sound as her feet left the ground, and this was probably going to be the only pleasant thing about returning to the ol' homestead. "I thought about hijacking the plane, but that wouldn't make it go faster."

"Christ, don't say that in the airport." She leaned back in his arms, examining him critically. "You'll get both of us arrested, you little asshole."

"Free showers and three squares a day," he fired back. "Sounds like a good deal." So far, he was doing all right.

Or at least, so he thought, until someone else laughed, clear and low and husky, and he saw who was trailing behind Helena.

Oh, God.

Social Purgatory

GET OUT OF THE house for the day, Helena had said; *it'll do you good,* she said. Hel Klemperer was getting on in years, and if she had a trip to the Portland Ikea in mind it behooved Rebecca Sommers to go along, lifting and hauling—because Beck had, in Granite River parlance, been Raised Right, even if her momma took off when she was just a sprout.

Besides, getting out of that goddamn hole of a town and into a city, if only for a few hours, sounded like heaven even if the only thing on offer was the meatballs in a Swedish furniture megastore's cafe. And, to top it all off, she was living on Aunt Hel's charity, so she had to pitch in.

But the Ikea was spitting distance from the airport, and Helena kept checking her phone—the same phone Beck did technical support on, since *the goddamn thing won't listen to an old lady like me*, Hel said, as if any piece of God's creation would dare to set itself against her will—every few minutes while wandering amid displays of beds, couches, kitchens costing a year's pay, and pillows in bright patterns. Beck should've known something was up, especially with the yearly Klemperer family reunion right around the corner.

She just hadn't thought Hel would be this overt. Everyone in Granite River had an opinion on the Sommers girl's life right now; she just had to bear with it.

So Beck smiled though her teeth threatened to grit like her father's when a malefactor temporarily escaped the long arm of the law, and she met Paul's dark, familiar gaze squarely. "Hi, Paul. Welcome home."

He set his aunt on her worn cowboy boots, steadying her rangy frame with thoughtless, habitual care. Ever since he got his growth spurt in junior high he'd moved like that, a bull suddenly in the middle of a china shop and cautious not to breathe too hard.

That boy was gone, though, and in his place was a muscular man with a growing-out mop of curly dark hair which obviously hated every moment it had spent under military supervision, a faded black T-shirt straining at his shoulders, equally faded jeans, and a pair of desert-taupe boots laced the way every other guy who'd escaped town by signing up to get shot at had theirs. He looked at Beck like she was something caught in the tread of said boots, and she didn't blame him one bit.

Her smile faded as they studied each other; Helena was outright beaming. She knew how to keep a secret, old Hel, but there was nowhere under heaven you could hide if she decided *not* to.

"Becks is helping me around the old place while her divorce goes through," the old lady continued, blithely, while Beck wished in vain for the earth to open and swallow her whole. It was getting to be a habit these days, along with nervously looking over her shoulder and jumping at stray sounds. "Come on, let's get going. Baggage claim is right down there."

"Only got carry-on." Paul hefted the ditty like it weighed nothing, still watching Beck like he expected her to shake a rattle and bite. "How's your daddy, Becks?"

"Still writing tickets." At least it was *Becks* and not *Mrs. Halston*, and he wasn't asking about Joe. Small mercies were the only ones ever granted. "You've had a long flight, I can carry—"

"Nah." He shouldered the bag, clearly unwilling to let her touch his belongings, and Helena was off and running again, grabbing his free arm. It was like watching a tugboat boss an airplane carrier, and Helena pulled her nephew past Beck with no further ado.

"We're stopping at the Pie Palace on the way." Hel's faded eyes shone with pride—of course, her prodigal was home for the first time since he'd left for basic training. Not only that, but he'd been wounded for his country, and her generation considered that far more honorable than making a good living and only slightly *less* honorable than dying for the Stars and Stripes. "We were just at the Ikea; you know they have everything there? Even towels and toilet scrubbers. Becks, honey, tell him about that kitchen we saw—they have whole *kitchens* in there—the one with the rails under the cabinets. Of course I'd have to rip out the old ones, but it's nice to think about. How was the flight? You get any peanuts?"

"They don't feed you on planes anymore." Paul let Helena drag him along; Beck drifted after them, watching her own black sneakers against heavily patterned carpet. Whoever had done the design in here evidently thought you wouldn't see the dirt of travel if you were too busy having an acid flashback. "Just pack you in like a sardine, and charge you for the kid kicking the back of your seat too."

"You coulda taken the train." Helena all but bounced; it was, Beck had to admit, really nice to see the taciturn old lady of the H & H

Wrecking Yard aflutter like a girl going to her first school social. "But then you'd be late for the party."

"Party?" Paul sounded wickedly amused, as usual. Looked like the Army hadn't killed his sense of humor; of course, he'd been born considering everything funny. In the old days, he'd always been up for a bit of mischief. "I thought you were gonna make me fix a couple cars and your sink, too. What's this party you're talking about?"

"Evil little boy. Your cousins keep asking me when you're gonna show up, and old Mabel Hutchins just called the other day asking if you still like carrot cake. As if *she* can cook anything without the fire department paying a visit; she'll probably get one from the new Costco in Parsburg."

"There's a Costco? Civilization at last. When you gonna move to a real town, Hel?" He didn't even glance back to see if she was following; Beck didn't know whether to be grateful or slightly insulted.

Hel kept downloading gossip all the way into the parking garage, and Paul eyed the new midnight-blue Jeep Cherokee for a few moments. Beck had Helena's keys since she'd navigated from Granite River, so she hit the locks and the hatch release; he hefted his bag in with a short exhale of effort. "Nice," he said, and shrugged his left shoulder, bringing some bloodflow back now that he was unencumbered. "But what happened to the truck?"

"Goddamn thing runs, but not well. That's your first project." Hel's grin was as wide as Beck had ever seen it, and she reclaimed her keyring with a flourish. "And *I'm* driving us home, Beck. If your daddy pulls us over, you can talk him out of a ticket."

Like he'll listen to me. But she had to put on a smile, because Paul was watching her again, that uncharacteristically somber expression drawing his mouth down. God help her if she pissed off his beloved aunt. Of course, God had been kind of stingy in the *help* department lately, but what did Beck expect if she didn't go to church?

"I'll do my best." It was enough that she'd escaped Joe, even halfway. As soon as he ran out of legal bullshit and the papers were signed, she was hell and gone. It didn't matter that she had no place to go.

Beck had made up her damn mind.

"We gonna rock, paper, scissors for shotgun?" Paul's capable, callused hands dangled, and she'd forgotten how his eyes had tiny flecks of gold in the darkness, and how he put out a colorless shimmer of heat even on warm days, a comfortably burning stove. For all that, he never really seemed to sweat.

"Oh, no." Beck's cheeks ached from the effort of wearing a pleasant expression. "You're the returned prodigal, you get shotgun duty. Besides, maybe you can make the radio work."

"It works just fine," Hel objected. The echoing concrete cavern of the parking garage was full of exhaust and a chill spring wind; of course, it was raining, a fine thin grey mist.

It was Portland, after all.

"It only plays country," Beck mock-whispered, and finally, *finally* Paul smiled. But he looked away immediately afterward, either unable or unwilling to grant her even that much.

Well, she couldn't blame him. After all, she'd married someone else.

"It plays all kinda music," Hel intoned solemnly. "Country *and* western."

"Christ." Paul scratched at the side of his neck, reaching up to pull-slam the hatch closed with just the right amount of force. "I should go get back on the plane."

Helena giggled. Beck escaped to the driver's side, clambering into the back seat and stealing the bare moment before everyone else piled into the Cherokee to take a deep breath. The flat-packs of new chairs and kitchen table Helena had selected after much dithering—waiting for the flight to come in, Beck now knew, and had to admire the sneak-iness—rested easily on the folded-down seat on the passenger side, smelling like raw lumber and fresh cardboard.

Tears stung her eyes as she dug in her cheerful, multicolored Tibetan sling bag for her own brand-new phone. More of Hel's charity, of course—Joe had "forgotten" to pay the bill on the old one and Helena had taken Beck into Parsburg, upgrading her own ancient flip-case and adding Beck to her phone plan for good measure.

Need one of the newfangled things anyway, the old lady had growled when thanks were attempted. *Shush, Becca. Figure out how to make this one work, will you?*

If not for Hel she'd be living with Dad, and while she loved her father she couldn't stand the pressure to go back to Joe. Connor Sommers meant well, of course, but he had no idea what Joe Halston was capable of.

Nobody did. Nobody but Beck, at least.

Doors opened and closed, the engine roused, and they were on their way, Hel still going a mile a minute and the radio thumping with some guy in a cowboy hat bewailing a lost love. Becks stared out the window, breathing deeply, swallowing hard, and grateful to be ignored.

IF THERE WAS such a thing as Purgatory, it probably consisted of an hour-and-a-half drive with the radio crackling twang-and-drang, your semi-landlady smoking like a Virginia Slim chimney, and your ex-boyfriend in the front seat joking with his favorite aunt while ignoring the hell out of you. It was only what Beck deserved, and even the stop at the Pie Palace—normally a treat her childhood self might have cheerfully stabbed someone for—was an exercise in endurance. Fortunately it was also a bathroom stop, so she could lock herself in a stall and let go for a few seconds, weeping silently into cupped hands before clapping a lid sternly on her stupid emotions and blowing her nose on single-ply toilet paper.

*Un*fortunately, though, as soon as she came out Helena left them both in the line with a stern admonition to remember she wanted a banana creme *and* a lemon meringue, thrust her wallet into Beck's hands, and took off to the restroom herself, leaving Beck and Paul standing awkwardly in a crowd of strangers.

Paul, slightly bloodshot after a long flight, studied what he could see of the menu over the long, sparkling glass counter. Business was good on a Friday afternoon; at least they'd missed the rush getting out of Portland. Another half hour would see them home.

What a ridiculous word, *home*. But Beck had to get used to being a guest everywhere she went; she wondered if her mother had felt this way in Granite River all those years ago. Did she ever think about the daughter she'd left behind?

God knew Beck brooded about it, every damn day. But Annelise Sommers had vanished, shaking the dust of the tiny town she'd been trapped in by love and pregnancy from her pretty big-city feet. No Christmas cards, not a single birthday card, nothing but silence.

She'd been too good for Granite River, and Beck was thinking she had the right idea.

"So," Paul finally said. "Uh, how's Joe?"

I wouldn't know. "Still working for my dad." Beck suppressed a shrug. "I'm staying with Helena for a while, waiting for all the paperwork to be finished. It's only temporary, I promise. As soon as. . . ." Thankfully the line moved, so she didn't have to continue. She could pretend her own fascination with the Pie Palace menu.

The place was still the same, a cross between fifties diner and bougie bakery; the line was out the door. Kids fidgeted with excitement, every booth was packed, but the *real* joy of the Palace was getting paper cups of coffee and a slice to go. Skipping school to drive to Parsburg was a time-honored Granite River tradition, and it usually ended up in Riverside Park with plastic spoons full of pie and maybe, if you were lucky, a little necking in the front seat. Chrome gleamed, employees in striped shirts bustled, and the good deep smell of baking sugar filled the entire place, spilling out into a damp grey parking lot starred with ornamental saplings and bushes bearing heavy new green buds.

"I'm glad you're there. She's getting older." Paul eyed her sidelong. It was almost like being in high school again, but of course, then they'd be holding hands. Did he still close his eyes when he kissed, or. . . .

Don't think about that. "She's in great shape though." Jesus, small talk was exhausting. But Beck had dues to pay, and Sheriff Sommers's daughter never let those mount up any interest. "Doc Hardaway says she's healthy as a horse. Probably outlive the rest of us."

"Yeah." His dark eyebrows drew together; he must have been on vacation from the Army for a while, because his hair almost hung in his eyes. He shook it away with a restless motion, and for a moment he looked just like he had years ago when contemplating something he truly disliked, like asparagus or a mention of his father. "But really, Beck, is she okay? And what about you? How are you doing?"

"She's slowed down a bit." The line moved again; maybe God was throwing her a bone in return for silent suffering. "But the wrecking yard's still going and she's in good shape. I'm trying to get her to quit smoking, but you know how that is."

"Yeah." There was a crash and tinkle of broken glass, a ripple of excitement; he flicked a glance over his shoulder, zeroing in on the noise. "Cleanup on aisle five."

The old joke hit her right in the stomach, just like one of Joe's casual suckerpunches. At least Paul wasn't being rude, just distant—and, she reminded herself for the umpteenth time, he had every reason to be. "Here." She handed him Hel's wallet and keys. "I'll be outside. Remember her banana creme."

He couldn't very well protest, and she made her escape. Even if she had to stand in the drizzle waiting, she could say she just needed some air. Her throat ached, her eyes prickled, and the urge to start screaming was well-nigh overwhelming. Luckily it was only fifteen minutes or so before he and Hel came out with a stack of pie boxes, and by that time Beck was in charge of herself again, rain-damp but ready for the rest of the drive home.

Familiar, Strange

THERE WAS PROBABLY a word for the weird double-exposure of visiting the place you'd grown up in, especially when it was a tiny burg tucked next to a river that used to carry away the effluvia of a now-closed and rotting textile mill. Jackson would probably know the precise term, albeit in German; Grey would call it *nostalgia* because he was into the five-dollar vocabulary lists too. A soldier was supposed to be at home anywhere, and really, if you weren't getting shot at, did you have any right to complain?

Even his own place in New Mexico, neat and tidy with beer in the fridge and Jacinta the concierge—they didn't call it that in the States, but the old woman, like Hel, made her own rules—glowering downstairs felt more like a stage set than a "home," albeit a comfortable one where he could lay his hand on a weapon at any moment.

Jet lag was dragging at his arms and legs, but Helena's fried chicken was just as tasty as ever and a good solid lump of it along with garlic mashed potatoes and a double helping of Pie Palace lemon meringue rested right behind his breastbone. Hel's manufactured home, at the end of its long gravel driveway, still snuggled companionably near the junk-yard's high fence topped with razor wire, though there was a new gate and actual security cameras. *Damn kids,* Hel said balefully, but Paul caught Beck's tiny grimace and shake of her pretty honey-blonde head, and figured that even though weed was legal now, the old drying sheds were still tucked among the rows of shattered, quietly rusting vehicles plundered for parts or just rotting into oblivion on their own terms.

Granite River had a few improvements—the elementary school had a new roof, a tiny espresso stand crouched proudly next to Sandra's Ice Cream Parlour on the two-lane loop on the way into downtown, and instead of plywood and broken glass on said downtown's facades there were a couple tourist-dependent attempts at gentrification, new arrivals with more money than sense thinking a small town meant *start over* instead of *morass.*

Oh, plenty was still the same—the Kwik-Kleen laundromat on the corner of Schillsterne Avenue, the dirt roads curving close to the railroad and veering off at the last second, the trampolines in weedy yards and the Safeway parking lot turning to an empty grassy lot at one end, not to mention the sense of pursed-mouth disapproval emanating from First Methodist and the slightly newer but still just as unforgiving Light of God Baptist. Chapper Hardwick's gas station was now a spanking-new Chevron, but Beaujolais Auto Repair was still in operation across from Sandra's, the stop sign holding an uneasy truce between them while the new espresso stand looked on. And this side of town was still the bad one; already this evening he'd heard the rumble of railcars both Hel and Beck ignored, familiar to them as their own breath.

He'd just lost the trick of unhearing it.

And then there was Rebecca.

Same quiet green eyes, thickly lashed. Same straight patrician nose, same high cheekbones, same wavy honey hair, just past her shoulders and layered instead of hanging almost to her waist. The pretty girl had turned into a knock-down drag-out stunner, but that wasn't any change; she'd always hit the breath clean out of him. Ever since fourth grade, as a matter of fact, when she'd kicked his shins on the playground and yelled *stop being mean!*

Same cupid's-bow mouth, now faintly chapped, innocent of any teenage lip gloss. She'd grown up, filled out, and though she could stand to eat a few more cheeseburgers, the curves on her just wouldn't quit. In school she'd worn some light cheap drugstore perfume. Now there was nothing but a faint breath of Hel's Dove soap lingering in her wake, and her fingernails weren't polished—used to be each was a different color, and how she loved the bright varnish—but bare and bitten savagely almost to the quick.

And she was right down the hall from Hel's guest room, using the pullout bed in the tiny annex Paul remembered smashing his thumb several times building onto the manufactured the summer before his freshman year. His father had sucked on can after can of beer while "supervising"; Paul and some of the cousins had done all the damn work. *Won't sleep in the guest room*, Hel had muttered to him on the porch, tapping a Virginia Slim into a green glass ashtray set next to a heavily painted yellow wooden rocking chair he remembered used to have a battered vinyl cushion instead of a new bright-red one from Ikea. *She's helping me in the yard and running that espresso stand for Mary Parrack, saving up.*

Beck wouldn't even *talk* to him. Probably barely remembered dating, as a matter of fact. Years ago, water under the bridge, and she didn't need to know that when he was getting his ass shot off in some hellhole, Boom swearing and Tax patching wounds while Grey and Klemp returned fire, Jackson doing his usual crazy shit and Dez wearing *that look* while he figured out how to get them out of yet another mess without casualties, the thing getting Klemp through was remembering a certain green-eyed girl's laugh, or the way she held her heavy hair up on a summer day, complaining about how hot it was while smiling ruefully.

Nobody needed to know that. What a man thought about when he was about to die was his own damn business.

Don't go, she'd said in the evening dusk years ago, her breath a sweet hot spot near his collarbone. *Just don't. Please.*

He'd already signed the recruitment papers, it was a done deal, and the fact that he'd planned on getting her a ring when he got out of Army basic was neither here nor there. He'd wanted it to be a surprise, but one thing led to another—he'd been tapped for "special training," then before he knew it Helena wrote telling him little Beck had married Joe Halston and Sheriff Sommers was like the cat that ate the canary because of it.

Well, live and learn. Joe was always hanging around, but Paul hadn't thought him quick enough to keep up with Becca Sommers.

Maybe he hadn't been, after all. Wasn't that what *divorce* meant?

Paul shifted; the bed squeaked slightly. It was the old iron bedstead from his father's trailer, and it made him uneasy. Same plaid comforter Helena always had in this bedroom, though, same slightly open window letting in a thin trickle of damp spring chill—it was a good thing he was used to weather changes, going from the desert to the Cascades was hard on the body. His ditty was in the closet, with the shotgun and the hanging blocks of cedar exhaling faint sweet perfume.

Hel believed in being prepared, and there was a thirty-aught-six right near the trim white-painted manufactured's front door too. She probably had a revolver on her nightstand as well.

Beck didn't like guns. Oh, she could plink with a .22, but her face always set with distaste when she did, and hunting with her daddy was a particular type of hell. Paul was hoping big bluff Connor Sommers wouldn't come by to say hello.

A train yowled in the distance, a big metal cat slinking along at midnight, and he dropped into a light doze. There'd been that one operation when they were inserted by boxcar, and Boom had found a harmonica somewhere.

Jesus, stop that shit, Dez had snarled.

Can't help it, Boom replied with a grin. *I got me a hobo's heart, Loot.*

Klemp smiled in the dark, wondering what his buddies were doing right now. That particular op had gone sideways as soon as they baled out of the moving train, and if *that* wasn't a metaphor for life, he didn't know what was.

Just as he was about to drop off completely, his body jolted, copper adrenaline coating his tongue and his heart leaping into overdrive. The bed squeaked again as he stiffened and his hand shot out, feeling for a gun that wasn't on the spindly oak nightstand because he'd flown commercial and left most of his gear at home. His breath came ragged and hot, sweat suddenly greasing every inch of him, and his leg gave a twinge.

Fucking hell, he'd said, *I'm hit.* And then the cottonwool fuzz of blood loss while Tax's face swam over his and Dez's tone took on that edge of *don't you fucking die on me, Klemp, or I will kill you myself,* and even Jackson started to look worried. . . .

He was rubbing at his left thigh, Klemp realized, running his fingers against layers of cloth covering the angry pink scar. *Medical leave,* they called it. What it really meant was *broken-down horse, ready for the glue farm.*

And now he was right back where he started, in Granite River. God *did* have a sense of humor, except it was more like Jackson's than Klemp's.

Soldiers normally didn't have trouble falling asleep—you learned how to flip the switch in basic, or you broke and washed out—but it took him two more tries that night, and he couldn't blame jet lag. In the end, he only got there by thinking about the annex, and wondering why pretty, bright, mischievous Beck had married Joe Halston, of all people.

And why she was so damn jumpy she couldn't even stand in line at the Pie Palace, or settle in her chair for Helena's fried chicken at dinner.

Set Terms

HER PHONE BUZZED at five a.m., but Beck was already awake and moving, the coffee burbling and Helena's breakfast ready at precisely five-ten so that when Hel appeared, blinking owlishly in her new, pink-plush velour bathrobe, the eggs and bacon were piping hot. Beck poured her benefactress's usual morning cup, added four rounded spoonfuls of brown sugar, and handed over the red NRA mug without a word.

No Sweet & Low, stevia, or other nonsense for Aunt Hel, by God. *It's either real or it ain't*, she was fond of muttering. At least with her first smoke of the day finished on the front porch, all she needed was a bit of caffeine.

Paul appeared in the kitchen at five-thirty, but by then Beck already had her coat on, her teeth tingling from mint toothpaste, and was on her way out. "There's bacon," she said over her shoulder as she grabbed her Tibetan sling bag, handling the balky front door with the speed of habit. "Eggs in the fridge, two pieces of bread in the toaster. Just push the lever."

"I know how to run a toaster," he mumbled, scratching at his stubble, and Hel's hoarse laughter followed Beck out onto the porch. It was going to do the old lady no end of good to have her favorite nephew back, for however long.

If Paul wanted Beck to make his eggs he should have been up earlier, but her conscience still pinched a little that morning. It was a familiar pang, barely noticeable. She didn't have nearly enough saved to get the hell out of Granite River and she was a burden on poor old Hel besides, so it behooved her to make herself useful.

The junkyard's "business car" was an ancient primer-spotted Taurus; Beck flat-out refused to take the Jeep and leave Hel home without reliable wheels. The sedan started reluctantly but without too much trouble, and she made it to the Coffee Tyme stand placed just at the edge of Sandra's Ice Cream Parlour's minuscule parking lot with a good ten minutes to spare.

If you're not ten minutes early, pumpkin, you're late. One of her father's chestnuts, old and hoary but still good.

Mary had closed up the stand yesterday; everything was in apple-pie order, including the new sixteen-ouncers. Beck got the big machine turned on, the till counted in, and everything was ready for the neon open sign to flick into buzzing life precisely five minutes before six.

Beck's boss, despite having a hard business head in other areas, didn't want her sole employee to open up earlier. *It's too dark at that hour,* she said when Becks tentatively advanced the idea that perhaps some of the truckers and construction workers driving through to reach sites in more-settled areas would see the sign and throw a few more dollars into the stall's coffer. *And too dangerous. Besides, six was early enough for my daddy, and it's early enough for me.*

There was no arguing with a Parrack, and Mary was doing her old acquaintance a favor besides. So Beck smiled, nodded . . . and turned on the sign five minutes before six, just because.

Besides, she'd seen the cruiser parked, windows dark and lights off, down the street on the other side of Jim and Molly Perkins's driveway. The county had come through and trimmed the dark, nasty holly hedge there, ostensibly so it wasn't a hazard but more likely because Jim Perkins was always writing letters to them about fixing potholes in Granite River instead of messing around with what he referred to balefully as "immanent domain, goddammit."

She wasn't wrong. A pair of sickeningly bright headlights flicked on, cutting through a faint misty dawn greying up the east and struggling through the harsh chill of early spring, and the cruiser roused. It swam silently for the tiny coffee stall—red-painted walls, cheerful white gingerbread accents, no restroom but you could use the one in Sandra's if you had to, barely enough room for Beck and Mary during the afternoon rush when the kids got out of the high school and the later one when the roughnecks were coming home for supper.

But it was a job, and the only one she could risk getting in this godforsaken town because Joe wouldn't dare mess with Mary even to hint that maybe it was best to keep Beck's hours to a minimum. In fact, everybody knew better than to piss off Mary Parrack. If Joe said anything but *yes ma'am* to that lady her nephews might get involved, or her uncle Craig.

Nobody wanted that, especially with both of Mary's brothers up-state. The Parrack boys had gone and gotten staties involved by crossing the California line, and it was mighty nice of Mary to be so understanding with Beck even if Dad's hands had been tied.

Once the staties got in the mix, the sheriff couldn't reach a quiet accommodation with a pair of local troublemakers to keep things neighborly.

Beck pushed the thick double-paned order window open, took a deep breath of damp, gravelly chill, and pasted on a neutral smile. The heater under the counter would take the edge off even the most frigid days, but she'd wait for the big, shining espresso machine to do its more gradual warming-up of the space.

It was better to wait and shiver a bit than to die of heatstroke come noon, when both machines *really* got going and the mist burned off too. They might have cloud cover all day, or might not.

You could never tell in spring.

"Hello, Becks." Blond, broad-shouldered Joe Halston rested his arm in the open cruiser window, a gleaming service watch on his thick wrist. His radio was turned down, not that there was likely anything happening in town at the moment, and he'd put on a dab of English Leather. He even smiled, and with his blue eyes open and warm like this, it was hard to see why she'd left. Oh, if you were from out of town and just going a bit over the speed limit, he might even be charming.

But the polite affability was a trap. There was always a cold spot in those waters, just waiting to shock an unwary swimmer.

"Deputy Halston." Beck killed the urge to fold her arms defensively, or to push her shoulders back. "What kind of coffee do you want?"

"Jesus. You don't have to be like that." He reached for his wallet, leather creaking as his belt shifted. That sound was as familiar as her own breath; it was her daddy hanging up his paraphernalia at night or taking his little girl for hot dogs in his own cruiser, the slight metallic sound of handcuffs and the jingle of keys, the big self-satisfied scent of men with short haircuts and live ammunition, an encyclopedic knowledge of traffic codes and the power to do whatever they felt like as long as some lawyer down the line didn't get their panties in a wad. "Drip, then. You got any scones?"

"Blueberry and plain." Beck didn't move. "What size drip, Deputy?"

"Will you cut it out? I'm trying to be nice, Beck."

Really? I thought you were just being very clear that you can find me any time you want to. "What size?"

He eyed the painted board of prices, and the flush had started on his neck. "Twelve ounce. Put a little sugar in it, willya?"

"You get two sugar packets. Or Sweet & Low." Beck's palms were damp, and she was very, *very* glad for the stall's walls. Sure, he could send the cruiser right through siding, two-by-fours, and drywall, but that would attract a whole lot of attention—and paperwork.

The most nerve-wracking time was right before she reached the stand's side door, because she had to park behind Sandra's and walk along the building. In predawn gloom and rain, it would be very easy for someone to simply appear while she was busy unlocking, and—

"But you know I like it sweet." Joe grinned. And God, now she was doubting herself all the way to Portland and back, because he sounded so innocent, so even-tempered.

But her heart was pounding, the fine hairs on her nape were tingling, and her vision threatened to turn into a pinhole. "My boss says two," Beck said steadily. The way to handle someone like this was to go grey-rock, she'd read. Make yourself uninteresting, and hope the predator would find something else to chase.

"Daddy's girl, always following the rules." Joe's smile widened. Looked like he was back to the Crest strips at night. Maybe he was hitting the gym over on Pleasant Vale Road twice instead of once daily, too, lifting iron while giving his opinion about perps and his ex-wife.

Soon-to-be ex-wife. God, she couldn't wait.

She punched the right buttons; the drip part of the big silver machine went to work like a spaceship cleared for takeoff. And Joe just sat there, smiling.

Waiting.

Her throat threatened to close. If she handed a drink through the window he could grab her wrist. Sure, this was a public place . . . but at this hour, if anyone came by all they would see was a sheriff's deputy getting some morning java, or maybe a jolt to get him home after a long night spent punishing evildoers. Even her father wouldn't find anything to fault his shining hope of a son-in-law for.

Beck had made the mistake, once or twice, of thinking *public* meant *safe*.

So she stayed silent while she poured twelve ounces of fresh drip coffee, making sure the sleeve protector was snugged tight and putting the cap on with more than her usual care. Two packets of sugar went on top, and she paused before setting the cup on the small metal shelf for lower-slung sedan windows rather than passing it directly across at SUV or truck height. "There you go. Two dollars even."

"Man, remember when coffee was fifty cents?" He tried to hand her a five, but she stayed well back, so he had to lay it down on the shelf. She whisked the bill away while he took his drink, a maneuver practiced so often as to be fairly instantaneous, and the cash register woke with a buzz and a rattle. "Hey, where's your tip jar?"

Not out yet. "It's around here somewhere," she said, vaguely, and now she had to give him his change. Already there was a prickling of sweat at the small of her back, and her knees were a little shaky. A restless night, no breakfast, and now this. "Three dollars is your change. Have a nice day."

"You said blueberry scones?"

You know I did. Or maybe he was treating her like a perp, forcing repetition to trip someone up in a story. She'd listened to her dad talk about questioning lawbreakers so often, she could recite the basic principles in her sleep. "Blueberry and plain," she repeated, taking care to make the words as flat and uninterested as possible.

"Well, maybe next time." He paused, settling his coffee in the drink holder. "You know, I can't keep your plants alive, Beck. That begonia thing on the front table's looking a little rough."

Of course it hurt. He was probably talking about the finicky velvet-red wizard coleus, the one she'd nursed from a two-inch cutting. Leaving it behind—plus the African violets, her beloved monstera, the ficus, and dear God, the aloe—was like abandoning hostages to a terrible fate. He was probably watering them with drain cleaner.

Assuming he could even *find* the drain cleaner.

Sometimes you had to leave things you loved, no matter the pain; it was a lesson she'd learned even before Joe Halston. Beck's teeth ached, because her jaw was clenched hard. Nobody else would hear the threat in his pleasantries, or believe her if she tried to explain it.

But Joey's so nice. Sure, he broke Tommy Lorton's leg, but that was a pickup football game, and so long ago, and look at how his older brother turned out anyway, it's a shame. Sure, Joe's a little picky about some things, but he's one of those law-and-order types, they're just that way. He's a good guy.

Even her father. *Pumpkin, what the hell? You could just talk to him, you know. Why won't you talk? It's all he wants.*

Everybody wanted to fucking *talk.* Nobody cared enough to actually listen, including her gruff, loving, but distant and puzzled father. Even Hel didn't want to know the ugly details—not that Beck could be induced to give them.

What was the point? So Becks simply shrugged, when what she really wanted to do was howl.

I won't tell a single person about it, Joe. Just leave me the fuck alone. God knows you're more interested in Amy Lorton anyway, as you so often reminded me.

That wouldn't get her anywhere. If she could just hold on, just get through this interaction, she might make it through the rest of the day as well.

It would be nice.

"I mean it," Joe persisted. "You could just come on home, Beck. We can talk about it. Hell, you can even keep working here if you want."

As if getting a job was some kind of gift she should be grateful for. As if he wouldn't start, bit by bit, dismantling her again.

Joe apparently thought he had her on the ropes, though. "We can even do that couples therapy you talked about. There's a place over Parsburg way, or we can go to Eugene if you want."

The thought of being trapped in a car with him for an hour, enduring his aw-shucks getting a therapist on his side, being ganged up on, then driving back while all the air leaked out of the car and she tried frantically to comb over every single change in his expression or breathing to find out when the explosion was going to be—Jesus, no thanks.

Beck just shrugged again. *I'm a pebble*, she repeated. *Just a tiny piece of grey gravel. Nothing to look at here. Nothing interesting. For Christ's sake leave me alone.*

"Come on, Beck." Soft and reasonable, his most winning tone. "You've gotta come home sooner or later."

He might be right. Still, Beck was going to reserve the definition of *home* to herself, like a judge on the bench. In this one small way, she could set the terms.

And they did *not* include going back to the trim little frame house on Passacola Street. Ever.

Some mornings were worse than others. This one, however, held a gift—another pair of headlights, a big green truck slowing as it came off the straight highway shot onto the downtown loop, bumping over cracked concrete and plainly heading for the coffee shack instead of the arthritic, antique gas pumps in front of Sandra's. They all still called it the Parlour, even though it sold all and sundries, not just ice cream anymore. It was how you knew someone was a local instead of a tourist.

Of course Sandra's was a glorified pit stop, like the rest of this fucking place. The more Beck thought about it, the more she knew her mother had the right idea decades ago.

She just wished Mom had taken her daughter along. The old sense of injustice rose to choke her, and that was the last thing she needed.

"Looks like I've got to get to work," she said, as neutral and even as possible. "Enjoy your coffee."

For a brief moment the flush rose from his neck to his close-shaven cheeks, his lip curled up, rage glittered in his blue eyes, and the other Joe—the one she knew, the one she suspected more than one perp had glimpsed—peeked through her soon-to-be-ex-husband's mask.

He grabbed his change from the shelf, dropped the cruiser into gear, and got out of the truck's way. Beck's hip hit the counter next to the tiny dishwashing sink; she let out a soft, shaky exhale before the truck's window rolled down and Gracie Molyneux, her reddish hair coiffed to heavenly perfection and her scarlet nails redone every week in Luella's Beauty Salon, grinned like a hyena.

"Mornin', Beck," she warbled, then began listing the drinks for the boys over at Molyneux's at high speed. God help Beck if she made the lady repeat herself.

So Beck listened, her hands already moving, telling the sour metal in her mouth and the pounding in her throat and wrists they would have to wait their turn. Joe had made his point, and she might have a few hours without being reminded of her problems.

That morning, it was enough.

Long Time Ago

THE H & H AUTO & Wrecking Yard was never what could be called a thriving concern, but at least it broke even—in one way or another. The property was valuable, and the business was grandfathered in under environmental regulations.

Not that anyone in the area would file a complaint. There were better things to do, even in Granite River.

When Uncle Herrold had been alive, the long low shop building against the southern fence where he rebuilt engines and conducted many a handshake deal hummed with activity all day long. And, often, half the night. Now, his sister kept two of the bays neat and tidy, and occasionally yanked a few parts from the rusting piles inside the fence for friends or desperate locals. Shiny new razor wire topped said fence, probably the single greatest investment in the place for about a decade, and Paul rolled out from under the ancient, faded blue Chevy truck.

"Did you not even change the oil while I was gone? Jesus, Hel."

"It still runs. Just not well." His aunt had settled on a stack of bald, ancient tires near the open bay door, hunching birdlike shoulders under her corduroy shop coat and blinking at a damp spring day. A few stray gleams of sun were working through thick cloud, and the smell—rotting leaves, wet black Oregon dirt, firs and balsam, gasoline and motor oil, old metal, upholstery breathing sun-scorched halitosis, all mixed together—all conspired to shout *hey, Paulie, remember this?*

Even the smooth concrete floor of the shop, quilted with tiny cracks and dyed deep with the sheen of spilled oil, not to mention splattered with paint so often the colors ran together into brownish mud, was an old friend. His father had sometimes put in shifts here, but generally quit after a shouting match with Hel.

I don't need your charity or your advice, Helena.

If Dad had bothered to listen once in a while, maybe he would've made it a few more years. Or at least lived in some comfort, rather than the ratty old falling-down trailer off the ass end of Old Marckola Highway, near where it jointed up to I5.

But no, the bottle had too hard a grip on Peter Klemperer, and what it didn't grasp his temper shattered.

"It runs, sure, but it won't *go* anywhere. Not until I get new belts on it and. . . ." Paul rolled back under for a moment—the old wheelie, its heavy-duty casters freshly oiled, was a lot better than any of the ones they sold nowadays. It should be, since Uncle Herrold had built the damn thing on the counter at the other end of the shop, amid hunching shapes shrouded in paint-spotted canvas tarp. Some of the machinist's helpers would sell for more than the shop itself, especially on the internet, but good luck with shipping. "At least there's no computers in this beast, like that new Cherokee. And why the hell is Beck driving the Taurus? The muffler's about to fall off."

"*You* try talking that girl into anything else." Hel had lit another of her damn Virginia Slims; perched on the stacked tires with her fleece-eared hunting cap on, she looked at least ten years younger. A strangely wizened child, she kicked her cowboy boots as she settled, clearly intending to supervise her nephew for at least a short while. "Way I recall, you had a gift for it back in the day."

Oh, for Chrissake. He slid out from under the truck again, thankful he wasn't on a flattened cardboard box or folded tarp. He'd worked on some bastard engines under some deplorable conditions; this was damn near a holiday. "Belts. Oil change, needs a lube job. Probably should take a look at the carb too. This thing's almost as old as I am."

"She's getting divorced." Helena took another drag. "Joe won't sign the papers, of course, but I think she'll outlast him. Even her daddy can't get her to reconsider."

"That's a new thing," he muttered, curling up to sit. The wheelie squeaked, his leg gave a twinge, and he suppressed a highly obscene term you could only let loose in the Army, not around a lady.

A thin, troubled silence filled the shop. If he didn't give a damn what Beck did, he would have already made a joke and Hel would have started filling him in on family gossip, not just town affairs. Instead, his aunt smoked, not bothering to lift her bright silver insulated travel cup, full of coffee probably tooth-rotting sweet, from its safe harbor against her skinny thigh.

She seemed a lot smaller than she had been, but then again, ever since he'd left she was just a cigarette-roughened voice on the phone, careful Palmer script on her regular letters, and a few pictures enclosed with birthday or Christmas cards.

Paul levered himself upright and grabbed for the hanging light hooked to the Chevy's open hood. There wasn't any mouse damage, thank God, Hel turned the key often enough to warn the little bastards away. "You can just spit it out, Hel."

The easiest thing, of course, would be to walk out to the highway and stick out his thumb. Even hiking with his ditty over-country to the Love's near Parsburg—or was it a Pacific Pride now? Truck stops were easy.

He could make it back to Portland or Eugene with little trouble, sleep in the airport while waiting for a flight, and be back in the good ol' Southwest, cleaning his apartment and waiting for dinner invitations at Dez and Cara's to impersonate a social life. There was drinking to be done, his stage-set apartment to rearrange—or maybe he could fly out to Vegas and tell Boom *I'm here early to help with the wedding.*

His buddies wouldn't ask questions, but Dez would get another one of his *looks*, and Boom would start wearing that worried line between his eyebrows. The last thing either of them needed was trouble from Klemp's direction.

"She coming to the reunion?" he said, finally. There. That was an acceptable question, right?

"Not if she can get together enough cash to leave town beforehand, I suspect." Helena kicked her boots again. "That girl came over every day your uncle was in hospice, and after the funeral too. Brought me so many casseroles, land sakes."

I'm sorry I wasn't here. While Herrold was sinking under palliative morphine, lung cancer raving through his entire bony body, Klemp and his buddies had been attempting to stay alive, hiding in sandy filth and praying for extraction. Coming back to base to find Hel's letter—*He's gone, went real quiet with the opiates*—had barely made a dent until he came down out of the red.

None of the others had asked why he went on a world-class bender after that operation. Sure, getting shot at made a man want some chemical buffer, but he'd lined up the glasses like he intended to kill his liver all in one go instead of drip by drop. Jackson had been the one to haul him back to base and pour him into bed, Paul still adamant he could get a few more in but too hazed to do much more than swipe at the ghost-quiet motherfucker.

"It's good that she's here." He eyed the rest of the engine. It was burning oil like a bombed refinery, and given the way it ground when the key was turned he probably should peek at the starter too. He was looking at a few days' worth of work if he took it slow enough to suit him, more if there were other problems lurking in the engine.

"She held my hand all through the funeral, too. But didn't go to your daddy's. *I* didn't even go to that, though Bob Brockhill told me it was real nice." Helena shrugged. "He brought over the flag from the coffin."

"That was neighborly of him." Paul had to suppress a smile; the bachelor Brockhill was always looking to do Hel a service.

"He expected me to feel bad about it." His aunt made a short, irritated noise. "The man's like an old hen."

"Maybe he just wanted to see you, Hel."

"Oh, I'm sure." At least her laugh was the same—raspy, warm, the safest sound in the world for a boy whose daddy had been in the Navy and ran his sinking, sagging trailer like a martinet sentenced to a broken-down destroyer as punishment for sins both military and personal. "Like you came home just to see your old aunt and attend a Klemperer hootenanny."

Yeah, about that. . . . He couldn't say that almost bleeding to death and being farmed out on medical leave naturally made a man think of family. What would be the point? "Should hold it in summer."

"Then *nobody* would show up. Spring's best." Just like she'd said every other year; Hel had never forgiven half the family for not showing up the one time the reunion was held in June. "Paulie. . . ."

He had a bunch of people calling him that hated little childhood nickname to look forward to. "Couple weeks, Hel. Can't say past that."

"I've got the room." She studied the glowing tip of her cigarette. "It's about all I've got, these days."

"Careful, you're sounding like an old lady." He found a folded red shop-rag right where it should be and scrubbed at his hands. "You could come south and live with me. Always sunny."

She waved the suggestion aside, just as she always did. A thin ribbon of smoke followed her hand. "I hate sweating."

"I have air-conditioning, Hel. I'm not a barbarian."

"Then I might think you're not related." Finally, though, she was smiling. "You should invite Beck."

"Not sure she'd want to visit." *Or that her daddy will let her.* "It was a long time ago."

"Funny. That's exactly what she says."

She doesn't seem to say much at all these days. Oh, Beck handled the social niceties, all right—but she kept directing the conversation at Hel or at him, gracefully avoiding anything else.

Which was thought-provoking, all right, but Paul had all the provocation he could manage at the moment. "You could leave it at that."

"Really." Hel took another drag, then slithered off her perch, catching up her travel cup with a swift habitual movement. How often had she sat there chewing something over with Herrold?

Too many times to count, probably.

"Suppose I could," Hel continued, brushing at the seat of her work jeans. "But I never did know when to quit. Especially with stray cats. You remember Princess?"

"How could I forget?" The cat, at first a dirty grey until Herrold washed her—losing a bit of flesh *and* blood in the process—turned out to be pure white from nose to tail-tip, with one baleful blue eye. A gorgeous creature, but only Helena had seen the potential in a shivering, manky, run-over kitten from a box on the side of Karkoe Road.

His aunt was the type who would carry stranded turtles across a freeway, disregarding her own life and limb to set a stupid reptile in cool tall grass, plucked from incomprehensible danger and saved through no fault of its own.

"That was a long time ago too." Helena stubbed her Virginia Slim out in a tall silverish ashcan that had never, in Paul's memory, been emptied. It just sat next to this particular bay door, solidifying year after year. "Still miss that cat. Never had a rat problem when she was here. Or voles."

For a one-eyed ball of fluff, Princess was a great hunter. It was a source of constant family wonderment, Hel listing the newest gruesome death for every nephew and cousin with deep relish.

"Good thing Becks isn't missing an eye." As soon as he said it, the joke fell flat.

Some were like that.

"Shoulda seen her when she got here," Hel shot back, turned on one booted heel, and headed for the house.

Which left him rubbing at his hands with the shop-rag, smearing oil and car-dirt around instead of taking it off the skin, and wondering just what condition Beck had been in when Hel decided another creature in her vicinity needed rescuing.

Heckuva Day

"CLEAN OUT THE JAR," perky blonde Mary Parrack said, opening the under-counter fridge and casting a practiced eye over its contents. "Looks like you had a busy morning."

"Must be the weather. Everyone needs caffeine." Beck took her time, spreading crumpled dollar bills and loose change across a small red plastic tray. She kept her entire body turned so Mary could glance over at any moment and check the tip-count.

Of course everyone asked some version of *you and Joe, huh?*, from Gracie Molyneux to stuttering, tongue-tied young Beavis McCall—the poor kid. Every time Beck talked to him, she wanted to say *forty bucks at the courthouse can change that name, Mac, and you won't have to put up with the bullshit.*

She didn't, though. Even well-meaning advice could be deeply unwelcome, and who knew that better than her?

"Take it all today." Mary straightened and glanced out the window, her chunky blue plastic earrings swinging. The three p.m. dead time was upon them. Most days Beck would go until six or seven, but it was a Tuesday, and that meant Mary took the afternoon shift. "God knows you earn it."

"That wasn't the agreement," Beck said, cheerfully enough. "Halfsies or nothing, Mary."

"Stubborn girl." Mary sucked at her top teeth for a moment, frosted lip gloss gleaming. At least working here didn't mean wearing a uniform *or* a nametag. It was the only job she could get without Joe making even more problems, and Beck's savings were pitiful.

As soon as the papers were signed, though, she could bolt from this godforsaken place. She finished dividing the morning tips strictly in half, Mary opened the register and transformed the coins into bills, and nobody had to go to the bank for ones or fives today.

Things were looking up. The Taurus didn't make any trouble about starting, and only backfired once when she accelerated onto Pamida Lane, near the defunct airstrip Yarley Bates was still attempting to sell.

The *For Sale Zoned Commercial* sign, old enough to be thinking about entering kindergarten, was looking as tired as she felt today.

The last gauntlet of the day was groceries. Hel called her order in weekly and Greg Finnegan at the Granite River Safeway had her card number on file, but Beck had taken over picking everything up. She scanned the parking lot carefully before walking in—no sign of a police cruiser, or of Joe's cherished, glossy red Ford half-ton.

Still, her heart beat thinly and she had to practice her smile in the rearview mirror for a few seconds before going in.

Same aisles, same canned Muzak, mostly the same linoleum. The place even *smelled* like it had during the two teenage summers she'd spent first bagging then checking—cardboard and plastic, old plywood, floor wax reapplied in eggshell layers, and a tang of spoiled dairy from the cases in back. The produce section had been redone and some of the flooring was being renovated, too—Greg thought corporate was using the entire place as a tax dodge, and Beck couldn't disagree.

Hel had added half-n-half to the list just that morning, so Beck had to go all the way to the cases in back to select a quart. And, of course, a squeaking cart hove into view just as she got there.

"Hey, Becks." Amy Lorton, her bangs frozen with hairspray, leaned on the cart's red push bar. She was flawlessly made up, as usual, from primer to finishing dust; her Uggs were spotless and her down-stuffed hunting vest the very pinkest of camo. A tiny golden heart hung on a whisper-thin chain, nestling just under the notch where her collarbones met the sternum, peeking out and glittering at Beck.

Who had one just like it tucked in the jewelry box upstairs, in the little blue frame house on Passacola. Joe probably even gave her the same speech when he handed over the small black velvet box. *Because you've got my heart, darlin'.*

Later, when the dimensions of the man she'd married turned clearly visible, Beck had quietly put the necklace away. Hard, small, and entirely impervious—the metaphor wasn't lost on her, especially the glitter that could fool an unwary onlooker into thinking it real gold.

"Hi, Amy." Beck's smile froze like a winter puddle; she let the heavy glass door swing closed with a thump. "How's your family?"

"Can't complain." Amy sized her up, head to toe, and the smirk on perfectly painted lips could have been maddening if Beck cared. "Tommy's working in Eugene. Lots of construction up that way now that winter's done."

"That sounds nice." She didn't give a rat's puckered ass, as Dad would say if he was sure Beck wasn't listening, what Amy's other brother was doing with his life. Still, it was better than talking about Joe. "Hel said your mom got a power recliner."

"Oh yeah, it helps with the arthritis, even got a heater in the cushions. We had to get . . . someone with a truck, to get it home." The tiny hesitation could have been gloating or the sudden consciousness of just who she was talking to.

In other words, Joe had helped, with that shiny red monstrosity of his. "That's good," Beck said, neutrally. "Give your mama my best, then."

"Sure thing." But Amy wasn't going to let her get away that easily. "Is it true? Paulie Klemperer's back in town?"

"For the reunion, yeah." Beck wished she'd waited another few minutes before coming into the store. She should have checked the lot for Amy's car as well as Joe's. "Hel picked him up at the airport yesterday."

If Joe found out *she'd* gone along, he'd ramp up his campaign. Every husband probably disliked their wife's ex-boyfriends, but hers had taken it to the *n*th degree. In school the two of them had been great friends, always getting into trouble together with or without Beck's help. But that was ancient history.

"Well. That must be nice." Amy's smirk intensified. Her purse, a knockoff Chanel, sat in the cart's front seat like the child she probably desperately wanted, its zippered top open and a wilted bunch of coupons, all neatly paper-clipped in different colors, peeking out.

The urge to take a few swinging steps, maybe throw the quart of half-n-half or a flat-out punch, filled Beck all the way to the top with clear red fury for a moment. Hard on its heels came bright blue shame, and her stomach rolled hard.

It wasn't fair to hope that Joe would suck Amy in and decide to let Beck go. "Helena's pretty happy." Hopefully her voice wasn't unsteady, and she wasn't shouting over the sudden rushing in her ears.

Amy's smile shifted a few degrees, hardening like cooked sugar. "Bet you are too."

"Me?" It wasn't hard to look baffled. "Hel's got me in the annex, I won't be seeing him much. But when I do, I'll tell him you said hi." She waved, turning sharply, and headed for the breakfast aisle. It was a straight shot from there to the checkout, and dreamy-slow Nan McKinnon, very proud of her red bagger's uniform, had spotted Beck on the way in so Hel's cart of groceries, kept in one of the back coolers until she could get in on Tuesdays to pick it up, would be waiting, neatly sorted and ready to be wheeled outside.

There. That was polite, right? Brightly colored cereal boxes turned into vivid smears on either side, but Beck kept going, one sneakered foot in front of the other. She didn't have nearly enough money saved, and the next hearing was Thursday. Each time, Joe had some new legal bullshit to gum up the works.

He was, after all, a cop. And what both of them were saving by not having lawyers involved—at Joe's request, naturally—she had to pay for in other ways.

"Well there," a pleasant baritone rumbled. "Hello, Miss Rebecca. Heckuva day, isn't it."

Speak of the devil. Beck froze near the section of breakfast shakes, trying not to feel like a teenager caught slacking. Her face felt frozen, but the accommodating smile was probably still there, a reflex every female learned early. "Hello, Judge Nelson. How are you?"

"Oh, gettin' by, gettin' by." Nelson, one of the two county justices handling most of the petty cases from Parsburg up north to Sinaida in the south, was a trim dapper bachelor, tall as Beck's father but considerably leaner. Steel-colored hair, neatly brushed, showed no sign of thinning like Connor Sommers's, though, and the judge wore a suit and tie even while off-duty. Some justices might wear shorts or pithy T-shirts under their robes, but Bugs Nelson—the nickname dated from his time on the Sinaida football team—was not one of *those*, no sir. "I hear Hel's hellraising nephew is back in town."

Of course everyone knew Paul had landed. Jungle telegraph had *nothing* on invisible small-town rumors. "Just flew in yesterday. I'll tell him you said hello."

"Might make him turn around and fly right back out." Nelson's wry grin was soothing, and he glanced down the aisle. If Amy Lorton saw him, she'd beat a quick retreat. "How's your daddy doing?"

"Fine, thanks." At least Beck could rely on this particular citizen of Granite River *not* to remark on her divorce. Judge Nelson was old-school. "You probably saw him earlier; isn't Tuesday the traffic docket?" It would explain why he was shopping at this hour; there must have been a paucity of disputed tickets and afternoon session didn't start until two-thirty.

"You remember that detail? I should have you clerk for me." Nelson shifted the basket on his arm. A whole chicken wrapped neatly in an extra plastic bag, carrots and celery, a bright-glowing lemon—looked like he had dinner all sorted out. "Any time you'd like to take the typing test, let me know."

"I'm dismal at typing," she lied. If she took a job in the legal system Joe would be all over her daily, not just whenever he could steal a few minutes from his own work. "But for you, I'd try."

"You're a good girl, Beck Sommers." Nelson nodded sharply, as if he was settling an argument in the ancient, creaking, wood-paneled county courthouse. "How's Helena holding up? Still got that junkyard running?"

Are you asking about the yard, or about the drying sheds? Well, what Beck didn't mention he wouldn't be called upon to do anything about, and if everyone in the town who grew—or processed--a little weed was hauled in there'd be nobody left to actually run the place. Plus, it was legal now. "Here and there. She keeps busy, and keeps me busy too. I'd better get her groceries home before the ice cream melts." *If Nan remembered to put the frozen stuff in, that is.*

"Can't have that. Say hello to your daddy for me, and to . . . well, to little Paul and to Helena." To his credit, the judge even looked faintly chagrined. He'd been about to say *and to Joe.*

"Will do." She pasted on another smile, hoping she'd be able to get out the door with a minimum of small talk.

But first, she had to endure patiently listening to Greg at the register, since it was the slow time for grocery stores too and her curly-headed former classmate was full of complaints as well as gossip. Beck was only saved when skinny, dark-haired Nadine Smalley shuffled up, her youngest on her hip sucking his thumb and staring wearily at the world. She had a full cart but the little boy didn't want to be in the seat, and Beck should have stayed to lend a hand.

But looking at the kid's chubby cheeks and mismatched shoes made her heart thump into her throat, Hel's groceries were warming up—Nan had remembered the frozen, thank God—and Beck wasn't sure her knees would keep their starch. She made it out to the car, loaded everything, punctiliously returned the cart to the lone return in the middle of the lot, and was blessed again by the sedan's ignition catching.

As it was, she had to pull over on the long curve of Tutman Road and sob into cupped hands, her shoulders hunched and her cheeks aflame. One or two cars rattled by, tires shushing on damp pavement that hadn't seen patching since the early nineties, but nobody stopped to "help" her with the Taurus or ask beady-eyed, pointed little questions. With spring right around the corner, there were hard little leaf buds swelling on naked deciduous branches, and she could hope she'd be gone before they turned into actual leaves.

She didn't think she could handle another day like today.

Home, Combat Drop

"IT'S SIMPLE," PAUL said. The entire manufactured was stuffed to the brim with the good smell of pork chops in Hel's rosemary glaze. "I take you to the coffee stand in the Cherokee, run down to Sinaida for parts, and by the time you're off work I'll have the Taurus less likely to explode on you."

"That's okay." Beck's chin had set. She set the forks down, one on each folded paper napkin. "It works, and it's fine."

"It's *backfiring*." He'd heard it, clear as day, as the Taurus approached down the long shallow bend of Cloepfer Lane. "That's the definition of *not fine*, Becks. Give me the plates."

"I've got it." She settled plain white Corelle moons on Hel's prized post-New Year's placemats, fabric painted with cherry blossoms. All the trivets were already arranged. "Thanks. I think Hel could use some help, though."

"You want me to go into the kitchen while she's cooking? Jeez, just shoot me." He tried a lopsided grin, but Beck simply hunched her shoulders, honey-highlighted hair bouncing.

It used to be easy to get a smile out of her. It *should* have been a snap, especially in Hel's dining room with the china hutch's smoked glass doors on one side, good smells riding the air, and the table decorated as if they were having company rather than just sitting down after a workday. Hel had coffee going, and the dark-brown wonderful note of roasted garlic meant she was mashing potatoes again.

And Paul, instead of being just pleasantly hungry and anticipatory after a day digging around inside an old-fashioned Chevy engine, was flat-out alarmed.

Not only did Beck try to unload and carry in all Hel's groceries herself, attempting to fob both him and his aunt off—well, she'd been raised right, and some of her protestations could be simple politeness—but she was also apparently dead set against Paul fixing the goddamn Taurus, and each time they had to pass each other she looked away, dark lashes sweeping down to veil any hint of actual feeling. Not only that, but. . . .

Well, there was the way she flinched if he moved too quickly. There was her carefully keeping Helena between them like a shield, and to top it all off, she wouldn't utter anything other than banal pleasantries.

The Becks he knew hated small talk with a passion, almost as much as she loved pulling a good prank. *I can play the game*, she'd said in high school. *I just don't like it very much.*

Well, now she was Olympic-league at it. Which would have been simply concerning and maybe a bit eerie, but added to the way she couldn't sit still and all but cowered if he got near the frontline of her personal space, it was giving Paul a few dark suspicions.

Something sizzled; Hel was cooking up a storm. His aunt hummed along with Patsy Cline warbling at low volume from Herrold's prized stereo in the living room, accompanied by the warm pops and cracks of vinyl meeting a needle. You could mistake that sound for a good fire on a cold day, and Paul had helped Herrold run the wires for recessed speakers into the dining room and kitchen as well.

Right before he'd left, as a matter of fact. It had been the last big project before basic training swallowed him whole, folding, stapling, and mutilating a wiseass boy into a man.

On the bright side, the music—and Hel's distraction—gave him some cover. Paul halted, aware he was between Beck and the kitchen unless she wanted to take a running dive over a breakfast bar serving as the demarcation between the two rooms. "Rebecca."

She turned sharply, her hip almost hitting the back of Helena's chair, and stared at him like he'd shouted. And there it was—that haunted, almost terrified expression.

No. Not *almost*. Beck Sommers was downright petrified, and covering it up with a champion method actor's skill.

Which hurt almost as much as the news she'd gone and married someone else. What the fuck had *Paul* ever done to scare her?

"Paul." Her chin leveled, and the only thing worse than the fear was how squarely she faced him, almost like a bareknuckle boxer bracing for a hit. You did that when you knew you were going to get a beating but couldn't back out; he should know, he'd gone enough rounds at recess, after school, or hell, even in basic. "It will be *fine*, okay? I don't work on Thursday. Maybe you could do what you need to then?"

That soft, placating tone, the question spiraling past tentative hope into downright pleading—Jesus.

What the fuck had *happened* to her?

"Maybe you could tell me what the real problem is." He tried for Dez's even tone; their CO had a way of suggesting things that made what he was asking seem not-quite-an-order but merely the only advisable, available course for a grunt in his crew.

Desmarais could bark with the best, but it was the fact of not having to that made him the Squad's leader no matter who wore the actual stripes. And the ol' Loot had managed to snag Cara, too; clearly the man knew something.

Beck eyed him, almost vibrating with unease. Anyone else would think she was just paying attention, but Paul knew better.

Even if he hadn't seen her for entirely too many years.

"It's just easier," she said quietly, the words almost lost under Helena banging a spoon inside a pot and working a cussword or two into Patsy's warble. "You start playing chauffeur, everyone in town's going to think. . . ."

Oh. Paul could have kicked himself. Gossip bolted through this place like spring flooding or a runaway train. Her divorce wasn't final yet and maybe she still churched, so the old Bible biddies would be looking for any meat they could strip off and plunge in their ever-clacking little mouths. "Some things never change." He couldn't even find a joke. "They're going to say it anyway, Beck. Might as well be comfortable while they do."

"Look." She shook her head. "You got out, okay? That's good, and I'm happy for you." She wasn't whispering now; the words were a low fierce hum as if they were teenagers again, pitched just perfectly to escape older ears. Helena was running a mixer, probably on the potatoes. "I'm planning my own escape, but it's going to take a while. So I'm trying to. . . ." Maddeningly, Beck stopped, glancing at the kitchen. "Helena's a lifesaver, all right? I don't want to make it harder on *her* either."

Harder for her? What the hell? "I could get a hotel—" he began.

"Oh, Christ," she hissed. "Don't. Please. Just don't."

How in the hell did I fuck this up? I wish one of the guys was here, they'd probably be able to tell me. "Hel didn't say anything, all right? I didn't know you were living with her; I didn't do this on purpose."

"She didn't say anything to me, either. One minute I'm helping her at Ikea, the next we're at the airport." One slim shoulder lifted, dropped; she'd kept her faded red jacket on, as if she was cold. She was certainly thin enough to need a little extra padding. "So let's just get along, okay?

I'm sorry, you have no *idea* how sorry I am, but can we please just get along?"

Why's she sorry about that? It made no goddamn sense at all, and for a moment he was simply rooted to the tannish carpet, new when the manufactured was delivered and religiously vacuumed but still showing wear on footpaths, like animal trails near water. "Jesus, Beck." For once in his wisecracking life, Paul Klemperer was perilously close to being at a complete loss for words. "This is me you're talking to, all right? You don't have to be sorry about a goddamn thing."

For some reason, that made her cheeks flush as if slapped. The color did her good, and her eyes glittered.

And it knocked the breath clean out of him once more. How did she *do* that? She merely had to exist in his general vicinity and all his internal thermostats malfunctioned.

Indeed, it looked like some things in Granite River were damn near eternal and unchanging, as the hymn said. Gossip, keeping a game face on, and Beck Sommers giving him heart attacks with a single glance—a gat-damn *tri*-fecta, Jackson would call it, his eyebrows lifting significantly.

Whatever she would have said was lost; the whir of a mixer stopped. "Potatoes are done," Helena called. "Get in here, kids, and help with serving up."

The words were so familiar he could have sung along, past and present fusing for a vertiginous moment. Flipping between the bits of the town stuck in nostalgic amber and the ones changed out of all recognition was a helluva jolt, like the parachute snapping open on a high-altitude drop or baling out of a moving train straight into fire.

Visiting the old hometown wasn't supposed to feel like a combat op, but what the hell did he know? He hadn't bothered to come back for visits, even after Herrold's funeral. And Hel had never uttered a word of even passive-aggressive complaint.

Beck was still standing by Hel's chair, still tense. Still bracing for impact.

So Paul did the only thing he could, backing away a couple steps, his hands up as if she were armed and angry. Or fearful, which was just as bad.

Nerves and bullets never mixed well.

He also nodded, twice, hoping she'd get the message. *Sure, Beck. We'll get along. Anything you want.*

Then he turned and plunged into the brightly lit kitchen, where

Helena handed him the old Wedgwood gravy boat. "Get that on the table, Paulie. And make sure there are napkins."

"Yes ma'am." Did his voice sound funny? Christ, he hoped not.

AS LONG AS HE kept Hel busy, Beck relaxed. So Paul did his best, and kept his aunt in stitches too. There were stories he didn't have to sanitize too much, like the varying consequences of Jackson's facility for languages or Grey's perpetual magic tricks. Helena knew his buddies' names mostly from letters and phone calls, since she had a deep suspicion of email.

However, it seemed Beck had finally managed to get Hel to trade in her old cell phone, and the two of them texted. "Sometimes people don't use punctuation," Helena said, severely.

Beck actually unbent enough to laugh, ducking her head shyly as if her hair was much longer and she wanted to hide behind it, a familiar movement. "I missed a comma *once*, Aunt Hel."

For a moment it was as if he'd never left. Paul's heart gave a funny twitch like it had decided to leave his chest entirely, and he wondered if he was having a coronary at the dinner table like Grandpa Mitch.

Gone between one and the next, Paul's father had intoned solemnly, every time he told that story.

The doorbell rang—familiar, jarring Westminster chimes. He was out of his chair before it finished, and only stopped the dive for cover by a wrenching, entirely invisible effort.

Beck started. Her knee hit the table leg next to her, and the milk in her amber glass tumbler rippled. "*Ow.*"

"I'll get it." Helena was already on her feet, dropping her napkin next to her plate. "And I swear, if it's that—"

"Hang on." Paul's hand flicked out with no conscious direction on his part, curling over Helena's shoulder. "It's dinnertime."

"Probably thinks I'm gonna feed him." Hel snorted. "Like a damn puppy. You just sit right there, Beck. I'll handle this."

Wait a second. "Handle it? Hel—"

His aunt escaped his hold by the simple expedient of walking away; he couldn't very well clamp down and hold her like someone Dez needed questioned. Paul glanced at Beck, who rose, rubbing at her knee. It had been a good solid hit.

The naked fear on Beck's face threatened to turn Hel's juicy rosemary-glazed pork chops to rock behind his breastbone.

Helena didn't stop for the rifle near the front door, which was a mercy. She did sweep said door open as if she was angry, and Paul's heart, which had been performing some interesting calisthenics in the last few hours, plummeted.

Under the glare of the yellowish no-bug bulb in the porch fixture, a big man with an iron-colored high-and-tight just like drill instructor's held his hat in one bony, liver-spotted hand. "Evenin', Hel." He clocked Paul, looming over his aunt's shoulder, and his dark eyes narrowed. Even after a full shift, Connor Sommers's uniform didn't dare to exhibit more than one or two creases beside the perfect ones at regulated angles. "Sorry to interrupt."

"Well." Hel put a hand on one hip, and didn't reach for the screen door's latch. "Evenin', Sheriff. We were having dinner." She pointedly did not invite him to come on in.

"I should've called; I was just driving by and thought I'd see my Rebecca." His holstered sidearm gleamed—old-fashioned revolver instead of new-issue Glock—and behind him, the short winter dusk had turned into a cold spring night.

Paul's back prickled. They were all clearly outlined in the door, for God's sake. Even cops were civilians; they had some good instincts, but not all of them.

"Connor. . . ." Helena turned her head slightly. "Go back to the table, Paul."

He knew finality in her tone when he heard it, but at the same time, Paul wasn't six years old anymore. "Sheriff Sommers. Been a while."

"Paulie." The sheriff looked sourly unsurprised. "Looks like the Army did you some good."

"Thank you kindly." He'd never been able to make this man laugh, and something told Paul it wasn't going to happen tonight, either. The polite thing was say *let me go tell Beck you're here*.

"We're at *dinner*," Hel jumped in, smoothly, as if she thought Paul was going to attempt it. "You can call her, Connor. I'm sure you've got the number."

Laughter threatened to crawl up Paul's throat. Very few people ever took the sheriff to task, but Hel was a law unto herself. Of course, Sommers had to know about the sheds in the junkyard, but Hel was local—just like he was—and most of the county had made ends meet with drying a little ganja every now and again.

Now that it was legal big greenhouses were going in, so it wasn't as lucrative. The real money lay in the grey, as usual. Not that it helped anyone currently in the system for possession.

Still, being in the middle of another family's business was never a good idea. In Granite River it was, in fact, a good way to end up a social pariah—or worse.

At least Connor Sommers loved his little girl. Maybe the man was trying to make up for her mother leaving, but his way of expressing affection was what Tax would call *suboptimal*. Grey would snort at the word, Jackson would nod if he found its use acceptable in the current situation, and Boom would swear under his breath.

He wished any one of them was here at the moment, and was paradoxically glad they weren't.

"Hey." Something touched his elbow. It was Beck, and a faint edge of her body heat was like a bonfire's breath against Paul's side. "I'm right here, Hel. It's okay."

"Honey. . . ." Hel didn't move, her head turned slightly and her attention clearly on the man outside. She looked like a thin dry tree in the face of oncoming flood, roots sunk and branches defiantly raised. "You sure?"

"For Chrissake," Connor Sommers said. "I'm her *father*, Helena."

"Really." Hel's tone couldn't get any drier. "I'd never have guessed." She didn't have to add, *The way you act. . . .*

It was implied, and if Paul opened his mouth he was going to start chuckling. Of all the things worth coming back to Granite River for, seeing Hel wag a verbal finger at Beck's dad was certainly in the top ten.

Beck slid past him. The small foyer area, its back to the living room, was impossibly crowded with all three of them, but Paul couldn't move. An electric current slid from the touch of her old, battered coat's bulky shoulder against his T-shirt sleeve and bare elbow.

Jesus. Just the same.

"It's all right." Beck put a hand on Hel's arm, too. Her fingernails were freshly bitten, no hint of white showing, and her wrist was far too thin.

He didn't like where all these clues were heading. Didn't like it at all.

"Fine." Helena half-turned, and reached for the latch. "But don't you fill up my ashtray, Connor, and I expect that girl inside to finish her dinner. It's a cold night."

"Yes ma'am." The sheriff's entire face relaxed for a moment when he saw his daughter. "Hi, Beck. I was really just drivin' by."

"I know." Two colorless words. "It's Tuesday."

Helena glowered through the screen door; the porch light shone on Beck's hair. She moved down the steps; her dad's cruiser was pulled up exactly where Paul would have parked if he suspected this place of being unfriendly. And Beck had her arms crossed high as she walked, looking very small next to her father's ramrod-straight back, his Sam Browne belt creaking slightly and his boots—still spit-shining after all these years, by gum—crushing driveway gravel and half-frozen weeds.

"What's going on?" The laughter had drained away, thank God, so Paul could sound curious.

"Damn man making a fool of himself," Hel snapped, but her gaze lingered past the sheriff's cruiser, scanning the end of the driveway and the bushes cloaking the private turn-off. It was dark down there, deliberately left that way so strangers didn't mistake it for the junkyard's entrance or a handy turnaround.

Paul couldn't sense anyone lurking, but Helena still watched. Her tension didn't diminish until Beck finished a short conversation, hugged her father, and turned back to the house, her head down and arms now wrapped around her middle. The sheriff watched her go, and even in the dimness the old man's expression was plainly worried and affectionate at once, pained and proud. Sommers's shoulders hunched for a bare, brief second, just like his daughter's, but he said nothing and straightened almost immediately when she turned at the foot of the porch steps to wave.

Like a little girl staying for a birthday party sleepover.

Sommers waved in return, settled his hat, and in short order his cruiser roused to humming life. He'd leave in a moment, sure—just not before the sheriff's daughter was safely inside. A faint flare of golden light was ol' Connor lighting a cigarette.

He probably needed it, after this.

Helena closed the door, throwing the locks with angry snapping motions. "At *dinnertime*," she hissed.

"I'm sorry. It's Tuesday; he does south county every week about this time after the traffic docket in the morning." Beck edged into the living room, almost pressing against the back of Herrold's old cat-shredded recliner. It was the only place she could go and get distance from both of them. "He had a call up near the bridge, too, and didn't think about it being dinnertime. He sends his apologies, Hel. Honest."

"At least he didn't bring that. . . ." Helena coughed slightly, against the back of her right hand. "Well, come on. It won't do to let good food get cold."

Beck's gaze flew to Paul. He couldn't decide if she was asking for help or dreading what he might say. "It'd be a damn shame," he agreed, cheerfully. "For a minute I thought he was here for me. I was trying to remember if I had anything in my pockets."

"You'd better not." But Hel laughed and motioned him along, a hen harrying her chick toward scratch. "Especially at the dinner table. Army should have taught you that, if I didn't."

"Basic training was a breeze, Hel." He found the next joke without any trouble. "It was like a Sunday afternoon here. I told my sarge once that my Aunt Hel hit harder, and about got my as—ah, my behind chewed into splinters." *There. We won't talk about it, Beck.*

His reward was seeing her relax a little when she realized he wasn't going to ask any questions. She let him carry the plates to the kitchen after dinner, and didn't find someplace else to be while he put the leftovers in Tupperware. Instead, she loaded the dishwasher, washed the pots and pans while Helena dried, and retreated to the annex when Helena settled to her eternal knitting on the old leather couch, turning the television on for the news the way she did every evening, hell or high water.

And Paul? He went to bed.

He had some thinking to do.

Thousand and One

THE OLD ANNEX couch folded out and its thin mattress wasn't bad, but Beck was painfully conscious of every sound she made, even simply breathing at midnight. Huddled in the dark of a strange bed, she had plenty of time to chew over the day, as Dad would say.

Honey, I just worry. And he did, but she had nothing to tell him. *You know I got your old room, we can fix it right up.* They could indeed, but he lived in town. Joe had a million reasons to drop by his boss's place and wear her down. *Will you just tell me what's wrong?* Oh, how she wished.

She'd thought about it, of course. But Joe knew what constituted proof and was careful to avoid it. Besides, Beck knew exactly what her father thought of "domestics." She'd heard it enough growing up at the dinner table, getting a sanitized version of his day after he'd patiently listened to hers. The stories changed as she got older, but his feelings on particular subjects didn't shift an inch.

It was far better to be thought stubborn and spoiled than risk forcing her father to fire a deputy. Not just any deputy, either, but *Joe*, the good kid, the basketball player, the solid guy, the Halston boy. No doubt everyone in town thought Amy Lorton was a necessary shoulder to cry on because his mean old harridan of a wife wasn't giving poor Joe a chance.

Beck shifted restlessly, held her breath when the house creaked. She'd just gotten used to Hel's spare room; the annex felt too echoing-large.

Her father loved her. She knew it as absolutely as she knew he wouldn't understand, because she mystified him as completely as her mother ever had.

Joe didn't even have to try; her father was automatically his ally. Not least because Beck would collude in the alliance, leaving certain things unspoken.

Can we please just get along? How many times was she going to have to ask a man that? At least Paul had backed off, and spent his time catching up with his aunt. Beck hadn't heard Hel laugh like this for years.

Since before he'd left, in fact.

He seemed content to let her business remain, indeed, *her* business. It was better than she expected and certainly more than she deserved, but her heart still hurt. It was probably natural; every woman over thirty inevitably had one she wished had stayed.

It didn't mean anything; it was just statistics.

Tomorrow she worked, and the day after was the hearing. It might even be the last one; she'd been reading legal advice columns on her phone during slow periods at the coffee shack. She could hope, right?

A train lowed in the distance, a long lonely sound, comforting and familiar. Would it disturb Paul? He'd slept in places even the trains couldn't dream of, and God how she envied that.

Joe had sworn he wanted to get out of this town too; he'd sworn they would leave for somewhere else, somewhere bigger. Once he'd made deputy, though, all that changed—and by then she was stuck.

She could have gone to college instead, she supposed. But the scare with Dad's liver right after Paul left kept her home that year, "just until things settle down," and somehow her escape velocity had petered out. The superstitious thought—that if she'd gone her father might really have died—waited until nights like this to come out and play.

At least she was warm. She wasn't sleeping under a bridge, and she wasn't in the house on Passacola. *That* thought caused a burst of relief, just as intense as every other time it occurred throughout the day. Embarrassment was excruciating but it was better than the alternative, and maybe it was the fuel needed to get her out of here for good.

Finally, when even the trains had stopped crying out, she dropped into a thin, troubled sleep. Even the distant heavy sound of a car door slamming outside near three a.m. didn't wake her.

GREETING THE SUN was a little easier when staying in bed was uncomfortable as hell. This time Paul was up before her and had the coffeepot running. It was probably childish to feel the slight bite of resentment at him taking the job and also, by the way, disrupting her morning routine. And doubly childish to think Aunt Hel probably preferred her nephew's coffee to her lodger's.

Beck liked early mornings, the hush and the chance to *think* without other people wanting, needing, expecting. Fortunately, Paul didn't take her question about how he wanted his eggs as an invitation, just said *scrambled's fine, please and thank you,* so that's what she did. She even had time for a few bites of toast before she kissed Hel's cheek and was out the door, pausing only to remind her landlady to text if she wanted Beck to pick something up on the way home.

The morning drive was pretty, dawn coming up earlier and earlier each day. The rain had stopped sometime before sunrise, which meant every fir tree was for a short moment edged in dripping gold. Even the weeds in the Parlour's parking lot had a brief flash of gilding.

Best of all, Joe apparently had business elsewhere, because his cruiser was nowhere in sight. She couldn't really relax until she was out of this town, but the lack of his quasi-regular morning visit was a gift. She put it to good use, reading about divorce procedures and proceedings on her phone, trying to think of things he might do Thursday to impede the process.

There wasn't a lot. Especially since he'd already been served with the initial papers, plus she was waiving alimony and any property settlement. He could keep the house, he could keep his pension; Judge McCready—Nelson's docket was mostly criminal instead of civil—seemed baffled that she didn't want anything.

But you are entitled to minimum support, Mrs. Halston. That's what the law says.

Was it wrong to hope there would be some kind of work emergency and Joe wouldn't make the Thursday hearing? Would that delay the inevitable? If it didn't, someone else's bad luck would be her good fortune, and Beck would hear about it through the grapevine.

One way, or another.

Maybe she wouldn't, though. She was considering getting the hell away as soon as the ink was dry on the decree, savings or no savings. At least she'd opened her very own account at a big national chain bank in Eugene with Hel's help. Though there was very little in it, the fact remained it was *hers* and she was off the joint one with Joe at the county credit union.

Freedom came in tiny, hard-wrung steps.

The morning rush started with Gracie Molyneux, as usual. Beck smiled, joked, made lattes, did not forget an extra shot of caramel for Phil Justy's venti mocha, and handed out small stickers to little people in car seats who couldn't have caffeine.

That last duty was pleasant, but oh it made her heart hurt each time.

Mary showed up to help with the lunch rush, and told her it was too nice a day to spend in the shack. "Get out to Cash & Carry . . . oh, you know what I mean."

"They keep changing the name," Beck agreed. Next to the register was a short list of necessary articles; Mary had brought the milk and other super-perishables from Costco, as always, but they needed more twelve-ounce cups and the backup chocolate syrup had just been opened, which meant it was time for a new jug. "Anything else?"

"You know you'll get right up to checkout before I remember." The other women clicked her tongue, giving a rueful smile. "Want to take my car?"

Everyone had an opinion on the Taurus, looked like. "I'll be fine." The last thing Beck needed was Joe or one of his buddies—her father's men, certainly, but her husband's *friends*—deciding to make trouble over her driving a car not registered to her. There were a thousand and one ways to punish someone when you had a badge.

Or when you had them trapped.

The Taurus had been sitting in the sun, so it started right up. Driving the thing was such a juggling trick she didn't really notice anything wrong until she crested Benson Hill.

For a moment the valley was spread out below her, faint traces of velvety green edging winter-naked limbs under a bright, freshly washed sky, the river a silver ribbon meandering lazily between overgrown banks and the town itself mostly hidden under tall firs. If it looked this way all the time, nobody would ever want to leave.

The problem, as usual, was other people. Necessary for infra-structure, but hell when you just wanted to be left alone.

The Taurus took the dive down the hill, sighing in relief as the engine wasn't called upon to handle an incline, and Beck touched the brake to prep for the curve at the bottom.

Or she tried to. The pedal gave easily.

Far, *far* too easily. *Oh, hell,* she thought, right before it kissed the floor. *That's not good.*

The hill was steep, and the curve at the bottom had eaten more than one unwary—or unsuitably lubricated—driver, especially late at night. Her father had been called out many a time to oversee scooping up the damage, especially if a car punched through the ancient arthritic guardrail and plummeted into the blackberry-choked ravine beyond.

The rail was more of a fond wish than a safety measure, and winter landslides inevitably took out portions of it.

Later, Beck wasn't quite sure what, exactly, she'd done. The handbrake was definitely involved, her right arm aching as she yanked *hard* and the car's tires squealing and smoking; she kept pushing the brake with her right foot too, as if it would suddenly remember what to do. The curve leapt for the Taurus like a hungry lion on a wounded gazelle, a hole in the rail like a bad tooth pulled from bleeding gums was *right there*, and she had enough time to think *oh, for fuck's sake* before the car tipped alarmingly, heading right for that empty space. The world shivered, a confused few moments' worth of weightlessness both eternal and blink-quick at the same time, and the only other thing she remembered of the accident was the terrific, shattering jolt as the old Taurus sideswiped a huge, much-scarred oak tree, half-dead from being uprooted by cold sliding winter mud, a good distance below the crumbling edge.

Some Luck

HEL WAS OUT OF the Jeep almost before Paul cut the engine. A big white tow truck, its lightbar blinking lazily, was there already—Lefty Beaujolais must've been having a slow morning, but then again, miracles could occur in a hot hurry when a local was in trouble. Heck Gonzalez from the Beaujolais shop had called Hel, and Paul's aunt had barely slowed down enough to say *something's happened, it's Beck* before heading toward the Jeep.

It didn't take a lot to convince her to let him drive, thank God.

Lefty, a shapeless and probably lucky fisherman's hat hanging from one hand as he scratched at his sweat-gleaming forehead, stood at the edge of the ravine right at the foot of Benson, where the bottom of Hill Road curved to hitch up to Old Marckola. Paul glanced at the seamed, ancient surface of Hill—not a lot of rubber, had a tire blown? There wasn't any debris either, just marks to show something heavy had gone straight over the edge.

That gave him what Boom would call *a bad ol' turn, good buddy*, and God only knew what would have happened if he hadn't caught sight of a familiar honeydark head, tumbled waves glowing in thick golden spring sunshine that did nothing to warm since the breeze combing firs and other trees was stiff today, chilly damp air rustling dormant blackberry vines.

Beck. She was alive, she was fine, and his heart decided it could beat again. At least, she was upright, and she leaned against the trunk of a county cruiser, hugging herself in that damn red coat. Maybe she just never took the thing off, like her mother's fire opal ring worn all through high school, or the blue baseball hat Paul had worn in sixth and seventh grade.

Kids—and soldiers—knew all about lucky pieces, not to mention walkaways.

Joe Halston loomed right next to her, his uniform not as crisp as Sheriff Sommers's but still showing a good deal of gym-steady muscle. His mouth moved—was he questioning her? Blond, blue-eyed, and clean-cut, he was still the picture of an all-American prick, and the way he hovered over Beck was depressingly familiar.

The way she shrank in on herself, looking anywhere but at him, was new. She was dead pale, two patches of hectic color bright up on her cheeks, and when she saw Hel her entire face crumpled.

Paul inhaled sharply.

"Son of a—" Lefty Beaujolais realized Hel was in earshot and swallowed the last word. "Paulie? That you?"

Hel made a beeline for Beck, who tacked drunkenly away from the cruiser with staggering little steps. Her black sneakers were a filthy, gravel-clotted mess, and when Paul got to the edge he could see why.

The car hadn't gone completely down the ravine. It had fetched up against a half-fallen killer oak a short distance below the lip, and was almost wrapped around the trunk. It was a good thing the passenger side had hit; the crumple zones had done their job, but it still could have been uncomfortable for anyone in that seat. Safety glass glittered, there was a sharp stink of automotive smoke but no gasoline reek, and the thought of what *could* have happened was a cold metallic taste in Paul's mouth.

"Hey, Lefty. Long time no see." He kept Hel in his peripheral vision as he offered his hand; Lefty smacked his palm into it and gave a squeeze as well as a few hard shakes, pulling him forward and clapping him on the opposite shoulder for good measure. "Hector called us. Thanks for coming out."

"Well, you know." Lefty's shrug was pure Granite River, years of history condensed into a single movement. He'd never said anything about wanting more than taking over the family business, and from the look of his businessman's gut he was doing all right. The engine grime on his big capable hands said he still knew his way around under the hood, too. "Jesus, some luck, huh?"

"Some luck," Paul agreed. Hel reached Beck and the two women turned into one, a statue of comfort plonked right on the gravel shoulder. Helena set about smoothing Beck's hair, patting her back, murmuring things Paul couldn't quite hear. "What the hell?"

"Said the brakes gave. She got on the 'mergency hand one and managed to slow the car enough. Bad luck that she hit where the landslide happened, but I guess she aimed for the oak. Smart, ol' Beck." Lefty glanced aside, uneasily. "Guess she also climbed out of the car and up the hill, and called Mary 'cross the street from us. You know her? Mary Parrack. Went to school in Sinaida, nice girl."

Just tell me what the fuck happened, man. Paul strangled a flare of livid impatience. Nothing in this goddamn village ever happened easily or quickly; it was all accompanied by standing around until someone else could be provoked into a decision.

Come to think of it, the Army wasn't any different, except for when you were out in the field. Then you were either bored to death and being eaten alive by some variety of rash or wildlife, or under fire with no goddamn time for anything other than bare survival and the prayer that you wouldn't shit your pants from fear.

"Don't know her," he agreed easily. "Some kind of coffee shop, right?" *The stand next to Sandra's, I saw it coming in. Okay.*

"Nice little business, nice lady. Anyway. . . ." Lefty shifted inside his coveralls, and cast another sneaking glance along the shoulder. Beck was talking now, short little bursts of words Paul couldn't quite hear. Just the tone—low, jagged, apologetic.

And terrified.

What he *wanted* to do was stride over there, grab her, and demand to know if she was all right before getting his arms all the way around and hugging her hard enough to leave them both breathless. Then he could get the chowder-to-cashews from Lefty, and *then* he'd like to have a private discussion with Joe Halston.

The deputy was watching this all go down, blue eyes narrowed, standing next to his cruiser. Shouldn't he be doing paperwork or something? And why was he looking at Paul instead of Beck?

Why, for God's sake, wasn't he trying to comfort her? Sure, they were getting unhitched, but. . . .

Oh, fucking hell. "Anyway?" Paul kept his tone neutral, returning his gaze to the Taurus. Yep, it had gone right off the edge there, already slewing because Beck was trying to make the turn, probably hanging onto the handbrake and praying. Looked like it had rolled once, a complete flip, then hit the oak.

It could have been much, much worse, and every inch of him knew it.

"Damndest thing," Left said quietly. "Joe showed up almost the same time I did."

"Maybe she called him, too." Paul didn't think it was likely. He and Joe had fought at recess, snuck beers together as teenagers, gotten into other kinds of trouble like every teenager in the River learned to do just to keep themselves amused. He would've said there were no surprises lingering in Joe Halston, but the man had married Beck, which showed some brains. And taste. "Or someone couldn't stop on the Hill, but saw. . . . ."

"She was down there, getting her purse. Girl went back *down* the hill, can you believe it? Sheriff's gonna hit the roof." Lefty sighed. "Gonna have to get out the chains. This is gonna take a minute."

"Yeah." *Getting her purse?* Paul eyed the marks on the side of the road. He wasn't the kind of tracker Jackson was—the crazy bastard could follow a hawk on foot—but Klemp and Grey weren't bad at it either. There were fresh scars where the car had hit, and smaller scrabbling ones where she'd climbed out the shattered driver's side window. There was a fairly easy route to the top, and the rain-softened bit at the asphalt's edge was probably why there was dirt on her red coat.

Right below the lip of the drop-off was a ledge, and Paul tilted his head as he stared at it. That would, he realized, be a great place to hide if you heard an engine approaching, and there were fresh marks on the wet moss clinging to grey volcanic stone.

"I hate to say it," Lefty continued, morosely. "But I think Hel might want me to just drag this back to the yard. It don't look too fixable."

"Just glad the important thing's okay." Paul's hands wanted to shake, but he kept them down, loose and easy. No need to stand at attention here.

"Few feet in either direction, wouldn't have found her until they start building houses along Marckola Creek. Or ever." Lefty heaved an only partly theatrical sigh. "I better get to work. Good to see you, man."

"Likewise." Paul shook hands again, glad the other fellow didn't play the dumbass squeezing game. "I'll ask Hel what she wants. I'd help you hitch up, but. . . ."

"I already radio'd Heck and little Todd Nipley to come out. Remember when there wasn't any such thing as cell service out here?" Lefty turned for his tow truck, consigning everyone else at the scene to their own devices.

But not without one last meaningful glance at Paul, and by the way his head turned slightly, Lefty wanted to look in Joe Halston's direction too. He didn't, but Paul got the idea it cost him some effort.

Gravel crunched under Paul's desert boots. It was no use, he was drawn, surely and invisibly as a needle pointing north, toward a rumpled head alive with honey highlights.

"—s-s-sorry," Beck said, repeating herself from the sound of it. "I sh-sh-should have . . . God. I'm s-so s-s-sorry, Hel."

"Oh, honey." Helena loosened her grip, but only to dig in her black canvas purse. "Here. Wipe up. It's only a *car*, Rebecca. It's a damn good thing you didn't go all the way down the ravine. Only thing I'm peeved about is you calling Mary first instead of me."

"B-b-but I have t-to get to the s-store," Beck insisted. Her hands were scraped and raw, not to mention crusted with drying spring dirt, and if she'd had any fingernails left they might have broken as she scrabbled for the top. There was a thin scratch-swipe on her cheek—a blackberry vine's work, and for a moment Paul wanted to liberate a flamethrower from the closest base and teach this hillside a lesson.

It was the sort of thing Jackson might suggest with a thin, cold smile, and Dez would consider the idea before sighing and turning to other methods. At least, most of the time.

Any one of the Squad could get savage in less than a heartbeat, a natural inclination polished until it shone like one of Tax's little in-country knives. It was why they'd been chosen for the training program, why none of them had washed out, and probably why the paper-pushers weren't trying to get one or two of them back in the saddle—God only knew what sort of covert shit might come to light if one of them didn't like a particular posting, or what would go sideways if one of them broke hard under combat stress in-country. Better to just thank them for their "service" and send them back to boring civilian life, knowing the law of decompression would catch up sooner or later and the problem would solve itself.

Dez had been more than halfway to imploding before coming across Cara; a woman like that would have no trouble keeping the ol' First Lieutenant on an even keel. Now Paul wondered what the hell he himself was doing.

There were wet, half-rotten leaves caught in Beck's hair, and down one side of her jeans. Mud caked that leg; it looked like she'd fallen, and slid.

"I have to." Beck took the folded black cotton bandanna Hel produced, and looked at the thing like she couldn't remember what it was for. "We need t-twelve-ounce cups."

Paul couldn't help himself. "You need to go to the hospital." He kept an eye on Joe, too, and didn't miss how the man stiffened, striding away from the cruiser and bearing down on them as if he thought he was John Law himself. Maybe he was trying to imitate Connor Sommers's absolute authority, but all Paul could see was a dumbass shirtwaist noncom ready to start barking.

"I c-can't." Beck's gaze turned to him, and the welling, sparkling water in her green eyes turned everything inside him over, like an egg flipped by a sure, deft line cook with orders to get out and no time to waste.

Or a light vehicle driven over an IED, flicked casually skyward by an explosion it wasn't built to handle.

"Hi, Joe." Paul didn't have to move far—just two steps past his aunt and Beck plus a single step sideways, placing himself squarely in the deputy's way. A siren rose, mournful and slow, in the distance. "You got taller."

The Last Thing

"HEY, PAUL." IT WAS Joe's butter-wouldn't-melt voice, the one adults invariably fell for when it was time to explain away a prank. Nice, even, polite, just doing his job. "Miz Helena. Sorry to make you come all the way out here."

Tremors jolted through Beck's entire body. She couldn't keep them down, and of course Helena would notice. Not to mention notice Beck's hands, and her face, and there were leaves in her goddamn *hair* as well; her coat was filthy and her jeans too. Her shoes were probably ruined, and buying another pair just put off her departure from this goddamn town a little longer.

And of course Joe was right here, and Hel had brought Paul.

"Joe." Helena's tone could best be described as *frigid*. She gazed over Beck's shoulder, dead-eyeing him, and a great scalding burst of shame wedded to love poured through Beck's entire body.

Was this what having a mother felt like? Christ, she wouldn't know. Mom had left before Beck was five, Dad had gotten rid of all the photographs, and why was Beck thinking about it now?

She had enough problems without her brain shivering like a tired animal, along with the rest of her.

Helena's attention swung back in Beck's direction. "Paul's right. You need the hospital. Is there an ambulance coming, Joe?"

Oh, God. "No." Beck tried to sound capable, mature, reasonably able to handle all of this. There was a siren getting closer; she hoped Joe hadn't called an ambulance anyway. "I told him not to bother. I'm fine."

"You need to be checked. You could have a concussion." Of course Joe would gang up on her now. The radio in his car squawked through open windows, a babble of police-ese, and there were locals around—Hel, and Lefty. He couldn't be seen doing anything other than the good-guy act. "I gotta fill out an accident report, too."

And of course you'll want me right in front of you while I give it, you'll make me repeat myself, and you won't let me go until I've agreed to something. "I'm fine," she insisted. "I'll take a sobriety test. Get out the breathalyzer. The brakes wouldn't work, I told you. It's an old car."

"Anyone can see you're not. . . ." Paul sounded baffled. "Who's on the way, Joe?"

"Nothing for us, I canceled a tow since Lefty was already here. It's probably Sam on his way to lunch. Boss is in court today." Oh, her almost-ex-husband would sound fine to everyone else, but Beck heard the edge under the words. This was messy, and it was *public*, but worst of all, Joe wasn't in control. He couldn't take her back to the blue house on Passacola with all these people watching, especially if Beck resisted.

After going off the edge into the ravine, not to mention clawing her way back to the top, Beck didn't feel like going anywhere quietly. Of course the rumormongers would start whispering, too. *Drunk in daylight, maybe. Poor old Joe, having to deal with that girl.*

Christ, she was so almighty tired of worrying what the people in this shitty little town thought or said.

"Well, then." Paul was directly behind her. It felt almost like having a big, heavy shield between her and Joe Halston, and she shouldn't like the feeling, or get used to it. "Can't do anything until the paperwork's done. The force is just like the service, huh?" Had he learned that brisk, no-nonsense tone in the Army? And dear God but he was storing up trouble, because Joe hated to be told what to do.

He was going to be furious, but that wouldn't matter to Paul. He'd fly out when the Klemperer reunion was done—Hel would have spent today on arrangements and calling everyone in town to make sure they understood their responsibilities.

No, Paul wouldn't feel Joe's displeasure. But Beck absolutely would, and the idea that she could just drop the divorce case, drop everything, and disappear with nothing but the few hundred bucks she had saved was powerfully attractive.

"Little less dangerous." Joe must have shifted, because gravel made a slight sound and so did his belt. The soft creak made the copper-penny terror against Beck's tongue double-thick.

Of all the times to have a stupid accident in an old clunker—and that was another thing.

"I'm so sorry," she whispered, her eyes filling with tears again. She just couldn't stop leaking, and her nose was full. She finally realized what Hel had given her the bandanna for, and swiped at her wet cheek. It stung. "Your car, Hel. I'm so sorry."

"Should've had Paul take you in the Cherokee." Helena shook her head. "You come on over here now, Beck. You're gonna sit down, I've got some bottled water in the trunk. Let me see if I can find the granola bars in my bag, I know I have some. We have to take you to Doc Hardaway if you're not gonna go to the 'Mergency.'"

I can't afford a doctor's bill. She didn't even know if she was still on Joe's insurance. Besides, the closest real hospital was the Kaiser complex in Parsburg. "I'm fine," she insisted, but nobody would listen. The siren in the distance faded—maybe it wasn't her father. No cruiser came floating ghostlike through shimmers bouncing from dry pavement—if it rained in the afternoon and the sun came out again, ropy white veils of mist would hang above the surface. Once he got out of court her father, not to mention Joe, would be called to the scene of other accidents.

Maybe Sam had pulled someone over. This was his part of town on Wednesdays; Joe would of course have an explanation for being in the area.

And he would be believed. "I should put her in my car," Joe said. "Standard procedure."

Beck stiffened, and opened her mouth to say *no thank you.*

"She isn't under arrest," Hel snapped, and her strong skinny hand closed around Beck's arm. There was simply no arguing with her right now, so Beck gave in. The worst had happened, and as long as she wasn't dragged back to Passacola or put in Joe's cruiser, she could figure out everything else later.

Including how to survive on a few measly hundred bucks, out in a world where nobody had ever heard of Granite River.

DOC HARDAWAY was attending a birth—Chanice Gonzalez, no relation to Heck, was having her second—all the way over at County General near Eugene, but his nurse Marge Gunderssen checked Beck's vitals, pronouncing her "a little shook but all right" and cautioning her to go to Parsburg or at least the urgent care clinic between Granite River and Sinaida if she wasn't going to come back to Doc himself, especially for X-rays. Whiplash was nasty, and there was the risk of hairline fractures in important bones.

Beck listened, nodded, promised, and asked for the bill. Her phone kept buzzing—Mary, texting *Are you okay* and *don't worry* and *let me know what happens*, her father with *Pumpkin are you all right call me, Joe got on the radio are you okay?*

She had to call them both, but in the meantime a text to her father would do. *I'm fine, at Doc H's office. Don't worry.*

"Admin's gone home for the day." Marge's faded blue eyes were still piercing, and she looked up from Beck's file—probably containing every bump and bruise she'd had since birth, Hardaway had delivered her up at General too—to exchange a meaningful glance with Helena. "You can see we're doing land-office business at the moment. You're gonna stiffen up good come tomorrow, honey. I can't give you anything for the pain without Doc signing off."

At least you're honest about it. There was never any real help for the pain once you grew up; Beck had learned as much just after high school. "I'll be fine," she repeated. "But I do need to pay, Mrs. Gunderssen."

"Well, you give me a cup of coffee next time I come through that shed of Mary Parrack's." Marge grinned, her strong white horse-teeth gleaming. At least the examining room wasn't cold, and there was nobody in the familiar tan-and-blue waiting area but Helena.

And Paul, his legs stretched out and an ancient *National Geographic* open on his lap. He got up in a hurry when they reappeared. "Hey." His dark hair was mussed, the curl asserting itself with a vengeance. "I heard from Lefty. They've got the car out and they'll take it to the yard."

It was all Beck could do not to cringe. "I'm sorry," she repeated. "The brakes just gave, Hel."

"I believe it." Helena sighed. "Thanks, Marge."

The ride back to Hel's was excruciating. Paul drove, with his aunt riding shotgun—so Beck had to sit in the back, again, and try not to cry. She'd have to wash Hel's bandanna with her clothes this week too.

For some reason, that insignificant task threatened to break her. It was just, as her middle school best friend Nat Broderick would say, *the very last thing.*

The Brodericks had moved away to Salt Lake City before high school. At least Nat had gotten out; they'd exchanged some letters, but the contact petered out. Back then Beck had all sorts of school friends, though, and there was always Paul.

Then they graduated, and now she didn't have a single goddamn person she could call "friend" in this town. Living on Hel's charity—not to mention Mary's—wasn't *friendship.*

Paul took the long way home; the short way followed Old Marckola for a while, and he probably thought she'd want to avoid Benson Hill for a while.

He was goddamn right, and that was upsetting, too. Plus she hadn't brought twelve-ouncers back for Mary. Another hard hot weight pushed up in Beck's throat, but she refused to goddamn cry any more.

A line of ink-black cloud was moving in from the south. More cold rain was riding its back, and the sun had to peer under its edge to see what was going on below. It was the light that made spring afternoons seem soft and promising, despite the bite in the shadows and the reminder of icy runoff in every creek. Every year some dipshit went swimming on the first warm day, and found out why hypothermia was always a danger in this part of the world.

Hel didn't even turn the satellite radio on. She stared out her window, her expression set, and checked her phone every few minutes—probably waiting for responses from the extended family. Klemperers, Siddons, Barranies, and associated others were due to start flying in over the weekend, or well on their way if they were driving.

Beck had even fucked up someone else's extended family reunion, which might've had a certain bleak humor if she wasn't so goddamn tired. She couldn't even think of a good prank to pull at this year's party; her sense of humor, not to mention any energy for hijinks, was done gone.

Paul hit the brakes at just the right time. Beck's entire body stiffened, expecting further assault, and she was helpless to stop it. He cut the wheel, and they bounced neatly into his aunt's driveway.

Cars just loved him. He returned the favor, and she wondered if he'd been a mechanic in the Army. There was no way to ask.

He'd certainly deflated Joe's plans to "take poor Beck to the hospital." The accident report was written out, nice and legal and signed.

"All right, ladies." Paul pulled the Cherokee almost up to the porch. "Front-door service. I'm gonna put this car away and close up the shop."

"Thanks, Paulie." Helena patted his shoulder, smoothing his dark jacket. "I might get little Georgie Ratner to bring us some pizza for dinner. He's delivering for Numo's in-town."

Oh, crap. She'd fucked up dinnertime, too. "Yes," Beck added. "Thank you, Paul."

"Ah." His dark gaze found hers in the rearview. "Don't worry about it. I could do some damage to last night's pork chops, actually."

"But . . . pizza." Hel sounded almost mournful. "Come on, Beck. You're going to sit right down and rest; I have some painkillers left from my back surgery."

Joe hadn't dared stop his wife from bringing casseroles out to Hel's after the surgery a few years ago, and running other small errands for her too. The idea of escape had been growing in Beck's head the entire time, a tiny seed sheltered and watered in the dark.

"Ibuprofen is fine," Beck managed, and reached for the door handle. Her phone buzzed again—maybe Mary, maybe her dad. Joe had the new number now, because she had to put it on the official paperwork.

And it had happened so *fast*, every inch of safety evaporating in a single afternoon.

"There's Lefty," Paul said as she opened the door. A Beaujolais flatbed tow truck was indeed turning into Hel's driveway, its glittering lights sending sharp darts right through Beck's aching head. The wreck of the Taurus hunched on its platform behind the cab, and she didn't want to see the broken glass and twisted metal.

Suddenly, it was the very last thing in the world she could stand, and Beck decided not to look back as she headed for the house.

Biggest Task

"PAULIE KLEMPERER." Heck Gonzalez grinned, grabbing Paul's hand and shaking hard. He'd always been stocky, built for power; now he was packed with usable muscle and his shoulders could fill up a doorway with no help or football padding. His smile hadn't changed, and neither had the sunny warmth in his hazel eyes. "Son of a *bitch*. Look at you."

"How the hell ya been, Heck?" The genuine pleasure of seeing Heck and Lefty was an antidote to the rest of the afternoon. "Hey, Lefty. Thought you'd get here before us."

"Cops." Lefty looked sour, and the bright sunshine coming under the edge of storm clouds picked out his stubble. "Even if they're local, they waste time like my daughter on her damn phone."

"I dunno, man." Getting older meant talking about *kids these days*, with a heavy helping of *this newfangled technology*. Paul's grin turned stiff, his face feeling almost unnatural. Of course, Joe and Lefty had never seen eye-to-eye, being from different sides of the tracks, so to speak. "What did we use to waste time on, do you remember?"

"Cheap beer." Heck gave one last hard shake of Paul's hand. "I keep telling him, he's an old man. Been that way all his life." He was wearing a natty goatee these days; Paul could remember when none of them had anything to shave but were eager to start. "Where you want this bitch, Paulie?"

"Yard'll do, Hel said to just pick a space. Back entrance is right over there." Paul dug in his jacket pocket for Hel's keys. In short order the gate was open, the truck was rumbling through, and the Taurus would take its place among dead auto soldiers.

The idea sent a bit of gooseflesh down Paul's back. Bad luck, thinking something like that before an operation. Except there was no op to be found here, right?

Most of him agreed, but his gut wasn't so sure. And every one of the Squad knew it was instinct you went with, even when everything appeared hunky-dory.

"Care for a smoke?" Lefty patted his breast pocket, his eyebrows raised. He knew damn well Paul would rather clean an entire transmission with his tongue.

"I'll keep you company." Paul braced himself for something possibly unpleasant as they ambled in the truck's wake. "Then I'll help Heck unhitch. Thanks for doing this, by the way." Towing was expensive, but anyone who fixed up engines in the county had an agreement or two with the H & H junkyard.

It was just good business.

"Yeah, well, it about gave me a heart attack to see Beck pop up on the side of the road. Going back down to get her goddamn *purse*." Lefty halted on one side of the gate, watching as Heck nosed the truck across an expanse of weed-starred gravel toward a line of rusty hulks with cataract windshields.

Paul would have to log the new entry in the ancient binder on a creaking shop shelf; Hel kept a running inventory in her head, but how long would that last? He should talk her into getting computerized. Maybe he could get Beck to help with that. "Well, you know, women. They've got their whole lives in little bags."

"Everyone else's, too." Lefty snorted. "Gonna have to tell Paige I saw you. She won't believe it." Apparently he'd married Paige McPherson, which was a surprise. The two of them had hated each other with resounding passion all through high school.

"Get out your phone, take a selfie." Paul found the right joke without much trouble. "Just don't post it. Everyone will want one."

Lefty didn't laugh. Instead, he dug a small plastic case out of his breast pocket. A few moments of fooling around produced a vape pen, and he sucked on its end, exhaling a pale cloud. "Fuck," he said, quietly. "Paige is on me to quit. Got me on this thing instead of regular smokes."

"Does it work? I might have to hook Aunt Hel up with one." Paul watched the truck; Heck was a goddamn master with the bulky diesel bastard. Besides, whatever was on Lefty's mind, he'd spit it out easier if he wasn't being stared at.

"Tastes like ass."

Paul refrained from the teenage *how would you know, you eat a lot of that?* If it had been Boom or Grey, the crack would have left his mouth without a pause, but he was supposedly an adult now.

Lefty took another couple pulls, working himself up to it. "I shouldn't say anything," he began, and paused when Heck dropped the truck into reverse. The beeping marred a quiet spring afternoon, echoing down rows of stacked, packed car corpses.

"About Beck, or about Deputy Halston?" It was a shot in the dark, and Paul didn't have Jackson's gift for those, or even Dez's. On the other hand, it was a *verbal* shot, and he was the Ghost Squad's reigning leader at those.

"Just watch yourself, Paulie. You know what Joe's like." Lefty's sigh was far too old for a kid Paul had known from grade school.

Then again, he was feeling a bit creaky these days as well. His leg was holding up, though. It hadn't given a single twinge since piling into the Cherokee to fetch Beck.

Christ, the thought of what *could* have happened turned him cold all the way through. A few feet, either way, and. . . . "Not surprised he ended up a cop."

"Yeah, well, half of Sommers's office is in bed with Dewey Johnson and that crew." Heck's mouth puckered up, sour as an unripe lemon. "You remember him?"

"He was a few years behind us, wasn't he? Cousins with Gavin Creslough? Hel told me Gav is up in county."

"Federal. Not eligible for parole, which means everyone can breathe a sigh of relief." Lefty exhaled another cloud of supercooled nicotine fog. "Little Dew got into meth and has a head for business. Woods are full of fuckin' labs, you can't even go hunting anymore without runnin' across one. You still hunt, Paulie?"

"Not really." Was it still called *hunting* when the killing wasn't dumb animals? Sure, some of the Squad's work was misdirection, confusion, extraction—a lot of euphemisms for causing and catching a shit-ton of murderous chaos while following orders—but those ops were definitely in the minority.

You didn't train men like Dez, or Jackson, or Boom, or even Paul's own sweet self for mayhem without planning to break some eggs, so to speak. It had never really bothered him much. Following orders and doing a patriotic duty for the Stars and Stripes while sending an allotment home to Hel was the best a kid from the wrong side of Granite River could hope for, the only real way out of grinding poverty and the hopelessness it caused.

Every time he pulled a trigger, he told himself Hel was a little safer because of it. It was probably a good thing he hadn't proposed to Beck before he left—what would Sheriff Sommers's law-abiding daughter think of some of the shit the Squad had to do? Had *done*?

"Guess the Army might take some of the flavor out," Lefty allowed, morosely. "But I ain't talking about that. Had a chance to look under that car when we dragged it uphill."

"Did you, now." This was the real business, Paul could tell. His pulse threatened to spike, and every edge was clear and sharp. He wasn't tasting metal like he would under fire, but the hair-raising adrenaline surge was still familiar.

"It was the brakes, like Beck said." Lefty glanced quickly at him, probably attempting to gauge Paul's response. "Damndest thing, Paulie. Looks like the lines were cut. Little bright nicks, shows up against the corrosion real nice."

Anyone watching would just think they were shooting the shit while watching someone else work, a time-honored good ol' boy tradition not just in Granite River but everywhere on the benighted globe.

Paul exhaled softly.

Dez's job was to lead, Boom's to blow shit up, Tax's to patch flesh and bone, Grey's to work intel as well as keeping them in contact with the mothership and each other. Jackson, of course, was the wildcard, the silent dog.

Klemp's job was to do what Dez needed, keep the transport running and find the road, as well as keep the leashes tight and everyone moving in the direction their CO decided on, preferably with a smile on their faces or at least a minimum of bitching. But his biggest task was to *anticipate*, so the entire squad functioned like a good engine.

He didn't have Dez to do the deciding right now, so he had to be very, very careful. Not just for himself, but for Helena, who had to live here, after all.

And for Beck, huddled against the back of Joe Halston's cruiser with him looming over her. You didn't need a dictionary to read body language like that.

Paul finally allowed himself a single syllable. "Huh."

A local, especially one he'd gone to grade school with, didn't need more. Lefty was deliberate, but he wasn't *slow*. Not where it counted, between the ears.

"Yeah." Beaujolais finished his vaping, and stowed the pen with finicky care. "Let's get 'er unhitched, then. Can't make Heck do all the work."

"You guys want to stay for dinner?" Paul suddenly wanted both of them out of here and heading back to town, but Hel would give him good old-fashioned holy hand grenades and double hockey-sticks if he didn't at least ask.

He also wanted to corner Beck and ask her a few questions. But she was so thin, and she flinched even when he *looked* at her.

Most of all, Paul realized, he wanted to go find Joe, and get a few answers the hard way. That wasn't the right move, but it was powerfully tempting.

"Thanks, but no; Wednesday's poker night. You're welcome for a hand or two, you know. Just knock twice on the back door."

"If I had a nickel for every time I heard *that*. . . ." Paul let the other man laugh, and even joined in. Others in the Squad would know what his expression meant, the smile that didn't quite reach his eyes. "Thanks, Lefty."

"Shit." But the other man looked pleased. "Glad you're here for Helena. Every time I see her, she talks about her Paulie."

Well, crap. But it was better than the alternative, so Paul set off for Heck, the tow truck, and the smashed Taurus.

IT TOOK ANOTHER forty-five minutes, most of which was Heck and Paul talking about old times. Hector had married too, no kids yet though, and both he and his boss were looking forward to poker night.

Paul made no promises but he did attempt to pay them, and Lefty actually looked a little offended. *It's an afternoon off, and besides, it's for Hel.*

Once the truck took the turn at the end of the driveway, its brake lights blinking rubies, Paul put the Cherokee in a handy shop bay, locked up, and walked to the other end of the building where the Taurus usually sat. All sorts of effluvia stained bite-size rocks on a dirt road or drive, especially near a yard or a garage.

He stood for a moment in the gathering dusk, head slightly cocked, and looked at the parking spot.

Yep. There, right where he'd expected, a slick of brake fluid glistened. Beck wouldn't have seen it; she'd left just before dawn, and she didn't check the underside of her vehicle for unfriendly items like he'd done hundreds of times while in-country with his squad. No, she'd probably been worrying about the workday, ditty-bopping along like any normal civilian. No rain today meant the sign was fresh.

How would I do it? Well, I'd park just out of sight near the yard's front entrance and cut through the bushes there, if I knew the layout. If I didn't, or not well, I'd. . . .

He glanced at the house. The porch light was on, a yellow beacon. Golden electric light in every window, and a shadow moving in the living room was probably Hel looking to see if he was coming in yet.

There was a weak spot in the bushes he used to slip through while walking home from the schoolbus stop years and years ago, but it was now choked with blackberry vines. That left parking on the shoulder between the yard and the private turn-in, and there was no sign in the gathering dusk. If someone had taken some care to close their car door quietly, he could simply walk right up the drive, slither under the Taurus, and if he had a penlight the entire shebang could be finished in a matter of moments.

The motion-sensor and other lights on the junkyard's fences and almost-neglected front office wouldn't catch that. The shop was wired with an alarm and exterior lights, but sticking to the overgrown side of the driveway made it child's play to get to a car parked right where the Taurus had been.

Beck, leaning against the back of Joe Halston's cruiser. For it to be pointed that way meant he'd come from the same direction she had—down Benson Hill.

Could be, Jackson would allow, his eyes narrowed and his tone soft, reflective. *But you've got to assess, asshole, not just assume.*

"Fuck," he muttered, and wished Dez was here. Or Tax. The medic could check Beck and maybe, with his easy, nonjudgmental manner, get her to relax a bit.

A hot, sharp bolt of lightning went through him at the thought.

The sharp sound of the screen door slamming cut the rush of rising evening breeze, the small sounds in the foliage from critters doing their evening chores, and a chainsaw running in the distance, probably down at the Markhams' place. They were the closest neighbors.

"Paulie?" his aunt called, and the note of worry in his name wasn't like Hel at all.

Don't worry. I'm on it.

Paul turned sharply on one heel, and strode for home. "Coming," he called back, as if she'd yelled him in for supper and he'd ignored the first warning.

He had to get Beck to open up. But if he couldn't, he'd have to settle for something else, like simply, directly solving the problem. As a wounded but still card-carrying member of Desmarais's crew of happy little maniacs, he had just the tools to do it with.

Or he could find them, which was really what all the training was for.

Accidents Happen

GETTING CLEANED up and taking a short warm shower was heavenly, but Beck was in the habit of not using too much hot water so it didn't last nearly long enough. Hel did indeed have painkillers left from her back surgery, and she wasn't taking *no, I'm fine* for an answer today. Beck dutifully swallowed the small tablet, and was about to get to work on the week's laundry—her coat needed to at least be run through the washer, too, which would make it damp tomorrow since it couldn't be put in the dryer—when Hel imperiously ordered her to the couch in the living room, turning on the television and pressing the holy remote into Beck's hand.

"You *stay there*," the old woman said, and there was no arguing allowed.

Besides, Beck's phone buzzed again. It was another text from Dad—voice could be spotty out in this area, but the little byte-packets of text worked just fine.

She couldn't put it off any longer. Hel's cordless sat companionably on the end table; Beck muted the Home Shopping Network and dialed.

"Hello?" A gruff bark, with an undertone of worry—oh, a landline connection was nice and clear, she could discern every shade of emotion in his familiar, beloved voice.

"I'm okay," she said. "Don't worry. It was just an accident."

Shuffling paper, sound of motion. He was probably in the office doing paperwork after a long day of waiting to testify in court or attending to other county business, shootin' the breeze with clerks or Judge Nelson or McCready, maybe talking to other law enforcement about this, that, and t'other. "Just an accident, hell." Another soft sound—he'd closed his office door. "I hear you almost went into that ravine off Benson Hill. Joe said you wouldn't get in a damn ambulance."

Of course Joe had gotten to him first. "There wasn't any need. I went to Doc Hardaway's office. The car hit a tree, Dad, I didn't go down the ravine."

"You could have." Now her father sounded deadly serious, a tone he rarely took with his beloved child. "You coulda been down there for hours, Beck. You coulda been down there for *days*."

She shut her eyes; the darkness behind her lids was comforting for once. "I know." She barely remembered struggling out through the shattered driver's side window and scrabbling frantically up the slope, convinced the car was going to explode at any moment and equally convinced the entire hillside was going to give way and bury her. "But I'm not. I'm fine. I handled it, all the paperwork's done."

"I don't care about no goddamn paperwork, Rebecca." Quiet, and final—if she'd heard this tone as a child or teenager, Beck would have been dead certain of being grounded for a month or possibly forever, with no phone privileges at all. "I'm glad you're all right. But you shoulda gone to the hospital."

"Hel said the same thing. I'm *all right*, Dad." She felt fifteen again, but she'd never been this scared. Not then. "Honestly."

"You ain't been all right for months, Beck. You won't even. . . ." He stopped, took a deep breath. Everyone in town knew Sheriff Sommers never lost his temper, even when meth-heads were screaming and spitting at him. "Joe was pretty shook, pumpkin."

I'll bet he was. The painkiller couldn't possibly be working yet, but a great lassitude swamped Beck anyway. She was just so goddamn tired; the television was a brightly colored smear hanging on the air. "I guess."

"Man can't help it, when his wife—"

"We're *getting a divorce*, Dad." She had to be an adult; teenage Beck wouldn't dare sound so sharp with her daddy. *For good goddamn reasons I can't tell you, because you won't believe me. Joe made sure of that.* "I don't want to talk about Joe."

"Fine. Lefty Beaujolais treat you right? I told him I'd take care of the tow fee."

"He was real nice, Dad. I can pay him." It was a lie, but what choice did she have?

"No, honey. I got it. Listen. . . ."

She did. She listened to him breathing, the faintly stentorian wheezes. Finally there was a click, and an inhale. He'd lit a cigarette.

He probably needed a bracer for this conversation. God knew Beck did, and she thought longingly of a tot of whiskey, or even vodka. She could still smell the mud, the rocks, and the scratch on her cheek from the blackberries throbbed. So did her hands.

Everyone was going to come by the coffee stall to take a look at her. Mary would do *land-office business*, like Mrs. Gunderssen often said.

"I hear Paulie Klemperer showed up with his aunt." Dad's tone was now excessively neutral.

Oh, for God's sake. "Helena didn't tell me he was coming for the reunion, Dad. I'm just as surprised as you are."

"Yeah?" At least Dad sounded thoughtful instead of outright disbelieving.

"Yeah. Haven't talked to him in years, and now this." There was nothing like the ring of absolute honesty when you were talking to your dad the cop. "It's kind of awkward."

"Guess so."

Beck's temper threatened to break. Of course Joe had been dropping intimations in Dad's ear, just like poison. Dad had never precisely liked Paul, and maybe that had been part of the attraction for teenage Rebecca.

But that wasn't the point now, and she couldn't get distracted. Beck had to be even more careful. It was galling—no matter how thorough, how self-effacing, how goddamn cautious she was, Joe would find a way.

The only solution was to leave entirely. She couldn't do it without money. And tomorrow was the hearing.

"The hearing's tomorrow," she heard herself say, dully. "Should be the last one. Then Joe and I can both get on with our lives."

"You sure you don't want to reschedule? You really should get checked out, Beck. Some X-rays, at least."

"I don't have a concussion. I'll just be a little stiff and I have a few scratches, Dad, but I'm fine. Honestly."

"I'd like to come out and see you, pumpkin." Of course he'd want to make sure his child was all right. It was a natural impulse.

"You should go home and get some rest. You're smoking in your office."

"Can't put one by my girl, can I. Sharp ears, like your mama."

Oh, God. Things were getting really bad if he was mentioning Mom. What would her father do when she left town? Would it be another betrayal he wouldn't mention, keeping it locked behind starched uniform shirts and the creak of leather? "I love you, Daddy." The sentence caught in the middle, like fabric on a protruding nail.

"Why, shoot, pumpkin." Now he sounded surprised. "I know that. You're my Becca."

"I'm sorry I didn't call. It was just so sudden; I was at the top of the hill and then the brakes weren't working. I used the handbrake, like you taught me." He'd taught her bootlegger turns, and she'd even practiced in Paul's cherished Camaro, both of them laughing like loons.

"Thank God for that." Dad took another drag. "You did real well. Joe said the car was busted good, but you'd aimed for a tree. Quick thinking."

That part was accidental. "It was so fast," she repeated. "Just, like *that.*"

"That's how accidents happen."

Well, that was true as far as it went. But they also developed over years, with shoves and pinches. With small insults, then larger ones. With checking-on-you phone calls and icy silences, and finally with hot, hard hands around your throat while your husband—the boy you thought loved you, the man you thought would help you get out of a trap—swore in a low hissing undertone and the world darkened at the edges, heavy gloom spilling toward the center of your vision like a camera shutter closing.

It took all kinds, as Hel said, to make the world go 'round.

I'm scared, Daddy. I'm so scared right now. "Everything's going to be okay, Dad."

"Of course it will, pumpkin. You can take that to the bank." Her father paused. "You know, I been thinking about retiring."

"Yeah?" That was like the sun deciding not to come up in the morning. "What would you do all day, then?"

"Oh, sell the house, buy one of them Airstream trailers. Your mama, she liked road trips. Said there was a lot to see in the world, but I always liked staying in one place. Let all that world come to me, you know?" He was moving again, probably pacing his office with the phone clamped to his ear, a trail of cigarette smoke behind him.

"It takes all kinds," Beck said. You could never tell what lurked under a parental exterior, or anyone else's. "I think it's a great idea, though."

"You don't want the house?"

I don't want anything to do with this goddamn place. "An Airstream sounds nice. For a while, at least." And maybe, if she could escape before he retired, he could visit her somewhere. In a different town, a different city. "There are people who do it all the time, and put pictures on the internet. You could get famous."

"Oh, I don't know about that." Connor Sommers considered the online world suspect at best, despite the ease and speed of law-enforce9-ment databases. "What time's your hearing tomorrow?"

"Eleven-thirty." Her throat was dry. Maybe the painkiller was beginning to work, because now she felt lightheaded. "I guess Joe probably asked for time off."

"I can pick you up in the morning, it isn't but a few—"

"No, Dad." It was far safer to keep him at whatever distance she could. Especially since she suspected . . . something, a terrible idea rising like bad gas from her subconscious mineshafts whenever she slowed down enough to really think. "I'll meet you for lunch, like we planned. It's better if it's just me and Joe."

Embarrassing Deputy Halston in front of his boss was a good way to get even more shit rolling downhill, and she had all she could handle.

Thankfully, Dad didn't push. "If you say so, pumpkin."

"I should go help with dinner."

"Hel makin' you cook?" A faint hint of disapproval.

"No, but at least I can set the table or something." The television screen blurred; Beck blinked furiously. "I'm sorry I didn't call earlier, Dad. I was just . . . holding it together. You know?"

"Yeah." The weight in the single word told her he did, in fact, know. "It's all right. Just . . . call me tomorrow morning, all right? And consider going back to Doc's, too, so you can get an X-ray."

"I'll think about it. I love you, Dad." Twice in one conversation, a new kind of record.

"I love you too, Becca. Bye."

She hung up, and it was official, she was *definitely* woozy. She had to think, she had to plan, but for once it could wait for morning.

Helena was due at the Grange early tomorrow, putting together all sorts of reunion stuff for next week; Beck could get a ride to the courthouse from someone heading to Parsburg for supplies. The important thing was, there was no way Hel could attend the hearing either.

It was safest for everyone; Christ alone knew what Joe would do. Even living with him for as long as she did, Beck had the feeling she'd underestimated a few critical things.

She barely remembered finding her purse in the crazily canted car half-wrapped around the oak tree, digging for her phone and almost sobbing with relief when it showed a single, lonely bar's worth of service—probably from the tower old Hank Gillespie had sworn would give everyone cancer. Beck couldn't even remember what she'd said to Mary, unless it was something like *I'm so sorry, I think I'll be late, I went off Benson Hill and into the ravine.*

A blip, a skip like a flaw in a recording or the cell signal dropping out, and she'd found herself wriggling out of the driver's side window like a groundhog looking for its own shadow. And she'd begun to climb, impelled by hysterical strength, absolutely certain she'd never reach the top.

Oh, she'd reached it all right, and peered over a concrete lip as the sound of an engine floated down Benson Hill. Wild thoughts of scrabbling up and flagging someone down died when she saw the cruiser, and Beck had flinched on a crumbling, slippery rock ledge, the instinct to hide clear and overwhelming.

He must've done a three-point turn on Marckola, because he'd come back up the hill next, while Beck crouched hidden, sweating and shivering. And he'd been going slowly, no doubt scanning the edge of the ravine. The hole in the guardrail was there, plain as day, but it had been since last November and the cruiser didn't stop. Instead, he accelerated up Benson Hill as Beck clung to dirt and wet, knobbled roots, her lips moving in silent prayer, trembling like a hunted rabbit for a fear-soaked eternity until another engine sound burped and bumbled along—the Beaujolais tow truck.

And then Joe had reappeared, after good old Lefty pulled Beck almost bodily up onto safe land. *Jeez, girl. You're lucky*

It didn't feel like it. Beck rested her head against the couch's frayed back and stared at the television, her gaze blessedly unfocused.

She just had to find a ride to the courthouse in the morning, and get through the legal dance. Maybe Joe would have run out of maneuvers.

Trembling, Beck drifted into an uneasy doze. She didn't even hear when the pizza arrived, and maybe it was the painkiller, because when she woke the next morning she was on the annex couch's fold-out bed and her phone alarm was shrieking it was time to get up and go to court.

There was even a note by the coffee machine; Hel had found her a ride.

Thick as Thieves

NORMALLY PAUL wouldn't mind helping Hel put together the god-damn Granite River Grange on Holtzmann Road for a party nobody was going to enjoy. He'd done it almost every year, growing up.

Well, that wasn't quite fair. The old folks liked the coffee, the cake, the casseroles, the barbeque, and the chance to get together and chew everyone's business down to the last bit of gristle and sauce. The adults would be busy cooking, cleaning, keeping an eye on the kids, and one-upping each other on the family ladder all week; some of them might even enjoy it, like Cousin Jeannie or Uncle Dreeson's second son Kenny.

The two of them had been rivals from the cradle.

Kids from every branch related to the Klemperers would be running around hopped up on Spring Break and a lot of food. The older ones would be looking forward to the lemons out of the huge vodka-and-ice-filled jars, wrapped in beach towels and cradled like babies for an hour or so while the big people talked. When the towel froze, the drinks were ready—though Uncle Dreeson, Aunt Stefanie, and several others preferred their booze in different forms.

Sneaking the leftover lemons was a game Paul was intimately acquainted with, and some years Beck had even helped with the operation. Nobody could divert attention or sweet-talk a suspicious adult like Sheriff Sommers's little girl.

"Put them over there," Hel said, and one of the cousins—Little Davey, Harlow Gripney's son, not to be confused with Big Davey who had married into the family or Davey Hutchins on Paul's maternal side—groaned as he hefted two folding chairs.

The kid, his hair cut into a fringe across his forehead they probably called *emo* instead of *grunge* these days, could have handled twice the load at double the speed. But he was only sixteen, snub-nosed, and sarcastic, his hands and feet a little too large and the rest of him not catching up.

Paul remembered him as a baby. "You're getting the day off school, Dave." He eyed the ladder and the pile of multicolored bunting Helena had made his problem. He'd almost rather be digging latrines, or marching with a full heavy. "You want to complain, I can take you right back."

He got a snort and an eyeroll in return, before the kid caught Hel glaring at him. "Nosir," Little Davey blurted, and hurried away with a chair in each hand, his shirttail flapping as if he'd forgotten to tuck in after his last piss break.

"That child." Hel's undertone was nevertheless affectionate. "Are you gonna be okay on that ladder, Paulie?"

"I've climbed worse," he informed her, absolutely straight-faced, and waited for the laugh.

All he got was a tight grin while Helena dug in her back jeans pocket for her new smartphone. She was checking that thing every few minutes like she thought it was going to explode.

"She's probably fine," he said, for the third time that morning. At least his leg hadn't given out while carrying Beck from the living room to the annex last night either; she was all bones and nervousness, and he kept thinking about that blackberry scratch on her cheek, dots of dried blood on a soft curve. "Just sleeping in."

Helena shook her greying head, glancing quickly at the Grange's ballroom. "She texted a bit ago; she got out of bed okay." The tables were already set up, Davey schlepping chairs with mutinous but reasonable speed, and everyone else was either in the commercial kitchen part of the building, the anteroom, or grabbing a smoke break. "The hearing's today. I asked Bree Markham down the lane to give her a ride to the courthouse."

"What hearing?" Paul's heart sank, squeezing itself like matter slung into a black hole. Boom was always going on about astronomy, and some of that shit was outright terrifying.

"*Divorce* hearing." Hel's mouth turned down sourly, and she gave that little glance again, checking the terrain or making sure nobody was in earshot. "She's hoping it's the last one. Not that you care, Paulie."

I'm giving her space, goddammit. Or he had been.

"Yeah, well, just how bad has Joe been stalking her?" The slick of spilled brake fluid was just a smudge today since rain had swept through just after three a.m., giving the entire town a good spring soaking. They had some sun at the moment, but it wouldn't last. "You might as well tell me now."

It wasn't the time to share some of his other suspicions. The words— *someone cut those brake lines, Hel, and the Jeep might be next or maybe he'll just show up with a shotgun like any other domestic violence asshole*—lingered on his tongue, burning worse than every joke he'd never told.

Why would Hel look startled? She stared owlishly at him, her phone dangling forgotten in one hand. Beck must have talked her into the hot pink silicon case for it, too. "I don't know about stalking. But. . . ."

Well, what the fuck would you *call it?* Paul's hands tingled, a familiar feeling. Everyone thought he was easygoing, of course. The humor helped, defusing him as well as the entire situation.

But his daddy's temper was behind it, and *that* monster had claws plus a long memory, not to mention the deep desire to slip whatever harness he wrapped it in and run amok. Funny, he'd thought the Army would help keep it down.

He couldn't decide if it had, or if it just sharpened the knives. "But what?" It took effort to keep his tone reasonable and his voice level. "If you didn't want me to ask, you shouldn't have dragged her to the airport to meet me. Without telling either of us, I might add."

Did his aunt—the closest thing to a mother he'd ever have—flinch, or was it just the rattle of chairs falling over?

"Sorry," Davey called, and added something in a half-whisper that was probably a swear word.

Just like Paul would have, at that age. And at that age Beck would have talked her dad into letting her help Hel put together another reunion, and they'd sneak a kiss or two in the kitchen, or in the short hall to the bathrooms, or. . . .

Jesus. She clearly didn't want anything to do with him, hadn't for years, and he should just leave well enough alone. But she was so obviously scared, so patently about to break, and—most of all—someone had just tried to kill her.

She could have fucking *died*.

The realization kept tiptoeing back into his head, over and over, at random intervals. Bleeding out under fire was one thing. He knew, signing up to the black-ops merry-go-round, that it was a risk. You got over it, or you washed out.

But imagining Beck's body in a crumpled, primer-spotted Taurus at the bottom of a ravine was something else.

"I'm an old woman." Helena's chin jutted slightly, and she eyed him much as she had his dad Peter once or twice. "I suppose I like to meddle, and that's between me and Jesus, Paulie. You two were thick as thieves, and I always wondered what happened."

"You and me both." *I don't know what fucking happened.* And why were they discussing this, rather than how long Joe Halston had been terrifying her? Paul never would have thought the asshole had it in him.

But he also never dreamed Beck would *marry* him. Maybe he'd seemed like a safer bet once Paul was gone.

She don't want to talk, Sheriff Sommers had growled into the phone the first time Paul had worked himself up to calling. He'd even written two letters in his eighth week of basic, but no reply ever came back. Hel hadn't been able to fly out for his graduation, and right after that he was tapped for the hush-hush shit.

It was the one time in his life his test scores had been good enough to mean something.

"It's ancient history," Paul continued, but he didn't believe it. "I'm more worried about how long Joe's been pulling this bullshit, Hel."

"This town. . . ." Hel shook her head, her mouth turning into a tight line before she forced herself to speak again. Her gaze fixed itself somewhere over Paul's shoulder. "Everyone's in everyone else's business, and that's what God intended when He made places like this, I guess. But I never thought anything was wrong, Paul. She never said anything, she never . . . I should've seen it before she . . . I should have done something."

Christ. "How long, Hel?"

"Last spring. She came for an afternoon visit, I could tell something was . . . anyway, she asked if I knew a place she could stay. Said she was leaving Joe. I got her a glass of iced tea, and—you know, it's odd. That was the day I found out you'd been hurt overseas. Got the call right after dinner."

Get to the point. But you couldn't bark that at your aging aunt, especially when her bony shoulders had drawn up and she looked like she was reliving something terrible. "Sorry about that." His throat was so dry it was difficult getting the damn words out.

The Grange's front doors opened and closed. Voices in the entryway were all familiar, all familial, and all unwelcome at the moment.

"What? Oh, honey, we're all proud of you serving your country." A tremulous smile, and Hel's eyes were suspiciously bright. "And I told Beck, *you just move in here, I've got the spare room and we'll figure it out.* Whatever happened with you and her, she's always been good to me, Paulie. Real good, and she didn't have to be."

It was just like Beck, frankly. And, he realized, Helena had probably been lonely as hell, especially once Herrold passed. "She's a good girl." The guy using his voice sounded like he had something cactus-shaped stuck in his craw. "Always has been."

"Yeah. Well, anyway, a town like this, you can't help but see people you'd rather not. I thought it was just that, but Joe's been doing everything he can to drag the divorce out and some days when she comes home, she looks. . . . She never says much, but I can guess he was waiting for her somewhere. Doesn't take a damn detective to figure that out, especially with the bruises." Helena halted, and her eyes turned round.

Paul couldn't tell what was happening with his own expression, but it probably wasn't pleasant. "Bruises."

"Don't get angry." Why was Hel, of all people, looking at him that way? And it was the sort of thing she used to say to his father, though with a lot more irritation back then. "Paulie? Just don't. It's not going to help."

He wished one of the guys was here. Dez would look thoughtful, a dangerous light beginning in his dark eyes; Boom would shift a little and his eyebrows would go up, sensing one of his beloved explosions. Tax or Grey would want more details, and exchange one of those *let's get planning* looks.

Jackson? Well, that motherfucker would be in complete agreement with what Paul found himself wanting to do at the moment. "What time's the hearing?"

"Don't. You show up there, God knows what Joe will do. I didn't think. . . ." Helena broke off, and her face changed. "Oh, shit. Here comes Gloria."

"Auntie Hel?" Gloria's auburn curls came right out of a Clairol bottle and the rest of her was built like one of Lefty's tow trucks. She'd married the older Jeff on the Gripney side when Paul was in middle school, and it was a solid bet that when Hel decided she didn't want to do the reunions anymore ol' Glory would try to take over. Which would touch off an interesting firefight with Cousin Jeannie and Gramma Mabel, that was for damn sure. "Do you have the key to the cloakroom? I thought we should make sure it's all set up too."

Paul didn't have any fucking idea what the cloakroom had to do with anything, but if there wasn't trouble already Gloria would *make* it, as the family saying went.

The urge to walk out of here with Hel's car keys, drive to the county courthouse, find Beck, and stand guard until he could get her alone to talk was goddamn well overwhelming. And, just for shits and giggles, he could call Sheriff Sommers and casually drop the news about some snipped brake lines. *What do you care about more, Connor? Your deputies, or your daughter?*

Except a cop would want proof, and Beck wouldn't thank him for putting her dad in that position. She was trying to get out of this as quietly as possible.

Again, it was just like her.

"—right, Paulie?" Gloria said, and the edge to her tone was like a buzzsaw across his already frayed nerves.

He realized he was considering taking a piece out of a frumpy, middle-aged woman in coordinated Lane Bryant earth tones and carefully matched Avon jewelry, for God's sake. She was family, and she wasn't bad. Just bossy.

"Don't drag me into it," he said. "I've got bunting to deal with."

"Surprised to see you, by the way." Gloria was even smiling, glossy brown lipstick cracking at the feather-edges of her lips. "I hear Beck Halston's down at the courthouse today."

"Gloria, for God's sake, keep your mouth on your own business," Hel snapped. "Let's go check that cloakroom, if you're so determined. Paulie, get on that ladder, I want those decorations hung."

I'll hang a few things, all right. Fifty other jokes crowded in his throat, and all of them had edges sharper than poor old Gloria could ever handle. "Yes ma'am."

Yeah, normally he wouldn't have minded this. It was just the same as every other family event, and there were a lot of them. Spending years fucking around trying to get himself killed with Dez and the crew was a goddamn vacation, comparatively.

That was a good joke. He had to tell Boom that one.

The ancient wooden ladder creaked as he made sure it was stable. His leg was itching again. And by God, if Hel didn't hear from Beck soon. . . .

There was nothing he could do. And of all the situations to be stuck in, he hated "can't do shit" the most.

Bigger Boxes

IT WASN'T THE worst she'd ever ached, especially since Hel had left another pain pill at Beck's place at the table with a Post-it saying *take it, DON'T argue* in her beautiful handwriting—they didn't teach you letters like that anymore, which was a damn shame.

Hel had also arranged for Bree Markham to give Beck a ride to the courthouse. *I got some shopping to do anyways*, the daughter of Hel's closest neighbor had said, settling her wide hips more firmly in the bucket seat of the blue minivan. *Want I should pick you up after?*

Maybe it was the painkiller blurring all the edges, but Beck for once didn't feel like a huge, deadly imposition. Even the car seat on the back bench didn't cause a twinge, just a hazy gratefulness that it was uninhabited and a deeper, more vivid one that she'd never buckled to Joe's pressure for kids. At first she'd just been too . . . raw, but later, the thought of one more anchor holding her to Granite River made her nauseous with something close to terror.

Was that how her mother had felt?

Beck emerged blinking into spring sunshine, clutching a manila folder full of precious papers, and her knees were warm gelatin. The county courthouse's granite steps, wide and clean, glittered with tiny mica pinpoints. Deciduous trees were full of ripening green buds, and the sky was a bright fresh-washed blue from last night's rain.

It was a distinct goddamn letdown.

Joe hadn't even shown up, but he *had* filed yet another motion—day before yesterday, as a matter of fact, and the process server handed her the papers right before the hearing. Judge McCready looked sour, but he unfortunately had to give it another week, banged the gavel, and ended with a *chin up and tell your daddy hi for me, Miss Sommers.*

Britney, the best of the court clerks, helped her figure out which piece of paper she had to file in reply, so that took a half hour. Nothing had really changed, despite all her hard work.

Maybe a lot of people felt this way standing on these very steps, breathing hard and trembling.

"Becca! Hey, Beck!" It was a man's voice, and Beck's heart leapt into her throat before she recognized her father, unfolding from the driver's side of his cruiser, parked in one of the *LAW ENFORCE-MENT ONLY* spots. Prime real estate, and technically he shouldn't be using it if he was just here to see her.

But her lungs expanded with a painful whoosh and she made it down the steps, every muscle creaking and twinging. He met her halfway, and when he hugged her, she breathed in his Afta aftershave mixed with the indefinable smell of *father* that meant safety, security, and refuge ever since she could remember.

"Hi, pumpkin," he said into her hair. "How'd it go?"

I hate everything, and my life most of all. "Joe filed another motion," she mumbled into her father's chest. "I have to wait a week."

"Oh, shoot. I'm sorry." He had to hold her carefully, keeping his sidearm well away, but it didn't matter. "Let me take a look at you. How you feeling? Got an appointment with Doc Hardaway for X-rays yet?"

"I've been a bit busy, Dad." But she made herself let go, and let him hold her at arm's length, inspecting her from neatly done French twist held by some of Hel's bobby pins to the semi-professional charcoal blazer and trousers out of the one suitcase she'd taken from the house on Passacola.

She'd chewed off everything else to escape the trap, and now she had to wait another whole *week*. She wasn't sure she'd make it. Her eyes were full of hot, heavy blurring, and her nose was filling up too.

"Oh, honey. Here." He let go of her, but only to dig in the pocket of his uniform jacket for a battered plastic travel-pak of tissues, *useful for more than catching snot*, as he always said. "Thought I'd take my girl to the Giblet."

She should have known; it was his favorite place to eat. Beck blew her nose, wincing as her back seized up a bit, and followed her father as if she were a teenager again, holding books to her chest on one of the rare but welcome occasions Dad signed her out of school and said *everyone needs a break now and again, honey, let's go do something nice.*

The patchwork of bruises all over her and the aches and twinges coming back as Hel's painkiller faded were yet another reminder that she had a price to pay for daring to attempt escape, and the interest on that bitch mounted daily.

THE GIBLET WAS just the same, even though old Molly Gibbs had retired to Florida and Buster Flanagan taken over managing the place. It was a cop joint, and Beck should have been nervous at the prospect of seeing Joe, or his buddies seeing her and reporting back. But dammit, she was with her *father*, and they'd been coming to this place since Beck was old enough to sit up and eat french fries.

She took a moment to text Hel a smiley face and a *I'm with my dad, I'll check in later*—and she did *not* forget punctuation. She texted Mary too, who replied with a solid wall of emojis expressing wholehearted support, righteous anger on Beck's behalf, and perhaps complete forgiveness for the inconvenience of her employee's car accident.

Beck's good mood lasted through the famous Giblets milkshakes, her usual double order of fries and side of salad, and even stood up to two of Connor Sommers's deputies stopping by the table to give their regards and hopes that she felt all right after her accident. Both Ed Smythe and Sam Neesdale were old friends—or they would have been, if she could trust anyone who talked to Joe on a daily basis.

Her soon-to-be-ex-husband. She could wait another week, if she had to. She'd done harder things, right?

It lasted all the way through Dad insisting on paying, too. He didn't ask about the divorce, or even much about the accident beyond the bare minimum. *I'm just glad you're okay, pumpkin.*

The inevitable waited until after she returned from the familiar, painfully clean blue-and-white ladies' room, a recent concession to female lawyers and clerks who now frequented the place almost as much as the cops did. Beck could remember when you had to knock on the door of the single restroom and pray there wasn't a guy in there.

She slid back into the blue gingham booth, glancing at the door—always check your exits, Dad said all the time.

Her father folded his hands on the cleared table, his refilled orange soda standing at attention in its appointed place. "So, Beck . . . are you gonna come home?"

For a moment she thought he meant the house on Passacola, and her skin crawled. Then she understood. "I thought I'd stay at Hel's for a little while longer."

"Why?" He didn't sound angry, just honestly baffled. "Is it *that boy*?"

The same two little dismissive words, every time he referred to Paul. Apparently it made no difference that she'd been living alone with Hel for almost a year now. "I didn't even know he was going to be here, Dad. He got wounded overseas, you know." That was no doubt why he'd come back; getting hurt probably made every soldier think about home. And Hel was getting older.

They all were.

"Probably up to no good." Dad's mouth turned down at either corner, and he shook his head. The door over the bell jangled; every cop head in the place swiveled to check out the new arrival. It was like seeing prairie dogs popping up from mounds on a nature documentary, a watchful herd instinct. "Just be careful, honey. Hel's all right, and so was Herrold. But ol' Pete was bad blood, and so's his boy."

The old reply rose in her throat. *You don't know him, Dad.* Another, sharper one lingered right behind it. *Paul never laid a hand on me, but your precious Joe did.*

She couldn't say either sentence, so Beck just pulled her bright embroidered purse closer to her side. The comforting crinkle of paper inside was another reminder that her chains were almost gone, the prison door was being wrenched open bit by bit, and she could move on to planning her final escape.

It was enough to make you wonder if life was just a succession of bigger boxes. You broke out of one only to run smack-dab into the sides of another.

"I never liked Pete," she said, carefully. "He was mean." *So's Joe, but he covers it up. And you're all fooled.*

Or maybe they just pretended not to see, like they pretended not to see Humphrey Castell's drinking problem, Jeremy Lee Benthan's gambling at the reservation casino, or Dewey Johnson's trailers out in the woods? Some things were dangerous to notice, but others. . . .

She didn't have any answers. At least in a bigger city everyone else might leave her the hell alone and there were international restaurants. Driving all the way to Parsburg for substandard Thai was what Hel would call a boondoggle and a half.

"Some men are." Her father studied the street outside the Giblet's plate-glass window, scanning for trouble or what he called *the ol' DLR, Doesn't Look Right.*

He was never off the job. After all, he was a cop, and even in small towns it was the kind of work that never slept. How many times had the phone rang in the middle of the night, Beck waking to a note left on the kitchen table?

Get a good breakfast, see you after school, love ya, Dad. She studied her slice of the table, the napkin her hands were busily folding into smaller and smaller halves. "Besides, I'm all grown up now. What would I do, live in the shed?"

"God, no." Her father actually sounded horrified at the prospect.

He hadn't done any woodworking since Mom left, but the garden shed was still his private space. "Your room's just the way you left it."

Beck decided a change of subject was in order. "Thank you, Dad."

"For what, pumpkin?"

"For this. You know, taking the time off." At least Joe hadn't shown up. "It means a lot to me."

"Aw." When he tucked his chin and regarded her like that, her father looked almost boyish. "You're my girl, pumpkin. Want me to take you back to Hel's?"

She should have gone to the Grange to help Hel with setup, but her head was throbbing, her shoulders felt like bridge cables, her back was a solid bar of steadily mounting pain, and her legs were unhappy with either moving or sitting too long. "Sure. If you've got time."

"Always got time for you." He took one last hit of orange soda. "Let's go."

It was even a nice car ride. She might miss the trees when she left, the mountains, and the coast within driving distance, although she rarely got that far even as a teenager. She kissed her father's cheek, promised to call, and let herself into Hel's house.

It wasn't until she locked the door behind her that her phone chimed with a text. She had to dig in the pocket of Helena's spare pink plaid winter coat for it, and when she did all the good feeling drained away.

An unknown number, and a simple message—a blurry but still reasonably clear picture of Beck and her father sitting in the Giblet's booth, a faint ghostly overlay of the plate-glass window. Beck was smiling, pushing her hair back, and her father was saying something.

Whoever it was had been close. Very close. Neither of them had noticed, even with Dad's cop senses. The message was clear.

I can find you anytime I want, Beck. How was court today? And Joe would smile, the grin some people even found charming . . . if you didn't know what hid underneath.

Oh, God. Beck barely made it to the bathroom. Her lunch came up in a tasteless rush, a total waste of her father's money. When the heaving was done she burst into tears, her purse discarded near the bathroom door on faded linoleum scrubbed once a week and the edge of a manila folder peeking out of its top.

All the paperwork in the world was useless. Joe wasn't letting go anytime soon.

Verbal Race

HE MADE IT THROUGH the entire setup without strangling anyone, dropping any bunting, or his leg buckling. It was, as Boom would say with a lopsided grin, *a goddamn miracle.*

He hadn't realized just how uneasy he was until he saw Beck in Hel's kitchen, wiping countertops while the ancient dishwasher chugged and purred. She'd been busy—folding laundry, vacuuming, and from the smell of lemon Pledge, even dusting.

"You should be resting." Hel greeted her with a hug, and if Beck closed her eyes and leaned in for a few moments more than expected, maybe it was because of the stack of paper set neatly on the dining-room table.

"Couldn't settle. You know how it is." She even granted Paul a shy smile, but her eyes were bloodshot and her nose pink.

She'd been crying.

"So, how did it go?" Helena prompted.

"He filed another motion. I've got to wait another week." Beck cupped her elbows in damp hands, and was now studiously not looking at him at all. "He didn't even show." The tremor in the words was audible, sure.

But only if you were listening.

"Well, *shit.*" Hel drew out the last word, but there was no venom in it. Instead, wonder and congratulation filled the single stretched syllable. "You got through another hearing, anyway. I say we celebrate."

"Dad took me out to lunch and there's leftover pizza. Celebration enough for me." But Beck's tentative smile returned, and Paul could admit it was like rain out in the desert. The sand, sagebrush, and cactus was a dream, and this was the reality—he was right back where he'd started, nostalgia and history both swallowing him whole.

"Beck." His voice sounded strange even to himself. "Can I talk to you for a minute?"

"Yeah, sure." Her thin shoulders hunched, but she made no demur.

He still had Hel's keys, so he could open the back gate to the junkyard. The chill of winter was giving way to the equally raw but somehow more promising cold of a spring afternoon, moisture clinging to blackberries, false grape bushes, frost-yellowed weeds, and clumps of crabgrass. Stubby saplings and scrub brush were reclaiming the yard's edges, and as the sun sank they were edged in gold. A soft breeze smacked wet, heavy branches and soughed through the firs surrounding both house and yard.

The Taurus looked even worse in daylight, caved in on one side, its windshield starred with breakage. Beck followed him at a distance precluding any chitchat, and only reluctantly stepped a little closer when he halted a few feet from the crumpled car.

"I'll pay Hel back for it," she said, a little too loud in the hush. The jagged edge of anxiety under each word taunted him. "It was stupid of me, I was in a hurry to get what Mary needed and I just—"

For God's sake. What had turned bright, laughing Rebecca into this anxious, placating shadow? "What did he do to you?" Paul half-turned, but couldn't look directly at her. If he did, he was going to grab her upper arms and maybe *shake* some sense into her.

That was the very last thing she needed, so he stared at her sneakers instead. They were battered black off-brand numbers, the tread almost worn through, and the hems of her jeans were frayed. The flannel button-up she was wearing had seen much better days, too.

"What?" Beck shifted uneasily. She was observing a very careful distance from him, and though it made sense, he didn't like it. "Paul. . . ."

No. He didn't like it at all. "I'm not going to ask about when I left." That was just to make it clear. "But when someone cuts the brake lines on your car, Beck, that's something I *am* gonna ask about. Especially when—"

"Brake lines?" She folded her arms, tight and defensive, and that scrape on her cheek was another poke to his temper. So was the edge of bruising visible just under her collar, and the way her cheekbones stood starkly out. He couldn't help it, he was cataloguing the damage, and each piece of it fed the slow fire that had been building in his guts all day. "Just what are you—"

"There's a huge patch of fluid under where you parked the night before." Paul realized he sounded like his father, and it added another burst of fuel to the burning. "The Jeep was out all night too, but it's—"

"Hold on." Beck tossed her head, a slight, familiar movement like a nervous horse. She used to move like that in school when a teacher was either moving too fast or not swiftly enough to suit her restless intellect.

"You're saying it wasn't an accident."

"Lefty saw it too. Lines nicked nice and clean." He watched the color drain from her face and could have kicked himself. He was handling this all wrong, despite spending the entire afternoon turning this conversation over inside his head.

She always tied him in knots. Most of the time it was fun, but not now.

"Lefty knows?" Beck sagged for a moment, closing her eyes. "God."

"I was gonna call your dad, but—" *But he hates me, and he probably wouldn't listen.*

"No." She didn't give him the chance to finish. "Don't, please. It'll just make it harder."

"Beck. You could have *died.*" And it sounded like Joe was working the legal system to keep her wrapped up as long as possible. Typical. "How could this get any worse?"

"It can always get worse, Paul." It wasn't right for any woman to look so haunted, but especially not her. Beck was paper-white, her shoulders curved inward as if she expected . . . what? "Always."

Now she was sounding like Sparky Lee Jones, who had trained the entire squad for mayhem. Stocky, plain-faced, and deceptively quiet, he'd been teaching soldiers how to do hush-hush shit that never saw congressional inquiry for decades. Hearing Beck repeat one of their teacher's cherished maxims gave him the willies.

He hadn't thought of Sparky in ages.

God damn it. "I am not gonna ask about a whole lot," Paul repeated, wishing he could get a little closer, maybe crack a joke and chase that terrified, numb look off her face. "But I am gonna ask about this, because—"

"You checked the Jeep?"

"Before we left this morning, yeah. I put it in the shop last night because—"

"Good." Her green gaze flickered past him, fastening on the crumpled Taurus, and she shrank even further, if that was possible. "I'm sorry. I know it doesn't mean anything, but I'm sorry, and I'll fix it. I promise."

What the hell? "The whole point of this is—"

"I *know*, Paul." There was an echo of the old Beck, but that girl had never looked this . . . this lost.

This defeated.

"Can you let me talk? Please?" And wasn't that a blast from the past, because he'd said it once or twice during their childhood spats. Paul's hands itched and the fury buzzed in his bones, demanding he find out just what the hell was going on so he could fix the problem.

Hard, and fast, and thoroughly.

While he was at it, he wanted to get a few more things straight. He'd told her he wasn't going to ask about it, but god *damn* the whole thing, he wanted some kind of answer about why she'd cut him off and married Joe. Sure, she'd pleaded with him not to leave and he'd never told her what he was planning, but—

"Can you please not yell at me?" The words trembled. Beck freed one hand, but it was only to wipe at her wounded cheek. The movement probably hurt, from the way she winced. She swallowed, hard, and it was official.

She was fighting back tears, again. Her eyes glimmered. It wasn't fair, they were already huge and thickly lashed, and he could have fallen into them forever if she'd just let him.

"Sorry." He forced himself to stay very still, to use the softest possible tone. "Look, whatever happened between us is history and it can stay that way, all right? But this is dangerous. You have got to talk to me so I can do what I have to."

"It won't matter." The highlights in her hair glowed, and she sniffed, heavily. "I'll take care of it. You don't have to do anything."

For the love of. . . . Paul didn't know whether to start laughing or turn around and scream at the junkyard like he was fourteen and getting rid of excess angst. He'd roamed the lanes between the stacked, rusting hulks all his young life, and it was still familiar territory.

Once more, the past looping over to catch on the present jolted him, and maybe that was why he took a step toward her.

Beck backed up in a hurry, much farther than she needed to. And she *flinched*, too.

In fact, she cowered like a whipped dog, her eyes widening and her heel catching on a hummock. She almost tripped, righted herself with a staggering lunge, and a small, wounded sound escaped her throat.

Paul stopped dead. He stood stock-still, and why were his ribs heaving? The pain was all through him, centered high up on the left side of his chest, and if he went down with a heart attack right here at least it would mean his leg wouldn't buckle ever again.

Beck regained her balance. Her breathing was just as ragged as his, and as always, she beat him to it. "Paul. Please."

If there was ever a verbal race Beck Sommers would win every time, and half of why he was so quick when dealing with the dimwits in the fucking Army was because of that training. She was in a class all her own.

She always had been.

"What." He sounded like he was being strangled. "The fuck. Did he do. To you."

"There's no proof." She backed up another step, like she expected him to close the distance and land a punch. "Whoever did this, there's no *proof*, and there never will be. You can't go in swinging like this is the playground, Paul. It's my fault, it's my problem, and I'll fix it, all right? You don't have to worry, and neither does Hel."

Like hell I won't worry. "I don't care about proof," he managed through the rock in his throat. "*I'm* not a fucking cop."

It was the wrong thing to say, he knew as soon as it hit air outside his mouth. But Jesus, the woman was infuriating. And his heart would *not* stop hurting, as if he'd been shot in the chest instead of the leg.

He could almost see the doors behind her eyes slamming shut. Beck drew herself up, and her expression was another familiar one.

She'd decided on something, and if he tried to stop her she'd simply wait for a little while and do it anyway. Just like the time she rode her bike down the tangle of trails on the side of Attenlee Mountain—really just a glorified, oversized hill, but dangerous all the same—the summer she was thirteen, arriving at the bottom banged-up and bruised with leaves caught in her long, gloriously tangled hair.

With her green eyes wide and sparkling, too, and the widest, wildest grin you'd ever seen. She always used to be laughing, his Beck, but now even getting a smile was hard fucking work.

Maybe it would become easier if he had some time to practice again. God knew there was nothing in the world he'd rather be doing.

"I'm very sorry for all the trouble." Now she was almost prim, like the time she informed Carr Henske that she was going to punch him right in the goddamn mouth if he said one more word about her vanished mama. "I'll be out of Hel's hair soon, Paul. You can count on that."

Paul had settled accounts with the little Henske shit his own way behind the gym after school, naturally, but that was beside the point.

The point was, *nobody* fucked with Rebecca Sommers on Paul's watch, and he was back on duty. He'd fucked up, sure—he should've told her what he had planned, or barring that, he should have stayed.

It didn't matter. He was here now, and not a moment too goddamn soon, like dropping into a hot zone to back up his squad. *Just tell me what to shoot at, Beck.*

"Look." He tried again. "Hel likes having you here, it's good for her. I just want to help, all right? Let me help you." *For once.* He managed not to tack the last two words on, but it was too late. She had already turned and set off, heading for the junkyard gate.

He could run after her, grab her arm. If he did, though, she might give another one of those flinches, or those terrible, hurt little sounds.

And all the work he'd ever done muzzling his daddy's temper in his traitorous bones and bloodstream, every joke in the world, wouldn't stop Paul then. He would find out from Hel where Joe Halston was living now, take his aunt's Jeep, and go talk with the bastard. It wouldn't be a pleasant conversation, and Sheriff Sommers might show up too if the neighbors noticed it.

And then he'd have to do something Beck wouldn't like at all.

So he watched her walk away, stiffly; she must've been hurting, but he was dismally sure she hadn't taken another pain pill or even some ibuprofen. Stubborn as the day was long, her honeydark hair alive with gold highlights, almost turning her ankle on another clump of crabgrass—he longed to run after, get his arms around her, and breathe in the smell of her hair. He wanted to wrap her in insulation, or the bubble wrap Grey swore was better than therapy.

Pop that motherfucker, the man always said, shoving a sheet of plastic into a squadmate's hands. *See if you don't feel better.*

Oh, he wanted to pop something all right. Two shots right into the cranium of everyone who had ever hurt her, right after he got some goddamn answers about brake lines and bruises, stalking and a woman's tear-filled eyes.

Paul swore, very softly. The breeze was just right, so she probably heard him.

But Beck just hunched her thin shoulders further and kept going.

Fight a Little Dirty

DINNER WAS—TO put it politely—awkward as all hell, especially with her and Paul both being painfully polite and attempting stilted small talk. But at least Hel was bubbling with news about the reunion preparations and commiseration about having to wait another week for the divorce, so the conversation kept going.

Beck accepted another pain pill and promised she'd go along to help with the rest of the setup tomorrow—Mary had given her the day off again, and she felt like the world's biggest bitch since she would rather peel herself alive and take a bath in lemon juice than deal with the extended Klemperer-and-assorted-others clan.

But it would get her to the Grange, and at some point, she could slip away.

At least she could go to bed early. She was bruised and stiff all over, but she managed a tolerable amount of leftover pizza and even a shot of smoky liquid courage from Herrold's leftover bottle of Glenlivet, kept religiously by Hel in the liquor cabinet against rainy days and truly special occasions.

And at least the Jeep was in the shop building for the night. If anyone tried to get in there, even Joe, the alarm would go off. But she didn't think he would, not tonight.

He'd let her wait and anticipate the worst for a while. There was always a cooling-off period after one of what she used to call his "fits," as if he was Shirley Mae Corrigan with her epilepsy or Grant Dutch with his Tourette's. The surprise of finding out, with a little online searching, how common Joe's behavior was—she hated calling it *abuse*, because it made her, in Dad's terms, *part of a domestic*—didn't go away over time.

It was all there, from the constant verbal takedowns to the slowly escalating physical pokes and prodding, from the weeks of breathless waiting to the explosions that left her shivering with terror, from the raging sonic assaults with the veins throbbing in his forehead to the terrible few times he closed his hands around her throat and *squeezed*. Each fresh instance she read on forums, in self-help listicles, or in survivor blogs was unpleasantly familiar, and like being suckerpunched in the gut all over again.

Joe hadn't face-hit or squeezed her throat that often—he was endlessly careful when it came to things neighbors might notice, and covering tracks was second nature to any man who liked to use his fists on wife or girlfriend. But even once was more than enough.

Beck lay in the dark, the pain pill wrapping all her aches in cotton. By this time tomorrow she would be out of Hel's hair, and the only thing she minded was having to leave her suitcase behind. She'd leave her accumulated tip cash, too—that should make up for some of the inconvenience.

She'd left the house on Passacola with a single piece of luggage, and now she was going to exit this temporary refuge with even less. Hopefully she was stripping away layers of a chrysalis, and would be able to fly at some point.

What the fuck are you considering, Beck?

Dad always told her to fight clean. *Don't lower yourself to their level, Rebecca.* Well, getting to adulthood meant inheriting a world where everyone else fought dirty; if she had to descend a few steps to make sure Joe would sign the fucking papers and also leave Hel and Dad alone, it was worth it. Beck Sommers was, as Joe reminded her often enough, no better than anyone else.

You think you're so fancy, Becks? Daddy's girl.

She turned onto her side, curling into a tight ball. Paul would keep quiet about the brake lines—he wouldn't want to disturb Hel, and besides, after tomorrow she'd probably never see him again.

I'm not a cop. Oh, he probably hadn't said it to be hurtful; it was clear he couldn't care less that she'd married Joe. It was simply the disdain for law enforcement you could find anywhere on the wrong side of the tracks, holding both resentment and justified caution. Just because her dad was a good one didn't mean all cops were, and Beck had realized as much by fifth grade.

Besides, Paul's family—Hel included—made a living any way they could, and not too long ago the drying sheds in the junkyard could have been a reason for Joe to call the feds in and get Hel sent to jail. Sure, it would be labeled as possession and intent to distribute, but what it *really* would have been was vengeance. There were cops who threatened Dewey Johnson's boys with similar things, and the entire bad-news crew returned that threat with interest.

The whole idea is stupid. It's dangerous. You could just walk away. Get on a bus to anywhere, and just leave the whole mess.

But that wouldn't fix the problem. Still, Joe wouldn't mess with Hel after she was gone, even indirectly; there was no reason to. Paul would stay for a bit after the reunion, another layer of safety for the woman who had always done her best for motherless Beck Sommers.

Whatever happened to us is history, Paul said, *and it can stay that way.* Which was just fine, even if Beck's breath caught and her eyes stung afresh. He'd probably forgotten her the instant he boarded the bus to basic training. Maybe he'd just been trying to let her down easy that entire last summer after high school.

It was embarrassing and painful to look back on that haze of sunshine, dusty heat, all the stolen kisses plus far more, and realize her own deeper feelings hadn't been returned. She'd thought Paul felt the same way, but off he went to the Army, never even calling once. Then there was Dad's liver trouble, another pillar of her world creaking ominously as it cracked instead of shattering, and the idea of going to college, alone and in a strange town, had quite frankly scared the hell out of her.

The truth was, Beck hadn't been brave enough to escape. As Hel would say, it was between her and Jesus to fix *that*, and the best time to get over her cowardice would have been years ago.

The second best time, like they said on the internet, was right-fucking-now.

Paul knowing about her status as a *victim of a domestic*—God, what a hateful phrase—was slightly concerning, but he was a local. He'd keep his mouth shut about it, the way everyone did about everything else.

The more she thought about it, the more what she was about to do seemed inevitable. But then again, so had marrying Joe, back when he promised they would get the hell out of this town together.

Sometimes she wondered if he'd have turned on her if they *had* escaped and settled elsewhere, but that was a useless question and she had more of those than she could handle already. Beck dropped into fitful slumber, and for once there were no nightmares.

A Little Recon

PAUL TOSSED AND turned all goddamn night. Rolling out of the sack at four a.m. wasn't unusual—not in the service, not on the Squad—and he could even tell himself it was to get the jump on Hel for once.

By the time Beck appeared from the annex, yawning, he had the coffeemaker going and a couple slices of bread ready in the toaster, bacon in the oven because Tax swore it was best cooked that way, a couple of eggs already in the pan, and for a few seconds the fantasy stole his breath.

It was a nice one, and it was simple—that this was just a normal morning and he could see Beck sleepy and tousle-headed every day because she'd consented to live with him. That she accepted the ancient blue-and-white miner's union mug from him because it was a habit, and that she stood near the sink all the time while he cooked, eyeing the stove with amusement.

The little dream didn't have the bruising on her shoulder where the seatbelt strap had kept her from worse injury, visible between the tank top she slept in and yesterday's threadbare flannel button-down casually thrown over it. The blackberry scratch on her cheek wouldn't be there either.

Well, he'd been dragged back from death while Tax swore in a monotone and the chopper heaved and thwopped through a dust-dry sky, and there was no better use for a second chance than spending it on making a few fairytales real.

Beck turned to look out the kitchen window, over what had been a vegetable garden when Herrold was alive. The old man had flat-out loved running his bright red rototiller. Dawn was coming earlier and earlier, but not quite early enough to catch either of them; misty grey hung between the firs at the edge of the pasture beyond listing posts hung with flopping deer netting.

Paul took a hit off his own coffee. His throat was dry. "You want eggs?"

She shook her head. Her profile was just as pretty as ever, and even her bare feet were cute. It wasn't fair; she blew all his internal thermostats at once, and didn't even notice.

The girl was oblivious, but maybe he had some leeway. He'd approach it like an op. Plan, prepare, perform. And maybe all the work he'd done since leaving this goddamn place would mean he had a chance of holding her interest this go-round.

Maybe this time, he'd be good enough.

"It's good weather," he said quietly, surprising himself. "Hated all the rain growing up, but once I was away, it was all I could think of."

Beck nodded slightly. Then she surprised him, too. "You must've been everywhere."

"Not quite. But a few places."

"Lucky." A soft, quick sideways look, as if gauging his mood. "What's your favorite? The desert?"

Anywhere I'm not getting shot at. "Desert's good. Lots of space, you can see what's coming but the sand gets everywhere." He waited to see if she'd smile, but there wasn't even a whisper of amusement. At least she still seemed interested, her eyebrows rising a little and her mouth soft, relaxed. "Jungle's green, lots of green, like here. Both are better than urban. It kind of. . . ." *Christ, don't tell her any of that.* Beck didn't need to know about dirty room-to-room fighting. "Here's about the best, though. Very few creepy-crawlies, good even temperature most of the time, rain keeps the moss between your toes nice and happy."

There. That finally earned him a small grin, immediately hidden behind the lifted coffee cup. But it was a start; he could risk a little recon, so he continued. "Where do you want to go, Beck?"

"Anywhere that isn't here," she muttered, and her slight grimace said she hadn't meant to let it out. *Truth hangs out in the bottom of a bottle,* Jackson sometimes intoned, but Paul thought you could find it right before the caffeine first hit, too.

"My CO's in New Mexico. One of my buddies is getting married in Vegas pretty soon." *Come along,* he wanted to say. *Change of weather'll do you good.* "Another's in California, and one's got family in Virginia. Jackson, well, nobody knows where he goes, but he keeps in touch."

"Jackson." She nodded again. "The wildcard."

So she'd been listening to him tell Hel stories. "He might make the wedding. You never know."

"They sound like good friends."

That was a civilian understatement. When the lead was flying and the mortars popping, not to mention the screaming and the blood spattering, it was your buddies who got you out safe, and vice versa. Even while almost-dying from a nicked leg artery, he'd known they wouldn't leave him behind.

That was worth something, in this world. They said blood was thicker than water, but buddies were goddam cement.

"They are." *They'll love finally meeting you. I'll never hear the fucking end of it.* Which was kind of putting the cart before the horse, so he decided there could be a little force added to the reconnaissance.

So to speak.

He'd been sneaky once before, keeping the secret of his proposal buried deep. It hadn't worked out, to put it mildly, so maybe it was time to get a little more direct. Paul did have to go past her to grab a plate for his eggs, sure.

But he didn't have to brush against her to do it, crowding her into the corner between the sink and the dishwasher. He didn't have to step so close he felt her body heat, the summery ripe morning-smell of a healthy adult woman filling his nose. And he definitely didn't have to look down at her, his face feeling a little odd because he couldn't tell exactly what expression he was wearing.

Beck held her coffee mug like a shield, but she didn't flinch this time. Her gaze met his, and he hadn't forgotten the thin threads of gold in her irises, the white scar along her hairline from a childhood accident involving a sliding-glass door, or the way she nibbled just on the inside of her lower lip when she was thoughtful, not quite showing her teeth.

It really wouldn't be that hard to lean down and find out if her skin was still as soft. He was pretty sure it would be, and pretty sure that even with coffee on his breath, he could wring a small delighted noise from her with a kiss the way he used to.

Maybe he just hadn't kissed her enough the first time around. He could fix that, too.

It doesn't matter what anyone did to you. I'll make sure it never happens again, Beck. An old promise, but still good. He was a lot taller, not to mention meaner, now.

Maybe she would have said something, because she inhaled sharply. Just then, Helena's deep, hacking morning cough sounded from the hall.

Beck shied away along the counter, coffee slopping out of her mug and probably burning her slim fingers. Paul had to grab a plate and rescue his almost-burning eggs, and by the time he'd accomplished that Beck had her toast and was heading into the dining room with a dripping coffee cup. Her place in the kitchen was taken by Helena, who gave something like an irritated grunt and headed straight for the coffeepot, her usual morning pack of Slims tucked in the breast pocket of her pink velour robe along with the rectangular shape of Herrold's old service Zippo.

Well, at least Paul had made it back to his own lines unscathed. He shouldn't have pushed, God knew what Beck thought of him at the moment.

God also knew he'd never had any moderation where she was involved. At least she hadn't flinched this time; maybe she still knew, on some deep level, that he'd never lay a hand on her.

But apparently Joe Halston had. If it was in-country, Paul could just exchange a quiet word with one of the Ghost Squad and the problem would get solved, hook or crook.

Out here, he was a little handcuffed, but he still—like Dez would say, quoting Sparky Lee—had options.

There's always options, son. You just gotta find the one you can survive with.

"Scrambled," Helena said as she turned away from the coffeepot. Next she'd head out onto the porch for her first morning smoke, and maybe he'd have a chance at the table with Beck. "And that bacon better not burn in my oven, you heathen."

"Burn your buns instead," he snapped in return, the tag end of an old family joke, and was rewarded with an unwilling, gravelly laugh.

Maybe he hadn't lost his touch after all.

Last Gasp

SHE TOOK CARE to make that morning just the same as any other. Neither Hel nor Paul would notice the divorce paperwork was still in her Tibetan bag; it was a bit big for a purse, but nowhere near Sally Beauchamp's huge canvas number or the diaper bags young mothers schlepped.

Her ID, all her paperwork, her bank card and a pittance of cash—the bulk was left in a neatly labeled envelope for Hel, on the end table next to the annex sofa—were all safely stowed, as well as a clean T-shirt and panties, a comb, and her toothbrush and paste. She'd made the bed and folded the sofa as usual, then packed away everything in her single suitcase, tucking it out of sight in the hall closet as usual.

Leave no trace, they said in the Boy Scouts; her father was also fond of that one while hunting. Well, she was going to be traveling as light as Rambo.

God, Dad loved that movie, even if the cops in it weren't perfect.

She did linger a few minutes in the shower. Who knew when she'd have hot water again, and a clean, private bathroom? You never could tell, and she might be looking at a lot of what they called rough living.

Now that she'd decided on a course of action instead of just simple endurance, everything was clear-cut and relatively easy. She even managed to meet Paul's gaze once or twice without blushing after that tiny kitchen incident.

Well, without blushing *much*. It was embarrassing as hell to have her hormones respond to a man who had outright rejected her, but if she'd survived the daily humiliations administered during most of her marriage, this was small potatoes indeed.

Besides, in a little while it wouldn't matter.

The long narrow Grange building was almost fully decorated, the familiar *KLEMPERER-SIDDONS-BARRANIE REUNION* message in removable letters on the sign facing the two-lane highway, the cloakroom ready, the kitchen sparkling. The only thing missing was Uncle Dreeson's prized Traeger smoker in the outside cooking area, but that would show up at midnight or so, and be tended until the reunion proper when his matching grill would arrive.

Today was for truly last-minute stuff, and the Grange was a hive of activity. Paul, returned after years spent in the service, was an instant celebrity hailed from every direction. Beck got smiles and waves probably sixty percent motivated by curiosity instead of mere politeness, and there were kids underfoot everywhere, not to mention swarming the Grange's dilapidated playground.

She remembered going down that slide at other reunions, laughing at some joke or another Paul made.

It was easy to simply start working, taking care of little things in each room so everyone could say they'd seen her. If Joe came along with his psych tricks to "help witness memory," she wanted the waters as muddied as possible. It also kept her one step ahead of Paul, who always seemed to drift into her vicinity after a few minutes.

Maybe he was genuinely worried, since the Taurus's brake lines had been cut. Beck might have thought she was going crazy again—the internet forums called what Joe did *gaslighting*, and wasn't that a nifty little term—except for the fact of a deputy's cruiser on Benson Hill, swimming lazily in front of the hole in the guardrail.

Like a shark.

Maybe Joe was following her for other reasons, or maybe he'd slipped out to Hel's place the night before. He might even have had some farfetched idea of being the hero to find her right after the inevitable accident.

Or maybe . . . just maybe he actually wanted her dead, instead of simply half-strangled and cowed by terror. Beck tried not to think it, but horrible implications and what-ifs kept tiptoeing into her head at odd moments. Each time, the worst seemed a little more plausible.

A little more likely, no matter how hard she argued with herself.

They'd been *married*, for God's sake. And while she hadn't precisely loved Joe—she could admit as much, now—they had still lived in the same house, eaten together, slept in the same bed for years. You could get irritated past bearing when you lived with someone, but wanting to outright erase them, perhaps in a fiery car accident? Or with collateral damage, because Beck could have easily run into someone else at high speed, desperately trying to brake?

It just wasn't rational. Still, Beck had been wrong about everything else in her life so far; misjudging just how far Joe Halston would go was par for the course. The important thing was to keep him from hurting anyone else.

If he could cut one set of brake lines, he could cut another, maybe on a brand-new Jeep Cherokee or a sheriff's cruiser. More worryingly, both her father and Joe worked with firearms, and accidents happened all the time. Covering up something like that wasn't quite child's play, but a deputy would know how to go about it. Frankly, Joe could get away with anything.

Anything at all.

"Beck?" Gloria Siddons was at her elbow, her smile only half predatory. Ol' Glory's usual earth-toned ensemble suited her better since she'd changed her hair dye, a little more sandalwood than obviously fake auburn.

"Hi, Miz Gloria." The same old greeting from childhood, falling off Beck's tongue in the usual polite way. At least this old biddy was easy to handle. "I love your hair today."

"Do you, now?" As usual, once her vanity was appealed to Gloria's temper turned sweet as pie, and she gave a wide, very genuine smile only faintly tinted with the nicotine from the menthols everyone pretended she didn't sneak after dinner. "Thanks, honey. You've always been the nicest little thing."

"I do my best." *If you only knew what I'm contemplating now.*

"The ice machine in that darn second fridge is at it again." Gloria waved her pudgy hands gently, her wedding ring and chunky gold Avon bracelets glimmering. "What *do* you do to make it behave?"

"Trade secret." Beck found a tired smile. Gloria would be dissecting this conversation all day with other gossipers, weighing Beck's behavior. "Say no more, I'll take care of it."

The kitchen had a secondary exit, and it was just about the right time for Beck to put her plan into motion. Paul was trapped in a knot of kids, from Little Davey to tiny Amanda Siddons, all clamoring for something or another, probably one of his funny cartoon voices. Helena, of course, was everywhere at once, making decisions and snapping orders.

For once, Beck was having some good luck. She made it to the kitchen with a dry mouth and pounding heart, waving at bald, potbellied Uncle Dreeson, who was by the main exit, discussing something barbeque-related with the two eldest Barranie brothers.

He didn't so much as blink in her direction. She was part of the wallpaper, invisible, and there were other women at the sinks with their backs to her, doing a preliminary wash of Grange-supplied kitchenware just to be sure.

Beck's red coat was still damp from the washer, so she'd be without a jacket for a short while. She settled her bag's strap—they'd think it was strange she'd worn it all morning, if they remembered—and plunged into the small stairwell to what everyone who used the Grange called "the kissing door." Some summer nights there was a lot of activity out here.

Maybe that was why this particular clan did spring reunions instead. Even Paul had a stubborn streak of propriety sometimes; there were, according to every Klemperer, some things you just didn't do.

At least publicly.

The most dangerous part was getting across the two-lane highway unseen. Fortunately, she could use a windscreen of cedars from the door to the edge of the parking lot, if she didn't mind her shoes getting wet from dew-heavy grass. Waiting for a clear spot with no cars in either direction took a few agonizing minutes, since family was still arriving to help. Not to mention it was get-to-work time along the Strip on 79th Avenue, and every local knew this was the best way to reach that slice of real estate.

This whole area used to be rural, but now it was something a little different. In another few years the gentrification along the Strip might move upstream and even swallow the Grange. The field would be turned into a gas station, maybe, fast food restaurants would go in on either side, and the slightly squeaky wooden ballroom floor would be torn out sooner or later.

God willing, she wouldn't be here to see it.

Beck darted across the highway, her bag bumping against her side, electric fear filling her mouth with copper. Plunging through the screen of scrub on the other side, she had a short jog down a mild hill to cross Grenley Road too, then she could take the footpath along Wilwault Creek and come up at the end of her old neighborhood.

The same shrieking, cowering internal voice yelling at her the day she left the house on Passacola was having a grand old time, and had been ever since she opened her eyes this morning. *You're crazy, Beck. You're insane. You did everything you could to leave that place, and now you're going back for a visit? What if he's home? Do you want to get caught? He'll hurt you. You know he'll hurt you.*

"He might even do worse," she muttered, saving that voice the trouble.

But that was the risk in fighting dirty, she supposed. She had burned a bridge, though nobody at the Grange could see the flames or the towering column of smoke.

She was committed, now.

THE GRANITE Landing development was relatively new, but most of the owners were the younger scions of old-growth local. You could even call Passacola Street one of the nicer places to live, and this comfortable-looking blue house, with its well-trimmed yard and newish board fence enclosing the backyard, didn't look like a trap.

It looked normal, and sane, like a place where only good things happened.

Hopefully nobody saw her creeping through the Philbins' always-unlocked back gate, or her two tries to climb the fence from the rockpile over their water feature. The fountain's plashing was nerve-wracking in the stillness, and when she landed on the other side of the fence with a jolt she had to bite back a tiny cry.

Even the deck put in two years ago was the same, the lawn furniture probably still in the shed Joe had built by hand on the weekends. Every time Beck saw the carefully stained wood and the three wide steps down to the yard she had to suppress a shiver.

He'd accused her of an affair with one of the deck builders, for God's sake. She'd known an explosion was coming, and had even been relatively certain it would be in that direction, but the venom in his accusations still hurt.

Innocence was no shield when Joe Halston truly decided to go for you. The funny thing was, he'd had that tendency from the beginning of their marriage—it had filled up the house with poisonous fumes, bit by creeping bit—but she hadn't noticed it until one day, *pow*, right in the kidneys.

The spare key was still in its plastic rock-shaped holder under the junipers. Joe had never found it, despite all his mowing and clipping.

The garage still held a familiar black car, and her heart was in her mouth before she saw the other side was empty. No shiny red truck he'd bought over her protests that they couldn't afford it, and both sets of keys—for the Jetta and the truck—would be hanging in his work locker, just where he wanted them. He'd stranded her here more than once, expecting her to beg for her own damn car.

Dad had bought her the Jetta, after all. Beck stared at its gleaming windshield, her head cocked and her eyes threatening to unfocus. Her heart hammered, and the top of her head felt very far away.

Don't do this. Just leave, just get out. It's not worth it.

After all, how long would it be before Amy Lorton was living here, finding out what Joe was really like? Maybe she'd be able to make him happy; God knew Beck had made every good-faith effort in that direction. She'd tried even harder than she had with Paul.

Her cheeks flamed with embarrassment. Of all life's humiliations, still being in love with the man who had dumped her so long ago had to be in Beck's personal top three. Maybe that was why Joe started going downhill—on some level, he must've sensed she'd just felt . . . affectionate toward him.

Just fond, instead of truly in love. Well, it had changed to outright fear soon enough, mixed with the paradoxical, wistful desire to somehow, perhaps, maybe, in some way help him see how much he was hurting her, how much he was *scaring* her.

The internet forums said the desire to save your abuser was normal, too. Even if Joe might not be what they'd *really* call an abuser—he didn't leave more than bruises most of the time and she'd never had a bloody nose but that once, and he'd only strangled her a few times but not until she passed out all the way—Beck figured the principle applied.

She stepped over the threshold, glad Joe's daddy thought security systems were a waste of money. According to Beck's father-in-law the best defense was a dog, but Joe couldn't stand the thought of the results deposited in his beloved backyard grass.

Instead, he opted for the gun safe, good deadbolts, and taking Beck to the range every once in a while. That last bit was ironic considering how he treated her, but Beck was a sheriff's daughter, so it was expected.

Halstons, born or married, knew all about keeping up appearances.

The door to the kitchen opened just the way it usually did. The familiar blue counters and country gingham touches were relatively clean except for a small pile of breakfast dishes—she'd receive a casual shake or slap if those weren't out of the sink in a hurry. She was a *housewife*, by God.

I fucking hated every minute of it, too. Beck could be honest about that now, at least inside her own head.

Her plants were gone, every single blessed one of them. Even the finicky aloe, and the circles in the dust told her they'd been removed recently. That layer of gritty grey would never have been tolerated before, especially on the glass coffee table he'd pushed her over once—thank God it hadn't broken, but she'd landed badly between table and couch and her neck had hurt for weeks afterward.

The huge plasma television was nice and shiny, though. There was a single empty microbrew bottle on the carpet next to Joe's big maroon recliner; his father had a matching chair in goldenrod. She almost picked up the bottle to rinse and put in the recycle, but what was the point? Still, she broke out in a sweat thinking of what might happen if Joe came home and it was still there.

Or if *she* was.

Beck climbed the stairs, quasi-familiar smells sending gooseflesh down her back even though he'd apparently gotten rid of all her pot-pourri and hand-scented candles as well as her plants. Had it always been so close and stale in here?

If her heart kept pounding like this, she might drop dead and *really* cause Joe some problems.

There was the master bedroom. Beck couldn't even look at the unmade bed. Trembling violently, she halted at her dresser.

The drawers had been ransacked and shoved closed. Of course he'd gone through her clothes once he found her goodbye note.

Joe, I'm leaving. We're getting a divorce. I've told my dad. Beck.

Her cedar jewelry box was where it should be. She could have emptied the whole thing, but that would make any criminal charges worse.

This is legally his house. You're breaking and entering at the very least.

"Only if I'm caught," she whispered. She'd talked to herself a lot before she left, roaming from room to room while Joe was on-shift, jumping every time the phone rang and generally feeling one thousand percent certifiable crazy.

Her engagement ring and wedding band were right where she'd left them. Had Joe opened this up to look? Was he planning on getting them resized for Amy?

It didn't matter. She could pawn them when she finally escaped this town and got to a decent city. It would be her own private *fuck you* to the whole situation.

She was entitled to at least one, wasn't she? She also grabbed her mother's fire opal ring too, relief dilating hot and sour behind her breastbone. The setting looked cheap, and maybe Joe had forgotten how she'd worn it all the time until she figured out neither her mother nor Paul were ever coming back.

Taking it off meant giving up hope. She'd held out as long as she could, but nobody could keep that up forever.

Beck had what she came for; she should grab her good winter coat and get the hell out. But instead, she turned right at the bedroom door, past the craft room that would, Joe always said, eventually be a nursery. It looked like a bomb had hit all her art supplies, and she didn't even feel angry, just weary. The door she was approaching would be locked, she would be saved from herself, and she could leave.

Instead, for once the spare bedroom *wasn't* locked. Joe had added a deadbolt with keyholes on both sides just after they moved in, with some weird idea of using it as a safe room during any potential home invasion.

Beck had known better than to argue, even that early in the game. When the infrequent guest stayed over—mostly Halston cousins—the room was aired and cleaned for their comfort, but the rest of the time she didn't dare approach the door, let alone touch the knob.

Which turned easily in her hand today, and she stepped inside.

Same old, clunky ashwood bedstead from Joe's childhood home, same pretty patchwork duvet with matching pillowcases she'd sewn herself, same small empty wooden Goodwill dresser under the window, same navy curtains half-drawn. The mirrored closet door was open, and that was the other strange thing—a large canvas duffle sat inside, just like the ones Army boys came home with.

Paul had one; he'd carried it from the plane to Hel's Jeep.

Beck approached the closet carefully, cautiously, as if she was out hunting with Dad. She dropped to her knees with a jolt, her ears almost tingling as she strained to catch even the slightest whisper of movement. Her pulse was thundering so loud she probably wouldn't hear a whole troupe of elephants on the stairs.

Beck suspected what she'd find when she unzipped the duffle slightly, but she wasn't truly prepared. She stared for a few moments, sweat prickling on her forehead, her legs quivering, and her hands curled into tight fists.

Just that swiftly, the plan inside her head snapped into a different shape. It was almost inevitable, because hadn't she suspected what she'd find—if not here then in the attic, or in the closet under the stairs?

Rebecca. It was her father's voice, blaring in her head like the Baptists' beloved trump of doom. *Don't you do what you're thinkin' about. It's wrong.*

That voice was right. It was probably even sane. But, Beck thought, with a burning bridge's smoke filling your head and your heart throbbing like the overdub in a horror movie, all sorts of things were possible.

Even revenge.

She reached for the zipper, sliding it closed tooth by tooth. The sound was very loud in the stillness. Everyone on the street was at work or grocery shopping on a Friday. Nancy Philbin would be getting her nails done, Mrs. Harker on the other side worked down in Sinaida. They were the biggest dangers; she'd chosen her time as well as possible.

Get the fuck out of here, Beck. Come on. She emerged into a thin wash of spring sunshine painting the backyard and re-buried the spare key's plastic-rock container, hoping Joe would never find it. Then she crossed the yard again, and locked the back garage door from the inside.

There was a certain grim enjoyment to be had from leaving him a conundrum. Was this how he felt while stalking her?

Beck had steadfastly refused to have the Jetta's registration changed to Joe's name or even put him on it, and Judge McCready had finally ruled yesterday that it was Beck's free and clear. It had been her last tangible gasp of teenage freedom, and she'd held to it grimly all through the marriage.

The real surprise was that he hadn't trashed the car like her art stuff. Probably because he knew just holding it was the best revenge.

However, Joe *didn't* know about the spare *car* key's magnetic holder tucked in a back wheel-well. Maybe he'd cut the Jetta's brake lines too, but she didn't think so.

It would cause a mess on the garage floor, and he wouldn't like that at all.

The little car's engine didn't want to catch, and she had a bad moment with the garage door open and the starter grinding, the paralyzing fear of some nosy noticing neighbor crawling inside her stomach like live snakes. Then it coughed into life, and she checked the gauge as the orange bar settled—half a tank.

That was plenty, for the moment. She just had to make it out of the development without being seen, *then* she could worry about finding a gas station.

Beck left the small blue house closed up prim and proper, almost exactly as she'd found it. She dropped the garage door opener out the window at the bottom of the driveway and drove away sedately, her knuckles white-gripping the steering wheel, unheeded tears slicking her cheeks.

And with a heavy canvas duffel bag in the trunk.

Makes a Man Reconsider

"HAVE YOU SEEN Beck?" The vertical worry-line between Helena's eyebrows was entirely usual at this point in the reunion preparations, but scrubbing her right hand on her jeans wasn't. That only happened under steadily mounting stress. "I can't seem to find her."

"Me either." Paul had been trapped by one adult family member or another all morning, and the kids regularly on some incomprehensible schedule you had to be under twelve to keep. Everyone wanted to know how the Army was, how he was doing, if it was true he'd been wounded, and by the way where was Beck, someone needed her for something.

Maybe some of the last group were truly anxious. Or Hel had been at work among them—*that girl helped me after Herrold passed*, was all she needed to say, and at least the Klemperer strand of the clan would know that meant they couldn't open their mouth on Beck's business.

At least not much, and not in Hel's presence.

Aunt Hel looked about to add something else, but a gaggle of kids parted like the Red Sea and there was Gloria, bearing down on them with a determined step. The first sharp jab of unease hit Paul then, because if the Siddons matriarch looked like this, something serious indeed was afoot.

"Helena." Even her tone was the complete antithesis of its usual syrup-sweet hum, but it was Paul she was looking at, and her eyebrows had drawn together just like Hel's. "Joe Halston's out front. Dreeson's talking to him."

Oh, no. "Don't worry." As usual, he had a joke ready to defuse any tension. "He probably just wants to reserve some of Uncle D's barbeque."

"Find Beck," Hel whispered fiercely, a general sensing battle and giving a last-minute order. In fact, she sounded a lot like Dez did the moment it became apparent the op wasn't going to get done without some shooting.

Or blowing something up.

"Nobody's seen her." But Gloria turned and marched away, the very picture of a bloodhound with a mission—and all in coordinated earth tones plus swinging, tasteful earrings, too.

"Paul." Helena's hand closed on his sleeve, and he realized he'd already started for the entryway. The ballroom hummed with conversation, and that particular pair of shrieking kids near the south end would play a few rounds of tag until being told to go outside with that noise, dammit.

"It's all right." He probably sounded thoughtful, a little absent, but a fellow Squad member would arrange himself in the backup position without question, assuming there was going to be something unpleasant in the next few minutes.

And of course Hel had raised him; she knew him better than anyone. He'd once thought Beck understood him better, but maybe not.

Joe's cruiser was pulled up almost to the Grange's steps, but parked neatly as if he only intended to jaw for a few seconds on a busy day. He was out of the car, trim and tidy in his uniform, smiling at Uncle Dreeson.

Portly, balding Uncle D was relaxed as usual, but his cold-coffee eyes hardly blinked. Of course, his branch of the family never met a cop they didn't loathe. Law enforcement returned the favor, mostly on the principle that transporters of illegal substances shouldn't drive so damn well and outwit them in most if not all cases while doing so. Since legalization, Dreeson'd moved his sons and himself into the clean sector of the same business their branch had been in from the beginning, and they were, by Hel's account, doing pretty well.

Which probably burned one or two law-enforcement biscuits. At least, Paul hoped it did.

It was a beautiful afternoon, fluffy clouds sailing across a blue sky, cold if you were just-arrived from the desert but balmy for a local. Joe grinned and waved, politely excusing himself from Dreeson and heading Paul's direction. Gravel crunched under Paul's boots. Helena had halted on the Grange's steps, and perhaps she looked worried.

I'm not going to hurt him, Paul told himself, but he wasn't sure if he believed it. "Hey, Joe."

"Hey, Paul." Even Halston's handshake was just right, again—the usual, normal pressure, no little squeeze-games. "I'll get right to the point."

I can't believe it's this easy. "I hope so." To a civilian, Klemp probably sounded sunny, open. Amused.

"Beck left a lot of stuff at the house, and she'd probably like to pick it up." Joe even managed to sound miserable but putting a good face on it, if you didn't know he was dragging out the divorce. Did he think Beck hadn't told Hel about yesterday's hearing? "I figured I'd ask you or Helena to help arrange picking it up, since she doesn't want to talk to me."

The kid Paul knew had always been a good liar, especially to adults. Looked like grown-up Joe followed suit.

"Thanks." It was the most neutral response possible. Paul's teenage self would have called bullshit, loudly and immediately, and probably followed it up with a right hook. "I'll let Hel know. Hey, I gotta tell you something."

"What?" If Joe's air of pleasant bafflement wasn't real, it was the best fake ever invented. As a kid he'd been great at the occasional prank and getting out of trouble with a bright, interesting, entirely plausible falsehood.

Looked like he'd been practicing ever since. Paul had spent his time learning other things, and one of them was not getting his ass into any trouble Desmarais and the rest of the squad weren't around to bail him out of.

But there was no reason he couldn't make a statement. "Tuesday night there was someone out on Hel's property." It wasn't a lie, and Paul wondered if the other man could hear the difference. "I couldn't sleep—the time change, you know." *Keep it vague. But not too vague.* "I had a bead on someone sneaking up our driveway, along the bushy side. I guess they were heading for the shop. You boys patrol out near her place; do you keep eye on things?"

"Much as we can. It's a big county, and not enough funding." Joe grimaced slightly, and if the thought of being under a scope as he crept around Hel's place vandalizing cars made him sweat, it was hidden by the uniform. "Listen to me. I sound like my father."

Was that little aside supposed to make Paul think of his? "Nah, not enough swearing." He waited until Joe was mid-laugh to change tack again, just like throwing a kick when your opponent expected something else. "You sleepin' okay, dude? You look a little rough."

Beck wasn't the only one who could play the social game, nowadays. The rules were just different in his bullring, and he'd had a few years to practice. Once you'd been under fire it simplified everything else in your life, and ideally it also cured the urge for pointless dick-measuring.

Well, nobody was perfect.

"I didn't know you cared." But Joe's blue eyes sharpened, and his smile turned hard. Looked like the message was getting through loud and clear. "How about you? We didn't really have time to talk yesterday; I hear you got wounded overseas."

"Nearly died." Another truth, but this jumped-up jackass would never know the real dimensions of the words. "Makes a man reconsider some things." *Like coming home for family reunions, and finally facing up to a few things.*

Joe nodded as if he understood. "That why you came home?"

"It was time." *Should've been here a lot earlier.* "Might stick around a while." Paul let his own smile widen, watched the implication hit.

"Don't know if you'll like it." Now Halston was paying attention, and those slightly bloodshot blue eyes were intent, laserlike. Maybe he wasn't sleeping at all; a busy man sometimes couldn't. "Town's changed, Paulie."

"Some things, yeah. Not others." For a moment, the sense of *déjà vu* was overwhelming. They had, after all, engaged in a version of this conversation when Paul was thirteen, the day he and Joe both realized they liked the same girl.

Oh, the words were different. But the look on Joe's face was the same. And he'd left Beck alone except for wistful glances all through middle and high school. Who wouldn't watch her longingly? She was the sheriff's pretty daughter, a good-grades girl, only mischievous once you got to know her.

Paul could still remember her on the playground at Marckola Elementary, her green eyes glittering catlike and the gap from one of her missing front teeth adorable. *Stop that! You're being mean.*

And just like that, Beck Sommers snapped a leash on Paul Klemperer. He'd worn it like dog tags ever since, and it was inevitable he'd come back. He'd fought it as long as he could, but achieved nothing except getting a chunk out of his leg, as well as a few other interesting scars.

And Beck had been dealing with this unholy mess all alone.

"She'll come back." Joe said it like he believed in Santa Claus, too. Maybe he was just very, very sure he could wear Beck down—and if all else failed, he could make it academic with a little more vehicle tampering. Or worse. "Once she gets this out of her system. After all, there's the house."

"I'm not interested in your divorce, Joe." Yet another absolute truth. The steady vibration in Paul's skeleton was just like rotors throbbing during the flight into a hot zone, all your equipment checked and buckled, the next round of getting shot at closing in with each thrum. "We've got a lot going on today. We'll let you know when Beck decides."

It was the just-following-orders schtick, something a soldier excelled at if he wanted to survive. Add to that a heavy dose of watching Aunt Hel be obdurate, firm, and invariably polite, even against the combined force of Dreeson, Herrold, and his own father, and Paul wasn't doing too badly.

Even if his right hand felt odd, like it wanted to curl into a fist. He had to concentrate to keep it loose.

He hoped the entire transmission was loud and clear. *I know what you've done, and if you come near Beck again, I will not hesitate.*

"All right." Halston settled his hat over his blond buzzcut. If Paul wanted a fight, he could say *yeah, cover up the bald spot.* He knew without a doubt it would provoke.

Halston senior wore a toupee, and Joe was always vain about his hair.

Instead, Paul watched Joe move away, and Uncle Dreeson, near enough to catch the general tone of the conversation if not the words, smiled like a vulture knowing there was always another meal somewhere. Helena watched from the steps, but if she was relieved it didn't show.

He hoped Gloria had cornered Beck, for once. It would mean he could drag his girl away for a plain discussion, and at the moment he didn't care if half the family was watching. Hell, he'd offer them popcorn and red velvet seats.

Only cowards did what Joe had to a woman, and those only stopped when someone they couldn't bully made the consequences clear— and applied them.

Paul was thinking it could even be fun. Any Squad member would find a whole lot of material to play with in Granite River. Half the population went around concealed-carry and the woods held both poachers and fishermen, with the addition of meth trailers and a whole passel of tents full to the brim with inhabitants of varying privacy requirements and nasty tempers to match. He wouldn't even have to visit any nearby military bases.

It was a cheerful thought, and one he clung to as he trudged back to the Grange. Dreeson fell into step beside him.

"I never liked that boy," Dreeson said, softly.

Neither did I. But that wasn't quite true. Sometimes he'd been the only friend Paul Klemperer had. "You never liked his father either."

"Suppose not," Dreeson allowed, and eyed him sideways with a strange expression.

TWO HOURS LATER, it was clear Beck Sommers had vanished.

Getting Through This

THE OLD SWEET Stoppe on the west edge of town still had pumps, and it was the only gas station in Granite River that didn't have some form of CCTV. She didn't know the kid working at the counter, either, which was a mercy. Paying cash to a stranger meant she'd leave no trace.

Her Jetta was a little creaky from disuse, but still remembered her. It probably knew the way back to her dad's house, and she could go and make a full confession now.

But if she did, Joe would wriggle out of everything—including attempted vehicular homicide—like he always did. Besides, she didn't have any solid proof; to provide any she'd also have to incriminate herself, because she'd just committed breaking and entering as well as theft.

No, there were better ways to do this, and if she was going to fall from grace, Beck saw no reason at all to halfass it.

The tank comfortably full, she and the Jetta headed north by long looping back ways, familiar as her own hand. Some of the logging roads had washed out over the winter, but she stuck to the ones slowly solidifying into stability, used by kids joyriding in beaters, hunters looking for good parking spots, and ATV riders. You never knew who you were going to find out here, and if you met on the road, you didn't stop for chitchat. You went on your way pretending not to see the other party.

It was safer.

Beck pulled over on Old Claypole Road. There was an interstate onramp just a mile up the way, and her fingers were shaking as she got her new phone out of its protective silicon case—Hel's was pink, Beck's red to match her old coat—and turned the damn thing off. Then she extracted the SIM card with the help of a pen cap from her purse.

There were no recent voicemails or texts, anyway. Maybe nobody even knew she was gone yet, and she'd been out of tower range for a good three hours getting the canvas duffel stashed. Coverage would pick up once she got on the interstate, but if she kept the phone powered down and stripped of its SIM she might be safe. God knew she couldn't just *drop* the phone like she had the garage door opener.

Hel had paid good money for it, after all.

She should have called Aunt Helena or Mary, left some sort of explanation other than a note on an envelope of cash tucked on the small table next to the annex's couch and her morning's text to Mary saying *I don't think I'll be able to make shifts for a while, I'm so sorry.* The urge to call her father, or put the Jetta into a smoking bootlegger's turn, heading back for Granite River and Dad's house on the west side of downtown, was almost overwhelming.

Did all criminals feel this lonely? It wasn't any big change from the usual human condition, as far as Beck could see. She'd thought she had friends, but then she married Joe.

You could be isolated even in a town where everyone knew your name, and everything else about you, too.

She tucked the SIM in her wallet, and pushed the now-dead phone into a snug little hole between a pack of travel tissues and clean pair of panties. She'd only taken three bundles of twenty- and fifty-dollar bills from the duffel, arguing with herself the entire time.

But her plan required money, she didn't have any, and if she was going to do this it had to be done right.

There were hotels between here and Parsburg that took cash and asked no questions. She might even be able to find working pay phones in the area if she looked hard enough, though she wouldn't need one until tomorrow morning.

Let Joe get home tonight and find the Jetta gone, as well as the bag. Let him have a little sleepless tossing and turning for once. It was only fair, right?

Dad would worry, but that couldn't be helped. Hel might worry too, but she'd probably also be relieved Beck was out of her hair and wouldn't be fucking up the Klemperer family reunion with marital drama. Paul would be glad Helena was safe, with no reason for anyone to mess with her vehicles now. Mary might be angry at losing her employee, but her cousin Ginny would be thrilled to work in the coffee shed; God knew she'd hinted about it enough.

All in all, everyone was probably glad to be rid of the problem Beck represented. And who knew, maybe she could get things settled with Joe and just . . . never go back. She had the car, her anemic bank account in Eugene, and her rings to pawn.

A lot of people started out with less.

Beck closed her eyes, her hands settled on the steering wheel. The Jetta was happy to be running again, and its engine-rhythm had smoothed out remarkably. There was even an ancient granola bar in the glove compartment, the kind with chocolate chips Paul used to like—she'd found it while checking for the registration, relieved that her license tabs were still good and Joe hadn't sweet-talked anyone at the DMV into altering the paperwork.

Maybe she should have done this sooner.

About the only fly in the ointment was her exhaustion, and her body's twinges and aches. No more pain pills, and the ancient bottle of dusty, bitter aspirin kept against emergencies—also in the glove compartment—wouldn't do any good.

Well, you've gone and done it now. You've committed some old-fashioned breaking and entering, you have a bag full of money—and worse—in the trunk, and you're about to do something else that will probably land you in jail along with Joe. Congratulations.

"Not helping," she whispered. Talking to herself again, crazy old Beck Sommers. "Let's just focus on getting through this, okay?"

It was the same thing she'd told herself almost every day of her marriage, even the good ones. At least she never had to be Rebecca Halston again. One way or another, she'd get her divorce.

Beck's eyes snapped open. She took a deep breath, checked over her shoulder, and pulled out onto Old Claypole. The Jetta hummed like it was happy, and she reached for the radio knob.

She loved Hel, but if she never had to listen to country music again, Beck would be a happy camper.

GRANITE RIVER WAS small, but Franklin—on the way to Parsburg, a blip on the freeway—was even smaller. Still, nobody there knew her except maybe Angus Polstrom, who was related to Dad and lived on the east edge of town. Parsburg also had Davy's Coach Inn, still used by truck drivers who didn't want the Love's a little further away if the wide gravel lot across Harnham Road was any indication.

Best of all, the Coach Inn took cash and didn't ask too many questions. Beck was sure couples sneaking away from other towns probably took advantage of the fact, imagining they could get out from under everyone's noses in their adulterous business.

The room was small, only indifferently cleaned, and the shower was only vaguely on the warm end of tepid even with the knob turned all the way over to hot. Still, Beck stood under it for a long time, sticky fearsweat washing off her skin and her limbs trembling fitfully.

She could get in the Jetta, go to the gas station and Wendy's near the main road without telling anyone where she was headed or when she'd be back. She could jump on the bed—though it would probably fall apart if she did—or turn on the ancient television bolted to the chunky pasteboard dresser and watch whatever the hell she wanted. For a few hours, this space was hers, and when she left the linens would be changed, the surfaces swiped, and she'd be forgotten.

It was lonely as hell, and it felt *great*.

Beck splurged on a burger and two large fries, along with a chocolate Frosty to dip them in. She settled on the bed, her flesh crawling only moderately at the thought of who else might have done what in it, and how filthy the place probably was under UV light or a microscope.

But it was good enough, and she ate without nausea for the first time in months.

She might end up living in the Jetta and working in a place like this, folding sheets and rubbing Pledge over the glassware. She kept checking the clock radio on the nightstand, probably off the actual time by at least five minutes if not more, and wondering if Joe was home yet, if Hel had found the envelope in the annex. Dad was probably still in the office, and he'd be worried once he found out she was gone.

Hopefully it wouldn't be for long. Depending on how this worked out, she could get a job and another phone in another city, and call him from there . . . *after* Joe was dealt with.

The Coach Inn had good cable, at least. Beck flipped aimlessly through the channels—the world was going on as it always had, taking no notice of a life wrenched violently off-track or a sudden descent into criminal behavior.

Had it always been this easy?

That night, as the usual spring rains swept in and tapped restlessly at the window, as doors opened and closed all over the motel and vehicles sat patiently waiting for their owners to return, Beck slept deep and dreamless. Maybe it was exhaustion, or just being fully committed to a dangerous course, or not having to be so goddamn quiet and mousy all the time.

Right before she dropped off, she thought of Paul. He was no doubt sleeping too; she'd likely never see him again.

It hurt, but so did everything else. Beck rolled over, mashed the pillow more firmly under her head, and was gone.

A Bigger Pond

SHE HAD LEFT a short note, written on a blank business envelope propped against the end table's lamp in the annex.

Thank you so much, Aunt Hel. Joe won't bug you now. This is all the tip cash I have; I'll send the phone back when I can so you can get a refund. I promise I'll pay you back for the car too. Thank you again, and I'm so sorry. Beck.

That, a grand total of fifty-two dollars in small bills, and Beck's suitcase sitting in the hall closet were all Klemp had to go on. She'd walked out of the Grange and vanished, just like Jackson or Grey when they decided a little AWOL was necessary. Paul hadn't twigged even when nobody could find her after Joe's little visit; he'd never live it down if any of the Squad found out.

"I don't understand." Helena looked a little perturbed, but honestly, if this wasn't perturbing, nothing was. "Did you tell her she had to pay for the Taurus?"

For fuck's sake. "Of course not." He stared at her clean, even handwriting—she still turned the end of her signature to a tiny heart, and the sight of it made his chest hurt *again*. The doctors clearing him to leave the hospital with his bum leg had sworn his arteries were clear; he was still in reasonably good shape although if the Squad was still a going concern Dez would run them all ragged for a few weeks before letting them go on an operation.

Just to be sure.

Hel popped up from her dining-room chair like a jack-in-the-box for the fifth time. "Just what did you say to her yesterday?"

"It wasn't an accident." He wished she'd sit down. He loved his aunt, but he needed some goddamn time to *think* and he couldn't do it with her asking these kinds of questions. Paul rested his elbows on the table and stared at the note, as if it would grow legs or a mouth to tell him what the fuck Beck had been thinking when she wrote it. "Hel, I'm gonna need you to calm down, all right?"

"*Calm down*, he says." Sharp sarcasm edged each word, and Helena's throat worked as she swallowed. Her ponytail was disarranged, and a thin tendril of grey hair fell into her sharp, worry-creased face. "What wasn't an accident, Paulie? What in the *hell* is—"

"The Taurus wasn't an accident." He didn't *want* to raise his voice, but the words bounced off every surface, almost rattling the china hutch. "Someone came up the driveway during the night and nicked the brake lines."

Hel dropped back into her chair, staring round-eyed at him. A short, dangerous silence crackled between them. His aunt folded her hands on the table, fixing him with a gimlet eye. "And you didn't think to tell me?"

If he was still a teenager, he'd be running for the hills. Not that it would do any good, with Hel in this state; there was nowhere on earth you could hide if she decided a boy needed a good scolding. "I was going to, once I figured out what the hell. Calm *down*, Hel. I need to think."

"You were *going to*? Christ Jesus give me patience, Paul James Allen Klemperer, I am about to go get me a switch or two and break them on that hard head of yours."

All four names. He was in trouble now, boy howdy. "If you think you can catch me, sure. Army taught me a thing or two, Hel, and I'll probably need it to get Beck out of trouble. I love you, you're practically my mother, but can you just *pipe down* for a goddamn second so I can fucking well *think*?"

Christ. I sound like my father. Again.

Keeping his temper chained in the pit of his stomach, usually a relatively easy daily chore by this point in his life, was not going well today. No, the beast wanted out, and if he let it escape Paul would find Joe Halston first, then go tell Sheriff Sommers a thing or two. After that he was going to go looking for a woman, and when he found her they were going to have it out, chowder to cashews.

But in this mood, he'd probably scare the fuck out of her because even if he'd never, ever harm her, he'd still be acting just like her goddamn husband.

Ex-husband. Whatever. A divorce could be helped along in all sorts of ways, from a lawyer to a rifle with a reasonably accurate scope, and Paul was goddamn good and ready to settle some problems the old-fashioned way.

You cannot do that shit. It's what you went into the service to avoid. Be smart, Klemp. Be like Dez, or if you have to, be like Jackson. Both of them would be telling you to stay cool right now.

Fraught quiet, full of the ticking of Grandma Owens's mantel clock on the sideboard, returned to Helena's house. After a short while his eyelids came back up from half-mast and he found his aunt studying him.

For the first time, Hel looked old, and very fragile. She'd always been slim but now she looked positively frail, and the laugh lines around her mouth and eyes had been joined by other wrinkles. If he'd been here all along, would he have noticed the aggregate changes?

Age crept up on you, just like everything else.

Well, she wasn't yelling, so that was all to the good. But she was eyeing him the way she'd looked at Herrold once or twice, when his uncle had made up his mind about some customer or fellow townie and no amount of argument would change what he'd decided to do about it.

Paul's father was known to have a nasty temper, true. But *nobody* in Granite River ever wanted Uncle Herrold mad. It was—like attempting to put one over on Dreeson—bound to end badly. Herrold had a long fuse; Paul had only seen it reach the end once.

Even though it had blown on Paul's behalf and Peter Klemperer never beat his son again after that day, Paul still remembered watching Herrold go at his elder brother like a mongoose after a snake—quick, oddly graceful, deadly silent, and giving zero fucks about his own survival as long as he put the other party down.

It had taken some doing for Hel to keep Herrold from bashing Peter's head in with a tire iron, as a matter of fact, and after that Paul lived with his aunt and uncle, rarely going out to his dad's trailer. Hel took over dealing with teachers and signing school permission slips, Herrold put his nephew to work in the junkyard, Beck was always around, and Paul's urge to throw a punch at whoever hassled him was reduced from a rolling boil to a slow simmer.

"All right," he murmured. "All right."

There was a suspicious glimmer in Helena's faded blue eyes. "Paulie?"

"What?" *Maybe I should call Dez. He'd know what to do.* The only thing Paul didn't like about being second in command was the prospect of having to make all the goddamn decisions if his wily, calm-as-fuck CO got tagged. He could do it, sure—but living with the result if he chose the wrong fucking course of action, especially under pressure, didn't sound like a happy trail.

No, he was comfortable with his role, and didn't want it to change.

"You mean that?" Helena's voice had never quivered like this before. Her eyes were very bright. "About . . . about me being your mother."

"Christ, Hel, you've been my mother since I can remember." The car accident that put Dad on disability had taken Paul's actual mother, who was—everyone said—the only person reliably able to calm Pete Klemperer down when he was on a tear. Paul wished he'd gotten that half of the genetic inheritance instead of the anger. "Didn't you know?"

"It's . . . well, it's different when it's said out loud." She actually sniffed, quickly looking down at the table and the envelope of cash lying between them, a silent and possibly frightened witness like a big-eyed kid peering around a corner, hoping the adults could stop the world from spinning off-course. "You're always joking, you know. It's hard to tell what you really feel."

Which was weird, because he'd always considered himself simple, direct, an open book. Did Beck have the same trouble reading him?

Hel reached out, her hand shaking just a little. Paul did too, folding his fingers around her smaller, more delicate fist, and found her skin was cold. "It's gonna be all right." He had no idea if he was lying, but what else could he say?

Maybe that was what being an adult really boiled down to.

"She's probably so scared." Hel's throat worked as she swallowed, hard. "Makes me wonder what else *that boy*'s done."

Well, Joe had been put in *that boy* category. His goose was well and truly roasted once Hel got two cents in with any town gossip. "You can't say anything about the brake lines, Hel. We don't have any real proof." Oh, *now* he could see what Beck had been thinking. Smart girl, the sheriff's daughter, and she obviously felt she had nothing left to lose.

Backed into a corner, any animal was dangerous. Even—and especially—those normally too tame to bite.

Hel's phone—the landline, not her cell—shrilled. His aunt jumped, a reminder of Beck's flinching, and Paul let go of her hand, dispelling the urge to dive for cover.

"It might be Beck." There was a handset with a long, tangled spiral cord at the wall end of the breakfast bar; Hel scooped the phone up, cutting off another bell-cry midway. It died with a tinny echo. "Hello?"

Even at this distance Paul could hear it wasn't Beck. Someone was yelling, and the tone—not to mention the voice—was familiar.

It was Joe Halston, and he was *furious*.

He demanded to speak to his goddamn wife, didn't believe Hel's assertion she wasn't home, and it wasn't until Paul took the phone from his aunt that Beck's ex-husband wised up a bit and stopped screaming.

By then, Paul had made a couple of decisions.

THE OLD A & W ON the edge of downtown had been turned into a Mexican restaurant, complete with cantina. Joe had already snagged a booth and the best side to sit in, with a clear view of the door and his back reasonably protected, though someone returning from the restroom would have a good shot at surprising him.

Nothing was perfect. Paul didn't like his own six to the front door, but if this helped Joe feel safer, it might give his questioner an edge. So he didn't protest, just slid into the free side of the booth and settled. The place was packed—well, it was a Friday night right before Spring Break, and the crowd could be good or bad.

Joe looked a lot better out of uniform, though his buzzcut, belt, and shoes still shouted *cop* to everyone who so much as glanced in his direction. Paul blended better, but then again, he had practice. Even his desert boots were pretty usual; a lot of guys around here had some military in their work history.

Or they pretended they did, because it was one more way to fit in.

"I'm sorry for yelling." At least Joe had cooled down a little. Now he would be wary *and* angry, though, and that was never a good combination. "Can you tell Hel I apologize? I'm out of my mind right now."

"Divorce does that." It did no harm at this point to let the asshole think Paul was on his side. It was just like dealing with a CO who had a stick up his ass and was determined to make soldiers do some useless bullshit that would end with one or more of them ventilated. Dealing with those was another of Paul's specialties even before he got his first sergeant nod, let alone his commission.

He could always blame some intransigence on Dez, who could return the favor, and between the two of them the squad sailed a bit more safely. It wasn't so much the in-country flying lead that got you, but the goddamn bureaucratic bullshit.

There was a pitcher of beer on the table, but Joe hadn't touched it. Two empty glasses stood beside it, so Paul poured. The waitress responsible for their slice of the cantina was a faded brunette with a tired smile who looked vaguely familiar, sort of like Stacey Hardamaker. Could have been her daughter, but hadn't Hel said that family moved away?

He couldn't remember, and it almost bothered him before he shelved the question as immaterial.

"It's not just the divorce, it's the. . . ." Joe hunched, resting his elbows on the table, and scrubbed at his face. Gym muscle rippled under his shirt. He was big—how many times had he used that size on Beck, scaring the hell out of her? The weedy high school kid wouldn't have been able to, but this was a whole different enchilada, as Tax would say with an eyebrow wiggle or two. "Look, you know how she is. She's always been a little insane."

For a moment the sentence refused to settle inside Paul's head, as if the other man was speaking some language he didn't even have the basics of. Then he realized Joe's game, and it really wouldn't take much to pick up the heavy glass pitcher and shatter it over the bastard's head.

Hell, starting a barfight in here would be easy. The only problem was the security cameras, though Klemp had avoided those getting a clear shot at him as far as possible.

That kind of thing was reflexive for any member of the Ghost Squad. The civvie across from him had no fucking idea what he was dealing with. Neither did Beck, or even Hel, God bless her.

"Well, she did take her bike down Attenlee that one time," Paul allowed. "And there was that whole thing with the mariachi band our senior year. Not to mention she married you, so yeah, insane kind of fits." *But if you think I'm going to believe she's a crazy bitch who's somehow ruining your poor innocent life, Joseph Halston III, you're sadly mistaken.*

Joe's shoulders stiffened. But he summoned a harsh laugh from somewhere, dropped his hands, and took a glass of beer. "The mariachi band? That was her?"

"I helped a bit." Any other day he'd be pleased that the secret had been kept so well. Beck always held that the best part of a successful prank was keeping your mouth shut afterward, and now Paul realized he hadn't heard her really, truly laugh once since he'd got off the plane. She used to find everything funny, for God's sake, a river of merriment hiding just under the surface. "You mean nobody figured it out?"

"Even *I* was accused of that one. But then, Beck's good at keeping secrets. She ran around town all the time, even after we were married." Joe grimaced, took a hit off his freshly poured, probably warm beer. "I hate to say it, but I gotta warn you, man. She's fucking nuts. Don't get sucked in."

Jesus Christ. Did Joe really think he was this stupid? "Must've made you mad." It was work to keep that same neutral, easy tone. All Paul wanted was to go over the table and choke the living daylights out of the man, but that wasn't going to get the intel he needed. "You always had a thing for her."

"Oh, yeah. Not to put too fine a point on it, you leaving town was the best thing that ever happened to me." A bright, direct blue stare, still bloodshot—what else was Joe creeping around at night doing, other than snipping brake lines? "Just being honest."

"Good." Paul smiled; a civilian would think it an engaging grin, but any member of his squad would notice it didn't reach his eyes. "Because I have to admit when I heard she married you, I almost wanted to go AWOL." *You probably knew that, and gloried in it too, you son of a bitch.*

"Yeah, well. Look, can you just . . . can you just tell her that it'll be fine, I'll sign over the house, I'll do whatever she wants, if she just *talks* to me?" Halston was off and running, now. "I don't even know what's wrong, I just came home from work one day and—"

If he didn't head the motherfucker off, they'd be here all night. "Joe." Paul kept his hands on the table, nice and flat to match the words. "She's gone." *Give me a clue. Something I can work with.* "Left a note apologizing to Helena and everything. I guess the accident scared her." *Was that all you wanted to do, frighten her?*

Paul had his doubts.

"Hell, she probably drove off the road while looking in her purse." There it was, that lying little sparkle in Joe's gaze. Some things changed in Granite River, sure—but others didn't. "We were buddies once, Paulie. I'm telling you, the girl is crazy. Just have her call me, all right? I can't help her if she doesn't talk."

It had the ring of an oft-repeated truism, and gooseflesh slid down Paul's back. He'd said pretty much the same thing to Beck.

No wonder she'd flinched.

"I told you, she's gone." Maybe that was a lie, maybe not. If he could just get a single smidge of something useful out of this guy, it'd be worth it. "Up and left. Vanished. Whoosh." He lifted his hands a little, adding a puzzled shrug. "I don't know whether to call her dad, or what."

"I wouldn't do that. You know how he feels about you." Joe took another hit off his beer. "You're sure she's gone?"

"She left the Grange sometime this afternoon. Also left money for Helena and an apology. That's pretty final." Paul had his subject running the right way now; Halston didn't even realize he was being interrogated. "Maybe she didn't like seeing my face."

"I dunno. She didn't talk about whatever happened with you guys. I didn't ask." Another ratty little eye-gleam.

Paul was suddenly one hundred percent certain Joe had asked, several times. He was pretty sure his own name had been used to torment Beck with, in one way or another, and even Hel's beloved Jesus was having a hard time keeping him from teaching this motherfucker the difference between a scared civvie girl half his size and a thoroughly trained member of Desmarais's happy wrecking crew.

After cracking Joe on the head with the beer pitcher, he could take the concealed piece Joe was wearing and finish the motherfucker off with it. The thought had a certain charm; their old trainer Sparky Lee often repeated that just because a weapon was in an opponent's hand didn't mean it couldn't be used by your own sweet self.

"She didn't talk about you either." Paul kept his own glass at just the right distance to serve as a preliminary weapon, but he didn't take a sip. "You want to tell me what's got you so upset? Did you see her?" When Joe cooled down a fraction more, he'd realize Paul might arrive at the idea that he'd murdered his wife in a divorce-sparked rage, and any attempt he made at damage control would hopefully give up some kind of clue.

"The Grange. It's walking distance from . . . we live near there, you know. Passacola, where the new development went in." Was Joe actually trying to *brag*?

"Nice part of town." Feed the ego, and a man would talk a little more. Paul hadn't learned that in the Army, or from Sparky's tender attentions.

No, that was a homegrown skill.

"Well, hell." False modesty, just the thing for a Sunday at either church you cared to attend in Granite River. "You marry Becca Sommers, you gotta provide something, you know? But it wasn't good enough, I guess."

The chilling thing was, Paul might actually half-believe some of this shit—*if* he hadn't seen the cut brake lines and a hundred other things. No wonder Beck was at her wit's end; the entire town probably believed Halston's bullshit.

"It's late, Joe." *Keep him on target.* "You want to tell me why you called my Aunt Helena, yelling so loud I could hear you across the room?"

"Well. . . ." Joe glanced across the crowded cantina like he thought someone was looking to zero him. Nobody was paying any goddamn attention; the screens over the bar were tuned to a basketball game. It wasn't like Joe to sit where he couldn't see the hoops; once he got some adult height the end of middle school his game had gotten a lot better, and the sport was a religion in this part of the world.

Texas had football, Oregon had March Madness.

"She came home," Joe said, leaning forward and pushing the pitcher aside. Now they were getting to it. "While I was at work. Took her car, which she could *always* have had, by the way."

Paul had his doubts about that assertion, but he nodded like a true believer, praise and amen.

"She took some other stuff, but it's not like I mind, all right?" Joe continued. "It's *our* house, you know? But she also took something that doesn't belong to her. Doesn't belong to either of us. And if I don't get it back, I'm not going to be the only one looking for her, you dig?"

Oh, shit. Everything snapped into place behind Paul's eyes, but he let the last sentence hang between them for a few seconds, ringing like a chow bell's after-echoes. *Beck, baby, what on earth did you do?* "Do I wanna know what this something is?" He did, very much—but he doubted Joe would tell him.

In any case, he could guess.

"Probably not. Besides, you've got Hel to think about." There was the threat, delivered so quickly and deftly there was hardly time to consciously register it. Oh, he'd learned that in the interrogation room, Paul bet. Next would come what Joe *really* wanted out of him. "Just, if you see her, tell her to come home. Or try to . . . I don't know. You could always talk to her."

"Not anymore." His brain raced; Tax said there weren't pain receptors inside the skullcase and he should know. But Paul would sometimes beg to differ, because right now he had a massive cramp right between his ears. "Not since I left. She's barely said two words in my direction, Joe. She'd talk to Helena more than me."

"Well, if Helena hears from her. . . ."

Hel always thought you were a little prick, but you're pretty sure you have me snowed. Because I went away. Paul could actually almost admire the slippery little bastard. Joe had called Hel's landline thinking he could get Beck on the phone and terrify the shit out of her, proving he still knew the number and that there was no place in Granite River he couldn't find an errant wife. Helena was an old woman, and tired; Joe could wear her down eventually. Paul was a bigger threat, but Joe probably thought of him as the stupid kid he'd been years ago, too quick with his fists to do any real thinking.

Maybe he was even correct. But when it came right down to it, Joe

Halston was small-town. A bigger pond's predators would swallow him right up.

And Paul was not the kid he'd once been. "You'll be the first person we call." The lie fell entirely naturally out of his mouth. The best trick of all was to stick the truth when you could, even if the other person wouldn't believe it—and when you had to utter a whopper, make it a good one. "Hel's really worried about Beck, especially since the accident. She almost died."

"Yeah." Joe paled, but not nearly enough to be the man he was impersonating for Paul's benefit—the guy still in unwilling love with a nutty girl who was doing him wrong. "Look, we both care about her, okay? That's what matters right now."

"You're right." Paul slid toward the end of the booth. He couldn't sit here a single second longer. "Thanks for the beer. Listen, if *you* see Beck or hear anything—"

"I'll leave a message for Hel." Joe didn't even ask for Paul's number. "She probably, uh, doesn't want to talk to me either."

"Well, you know how women are." With a wink and a grin, Paul got the hell out of there before he was even more tempted to do something he shouldn't.

Beck. What the fuck did you take, baby? What in hell's name are you thinking?

He mulled it over all the way home to Helena's, and each mile passing under the Jeep's tires made him more and more nervous, if that were possible.

Make It Simple

FOR THE FIRST morning of her criminal career, it wasn't bad at all. No phone alarm, no immediate thump of guilt under her breastbone, no snap of Joe's belt if he thought she was being lazy, no scrambling to make breakfast, no uncomfortable conversations or false, necessary cheerfulness.

There wasn't any coffee until she left the motel room, but that was a small price to pay.

It was sheer luxury to lie in bed with the television on and not have to smile at anyone. She didn't have to apologize or refuse well-meaning charity, and she especially didn't have to watch her mouth.

For once in her life, Beck Sommers could say what she damn well pleased, and she liked the feeling. The fact that it was because she was completely alone was pleasant, too.

The water seemed a little hotter this morning, and she took her time in the shower. She also waited until the parking lot was empty, about an hour before official check-out. A simple drop of the room key into a slot, hearing the clatter as it landed, and she was free to go wherever the hell the Jetta could take her.

Joe must be out of his mind by now. If he came home at all last night, that is.

How many nights had she lain awake, hoping he'd be busy with Amy or whatever else kept him out until he had to get to the gym before work? It was impossible to relax when any moment might bring the rattle of the garage door and his footsteps on the stairs. If she was lucky he'd just visit the bathroom and then get into bed.

If she wasn't, if someone had ignored or disrespected him during the day, goodbye to any chance of sleep the rest of the night. He was so affable outside the house, but he kept a running log of every slight. And eventually, every tally-mark was taken out on Beck in private.

And with interest.

It probably ran in the family. Yolanda Halston wasn't local, and she rarely said boo outside of church. She was nice enough, Beck had always thought, but wishy-washy.

Now she wondered. Joe Senior always had a little gleam in his blue eyes when he looked at his wife, and Beck now knew the look intimately.

In any case, there was a pay phone in the parking lot of last night's Wendy's, and she'd written down all essential numbers in her old address book yesterday since her phone was going to be out of commission. God, how the world had changed since she was a kid.

I sound like Helena. The thought gave her a smile, and there were quarters in the Jetta's ashtray—innocent of any cigarette fallout and thus a repository for hair clips, loose coins, and pocket lint. The tiny grin died as she dialed, plugging her other ear against the parking lot's noise. He'd be able to tell she was at a pay phone, but she might be able to get a burner today.

If she was lucky. A lot depended on how this conversation went.

He must've been practically sitting on his phone, waiting for it to ring. "Hello?" His official police bark, all business even on his cell, stung her ear.

"Hello, Joe." No betraying quiver in the words. All things considered, Beck thought, she sounded pretty normal.

"Jesus *Christ.*" Joe had to be at home; he wouldn't hiss like this in public. "You think this is funny? Where the fuck are you, Becca?"

"I could tell you, but I'll be gone in a few minutes so I don't think it matters." *Get it over with. Don't haggle, and don't explain.* She'd practiced this call in the shower, trying out different scripts. Most of her planned words had vanished, though, a verifiable instance of pre-staircase wit. "I'll make it simple, Joe. Give me my divorce, and I'll tell you where to find the bag. Keep dragging your feet, I'll call Dewey Johnson and tell him you don't have his property." She had the first two fingers of her free hand tightly crossed, but not because she was eight and felt bad about a fib.

No, she was all grown up, not to mention hoping, wishing, and praying she had correctly guessed who her cop husband was in an even dirtier bed than Amy Lorton's with. Dad didn't talk about Dewey, but Joe did, and every time he mentioned Granite River's local meth powerhouse it meant Beck had to be on her toes.

Cold, reptilian silence poured through Joe's smartphone, beamed invisibly through the air, hit a tower, and was translated to phone lines, then funneled to her ear. She shivered, and a car door slammed in front of the gas station.

"You have no idea what you're fucking doing," Joe said, conversationally. "You meet me somewhere, and bring the bag. That's the best offer you're gonna get, Becks."

Just how stupid do you think I am? Well, she *had* married him, and for all the wrong reasons, too. "Guess I'm calling Dewey, then. He always liked me in school." *Oh God, Beck, don't poke the bear like that. He's going to be so angry. So, so angry.*

But he had to catch her to make her pay, and if he was busy avoiding Dewey Johnson—and his ATV-riding crew—he might not have the time to look for ol' Becks.

"So you're fucking him now too? Does Paulie know?" Of course he'd pick the most horrible, hurtful thing to say.

"I know about the brake lines, Joe." Now she was wishing she'd used the Wendy's restroom before making this call. What was it about being scared that made you want to pee so bad? Were you just lightening for takeoff, fight-or-flight dumping everything extraneous out the hatches?

"Why, what brake lines, sweetheart?" The mock-puzzlement in her husband's tone made all the fine hairs rise, from her arms to her nape and all the way down her back. "That Jetta of yours might need some service. I coulda taken care of that for you, if you'd asked."

He's bluffing. She couldn't be sure, though, and she needed the car. The panicked desire to blurt out where the money was, that she was sorry, that she just wanted him to sign the fucking papers made her writhe internally with shame, but she was over the river and through the woods, as Dad would say.

There was no backing down now. She'd dynamited this particular bridge—not that it was ever in great shape to begin with, but now it was completely gone-a-roo, as they used to say in elementary school.

"You have until two p.m." She had practiced this part too, over and over. "You can ask any clerk at the courthouse for the right papers, it shouldn't take more than ten minutes to sign them all. I'll call them to confirm, and once that's done, I'll call and tell you where it is. Then we never have to see each other ever again."

"You are crazy. You are fucking *insane*." He was gathering steam, and soon would come the sonic assault to turn her into a quivering, submissive heap.

Not this time. "I'm also tempted to go spend some money," she said, level and cool. "How much do you think I can get rid of before you eventually sign? The drugs, well, they can just go in a river somewhere."

"You fucking *bitch*—"

So they'd reached that part of the program. He'd have to go to the gym to calm down. Well, the day was young, she'd left him plenty of time. "Then you should be glad to get rid of me, Joe, because I'm just getting started. The longer you wait, the worse this gets. Bye-bye." She chirped the last, her usual teenage adieu on nights when her ear ached from the phone clamped to it and her dad would holler *Becca Jane, get off the goddamn phone or I swear. . . .*

Then, she hung up.

She *hung up* on Joe Halston. Beck stood, rubbing her fingers against her jeans since God alone knew what was on that handset, and stared at the pay phone as if it would turn into a snake and lunge for her.

But nothing happened. People were buying gas, pulling up to the Wendy's drive-thru, heading for the freeway as if it was any other normal day. The world kept spinning on.

God, she should have done this *ages* ago. A burst of exhilaration staggered her, and the flood of sick dark terror right alongside it almost made her want to bend over and splatter her breakfast sandwich all over her sneakers. But people might remember that. She was already on Wendy's security cameras, but then again, Joe could trace the phone number. He was probably doing it right now, calling in a favor.

She might as well pee, and then she could find another hotel. She might even be daring and get a burner phone, too.

Go figure, all her childhood and teenage mischief-making, usually with Paul as an accomplice, had just been practice for this. Kid games, preparing for deadly serious adult ones.

So far, Beck thought, she was doing pretty good. And it was a nice change.

Picked a Fine Time

HEL WORKED THE phone tree all Saturday morning. Old-growth Granite River knew Beck Halston was missing before any of the younger set caught on, smartphones be damned, but Paul was still willing to bet that by noon everyone in town and most people halfway to Eugene had a theory or a sighting. The landline rang off the hook, and Hel's smartphone kept beeping until Paul turned all notifications off except those from his own cell—and Beck's.

Paul paced, cracked jokes when Hel started to look too worried, ran the coffeepot, greeted Aunt Gloria with a smile when she arrived, and thought, furiously.

The only surprise was that Gloria wasn't alone. Dreeson followed her royal-blue Lincoln Continental in his old, cherry-perfect square-body green Chevy truck—the old girl purred like a kitten, and Paul remembered working under that hood as Herrold and Uncle D chatted or offered advice.

His heart sank, but Gloria wasn't wearing her tragic face. She was all business, bustling past Paul and digging a cell phone out of her huge rhinestone-studded purse, shocking against the earth tones she liked to wear. She also produced a fresh pad of legal paper and a brand-new package of blue Bic pens.

That was even worse than the breathless recitation of some misfortune—an accident, a body found. The next step after "Gloria with a legal pad" was calling out the National Guard.

Dreeson halted on the porch, and beckoned. "I need a smoke, Paulie. Come on out here."

Oh, shit. "Did you find her?"

"No. Y'all weren't raised in a barn, get *out* here and shut the damn door." Uncle D had zero patience for anyone other than very young children or Aunt Rose, and even less for obtuseness. "No need to make Hel worry."

Oh, Jesus, Beck, what the fuck have you done? He stepped out, closed the door softly, and eyed the treeline. Nothing lurking there. A cool misty spring day, just enough precipitation to flick the wipers every once in a while, lay hushed and serene under a soft grey sky. "Whatever it is, it's not Beck's fault. It's Joe Halston's. You've got to know that."

"Wellnow." Dreeson produced a familiar-looking case. He had a vape pen like Lefty, and for almost the same reason—Aunt Rose had put her foot down, Helena said, and locked Dreeson out of the house until he went and bought it. She also locked him out if he fell off the wagon and snuck a Camel, so it was something of a family game to catch him at it and text a photo to his round-hipped, soft-spoken, absolutely fearless wife. "So you did learn something in the service. I had my doubts, young man."

At least it was *young man* and not *boy*. "I did my duty. Sir."

"Don't be like that." Dreeson fired up the vape, got a nicotine hit, and exhaled harshly. His plaid button-up was crisply ironed and starched; so were his faded jeans. The silver caps on his cowboy boots' toes winked merrily. "Christ, I hate this thing."

"I can send a picture to Aunt Rose." Paul strangled a flare of impatience. The ruler-by-default of the Klemperer clan, always soft-spoken, took things in his own good time and held it was better to work smart than hard. Some men moved too fast for the world, but Dreeson ambled, somehow always arriving at the critical point well ahead of anyone else. "Tell her she has to reward you."

"If I thought she'd listen, I might let you." Dreeson even half-smiled at the thought, a wolf's grin under his many-times-broken nose. "I've got my boys and some friends looking for Beck."

Paul's entire body went cold. He measured the distance between them, a reflex trained in so hard it didn't matter that Uncle D was family.

There was no pleasant reason for Dreeson's boys *and* friends to be looking for someone. Ever.

"Not that way." Dreeson was, Paul realized, watching him sidelong, very carefully. Like a man gauging a rattlesnake's mood. "Jesus, Paulie. We're looking to *protect* her." He paused. "Still hung up on that girl, even after the Army. That's something."

Thanks for the commentary, Uncle D. "Protect her from what?" That was the important question. His uncle wouldn't mount a response this size just for a single wife-beating deputy.

Just what else was Joe involved in?

"Well, to understand that, you gotta understand what's been through here last few years, Paulie. Weed's legal now, you know." Dreeson's quick smile was almost impish for a moment, and he coughed another cloud of white vapor. "Almost makes me like the guvmint, for once. You remember Dewey Johnson."

"Couple years after me in school, but yeah. Poor kid. Math whiz." *Scrawny, but tough.* The middle brat in that particular subdivision of the Johnson family wasn't easy to provoke, and for the most part he avoided trouble because it took only a couple fights before everyone knew it wasn't worth it.

If you got him riled, he'd *finish* the fight, and even kids didn't mess with that kind of crazy.

"Well, he's in business," D continued. "Doing well for himself, too."

"Meth." Or so Helena hinted. Paul's hands itched to grab his uncle's shirtfront and *shake* the man, but that was a bad idea, even for one of the Ghost Squad.

Dreeson nodded, slowly. A patch of bare skin near his temple gleamed; they'd scraped a melanoma off there five years or so ago. "So you *have* been listening."

"Since I got off the plane." *Just caught on too late to do Beck any good. But I'll fix that.* "Plus, Hel writes letters."

"Used to be the only way to get news." Dreeson chuckled, a soft sound lacking any real amusement, and that was the signal he was finally down to brass tacks. "Well, Dewey's got a way of convincing people, as well as a little business sense. Every once in a while there's a bust to keep the staties happy, but most of the time nobody works too hard unless it's a territory question. All in all, I'm glad to be legal these days." He rolled the vape pen between his fingers; most of the addiction to coffin-nails was having something to play with while you gave a matter some thought. "Anyway, that Halston boy's one of Dewey's many friends and admirers."

Oh. Several pieces of the puzzle fell into place. "Joe said Beck went to their house yesterday while he was at work. Took her car and I guess some of her clothes." Paul took a deep breath, bracing himself. "But she also took something else."

What were the chances it was, say, something Joe was holding for the Johnson kid? Who apparently was tough enough to run a little meth empire out here in the woods—a surprising turn of events indeed, but if Paul could change over the intervening years, a math whiz with a crank habit could certainly do so as well.

"I was hoping you wouldn't tell me that." Dreeson's sigh was heavy and familiar as an autumn downpour.

"What, you just told your boys *and* friends to look for her on a hunch, or because Hel asked and she's a nice girl?" It wasn't entirely out of the question—but it would be entirely out of character.

Uncle D protected his own, but he didn't bestir himself too far for anyone else.

"No." The old man sucked on his top teeth for a moment, his face puckering. "I did it because Sheriff Sommers is retiring soon. And he's been making noises like he might want to clear his conscience before he does."

"Wait." Hel had never said a single thing about *that*. "You mean Beck's dad. . . ." Good ol' fashioned Law-N-Order Sommers, who got reelected every damn time no matter who ran? The man even the Baptists and the First Methodists agreed on?

"Involved with little Dewey Johnson, and has been for years. Boggles the mind, don't it? But I guess he wants to leave little Becca looked after." Dreeson coughed into one liver-spotted hand, a deep, familiar smoker's hack. The vape wasn't helping *that*. "So, Joe having his daughter was sort of insurance, I guess. Then she up and leaves him, and Dewey, I figure, might be wondering just what she knows."

"Oh, Christ." Paul could barely believe his ears. "Not about her father, I bet. It would absolutely . . . wow."

"But mostly they're looking for her because I started thinking, what if Joe got his hands on little Becca and did something?" His uncle's tone had dropped, soft and reflective. "Boy's got a temper. Not like yours, or even your daddy's, but he's always been a little shit."

It was unpleasant to hear his own worst fears delivered in such a casual, logical way. "That's part of why I went to see him last night, just to get a read on the whole thing. He's frantic, but not like he'd be if he. . . ." *If he's done what those type of guys usually do.*

Paul didn't want to think about that. Because what if he was wrong, and Joe just that good of an actor? Was Beck lying in the woods somewhere, still and pale, leaves tangled in her honey-kissed hair? A cop would know how to weight a corpse; this was a country of rivers. There were also the local quarries, deep and dark, plenty of secrets hiding under cold water's placid surface. If that failed a heavily wooded gorge would do just fine, and there were a million of those around. There were dead all over the hills and into the mountains, moldering with no chance of discovery. The Last Judgment would get awful crowded out here, with all the murdered getting up and shouting *hallelujah* at once.

No. She can't be. His guts were cold. Klemp thought he knew every shade and taste of fear—hell, every man on the Squad was a connoisseur of that particular emotion.

But never, even under fire, had he felt this particular brand. And he hated it.

"Well, that's good; Hel will be relieved." Dreeson was too, to judge by his slight nod. "But it still seems like little Becca has a way of bringing down her ex-husband and Dewey Johnson both, if the staties believe the nice sheriff's daughter some of 'em have known for years. There's some locals up in there too, you know."

"And her father. . . . Good God." If Beck found out her dad was a little less than holy . . . Jesus. It would be like the world ending, for her.

Her father was really all she had, especially with Paul off seeing the sights and trying to get himself killed all over the globe.

I should never have left. But what would he be if he'd stayed here? Another version of Joe?

Or maybe worse?

"I hope she knows what she's doing." Dreeson dug in the pocket of his jacket, extracted a sleek black phone, and glanced at its face. Looked like he'd adapted to the pace of modern technology just fine. "Or that one of our boys gets a bead on her—so keep your boots on, because if that happens you're gonna be the one making her listen to some sense."

"Of course." He wanted to say *duh* instead, but while you could occasionally mouth off in the almighty US Army, backtalk to Uncle D was an entirely different jar of angry wasps.

"Good. Now, if Dewey's boys get their hands on her, they're an enthusiastic bunch, and they . . . well, but Dewey might see reason." Dreeson was still watching Paul in his peripheral vision, casual but careful. "He might even have a soft spot for her. Christ knows half the boys in town did."

Yeah, and you always gave her the strawberry suckers from the jar on your desk when we were kids. Everyone else got whatever, but you saved those for her. "Guess I'm in good company, then."

It wasn't really a joke, but Dreeson cawed with actual laughter until he coughed again, and Paul was honestly concerned by the time he stopped.

"Jesus, kid," Uncle D rasped. "You're still funny as fuck. That's good."

Surely the sky was going to start falling any minute. It was profoundly uncomfortable to be actually complimented by the man nobody could ever please. "Thanks? I guess?"

Beck had to be alive. She *had* to be. It wasn't possible that Paul had misjudged Joe that badly. But still, the nagging worm of doubt was in the apple now, and Christ he wished he had some backup.

If he was wrong. . . .

Don't think about that. It was a contingency even the Squad's number-two officer wouldn't plan for. Planning was the same as admitting a possibility, and that was too close to tempting fate.

But oh, God, if Joe had done something irrevocable to Beck, not even Vincent Desmarais would be able to get Paul out of the stockade. Because Klemp would carefully, calmly hunt Joe Halston down.

And he would make the bastard's agony *last* before finishing the job.

"Don't thank me." Dreeson wore his watch's face on the inside of the wrist, like Paul and the rest of the squad. His nephew had never noticed before, growing up. What else hadn't Paul seen? "I called Sommers this morning and invited him on out here. My guess is he'll be a little less than happy."

"Great." The morning just kept getting better, like that whole mess in Tangiers, one of the first ops the Squad ever ran. Every single one of them had caught lead during that bullshit, and they'd lost Footy Lenz. "This'll go well. I'm almost positive it will."

Footy would've loved Beck. *A real doll*, he'd say.

"You can't punch him, Paulie." Did Dreeson actually sound worried? Wonders never ceased. "Not if you plan on marryin' that girl."

She's still married to Joe. Technically, at least. "She wouldn't have me."

"You ever ask?"

"No," Paul had to admit. "I did not."

"Then you're a jackass." Like all Uncle D's character judgments, it was delivered in a flat, nasal deadpan. The chilly breeze swirled around both of them, rattling the branches along Hel's driveway. "You got any coffee?"

"Two sugars and stir once," Paul recited, rolling his eyes, and went dutifully to fetch his uncle's java. They said you always turned into a kid whenever you went home again. For the most part, it was true, not to mention as uncomfortable as wet, sandy skivvies.

Fifteen minutes later, Sheriff Sommers did indeed arrive.

ONCE MORE, THE sheriff parked just where Paul would have while visiting potentially unfriendly territory, but this time he ambled slowly toward the porch, his gaze roving the front of the manufactured and coming to rest on Uncle D like a man finding a snake in a woodpile.

"Dreeson," he said, when he got to the bottom of the porch steps.

Uncle D lowered his coffee cup. "Connor."

Sommers eyed Dreeson's nephew, and a muscle in his cheek flicked. He'd nicked himself shaving that morning, and Paul was suddenly aware of his own stubble.

He hadn't even had a chance to shower yet. "Sheriff Sommers." Might as well save the man the trouble of having to open his mouth.

"Paul." Not *Paulie*, and not just a grunt. If it was an olive branch, it was a polite but distinctly underimpressed one. Then he got right down to business. "Where's my Becca?"

I wish I knew. "Joe call you?"

"No, not since. . . ." Sommers's expression didn't change, but his right hand was suspiciously close to his sidearm. "Paul Klemperer, you tell me where my daughter is. Right now."

"If I knew, I would." It was just like giving Dez a sitrep when an op had gone half sideways and was looking for the other half. "Joe came by the Grange when we were doing setup yesterday. Maybe she saw him, I don't know."

"What the hell does that have to do with—" Sommers wasn't thinking like a cop, or he would have let Paul continue. All Paul's young life the sheriff had been a stony monolith, the lawman almost impossible to read, but at the moment he was just an angry father, and under the ire was a bald edge of devouring fear.

It was uncomfortably like seeing old Sommers naked. Paul almost winced at the thought. "He said he wanted her to pick up some things from the house. Guess she up and did that while he was at work. He also called Hel yesterday evening, yelling his head off, and I went to meet him out at the old A & W."

"Casa Buena now," Dreeson supplied softly. "Manny and Liza's place."

Sommers already knew, and visibly didn't give a good goddamn whose place it was. "Where is Becca?"

Paul added the kicker. "Joe says she took something that didn't belong to either of them, Sheriff. And Uncle D was just explaining to me what that probably means."

A few years ago it might have given him some satisfaction to see one of Granite River's unquestioned authorities turn pale as an alligator's belly and all but stagger. The sheriff recovered quickly, though, and his right hand moved away from the gun butt.

Which was a distinct relief.

"Time was you wouldn't need an explanation." Sommers reached blindly for the inside pocket of his uniform jacket. His nametag glinted dully as he pulled out a pack of Pall Malls.

"Thought you quit." Dreeson took a last swallow of coffee that had to be cold by now, then grimaced, showing his strong, yellowed horseteeth.

"I did too," Sommers replied grimly. His big, square hands held the faintest tremor. "*Fuck.*"

Maybe Paul was finally one of the grownups, if the sheriff was swearing in front of him. "She left a note for Hel. Said *I'm sorry, now Joe won't bother you anymore.*" There was no joy in giving that particular detail, not now.

"He wouldn't sign the divorce papers. Kept filing motions." The sheriff clicked a battered blue plastic lighter and inhaled, sharply; the morning marine layer was burning off and they might get some real sun later in the afternoon. "I know he loves her, but—"

"You think so?" *I could be out there looking for Beck instead of listening to this horseshit.* The urge to get in Hel's Jeep and start driving backroads was almost physical, prodding him in the back like a rifle muzzle. "Is that why he whaled on her? Or why he stalked the shit out of her? Or—"

"Hold up." Sommers tensed, lowering his burning cigarette. "He hit her? Joe Halston laid hands on my baby girl?"

"Didn't you know?" Paul's voice was rising, and a tiny internal whisper that sounded very much like Beck's was telling him to *calm down, if you get started now it'll just make things worse, come on, Paul, help me out.*

Christ, he wanted to. If she would just *let* him.

"I didn't think he'd. . . ." Sommers glanced at Dreeson, who was checking his phone again, either unconcerned or wanting to look that way. "You're sure? Paulie, you'd better be damn sure what you're telling me."

So now he was *Paulie* again. "If I could tell once I saw her again, what stopped *you* from figuring it out? Some cop you are." *Fuck, Paul, calm down.* "And you let her marry the bastard. Probably even gave your blessing."

He wasn't calming down. The knot in his gut was getting worse by the minute, and the image of Beck lying on the forest floor, a crown of last year's leaves tangled in her hair, just wouldn't go away.

"I ain't gonna apologize for keeping you away from my daughter." Sommers's chin jutted out. Beck did that too when she was getting stubborn, though on her it was adorable.

On her father, it was purely bullish. But the old man, a figure of terror and wonder all during Paul's youth, was just that—old. He looked surprisingly frail at the moment.

Like Helena, like Dreeson. As old as Herrold, if he'd still been alive. Old as Paul's own father.

When the hell had that happened? "Well, you did a great job of it." Paul could barely get the words out, and for once there wasn't a single joke trying to escape his brain and bolt through his mouth. "Tip-top. Marvelous work, Sheriff."

"I don't. . . ." Sommers glanced at Uncle D. "Dreeson? Joe Halston hurt my daughter?"

"How deep you in with Dewey Johnson, Connor?" Dreeson apparently didn't feel like rehashing Beck and Joe's marital problems, and Paul supposed they could all be grateful for the subject change. "How hard is he gonna look for your girl?"

"Deep enough." Forget pale, the sheriff was now flat-out ashen. Acrid smoke lifted from his forgotten cancer-stick, dangling in one callused, capable hand. "Staties raided Chapwick's this morning."

Chapwick's? It took Paul a second to remember the name. It was an ancient building on a waste lot in the northeast end of town; back in high school, everyone swore it was a real, actual biker bar. Some kids even claimed Hell's Angels could be seen out there, not that anyone ever went to look. Not even the real troublemakers. "That old place?"

"Dewey's in-town headquarters for the last couple years. Got him some professional muscle helping to run the meth up, down, and east too, and they do some of the changeovers there." Dreeson shook his head. "Now why would the staties go near Chapwick's, Connor? They get themselves a tip or something?"

The sheriff's answering shrug was a marvel of ambiguity.

Every time Paul thought he had some kind of handle on this situation, something else popped up. "Did they get him?" If Dewey was in a holding cell, even temporarily, it meant they could deal with Joe first and maybe tie everything off relatively quickly.

"'Course not." The sheriff tipped his head back, his jaw working.

"Now he'll be madder'n hell," Dreeson said. "And holed up in the back forty like a tick in a dog's armpit. Gotta hand it to your Rebecca, she picked a fine time."

The implication took a moment to sink in. If Dewey had been tipped off to a raid, what better place to hide something incriminating than with a deputy? But Beck had whatever-it-was now, and Dewey Johnson would be suspecting a doublecross. Which was probably part of her plan, fine—but what she didn't know stood a very good chance of killing her.

If Johnson caught Beck, he'd make an example of her. Joe might be able to save himself by getting his hands on her and whatever he'd been holding, but that wouldn't end well for her either.

"Christ," he muttered. "We've got to find her."

"We'd better find Joe, too." Sommers brought his chin back down, and the light in his hazel eyes was uncomfortably close to the glint in Dreeson's cold-coffee gaze when real business was being discussed. "He called in sick today."

Which meant Beck's husband was most likely out hunting, and the sheriff probably couldn't reel him in even with a plausible lie.

And all Paul could do, for the moment, was sit here. "Son of a *bitch*," he muttered, and thank God there wasn't anything around to kick but Hel's porch.

Just then his back pocket buzzed like an angry rattler, nearly sending him out of his skin. It was just his phone, though, and for one lunatic moment he thought it might be Beck calling.

It wasn't.

Familiar, Cage

THE ONLY THING not to like about her new criminal life, other than the heart-pounding terror and the feeling of all her nerve endings rawly exposed, was all the fast food. She'd gone from anxiety-induced nausea to being ravenous, but there was only so much grease she could stand.

Which explained why she was in the produce section of Goshen's shiny box store on her way back from Eugene, far enough away from home she didn't think anyone would recognize her. Especially with her hair braided tightly back, a new black baseball cap pulled low, her navy-blue belted Thinsulate hunting coat instead of the red jacket she'd taken to Hel's and worn almost religiously ever since, and a pair of sunglasses she hadn't put on since high school.

They were Paul's, and too big for her. Now wasn't the time to think about why she'd left them in the Jetta for years, jammed in the catch-all cupholder along with spare change, a tire pressure stick gauge, and two different kinds of slowly congealing lip balm. It was always good to have a spare set of shades, right?

Her conscience pinched at spending cash from the duffel. The bag was almost as big as she was, and stuffed to the gills with little baggies of crystalline drugs as well as neatly rolled or banded wads of green. It was probably a drop in Dewey Johnson's bucket, and if it got the papers signed, Beck had no problem telling Joe where to find it.

Well, where to find *most* of it. She'd done a lot of driving today, from the back of beyond to Eugene and now to Goshen, a regular Saturday car tour. It was true what they said about criminal careers— they started small, but the temptation to keep going was irresistible. Either church in town would happily thunder about the primrose path being wide and easy, leading right to hell.

Was it still a downward glide if you'd been in a personal hell for years already? Beck settled the shades more firmly on her nose and eyed the apples, turned weird colors by scratched, pitted dark lenses filtering fluorescent light.

She could just take all the cash and keep going. It kept occurring to her at random moments, when she wasn't brooding about how furious Joe probably was, or wondering if her father had even realized she wasn't simply busy and letting calls go straight to voicemail.

Helena was probably relieved to have her house back to just-family; the reunion would be going full-tilt on its first day of meetings and greetings by now. If Paul thought about her at all, it might be with grudging acknowledgement that she had done something right by getting out of his aunt's hair for good.

A prepackaged salad was better than drive-thru grease, and maybe tonight she could even sit in a decent restaurant somewhere. It sounded great, except for the guilty certainty that everyone in the goddamn store was watching her.

She'd planned to get a cheap fishing cooler and some ice too, maybe a half gallon of milk and a box of sugary kid's cereal to celebrate her freedom—for however long it lasted—but that would mean laying out even more drug cash, and the two burner phones in her basket with their fluttering receipt, already paid for and loaded with minutes in the electronics section, were her significant investment for the day. Maybe either of them could be tracked off the cell towers, but until she actually made a call they were safely anonymous.

Beck's nape crawled. She set off for the front of the store, her damp sneakers occasionally squeaking on vinyl flooring made to look like wood in the grocery sections and plain old linoleum in the rest of the store. A skinny blond guy almost lost in his faded, frayed fatigue jacket ambled in her wake, his combat boots making similar sounds at random intervals. It was a good bet he'd never been in the service; no soldier would walk that way.

He could be following her. She turned down the beans-and-soup aisle as if she'd suddenly remembered something she needed, and he walked past without missing a beat. Her heart beat thinly in her throat, and she tasted copper.

Jesus, Beck. Get it together.

Hopefully Joe wasn't willing to risk Dewey's wrath. If he made it to the courthouse and signed the papers, she was more than willing to let him know where the duffel was. While he was busy picking it up she could sign whatever was left on her half of the paperwork and be out of town before anyone who recognized her had a chance to gossip.

If anyone cared, that was. Beck could call Dad from a reasonably large city, reassure him, and if she was careful she could vanish entirely from the area, not to mention Joe Halston's life. He'd marry Amy, and maybe she could deal with him. Beck could get a dead-end job somewhere far away, or maybe go back to school.

And she would never have to see her fucking hometown again.

Goshen was far larger than Granite River, and the checker was an absolute stranger. Beck had almost forgotten what it felt like to just buy something without having to ask after someone's family, and it was *glorious*.

The guy in the fatigue jacket was at one of the brightly colored coin-op machines in the store's entryway, working a claw over a snowdrift of cheap toys. Those games were all rigged, but Beck wished him luck. She swung the plastic bag carrying her purchases like an excited kid, and dropping into the driver's seat of her car was a relief.

So far the Jetta was holding up, and so was she. Clouds were breaking over the mountain, and thick gold spring sunshine turned the half-full parking lot into a gleaming wonderland for a few moments.

The glare off wet pavement was so bright she kept the shades on, and as she put the Jetta in reverse, she twisted to look out the back window, resting her arm along the passenger seat.

The blond in the fatigue jacket was across the aisle, looking at her car. Beck's heart leapt into her throat again and began pounding, hard, for the fiftieth time that day. She'd had an entire year's worth of cardio this week; maybe she'd even fit into her old high school jeans by now.

"Fuck," Beck whispered. "Oh, *fuck*."

Not only was the blond watching her car, but he had a phone clamped to his ear, and his mouth was moving.

Beck already had the car in reverse. She could gun it, maybe, and catch him between its trunk and the blue SUV parked on the other side. She could add vehicular homicide to her list of crimes.

Dad would be so disappointed.

Instead, Beck finished backing out, pawed for the gearshift, and dropped the Jetta into drive. The blond's mouth was still moving. He squinted against the glare. Was he talking to someone else and just letting his eyes wander, or was he repeating her plate number to a very interested party on the other end of the call?

Get out of here, now.

Beck did not peel out of the box store's parking lot. She managed a sedate pace until she reached Goshen's main drag, then headed for the freeway.

It took a good twenty miles at cruising speed before her hands stopped shaking.

TECHNOLOGY WAS great, but its relentless onward march meant pay phones were seriously endangered. Which was why she'd bought two burners; Beck consulted the list of numbers she'd written down, flipped the first burner open, and dialed.

She was lucky; an unfamiliar voice answered on the third ring.

"Linlane County Court Clerk's Office," it intoned. "How canna helpya?"

Beck gave the case and docket number, her own information, and waited, her legs feeling distinctly noodlelike. It was a good thing she was sitting down.

The clerk came back on the line after a short interval spent clacking at computer keys. "Nah, nothing's been filed today. Looks like you got a court date next week, though."

Bitterness filled Beck's mouth, but she was used to projecting cheerfulness around that terrible taste. "Ten a.m. on Thursday, right?"

"That's the one. Yeah, nothing's been filed." The clerk paused, probably used to these sorts of calls. "I'm sorry."

"It's all right," Beck lied once again. "Thank you so much. Have a nice afternoon."

She hung up and stared out the windshield. The laundromat on Heb City's Bleecker Street—the town was even smaller than Granite River, if that was possible—had a bank of plate-glass windows, and they glowed with reflected sunshine. So, Joe hadn't signed.

Either that, or he had and it simply wasn't filed. Maybe she should give him another day?

Oh, please, Beck. Don't be a dipshit.

The only thing worse than hearing his voice in her head with one of his favorite disparaging terms was knowing she would probably never be free of it. Memories crowded her—Joe with his arm over her shoulders at county staff barbeques, Joe tall and trim in his tux on their wedding day, sweeping her up to carry her over the threshold of the house on Passacola Street. Or even earlier, young Joe with his arms around her, the week after she figured out Paul wasn't calling because he didn't want to.

That evening Joe had been so gentle and careful, as if she were made of spun glass. *Don't worry, Beck. I'll never leave you.*

She'd thought it was a promise, not a goddamn threat.

Of course, by that point she'd known exactly what she had to do, and how to do it. The very next day she'd driven out to Eugene while Dad thought she was spending the night at Jenna Blackminton's. There had been the cramps tearing her in half, the bright red clotted mess, the stained pads, the awful distorted underwater feeling of the meds. *You should have someone with you, honey,* the nurse had said.

I'll be fine, Beck answered, grimly; she'd been repeating it ever since. And the following spring, she married Joe.

He'd been so nice at first, tender and almost breathless like he couldn't believe his good luck. Whatever had turned him mean was probably her fault. It was a solid argument for never getting involved with another man again; she was zero for two now, and maybe she should be grateful she was finding this out in her early thirties instead of later.

Yeah. She'd get right onto the gratitude as soon as she figured out what to do next.

Threatening to call Dewey Johnson was all very well, and she'd hoped it would do the trick. But if Joe was calling *her* bluff—God, she remembered Dad teaching her to play poker at their kitchen table when she was nine, and intoning *you better be real sure you can back that up, Becca Jane*—then the best thing to do was probably just call her goddamn husband, tell him where the bag was, and get the hell out of town. Drive as far as she could, live in the Jetta if she had to, and try to forget Granite River and everything about it.

Just like her mother. But Dad had never hit Mom, and he would've given her a divorce if she'd asked, wouldn't he? She'd still just disappeared, like a ghost.

So Beck knew it was possible to vanish, for any reason at all. Once you had that proof, what really stopped you?

"I'll call again in the morning," she said, almost startled to hear her own voice. The radio, turned down super low, gave a few beats of pop encouragement; she had it tuned to the Top Forty station across the valley and none of the songs were familiar anymore. "Just to make sure. Then I'll decide."

There were the drugs in the bag, sure. And so much cash—how long before she was tempted to go back to the well, as it were, and take a little more? A soft, cold breeze trickled through an inch of open window on the driver's side; the Jetta's heater hadn't lost any of its punch and warm air still lingered even with the engine off.

But there were other things in the bag as well, like the snubnose .38 with a handful of ammunition in a cloudy, much-reused Ziploc rubber-banded to its butt. The gun might be evidence, or it might be insurance. Then there was the hard plastic case, about the size of her mother's jewelry box, and the things in *there* gave her a lot of food for thought.

Dad drove up to Eugene every once in a while, too. He had a few friends in state law enforcement, and most of them knew Beck by sight if nothing else. They might listen to her.

Would her father be proud if he thought that was her plan all along? Of course she couldn't go back to Granite River anyway; she wouldn't be just gossip fodder but outright persona non grata.

That Becca Sommers, she went squealing to the staties. Nobody liked a stool pigeon, not even Dad.

The sun had dipped behind the brick buildings on the opposite side of the street. Shadows thickened, and there was another small motel out on the highway between here and Franklin; a brand-new Chevron station had gone in there a couple years ago, companionably sharing parking lots.

What would it be like to live somewhere she didn't know every inch of? How far could she get as an anonymous stranger instead of Connor Sommers's little girl? Granite River was a cage, certainly—but it was *her* cage, and she'd already been too much of a coward to leave once.

Her stomach growled, and Beck blinked. Dusk had fallen while she sat here woolgathering.

She started the car, grateful the battery wasn't going, and put her seatbelt back on.

Nasty Prayers

IT WAS THE REUNION'S first afternoon out at the Grange, but Paul wasn't there. Neither was Aunt Helena.

Hel's landline was still ringing, but the calls were no longer frenetic; there were even a few ten-minute gaps of silence. There was nothing to do but pace, rack his brains over and over for anywhere Beck might go to hide, discard the idea of driving in a search pattern because what if someone called while he was out of cell service?

Paul was used to killing time; the Army made it a goddamn Olympic event. You were either shagging ass in training, getting shot at, or bored out of your skull waiting for command to get their shit together and the green light to show. Soldiers found ways to murder each passing minute, some of them astonishingly creative.

At least he'd had one reasonably good phone call today—Tax, pinging from the road.

Hey, mothafucka, how you doin? I'm driving out to help Boom with the wedding and Dez says I'll be in your red neck of the woods. Wanna grab a beer?

Either his squad leader was sending Tax to check on him, or good ol' Arthur Tachmann was a little nervous at the thought of driving out to Vegas and making a good impression on Boom's intended without backup. Plus, why stay in a hotel when you could bother a buddy? It was cheaper, and a helluva lot more fun.

Maybe this would even be an amusing incident by the time his squadmate blew into town. If they found Beck alive and well, Paul would take any shit the man could come up with.

Family dropped by Hel's all day, some bringing food, others just checking in, a few with things Hel might actually need. *I don't see what the big deal is*, Cousin Marcia had said, *she probably just left town like her mama did.*

Hel had lit into her but good. Marcia took it chin-up but left right after, and Paul thought another family feud had been planted.

There was no shortage. Christ, it was like he'd never left.

Dreeson was in Herrold's old recliner, either napping or doing a good imitation. Every once in a while his phone went off, but most of it was regular business. Some calls Uncle D didn't even answer, just glanced at the phone's face and shook his head slightly. He only moved for more coffee, to visit the head, or to accompany Helena out onto the porch for smoke breaks.

He knew better than to vape inside Hel's house. Even Herrold had never smoked in here.

Gloria was on her own phone and in her goddamn element. Reunion plans had to be shuffled, possible sightings of Beck weighed for veracity and passed to Uncle D for further investigation or a slight disgusted headshake. She also bustled into the kitchen and began making dinner as the sun fell, saving Hel the trouble.

Aunt Helena was, quite frankly, in what Granite River gossips referred to as "a state." *I told her not to worry*, she kept repeating. *I told her I'd help. That girl, always holding up the mountain. What's she trying to do, get herself hurt? Poor thing.*

Beck would be shaken until her head bobbled, given a good scolding, and cried over, if—no, *when* she eventually showed back up. Hel still didn't know about Dewey Johnson possibly being involved with this mess, and Paul wasn't looking forward to her finding out even if Uncle D was adamant she shouldn't be worried even more.

Connor Sommers had left to look for his daughter. He didn't see the benefit of staying here, and Dreeson promised to call him the second they had hide or hair of Beck's whereabouts—or Joe's. The sheriff had aged twenty years during the conversation in front of Hel's house, and Paul couldn't even feel good about finally seeing the man break.

It was, like a great many nasty prayers, a distinct letdown once answered.

Hel insisted on them all sitting down for dinner—some kind of casserole, which Dreeson unbent enough to compliment but Paul barely tasted. Three-quarters of the town had called Helena today, and the remainder probably would after eating.

All day, the same thoughts kept crowding Paul's head.

Where are you, Beck? What the hell are you thinking? And the image of her still and quiet, leaves in her hair, simply wouldn't go away.

According to Dreeson, Dewey Johnson's boys were all over town. The woods were alive with the sound of ATVs, and Joe Halston wasn't in any of his usual haunts—work, house, gym, Amy Lorton's trailer out on Brickell Loop—either.

After-dinner coffee was burbling into the pot, Gloria and Hel scraping dishes in stony silence, when Dreeson's phone dinged again.

The old man excused himself into the living room. Looked like it was a business call.

Paul went down the hall, past Hel's bedroom, past the spare that used to be Herrold's where Paul's own luggage was sitting, into the annex.

Beck had left the couch neatly done up. There was no trace of her in the bathroom, everything was packed in her one suitcase. Soldiers were used to living light if they had to, but she was taking it to the next level.

It was like she was afraid to even breathe too loudly, afraid of taking up any space at all. Where was the fearless, laughing honey-haired girl who had, for a few brief glorious years, seemed to like him better than anyone else?

I'm sorry, you don't know how sorry I am . . . I'm fine. I'll fix it. Hel won't have to worry.

And Joe, with his nasty little accusations. The bastard wasn't satisfied with winning the most beautiful woman in the world, he had to go and treat her like shit. It boggled the goddamn mind, right next to Dewey Johnson turning into a homegrown kingpin and ol' Law'n'Order Sommers proving just as criminal as the rest of town.

Paul could blame the buckling on his wounded leg, but the good one went too and he dropped heavily onto the couch Beck had slept on. Christ, he'd even pushed her out of the spare bedroom. No wonder she felt like she couldn't stay.

"Paul?" The voice came from the shadowed annex entrance; Klemp tensed, his hand blurring for a weapon he wasn't carrying. "You in here?"

He'd had no idea Dreeson could move so quietly. "Yeah. What's up?" *Tell me you have something. Anything.*

"We've got something," his uncle said.

Run Warm

BECK REMEMBERED the Lamplighter Inn between Franklin and Heb City as kind of rundown, but it had apparently been gentrified a bit since she was last out this way. The new gas station had brought a McDonald's with it, and an old barnlike building that had once sold rockhound equipment and semiprecious stones—gone out of business in one of the recessions—had been converted into a down-home restaurant only too happy to service travelers.

The hotel wasn't pay-by-the-hour anymore, but it was just on the edge of "takes cash, no questions" and the front desk was staffed by people she'd never seen before. She had to hand over her ID, which was panic-inducing but she figured Joe couldn't put out an APB without her dad knowing, and *that* would bring the whole house of cards down on her soon-to-be ex-husband.

It might almost be a relief.

Her nerves were shot, but she managed a meal at the restaurant anyway. It was nice to eat something that wasn't congealed lard, but she missed Hel's kitchen, not to mention her own.

The Lamplighter had a bar, too, but that would be pushing her luck. It was a shame, because a few belts of even substandard bourbon would have been *great*. Instead, Beck took a creaking elevator to the second floor, checked the room number three times—her eyes were grainy and the rest of her felt like she'd been thrown down Attenlee Mountain—and put her key in the lock.

This room was much nicer than the Coach Inn's offerings. Beck fumbled for the light switch, lifting the strap of her Tibetan bag over her head, and barely had time to gasp as a hand clapped over her mouth and she was mashed against the door, the man behind her pressing obscenely close.

She was caught.

"SIT DOWN." PAUL'S hair was wildly mussed, and her own wasn't much better. He also had a bloody lip, since Beck's thrashing had brought the back of her head right across his mouth. He shook his right hand absently—she'd sunk her teeth in hard, vainly attempting to scream until his repeated *shhh, Jesus, Beck, it's me, relax, stop it, it's me, you're safe* penetrated deep red terror.

She'd kicked his shins repeatedly, too, but her black sneakers weren't robust enough to cause any damage. Paul had always been strong, and held her motionless as if it was no big deal.

Like Joe could. Beck wiped at her mouth with the backs of her fingers; she didn't resist when he pushed her gently into the room's single chair, an old 70s-era wooden affair with a faded pink cushion.

She ached all over, her throat was full of sour heat and the ghost of bleu cheese from her recently consumed steak salad. She could probably vomit right now—didn't some vultures do that in self-defense?

Beck was honestly considering it.

Paul stalked to the window, making sure the heavy striped drapes were closed, then turned on one heel and fixed her with a glare. With his hair shaken down over his forehead, his black hip-length jacket unzipped, and his hands tense but not quite fists he looked about sixteen again, in that volatile state just before nothing she said would stop his scrapping with other boys.

Beck hugged herself, huddling in the chair. It squeaked as she shifted, a tiny forlorn sound. There wasn't enough air in the room, she couldn't get any oxygen. Tiny black flowers bloomed at the edges of her vision.

Oh, fuck. No. No, no, no. What is he DOING here?

"Shit." At least he didn't sound angry—yet. "Look, Beck, it's me, all right? You're safe. Calm down. Try to breathe."

I am. I'm trying so hard. It's never enough. Beck realized the faint whistling sound in the room was *her*, gasping like a landed fish. She shuddered, every muscle straining painfully, frozen in place.

Dad knew she didn't like hunting, but he was perplexed that she felt the same way about fishing. *They don't even feel it, Beck.*

But the glassy suffering in a fish's eyes while they flopped, the tiny breathless movements with their mouths, the gills flaring desperately—it made her feel faint each time.

"Oh, *fuck.*" Did Paul sound disgusted? He probably was. A hot dot of moisture trickled down Beck's cheek. She couldn't *breathe*, she was going to pass out.

His hands closed around her upper arms. She slithered from the chair despite her muscles' seizing, and somehow Paul was on the floor too. He got his back against the bed and stretched his legs out, settling her in his lap. Then his arms closed around her, his chin resting atop her head. "Easy," he crooned, the word reverberating under her cheek. "Easy, sweetheart. You're safe now, all right? Safe."

Nothing's safe. And yet, air returned in sips and starts, creeping past the blockage in her throat, seeping into her lungs. Then the uncontrollable trembling started, and while that was embarrassing it was also a sign the worst of the panic attack was over.

Finding a term for the internal earthquakes and vapor-locking had comforted the hell out of her. The internet was magic—it had a diagnosis or at least a name for everything, once you figured out how to ask the right question.

The only thing worse than the embarrassment was the unwilling, undeniable comfort. Her ear was mashed against Paul's chest and the sound of his heart thumped along, not too fast but not slow, either. He'd always run warm; she used to make a game out of slipping chilled hands under his shirt during wintertime.

He'd never complained too much.

And God, but he felt just the same as he always had, a reassuring hot glow somehow blocking out the rest of the world. He'd been solid even as a kid, now the muscle was comforting despite its echoes of casual, destructive male rage. Paul always smelled of soap and healthy heat before, but now she caught a hint of fabric softener, a bit of aftershave, fresh night air—maybe he'd been driving with the window down—and the underlying current of *Paul,* a riptide threatening to swallow her all over again.

She was caught between past and present, and there was no manual or research in forums that could tell her how to handle being in the lap of a man who had rejected her years ago—not now, not at any time, let alone a few days into her nascent criminal career.

The hum of traffic from the highway crept through the room. Somewhere down the hall, another room's door opened, then closed with a bang.

"H-how did you . . .?" She regretted opening her big mouth immediately, because Paul tensed and she was suddenly sure he was going to shove her away and yell at her for. . . .

For what? What the hell was he *doing* here?

"One of Uncle D's greenhouse boys has a second job out this way—Claude, the skinny one, Hal Slissburg's second oldest. Took a phone picture from behind one of the fake trees in the foyer." Paul sounded, of all things, amused. "Kid always wanted to be a ninja. Dreeson's actually kind of proud."

Dreeson? But why would he. . . . "Uh." She had no goddamn idea what to say. "Oh. I see."

"I think we should talk." Paul didn't move. It was like any other time she'd cuddled with him, right down to the definite signs of interest below the belt. She had to pretend she didn't notice. Maybe it was just an uncontrollable reflex on his part, or something. He'd just gotten out of the service, after all; maybe he hadn't had time to find a date yet.

Oh, yeah. Talk. That'll be great. "I'm, um. . . ." Beck took a deep breath, trying to ignore the hot, welling, shameful sense of comfort *and* the knowledge that he had to still be attracted to her on some level.

Any port in a storm, wasn't that the saying? Beck was everything Joe called her, and worse, because she wondered for a few seconds if she could use that to somehow get out of this impossible fucking situation.

How, in God's name, had she ended up here?

"I'm not sure that's a g-good idea," she continued, hating the quaver in her own voice. "I'm kind of in some t-trouble, Paul, and I don't want to drag anyone else in after me."

"You're in trouble, huh?" Gentle sarcasm turned into a laugh near the end of the question. "Gee, I would never have guessed."

Oh, for God's sake. Beck tensed, shifting. She meant to express her willingness to move away so he wouldn't be embarrassed, but Paul didn't appear to notice the movement. "Can you let go?"

"I could." Thoughtful, as if he was considering the notion. He rubbed his chin against the top of her head, an absent caress, and a bit of stubble rasped against her rumpled hair. "Unfortunately I don't want to, because Christ only knows what you'll take it into your head to do next. So I think I'll just hold on for a bit until we get a few things straight."

Was he going to hurt her? He could; she knew very well how a hug could hold a sharp bright flare of pain, or turn into grinding agony when a man clamped down. Beck froze.

"Are you listening to me, Beck?" Soft and gentle.

It was hard to be alert for hidden menace in the tone, between his heartbeat thundering in one ear and that treacherous, unwelcome feeling of safety. "I am," she whispered. She knew the penalty for inattention.

"Okay." Now he moved, but not to dislodge her. Instead, Paul settled himself a little more comfortably, as if he intended to stay for a while. "You've got something Dewey Johnson wants back, and your ex—who tried to kill you a few days ago—is looking for you. Sound about right?"

A Bad Patch

OF ALL THE THINGS he thought a trip home for a family reunion would hold, sitting on a hotel-room floor with Beck Sommers shivering in his lap hadn't even been in the ballpark.

She'd fought hard, too. Her daddy had taught her a bit of self-defense, and Paul's lip was already swelling. She'd gotten a good few kicks in, and bitten his hand so savagely a thin scrim of blood was tacky-wet in his palm. Paying cash, moving from motel to motel—smart girl, and if not for Claude picking up an extra maintenance shift on the reunion's inaugural day because he was saving to marry Joann Briggs, Beck would absolutely have pulled off another night in the open.

But he had his hands on her now, and the relief was making him a little giddy. Not to mention distracted, because the warm living weight of her, the feel of Beck in his arms again, was not at all as he'd imagined.

It was far, far better.

"I don't even know why I did it," Beck whispered, and the way each word staggered under a full rucksack of heavy terror did something strange to the inside of his skull. Gas fumes, a colorless shimmer, just looking for a spark. "He n-never let me in that room. It was always locked."

"Did you go to get your car?" Interrogating shaking, terrorized victims was his least favorite duty. Boom was better at that deal, but he hated it just as much.

It was a lot easier when they were hostile.

"And my r-rings." Beck nestled against him as if she didn't mind being there, and it was enough to short-circuit any bit of critical thinking he could ever lay claim to.

But he had to keep her talking, and figure out just what the hell she was thinking. At least the image of her sprawled on the forest floor, or motionless under several feet of cold dark water, was gone. Every time she inhaled, it was proof she was alive, and fine, and right where she belonged.

It was also a reminder that he had to keep it that way. Paul

Klemperer found, to his relief, that he was done fucking around. Joe Halston was about to enter the "find out" part of the program, but that could wait.

Everything could, now that Beck was safe.

"I was going to pawn them once I got away. The engagement, not my mom's. . . ." Her voice strengthened a little. "Then I found the bag, and I took it. I thought if I had it I could make Joe sign the. . . ." A shudder passed through her, crown to soles, and Paul's arms tightened.

He didn't want to crush her, but god*damn*. "Okay. We'll solve that problem later. Where's the bag now? In your car?"

She stirred, but didn't speak for a long moment. The room wasn't anywhere near soundproof; he could hear the freeway outside, a seashore hiss. Maybe he could talk her into going to the beach—she'd loved that as a kid, and perhaps salt water and a bit of sun could make her smile again.

Finally, Beck sighed, wearily. "Is that what you want?"

What the fuck? "What I want," he said, steadily enough, "is to get you out of this situation in one piece, and take you back to Helena so she can stop worrying. And hell, to your father too, because I'm not used to seeing Sheriff-fucking-Sommers looking scared."

That got a reaction. "My dad?" Beck stiffened, but she didn't struggle. "He . . . he knows?"

He could get all sorts of revenge on Beck's father right now, couldn't he. All it would take was telling her the bare truth. Hell, he could even make a few jokes about it, and good ones, too.

Paul strangled the urge, hating himself for even thinking it—it was the sort of thing you considered in-country, not out in the civilian world. "I don't think Joe being dirty surprises him much." There, that was also true. It might even qualify as kind. "Half of town probably thinks Joe's stashed your body someplace, by this point."

"Half the *town*?" Beck's tone hit a pitch close to *perturbed* and she wriggled, attempting to break away.

Before he left, that might have been an invitation to a different sort of game. Now, though, Paul simply loosened his arms a bit.

But only a little. "Did you honestly think we wouldn't notice you disappearing in broad daylight from the Grange? Or that Hel would read your note and go *oh, okay, guess she's fine*? Did you really think, for even a minute, that *I* wouldn't come looking for you?" For the second time that very, *very* long day, Paul realized, he was in danger of absolutely losing his shit.

And that would scare her even more.

"I thought. . . ." Beck moved restlessly again. "Um, maybe this isn't the place for this conversation?"

Oh, no you don't. She could fob off everyone else in town—or the entire fucking world—with polite small talk, but not him. Not now. "We don't have things straight yet."

"What do you *want?*"

Oh, was she asking for his Christmas list? "I want to know why you didn't call me the first time Joe hit you." *Don't do this to her, Paul.* But it was no use, he couldn't stop. "You could've gotten the number from Helena. You know I would have come home and—"

"Call you? Why on earth would I call you?" There was a flash of the old Beck, the rare lightning spark of her anger.

It was a long country mile away from a laugh, but at least it wasn't numb apathy or brittle cheerfulness. Progress was being made—after a fashion.

"Is it because you knew I'd kill him? Is that it?" All the questions he never thought he'd be able to ask wanted out toot-fuckin'-sweet, as his old drill instructor used to yell while rousting recruits from their beds. "Were you just scared of me, because you think I'm like him?"

It made a mad type of sense, Paul had to admit. Maybe she thought the simmering rage, his constant childhood companion and invisible squadmate, would somehow turn on her. If he hadn't gone into the Army, if he'd stayed in this goddamn hick-ass slice of the world, would she be right?

"Paul. . . ."

"Because I'm not." It felt good to say it out loud, and even better to know it was true. "I found out I wasn't a long time ago."

"Oh, *God.*" Beck gave a despairing moan, and made another restless wriggling movement. "Why the fuck would I call the guy who dumped me right out of high school to report my abusive husband, Paul? What goddamn sense would that make? Let *go.*"

He didn't want to, but she slipped free, scrambling aside in the cramped space between the bed and the postage-stamp table with its blocky, solid chair.

Beck pulled up her knees, hugging them tightly, her shoulder socked hard against the bed as if she couldn't stay upright without its help. And finally, she stared at him through a tangle of her beautiful honey-lit hair, a wild creature trapped and exhausted but still defiant, just gathering what strength it could before it battered itself to death on the cage bars.

Dumped you? There had to be an explanation, and the simplest was no doubt the correct one, for once. "You probably didn't get my letters." But he couldn't really blame Connor Sommers.

Paul had, after all, given up too easily. He should have come back at least once, on leave or AWOL, and heard the truth right from her lips. He should have forced her to say it out loud, taken the hit like a man. Instead, he'd punked, using the easy way out.

The coward's way.

"You sent. . . ." She sagged against the bed even further. "Dad. Of course."

"I called, he told me you didn't want to talk. Then I think he blocked the number, it just gave a busy signal each time I dialed." The base only had four pay phones, but a father in law enforcement could get a whole area code blocked with a single chummy call to the local phone company if he had a mind to. That should've been Paul's first thought, but he'd been too busy being butthurt. "Then I wrote a few times. No answer. It made sense, I figured it was your way of letting me down easy." *I was a stupid kid, Beck. I fucked up. I'm sorry.*

"Oh." Just the single syllable, soft and drawn out like she'd just solved a particularly complex math problem.

Paul immediately felt like a jackass. Why was he bitching about ancient history? He was here now and he wasn't letting go of her easily this time, but that part could wait. Beck looked on the edge of a complete nervous breakdown, and he still didn't have the answers he needed to keep her safe.

"Look." He didn't move, hoping she'd calmed down enough to see reason. "We can argue about that later, if you want. Right now, I need to know exactly what you're holding so I know how bad Dewey wants it back, and where it is so I can figure out which way to get you out of this."

"I have a plan." Beck sniffed, hard, and rubbed at her nose with the back of one hand. "I'm not stupid."

"No." Christ, if she started crying he might really come unglued, and that would scare her even more. "You're the stubbornest person I've ever met, but you're not stupid."

"Maybe I am, though." She said it almost mournfully, carefully watching his expression. "After all, I married Joe." Her eyes glittered; she pulled in on herself a little more, as if she expected an explosion.

"Yeah, well, that makes him a lucky bastard." It was out before Paul could stop himself. "It doesn't say anything about *your* intelligence."

For once his goddamn mouth won him one, because Beck smiled. A tiny, fleeting quirk of her pretty lips, but it was there and verifiable, as Grey would say.

Beck weighed him again, for a long breathless moment. "It's a bag," she said. "A big canvas one like soldiers carry. Money, drugs, you know." Another short pause. "I hid it. I don't have it with me."

Hallelujah. Finally, he was getting somewhere. But a ditty full of greenbacks, while concerning enough, wasn't worth the kind of commotion Joe was risking—or Dewey was making. "What *exactly* is in the bag, Beck? I need to know."

She hugged her knees even tighter. Those big, distrustful eyes of hers were going to kill him. "It's heavy. There's a lot of cash. The meth's probably worth more though, it's all bagged up and ready for sale." She took a deep breath; some of the shaking had gone down.

So far, so good—the more relaxed she was, the better he'd keep his own silly self on the rails. "And?" he prompted.

"And a plastic case about this big." She freed one hand, sketching a rectangle in the air, a tentative approximation. "It's full of jump drives."

Why the hell . . . oh. "Oh," Paul said. The bottom dropped out of his stomach, but at the same time, there was a certain relief in finding the bottom of the hole. *Now* everything made sense—Dewey was a thoroughly modern CEO, of course he'd need safe information storage. "Oh, shit."

"I hid those too." Her chin lifted slightly, again. Another welcome echo of the old Beck.

"The staties raided one of Dewey's hubs this morning." Slow and easy—he hated giving her bad news, that hadn't changed. "He was tipped off, probably by Joe. Which means you're holding his escape plan, or his backups."

"I *what?*" Beck stared at him, thunderstruck. Then she dropped her forehead to her knees, her shoulders shook, and all Paul could do was stare.

Finally, his Beck was *laughing.* But it wasn't with merriment, or with the deep shared enjoyment of a successful prank pulled off. Instead, deep, wracking chuckles burst out of her, each with a sawtooth edge he recognized.

Sometimes, after a truly bad patch, soldiers laughed like that. Usually their buddies dragged them away to stand under a hot shower, then stuffed them with as much chow as they could handle, finishing off with as much booze as could be found.

The chow was optional, really, and the entire treatment plan was only possible on-base. If you were in-country and a buddy started laughing like that . . . well, you never wanted to spook a soldier who had decided everything was so fucked he might as well giggle.

He knew he should move her out of this damn hotel—if you could find your target, the opposition could as well, another of Sparky Lee's homilies—but Claude was one of Dreeson's boys, he could probably keep his mouth shut for at least a few hours, and this wasn't a bad choice for a hidey-hole.

Beck was painfully thin. It wasn't any work to gather her up and get her onto the bed. When the laughter stopped she just curled up in a tight ball around that bright embroidered bag and closed her eyes, checking out for the duration, and that was probably a hopeful sign.

If ever a woman needed some rest, this one did.

Lying down beside her was tempting, but he took a guard post in the hallway near the door instead. His father's old hunting knife—he was almost regretting not bringing a full load of gear—was oddly comforting under a pillow taken from the bed, and before he did a final sweep of the room he watched her for a long moment, drinking in the fact that he'd found her, she was alive, and she was safe now.

Why the fuck would I call the guy who dumped me right out of high school?

It was his own damn fault, and worse, she'd suffered for his fuckup. That was inexcusable, but maybe he could make it up to her. Maybe she'd at least let him try.

He wasn't sure if she was awake or not. Paul took care of the lights, leaving the one in the bathroom on since she used to sleep with a nightlight.

Scared of the dark, his Beck. Well, she should be. He knew what lived out there; what else did his squad hunt?

Paul settled on his patch of nylon motel carpet, glad he wasn't sleeping outside, and dropped into a light doze.

Ancient History

REBECCA SOMMERS had sailed right off the edge of the world, out to where no normal rules of behavior applied. There was no other explanation, really, and to make it worse, she'd slept in her bra. Which was the final unbearable insult, and getting the damn thing off under her shirt as she surfaced from heavy sleep, not to mention dragging it out an armhole and hurling it across the room, was incredibly therapeutic.

She didn't expect Paul to pop up like a jack-in-the-box near the door, and Beck let out a short, girlish scream before clapping her hand over her mouth.

Great. Wonderful. Fantastic. I've turned into a horror movie actress. "Jesus!" she blurted, through her sweating fingers.

"Nope." Paul shook his head, rising fluidly from an easy crouch. He turned the motion into a stretch, with enviable grace. Had he slept in his boots? "Just the mailman, Beck."

The old joke threatened to touch off a spate of high-pitched giggles; she could just feel them bubbling behind her breastbone. Maybe Joe was right and she *was* crazy. God knew she felt halfway there.

Still, she'd slept so hard she felt a little woozy, not to mention far more rested than usual. She still hurt all over from the accident, but it was hardly worse than the aftermath of one of Joe's fits.

She could ignore it.

Paul bent to pick up a pillow—had he slept on the *floor?* Good Lord. He tossed it onto the bed and followed at a much more sedate pace. In fact, he folded down to perch on the foot like he expected her to shoo him away, yawning and rubbing his neck.

She didn't miss the hunting knife vanishing under his jacket, either. A jolt of fear smacked against common sense; she'd passed out and slept all night with him in the room. Besides, it was *Paul*. He wasn't going to stab her.

If he did, would it hurt more or less than a broken heart? She didn't want to find out.

He studied her for a long moment in the dimness. Thin grey morning tried to get past the drapes, and the bathroom light was on. "Feel a little better?"

How on earth could she answer that? "I suppose." Now she regretted throwing her bra. Her mouth tasted like morning and she felt greasy. Still, the clarity a solid night of rest could bring was welcome, and she could use every bit of it. "What are you really doing here, Paul?"

"Good morning to you too." He rolled his shoulders, grimacing slightly. "First, we need breakfast, then I'm gonna stash you someplace safe while I tie this entire mess off. After that, I'll pick you up and take you back to Hel so she can see you're all right."

Oh, Christ. The thought of facing Helena right now was almost as terrifying as the prospect of seeing Joe. Beck shivered. "Is . . . is she really mad?"

"More worried." Wildly rumpled, Paul should've looked like a kid again. Instead, he was all adult, and thoughtful too, scratching at a stubbled cheek with blunt callused fingertips. "She'll be better now, and the reunion will keep her busy."

"God." She was ruining an entire family reunion, and it wasn't even her own. "I'm so sorry."

"Are you kidding? Everyone in town will come by, and they'll bring food." Now he grinned, but his eyes were serious and level. "It'll be the biggest Granite River bash in years."

"I figured I had a few days before anyone really noticed I was gone. Especially my dad." Beck pulled up her knees—she hadn't even crawled under the covers—and hugged them, wriggling her sock toes. At least her purse was safe, right next to her on the bed.

It was all she had left.

Paul stared at her. "You figured you had. . . ." He gave a tiny little headshake, a curl over his forehead flopping, like she was too stupid to be believed.

"Well, my criminal career got off to a great start, even if it was super short." Beck tried not to sound defensive, and probably failed miserably.

"Criminal career?" Now he looked puzzled, as if she was speaking a foreign language. "How do you figure?"

"I successfully did some breaking and entering, since it's technically Joe's house. Then there's the attempted blackmail. I've spent some of the money and the other stuff is probably evidence, so that's tampering." It wasn't much of a list, but each was a quality item, as Hel would say. "I was hoping Joe would sign the divorce papers, I'd call him from a burner and tell him where the bag is, then I'd leave town. I thought if it got really bad I could probably trade the jump drives to the staties for some kind of immunity."

"A good plan, all things considered." Paul nodded, rubbed briskly at his face, and exhaled sharply. It was his old *let's solve a problem* sound when they had to pull off a difficult prank without being caught, like the time they'd TP'd the county fire station. "What happened to law school? You were pretty determined when we graduated."

"I was going to college, but Dad had a medical scare. His liver. So I stayed home for a year to take care of him, and then . . . well, I married Joe." She decided that was a reasonable enough Cliff's Notes explanation. He didn't need to know about the rest of it; she was causing enough trouble as it was. "Dad said I didn't want to talk to you?"

That was news. They'd had one painful conversation about Paul leaving, Dad insisting it was a good thing, Beck in tears with a bigger secret trying to wriggle out of her mouth.

But Paul said he'd called more than once and even sent letters—letters, plural. That bothered her more than a little, even if her father was only trying to protect her.

He never liked to see his baby girl cry.

"Yeah. I didn't push, figuring you were mad because I went when you asked me not to." Paul shrugged, his gaze dropping like there was something incredibly interesting on the bed near her feet. "And then I thought, well, she's probably relieved, and letting me down easy. You know, being kind. Like you do."

Oh, God. "I thought you'd dumped me," Beck said, blankly. "Paul. . . ."

"We'll get that settled later. For right now. . ." He leaned forward a little, and extended his left hand. "Fair warning, Beck. I'm not a dumb kid anymore. I mean, I may still be an idiot, but I'm all grown up and I learned a thing or two in the service. All right?"

In other words, he wouldn't rehash the whole long-ago boondoggle if she wouldn't. Which was a relief—if she had to tell him the rest of it, the trip to Eugene and all the blood, what were her chances of getting any help at all? Thinking that way was awful; it made her the manipulative, selfish bitch Joe always accused her of being.

Right at the moment, though, Beck didn't have any other options. "We can both be adults, then." She had to take his hand, and the touch sent a shock all the way up her arm.

Like it always had.

"We always were a good team. Partners in crime. Remember our senior prank?"

The situation wasn't funny, but she had to smile. "The mariachi band." Hiring them to follow around the principal for a couple hours in the middle of the day had been a difficult, delicate bit of mischief; they'd saved and planned for months, and gotten away with the whole deal. "Principal Skinner retired a couple years ago."

"Not a moment too soon, I'm sure." Paul didn't let go. He squeezed her hand again, gently. "You want to take a shower? Then we'll get out of here."

Well, she had one clean pair of panties and her toothbrush, so it was kind of like camping. At least there was running water. "Okay." She had to tug twice to get her hand back. "Paul?"

"Yeah?"

"Thank you. You don't have to do this, you know."

Then she could have kicked herself, because he turned even more somber, his mouth tightening and his eyes opaque. "Yeah, I do." He checked his watch, the face inside his wrist—he'd slept in his clothes too, and was probably feeling as gritty and greasy as she did. "Get cleaned up, baby. We've gotta get out of here."

Her legs were a little rubbery, but she could manage. It wasn't until she closed the bathroom door she realized he'd called her *baby*, just like he used to, and tears stung her eyes. She was even crying before coffee, for God's sake.

The online forums said it took an average of seven tries to leave your abuser. For her second attempt, Beck figured she was doing pretty well.

But oh, the cost was high.

Scout's Honor

IT WAS LIKE BEING in high school again, driving the Jetta instead of his Camaro, but with Beck in the passenger seat either way. Except she wasn't scanning the radio to find them some good tunes, singing along with an oldie or a new pop song, telling him about something interesting and weird from her constant reading, bubbling with plans for an art project or a prank, sharing school gossip, or even humming while she watched the scenery change out the window.

Instead, she huddled silently on her side of the small car—he had to put the driver's seat back all the way—while viewing every intersection with trepidation, watching the side mirror like there was someone behind them and clutching a latte from the drive-thru Starbuck's on the edge of Franklin. Even the plain scone she consented to for breakfast didn't break her mournful quiet.

It was like traveling with a ghost, or a cuffed-and-stuffed asset.

Direct questions got responses, that was all. She'd done pretty good for a woman on the run, popping the SIM out of her mobile and finding pay phones, staying one step ahead. Some guy had seen her in a Walmart parking lot, but she couldn't be sure—maybe one of Dewey's, who knew?

She had no luggage, just her car, a couple burners, her purse, and the clothes she was wearing. Traveling light even for a soldier, although you could be dropped into anywhere with a knife—or even just a stick—and survive.

He should know.

Paul took a long looping route through the fine, bright spring morning, testing the Jetta's responses. It held up stunningly; Beck, well trained by her father, had taken her car in for regular maintenance. The trees had decided all at once winter was finally over, and new green edged each branch while spring runoff cascaded through every creek, river, and culvert. The playground equipment at the Grange would dry off quickly, and the kids were probably having a ball.

He'd made a few phone calls while Beck was in the shower; it wasn't quite time for him to drop completely off the map yet. Tax was inbound. Hel and Gloria were at the reunion for the Sunday sack race and bingo, safe among the crowd; they'd be relieved to hear from Dreeson that Beck was now safely under a wing and Hel would impress upon Gloria the necessity of keeping that information close for a while—it would help with bragging rights later, when Gloria's retelling of this incident would be in high demand.

Uncle D's boys, not to mention the rest of the clan, would be on guard. Dewey probably knew better than to mess with the Siddons, let alone the Klemperers, but meth-heads weren't known for good risk assessment.

Dreeson said Dewey didn't sample his own merchandise. That was either a sign he could be reasonable, or that he was so bugfuck crazy he didn't need the chemicals to lend a helping hand. Paul couldn't guess, he'd barely ever seen the kid in school.

As they got closer to Granite River, Beck's tension increased. She'd taken down barely enough of the latte to stave off caffeine withdrawal. Her hair was drying, a wild glory of ripples and highlights, and the scratch on her cheek was healing nicely.

The silence stretched, and stretched. Finally, when he got off the freeway and onto the long gentle loop of River Road, he broke. "Can I ask you something?"

Beck stirred. "Sure." She took another small sip of latte; it was a victory.

A tiny, tactical one, but sometimes that was all you needed. "How bad was it with Joe?" He kept an eye on the rearview. The Jetta would almost certainly be seen by an unfriendly, but his route was designed to confuse and throw off Dewey's hounds before arriving clean at the rendezvous point south of town, halfway to Sinaida.

He'd feel a lot better about this once Tax arrived.

"Bad enough," Beck finally said, almost inaudible under the engine noise. "My own fault, really. I married him for the wrong reasons."

Because of me? How could he ask? It was a complete asshole move to even *think* it. She was a brutalized civilian trapped in a high-pressure situation, the very last thing she needed was him dragging up old hurts. And only a bigger douchebag than Joe Halston would be thinking of using the current situation as leverage.

But God how he burned to know, especially since she'd apparently thought Paul's silence was intentional. He could have solved everything, changed the entire course of his goddamn life, by simply opening his mouth at the right time.

Which was darkly, hilariously ironic. God had a worse sense of humor than Paul's own, and that was saying something.

"I mean, it started out fine," she continued. "I always knew he liked me. It was good to feel . . . wanted. But then it got worse, little by little."

That's how it generally goes. He kept his trap shut, because she finally seemed disposed to talk. But what the hell did she mean, it was good to feel wanted?

Hadn't his own wanting been enough? God knew it seemed endless enough, to him.

"Maybe Amy will help him, I don't know." She took another bit of latte down, staring out her window. "All I wanted was for him to sign the papers and leave me alone."

"Amy?" It was the second time an *Amy* had been mentioned in the past couple days, and it nagged at him.

Fortunately, Beck didn't let him linger in suspense. "Lorton. She and Joe are a thing."

What. The fuck. How a man could want anything else when he had Beck's attention? "Uh, didn't he put one of her brothers upstate? And broke the other one's leg?" Paul hit the brakes for the upcoming curve; the road was a little more overgrown, but he still knew its tricks.

"How did—oh, Hel." A soft, pale laugh, not like her usual golden giggle. "I honestly didn't know you were flying in, by the way. I thought she just wanted some stuff from Ikea."

"Still have to put that together for her. We'll do that after the reunion." Maybe he could invent enough things to do for his aunt to keep Beck around after all this, keep her interested. He slowed further, River Road beginning its back-and-forth descent into the valley.

"Can I ask where we're going?"

"Oh." It hadn't occurred to him that she wouldn't just trust he had a good destination in mind. "Down near Sinaida. We have a rendez-vous."

"Sounds enticing." Another little sparkle of the old Beck, fading under fresh anxiety. "Who are we meeting?" Excessively casual—he might not have heard the faint whiff of suspicion if he hadn't grown up with her.

God, just being around Beck was a gulp of air to a drowning man, or landing at base after a hard patrol. Like walking into a safehouse and knowing beyond doubt your trail was clear, like having your favorite home-cooked dish after starving for weeks. Every sharp edge inside Paul settled like a dog's hackles, lying nice and flat, and he could breathe again.

She'd been left in enemy territory, unsure of rescue. It was a wonder she wasn't *more* distrustful, but Beck Sommers had run out of options in a big way.

He was a terrible human being, and not just because you didn't get into heaven by murdering for your country, though everyone said that was the deal. No, he was a complete dick because he knew her lack of any other alternative was leverage too. And the temptation to use it was overwhelming.

"Backup." To a buddy, that would be the end of it, but Paul belatedly realized she needed more context. "Uh, Tax is driving up from Cali. He's on his way to Vegas to help with planning Boom's wedding—I think he gets bored off-duty, and Boom's a little nervous. But Tax'll stop here and help tie this off."

"It sounds so easy when you say it that way."

I've trained for worse. Hell, we've done worse. She probably wouldn't find that comforting, though. "A lot will depend on how hard Dewey wants to make it. If he'll take his shi—his stuff back and leave you alone, I won't push it. We'll deal with Joe afterward."

"You'd think he'd be glad to get rid of me," she said softly, still looking out the window. The hills were greening up, so many different shades of rain-washed verdant growth covering craggy granite. Runoff foamed down hillsides, cutting through sheer rock; the creeks would all be roaring wherever there was a bit of drainage. It was a lovely time of year, especially with the sun herself sitting right in the passenger seat. "Considering how he. . . ."

He wanted to press, wanted her to pour out the details so he could reassure her. Well, that wasn't quite it.

Paul wanted to know what Joe had done to her, so he could visit every single inch of it back on his old semi-friend. With interest.

But saying that probably wasn't a good idea. He couldn't figure out what would be, either.

"Paul?" Now Beck sounded even more anxious. "I'm glad you're here. Not just because of all this."

"Likewise." There was something in his throat, and his hands ached. He was squeezing the steering wheel like it was a neck needing a good wringing. "I've missed you."

"Really?" She took another hit off her latte, a good gulp this time instead of a tentative sip. The breathless static of her unease abated a little, then a little more as he pressed the accelerator and the Jetta took one of the prettier hills on River Road.

"Scout's honor, babe." The foliage had changed, some of the signs were updated, and a lot about the old hometown was altered beyond recognition. But the road was a familiar skeleton; he knew just where to brake, where you could push it a little, how each curve set up for the one beyond.

It was a nice change.

SINAIDA WAS BIGGER than Granite River, half an hour south and boasting a Holiday Inn on its northern end as well as a pho restaurant Beck looked a little longingly at as they passed.

He disliked the idea of leaving her alone even for an instant, but he had to check them in. "You got sunglasses? Great. And a hat? You're a natural, Becks. Now, stay here. *Right* here. Do not leave the car."

"You don't have to repeat yourself. I'm not a dog." The old Beck was peeking out a little more frequently now. Each time, he felt almost like cheering.

"Sorry. It's the Army, I guess." And the fact that if she vanished again, he wasn't quite sure *what* he'd do.

Everything went like clockwork, though, and a short while later he closed the door of a much nicer double room than the Lamplighter's, eyeing the secondary locks. None would present any trouble to a professional entry team, but those caused a lot of noise. Amateurs caused even more.

Dewey wouldn't want to be loud; his kind liked soft, quieter targets. Joe might not care about an exit plan if he could get to his ex-wife, which would make him both loud and desperate, but that little thought Paul kept strictly to himself.

Beck headed for the bathroom like a woman with a mission, and Paul dug his phone out.

Less than ten minutes later, as Beck settled on the bed nearest the glass door to the postage-stamp balcony—a polite fiction that let the company charge more for a few square feet to shit, shower, and sleep in—a familiar series of knocks tapped at the door.

Shave and a haircut, but without the two bits. Tax was, like Paul himself, a goddamn comedian.

Beck was off the bed like a shot, grabbing her purse and swallowing a gasp. Their gazes met, and the naked fear in hers told him more than words ever could about Joe Halston's marital methods, so to speak.

I should just fucking kill him. The concerning part was just how seriously—and frequently—Paul was contemplating an actionable plan in that direction.

"Relax, okay? It's friendly." He didn't check the peephole; that was a good way to get yourself shot in the eye. Paul did make a point of keeping the chain on and peering through the door, like whoever was outside couldn't just pop it with a good hard kick. "Very funny, Tax."

"I couldn't resist." As usual, the corners of Arthur Tachmann's dark eyes held a few sketched-in laugh lines. With thick, jet-black hair growing out just like Paul's but ruler straight, he was saved from baby-face—he barely stubbled up at all—by a regal nose and high cheek-bones, and he wore the same off-duty uniform Paul did. T-shirt, jeans, hip-length jacket with good pocket space and just enough flow to hide a few surprises in, a service watch, and boots. The only difference was his footwear, jungle green instead of desert taupe.

Medics were all crazy—scrambling out under fire to haul wounded to safety, or attempting to patch up a bleeding human body while flying lead filled the air, wasn't a game for sane individuals. But Tax was a step past, which was frankly necessary to keep up with the rest of the Ghost Squad.

He gave the room a once-over while Paul checked the hall and closed up. Good God, it was great to have backup.

"Beck, this is Arthur Tachmann. Tax, this is Beck Sommers, and she's a lady." In other words, *keep your mouth clean and your paws off, asshole.*

Some things had to be said, even if unnecessary.

"Always stating the obvious, Klemp." Tax's eyeroll was a mere flicker, generally deployed behind a barking officer's back. He straightened, and went in for a handshake while doing his best to ooze reassurance. "How do you do, Ms. Sommers? It's a pleasure to finally meet you in person. We've all heard a lot about you."

Oh, shit. "Uh, actually—" Paul began.

"Really?" Beck gave Tax her hand like a queen accepting homage. "And likewise. Paul's always talking about his buddies. Did you really get food poisoning from a scorpion in Thailand?"

Double shit. If Tax was still upset about that particular op, the story wasn't quite as funny. "Uh—"

"I've eaten a lot worse, especially around him. The man can't cook worth a damn." Tax set right to work charming and smoothing the waters. He was good at it, the bastard. "Speaking of which, oh Klemp my brother, I bring greetings from my mama, and a couple jars for you."

"Wait a second." Paul could barely believe his luck. "Your mother sent kimchi?" Mrs. Tachmann came from Korea, was half her son's size, and put up with absolutely zero shit from anyone. She also made amazing fermented things, and wasn't shy about sharing.

"And those broccoli-stem pickles you like so much." Tax's grin was easy and neutral, but he stood right where he could watch Paul's six, and vice versa. "But everything will stay in my luggage until I head out. I'm not bunking with you after kimchi. My sinuses can't take it."

My friend, I am going to strangle you. "Oh, like I can stand the way you snore." Paul aimed the next bit at Beck. "He leaves the toilet seat up, too. Be warned."

"Oh, it's on now." The medic all but rubbed his hands together with glee. "I'm going to tell her everything embarrassing about you, Klemp."

"Go ahead," Beck said. Her eyes were sparkling, and for a few moments, at least, she didn't look afraid. "I grew up with him; I might know a few things you don't."

"Mutiny and insurrection, that's what this is." Paul folded his arms, leaning against the wall separating bedroom space from bathroom and hall. "On second thought, Tax, you can just keep driving."

"Look, man, I told Boom I was stopping to visit you and he accused me of being scared of weddings." Tax shrugged, spreading his hands. A familiar gun butt nestled under his left armpit. He was carrying with a permit, of course, and no doubt had at least four knives on him plus even more gear in his car.

Paul was never going to hear the end of flying home without a full kit and calling for backup. "He's got a point. You're terrified of white dresses."

"Look, it was dark, and better shooting than sorry, all right? Jeez." Tax sobered. "So. . . ." He glanced at Beck, a quick weighing, and of course he saw a woman strung to the breaking point. Any medic worth his salt would. "I'm starving. Get me some room service if you're going to interrupt my very nice vacation, willya?"

It was, Paul thought again, goddamn good to have buddies like his.

Life Lesson

IT WAS A SIDE of Paul she'd never seen before; Beck was alternately comforted and chilled.

On the one hand, it was nice to feel like the two guys in the room knew what they were doing. On the other, this version of Paul Klemperer was a stranger. He was utterly serious, not to mention completely in control, occasionally leaning forward a little over the table now laden with room-service dishes to make a point or exchange more slang with the new arrival.

Beck picked at her french dip and side salad, but both of them went to town on the menu. Apparently the Army paid well enough for that. Paul was on medical leave for his wounded leg; she wondered if the other guy was really on vacation, like he said.

Tax seemed a little too . . . intense, for anything as mundane as a vacay. Paul's coworker—if that was the right word—smiled a lot, but his dark eyes stayed still and cool, assessing. He listened quietly to Paul's rundown of the situation, and didn't even blink at the term *abusive ex*.

"The brake lines," he said, meditatively, reaching for his root beer. "You think it was a hero move, or a hit?"

"Beck?" Paul must have seen her confusion, because he continued. "I hate to ask, but you lived with the man. Do you think Joe meant to kill you, or do you think he wanted to be the hero and rescue you after an accident?"

"I. . . ." Her stomach knotted up; she twisted a wine-red linen napkin, her fingers aching. Hearing her own worst thoughts articulated by someone else was both validating and terrifying. "He was following me. That day." The reflexive urge to smile—to smooth it over, deflect anything other than cursory interest—threatened to close her throat to a pinhole.

Paul sat on the bed; there were only two chairs so they'd moved the table. Just picked it up and carried it over while talking about something else, without any verbal direction to make the task go more smoothly.

It took a *lot* of working with someone to get so comfortable. She'd once been like that with Paul.

Not anymore, though. And never again, she suspected.

"He follow you a lot?" Tax asked, and Paul shook his head slightly. It was just a flicker of motion, but the other man subsided.

Of course Paul would know she'd been about to say more. He had always been a good listener, despite the constant jokes and teasing.

"All the time." The woman using Beck's voice sounded very small. "But after the accident I climbed out of the car, and at the top. . . . It's stupid. But I heard someone coming and I sort of crouched on the ledge there, so he couldn't see me. He turned around, down at the foot of the hill, and came back. I peeked; it was him. It was his cruiser." *Shut up, Beck. Just answer the question.*

Except she'd forgotten what the question was by that point. Jesus.

"He played it like the tow truck was there first," Paul said. "I believed him. For a few minutes."

"Then?" Tax dragged two french fries through ketchup and tossed them down the hatch. His table manners were exactly the same as Paul's—always good because he'd clearly been raised right, but with a military upgrade to both speed and efficiency.

Paul's expression hardened, the stranger wearing his face suddenly unreadable, a blank granite cliff. "Then my old pal Lefty dropped a quiet word about the brakes being tampered with, and the entire situation underwent a drastic reassessment."

Had Paul really been suspecting Joe, even though she hadn't said anything? Beck's hands decided to twist the napkin the other way, just for a change. A little feeling returned to her fingers.

Tax nodded. His dark eyes narrowed, and he regarded his plate like he wished there was more left on it. "Spoken like a true sergeant."

"First Lieutenant now, buddy. Try some respect."

"I was just giving you a chance to bust that out and impress the lady." Tax settled back in his chair, and a cat could not have lounged more elegantly. "So, Ms. Sommers. You want to hang this Joe guy legally, or personally?"

I just want him to go away. Beck couldn't make the words come out. The table blurred a little; her eyes stung. *Oh, for God's sake, don't cry now.*

Maybe it was only on Paul's say-so, but this stranger believed her about Joe. The shock of validation was like reading a well-articulated forum post and recognizing her own feelings, but far more powerful.

"Either way he's going to leave you alone, Beck." Paul said it like a promise.

It didn't seem possible. "That would be nice." But Joe was likable, and Joe was a deputy, Joe was a good ol' boy and that was what counted when consequences were handed out, especially in Granite River.

He wasn't going to leave her alone until she was completely out of reach. Even half the globe between them might not be enough.

"I don't know what to do." She had been plodding steadily for so long, the divorce a tantalizing carrot dangled in front of her. Now she could see the stick it was tied to, and it was horrifying to have literally zero idea what to do next.

"You've got combat fatigue and no training." Tax shrugged, as casually as he would while saying *it's raining*. His T-shirt strained at his shoulders; he was far leaner than Paul, but she suspected he was just as strong. "So, yeah."

"Exactly." Paul's knee bumped hers under the table. It might have been an accident, but Beck was still grateful for the small contact. "He's a medic, he'd know."

"Shoot you in the as—uh, the rump, and stitch you up after." Another very charming smile, and their guest added a slurp of root beer for emphasis. "All right, Klemp. What's the play?"

"You're gonna dive with our football." Paul reached for his own drink. "I'm gonna muddy the water, feed the shark, and do a blind drop with some dogs."

He might as well have been speaking Icelandic. *Is all that in code? Like spies?*

Tax nodded as if that made perfect sense, and shook his hair out of his eyes with a quick, irritated flicking motion. "Double insurance. You sure the shark isn't just keeping something worse out of the pond?"

"That's the next guy's problem." Paul grinned like he'd just won three dusty playground fights in a row and was ready for more.

"Which means it's not ours." Tax's laugh was soft and genuine. "Classic."

"You don't have to use code words," Beck said. "I can just go to the bathroom, if you don't want me to know."

"Sorry. This sort of thing has its own language." Paul's smile vanished, the sun behind a thick veil of winter grey. "It just means you're gonna miss a little bit more of the reunion, Beck. But I really do need to know where the bag is."

Of course you do. It was ridiculous to think he was going to take the cash and vanish, leaving her stranded, but a tiny little worm of doubt in Beck's chest would not stop chewing. Maybe she'd doubt everyone for the rest of her life, including Dad.

How often did Paul deal with *this sort of thing*, that *had its own language?*

But she had other questions, maybe less important but still burning a hole in her stomach. How many letters had Paul written to her? She hadn't even noticed Dad picking up the mail more than usual, though he'd been home on leave with the liver problems and she'd been taking extra shifts stocking shelves at Safeway between driving him to doctor's appointments. Or had Dad quietly dropped a word to Horace Lettinger, who had delivered the mail on their street all Beck's life?

Horace must be ready to retire soon. Beck hadn't seen him in ages; they used to leave a Ziploc of cookies and a small gift for him in the mailbox every Christmas season.

Maybe the two men noticed her hesitation. If she was lucky, they'd think she was about to cry again. *Just like a girl*, a tiny, hateful voice sneered. It wasn't even Joe's, simply the generalized, low-grade self-hatred of living in a man's world.

Either way, she despised hearing it.

"The bag's out at Clemens Mine," she heard herself say, dully. *Be smart right now, Beck. Don't tell everything, even if it's Paul.* Who knew when he'd decide she was too much trouble? "Our place, I mean. Where we used to go. The case with the jump drives. . . ."

"I'm gonna need all of it, Beck." Paul hadn't learned that quiet, matter-of-fact tone from anyone in Granite River, even his Uncle Dreeson. It was probably something the Army had taught him.

And she was a fool. It was stupid to trust anyone.

She could have asked Hel to smuggle a letter to Paul years ago, but every time she'd sat down to write it amounted to the same thing, over and over again, and the shame all but drowned her.

I'm scared, and I was late. Are you really done with me?

While Dad was busy blocking Paul's calls and probably tearing up his letters, she'd been scraping together every cent she could find and trying to decide what lie her father would believe so she could make a trip to the clinic in Eugene. Then, when she'd decided on a good whopper to cover her overnight absence, she'd hoped like hell Dad wouldn't have a reason to call Jenna Blackminton's house and find out she wasn't there.

Even if she had technically been an adult at that point.

Nobody in Granite River could have really helped her, or kept their mouth shut if they did. It was one more secret she'd folded up and stuffed into the darkness at the bottom of her brain, only so many of them were spilling out into daylight now.

So Beck told Paul almost everything he wanted to know, excused herself, and fled to the bathroom. Running water was a dead giveaway for a crying fit, but she had learned how to weep silently.

Just another life lesson.

SPLASHING HER FACE with cold water didn't help the puffiness around her eyes or the red in her nose, but she couldn't hide in the restroom forever. Beck emerged to find Paul standing to one side of the window, carefully not touching the drapes as he scanned the parking lot, a sleek black phone to his ear.

A wave of bright red terror scorched her from toes to scalp; Beck barely registered Tax at the room's television, fiddling with the button-laden remote. "Channel Seven, copy," he said, briskly.

"You want to just tell me?" Paul turned away from the window, and his gaze settled on the flatscreen TV's glowing, glassy eye. "Yeah, it's on."

Channel 7 was the local news affiliate, and it was just about time for the midafternoon roundup. Beck's right hand hurt, because she was clutching the bathroom's doorframe.

Tax pressed another button. Subtitles rolled across the bottom of the screen, a few moments behind words falling from the lips of a very attractive bleached-blonde newscaster in an earth-tone blazer Gloria would probably kill to wear.

"*—on this developing story once we have it. Once more, a sheriff in Linlane County has been gunned down in cold blood, which brings the toll in the past two days to three dead and several injured.*"

"Dewey's boys?" Paul said, and Beck couldn't look away from the screen.

It was an official photograph; she remembered knotting Dad's uniform tie for him that day four years ago. *You look like a movie star,* she'd teased, and for a few hours that afternoon, she hadn't been worried about Joe because she was with her father.

Returning to the house on Passacola afterward, she'd started thinking about how, exactly, she could try to escape. That had been her first lunge for freedom, packing a suitcase and going back to her childhood home. But Joe swore he'd do better, swore he'd changed, even cried. He wore her down little by little, Dad agreed with him because Joe was such a nice boy, and eventually she'd gone back to try and make her marriage work.

Once the second honeymoon wore off, he'd escalated quickly. *Run to your daddy again, Becks. See what I do.*

"Great." Paul rubbed at his eyes with his free hand. "What about Hel?"

Oh, God. Had Joe gone after her, too? Beck had been certain Aunt Helena was relatively safe, since the entire town knew what Dreeson, not to mention the rest of the extended clan, would do to whoever hassled her.

See what being a criminal gets you, Becca? Her father, sternly, the time she'd skipped school in fifth grade and been not just caught, but righteously busted. *You stay on the straight and narrow, now.*

Well, she'd tried. And she'd tried stepping off. Both were rigged games, like the carnival at the county fairgrounds each year.

"Yeah." Now Paul was looking at her, and she couldn't tell what he was thinking. Funny, he used to be an open book—or maybe she'd just *thought* so. She would never have dreamed he'd desert her, but she'd made whatever peace she could with it; the fact that it hadn't really been him but circumstances was beside the point.

Because she hadn't thought he'd come back, either, and here he was. Just in time for her to royally fuck up his life as well as her own.

"Ma'am?" Tax was right in front of her, blotting out the television and her father's worn, beloved face. Of course, to him it would be a stranger's. "You look a little pale. Let's sit you down."

I don't want to sit down. A scream was crammed in Beck's throat. She could make it to the door, maybe, somehow unlock it and get into the hall.

They'd probably be glad to see her go, taking all the problems she represented with her. Her purse was on the bed; if she could grab it and get away, maybe. . . .

Maybe *what?*

"All right." How could Paul sound so *calm?* "Tonight, after dark . . . yeah, of course." Another long pause; it had to be Dreeson Klemperer on the phone. Before the state legislature decriminalized weed, his grow-and-ship operations had been considerable; he'd gone legal now, and Dad sometimes looked sour when the fact was mentioned. But Dreeson was old-growth local. He knew the rules, and he had a collection of felons who couldn't get work elsewhere employed in his greenhouses plus the brand-new processing facility out on Bear Road. "Nah, I got all I need. I'm gonna give my backup your number, though." Another pause. "No, I don't *expect* it to go south, Uncle D. But I'm prepared." A small, tight smile, another entirely new expression on a man she didn't, after all, know anymore. "Give her my love, tell her it's fine, all right? I'll check in later."

He hung up. Tax's hand was on Beck's arm; he guided her to the closest bed. All the strength ran out of Beck's legs. Now she could see the TV again.

The news had moved on. Traffic, weather, politics—her own tragedy was just a juicy tidbit, bleeding and leading.

"What's up?" The new guy straightened, turning to face Paul. "Is the guy on the news one of ours?"

Once more, all the air had left her immediate vicinity. The television turned into a blurry, glowing smear. Her heart thundered in her ears. Maybe she'd have some sort of cardiac event and save everyone the trouble.

Gunned down. Cold blood. Death toll. The words kept dancing inside her head, white letters on subtitle black.

"Beck." Callused, strangely gentle hands cupped her face. The bright smear of the TV vanished, eclipsed by a shadow. "Beck, sweetheart, breathe. Breathe for me. Come on."

No. I should just stop. It would be best for all involved, don't you think?

"She's having a panic attack." Tax sounded amazingly calm. "You want her sedated?"

"Watch the parking lot," Paul snapped. "Beck, baby, look at me. Look."

She didn't want to. His face warped and changed through a film of tears, and the absolute terror locking up her joints and stealing her lung function added another layer of distortion.

"Yessir." Tax vanished, the sense of his presence leaching away.

Paul didn't move. Beck's hands jumped up, tiny pheasants fluttering to draw predators away from the nest. The left smacked Paul's shoulder, a small, ineffective sound.

"Dad," she heard someone say. It was a child's voice, breathless and despairing. "My dad."

"Shit," Tax muttered from the window.

Paul ignored him. "He was airlifted to County General. He's in critical condition, but he's not dead."

What? It had to be a lie. Joe sometimes did that, lied and later laughed. *It was a joke, Becks. Jeez, lighten up.* Or he lied, then lied again, until she was so confused she didn't know which way was up.

"I need you to breathe, Beck. Just inhale with me, all right?" Paul's face swam back into focus.

He stared directly into Beck's eyes, and it wasn't a stranger in front of her anymore. It was the boy she'd faced down on the fourth-grade playground, yelling *stop it, you're mean!* The boy she'd ignored all through fifth and sixth, the boy who had shown up the first day of seventh at Granite River Middle School and dropped into the seat next to her at lunch, ignoring her frosty silence and keeping the rest of the table in stitches with a running patter of filthy jokes.

Eventually he found out how to make her laugh, and from then on, she was a goner.

It was the same boy who'd brought his first car to her house, and only smiled when her dad refused to even address him by name. *You stay away from that boy,* Dad always said, and she didn't listen.

You just don't know him, she'd always said. Well, now Beck didn't know him either, but he looked so much like when she *had* known him, she couldn't keep anything straight.

"He's . . . in the hospital?" Her throat was so dry, the words were papery cornhusks.

"Yeah. In critical condition, but alive and under guard, Dreeson says."

That won't stop Joe. Nothing does. "I have to. . . ." *I have to go there. I have to see him.*

"You have to breathe, and in a little while, you're going with Tax. He's going to look after you while I take care of this." Paul leaned forward. She almost flinched, expecting his hands to clamp down, expecting sudden pain.

But he pressed his lips to her forehead instead, and the distracting, half-familiar smell of fresh air, clean laundry, and a ghost of aftershave over a simmering well of male heat swamped her.

He stayed like that, bent over, his mouth against her skin. Cold and hot washed through Beck in successive flashes, and what the hell, even her own body was staging a revolt. She was through the looking glass.

That book had scared the shit out of her in high school lit. Paul was the only one who had listened to her halting explanation of why mirrors possibly weren't safe and how she couldn't ever look in one again.

Okay, had been his only comment. *I'll tell you when you've got something stuck in your teeth, then.*

He had a way of reducing problems like that. Eventually she'd lost her fear of reflective surfaces, but so much from childhood was roaring back into fashion at the moment.

"It's gonna be all right," he murmured, the words sinking into her flesh, spilling down her back along with the shivers from his lips against her skin. Or, not the words themselves, but the tone—very soft, dead certain, utterly comforting.

It was the voice he'd always used just for her.

"I am gonna *make* it all right," he continued, pulling away a bit. "So take a breath, Beck. For me. That's all you've got to do. I've got the rest."

The iron bands around her ribs fell away. A long, shuddering inhale filled her straining lungs, and she was dimly aware she was sweating again. She didn't have any clean clothes. Her stomach was rolling like an overpriced carnival ride, her hair was a mess, and Paul was nose to nose with her, staring like he could see right through to the back of her skull.

Her father was in the hospital, and she should never have let this man go. When he found out exactly what she'd done all those years ago, she was going to lose him again.

But first she had to survive this. And she was just as hypocritical as any old-growth local pretending not to see the obvious, because she wasn't going to tell him her last secret.

Not just yet.

"I'm okay," Beck lied. "I'm *fine*. What do you need me to do?"

Personal Best

"I DROVE ALL THIS way to play grabass in the woods with crackheads, my man." Tax folded his arms, leaning against his charcoal Honda. The SUV had all-wheel-drive, was freshly detailed, and had started out from home pristinely waxed. "And you've got me babysitting."

"First of all, this is Oregon; it's meth, not cocaine." Paul couldn't see Beck, closed solicitously in the front passenger seat. The window tinting was just a step away from illegal, and the California plates simply added to the camouflage. "Second, this is only rural, not the woods. I can take you to the actual woods if you like."

"Maybe after the wedding." Cold breeze riffled Tax's hair, and his grin meant he was prepared to do some serious roasting of his buddy. "If she'll let you out to play with your friends."

"She's my girl, not my mother." Of course Paul could have refused to take the bait, but what fun was that? "Grow up, asshole."

"Dez is practically hitched, Boom is making it official, and now look at you. Looks like there's a trend going around, like that time we decided to play *Will It Piña Colada?*"

Dumping whatever you could find into a blender and making your buddies drink it was an honorable old Squad tradition. Nobody had gone blind yet, but there was always a first time. "I don't think she wants to be married again so soon." Paul should have known better than to show any weak spot. He was *never* going to hear the end of this. "Look, it's complicated. Besides, the last thing she needs is a rebound."

It was the height of douchebaggery, not to mention arrogance, to think that with all this going on, maybe he had another chance with Beck. Especially with her dad in the hospital. Dreeson didn't know if that little event was courtesy of Dewey Johnson or Joe, since there had also been another shootout with deputies out on Old Marckola and Sam Neesdale had exchanged fire with some of Dewey's boys down near the river less than two hours later.

At this point, Paul figured whoever had shot the sheriff was pretty academic, and it was looking like the deputies catching lead was only a matter of time. Pretty soon they'd call the staties in.

Beck looked so lost, so small. Tax had produced a painkiller and a sedative, and she'd taken the tablets from a virtual stranger without question, dry-swallowing them and blinking at the medicinal taste.

A good little girl, trapped in a nightmare.

"Sounds like this Joe guy was her rebound, frankly. I say we run this like Baja. Shoot him, hide the body, and we can get you married in Vegas along with Boom." Tax wasn't going to let a good advantage go to waste, and if he was mentioning Baja it meant he'd gotten over that particular off-the-books operation. It hadn't been bad, just . . . complex. "Seriously, though, she's a nice lady. I like her."

"Just don't like her too much." It had to be said, even to a buddy. There was R & R, and then there was *serious*. "Stay deep, and stay *down* unless you hear from me."

"Relax, will you? I'll take very good care of your girlfriend. I won't even tell her any of your truly disgusting habits." Tax scratched at his cheek, callused fingertips making a slight dry sound. His dark gaze flickered up, checking Paul's six, and returned. "What's she going to do if I have to get persuasive with one of the locals?"

"Well, she's a civilian." He couldn't find any other way to say it.

"Yeah. Didn't Dez's old lady hit you on the head with a milkcrate?" When Tax was genuinely amused, he ducked his head to laugh and a flash of the kid he must have been showed, lightning-fast and just as quickly gone. "This one better not try to brain me with anything."

"If she does, you'll take it like a good recruit." He clapped the squad's medic on the shoulder, a companionable punch. "Hey. Thank you."

"What the fuck for?" Tax answered the blow with a light, stinging one of his own, and stepped away. "Wait until the guys hear about this, Klemp. Just you wait."

None of them ever lived *anything* down. The constant razzing stood in for affection, sort of. You couldn't admit you were scared enough to shit peach pits, but you could hassle your buddy and get the favor returned, a pair of guardrails keeping adrenaline-junkie soldiers on some approximation of the right path. "Well, pretty soon someone else will get a bright idea and the time to engage it, and we'll be ragging on *him* instead. Be careful, you hear me? Crank makes these assholes unpredictable."

"Yeah, yeah." Tax gave an insouciant salute, reaching for the driver's side door. "Don't get shot up somewhere I can't patch you."

He must be worried. It was, after all, Tax who had hovered over Klemp on slippery metal grating as the helicopter banked, attempting to plug the artery-pulsing hole in his buddy's leg. The medic's refrain in those situations was always the same.

No you don't, you bastard. Don't you dare. There is no fucking dying allowed today.

Paul had to give his best parting fire. "Yessir, I will only get my ass shot up in the approved manner sir, thank you sir."

A cheerful flip-off over his shoulder, a laugh, and Tax got in the Honda. The engine started, and Paul wanted to tap on Beck's window. *Wear your seatbelt. Be careful, do some deep breathing, let Tax do what he has to.* And, of course, the most important thing. *I'll finish this off, and I'll give you all the time you need. But if you think I'm letting you go again, Becks, you're dreaming.*

It was just that simple. Almost, in fact, as simple as what he intended to do next.

BECK'S LITTLE CAR was a valiant soldier, and it had been up this way recently. Beck had told him about the washout halfway up Clemens Mountain—another glorified hill, really, but so craggy and covered with firs and wild apple, not to mention Oregon grape and banks of ancient blackberry tangle, nobody was going to tell it as much to its face.

Way back in the nineteenth century the gold rush had come through this part of the world, and the old Clemens Mine had given up a bit of silver before pooping out and taking the fortune of that entire family with them. The last scion, ancient, crotchety Herbert Clemens, lived on the other side of the mountain in a shack with a well and a tapline the power company never got around to doing anything about.

It simply wasn't worth it to send a crew back to cut him off. Not with the trigger-happy neighbors out that way.

The meadow spread before the old mine entrance was a favorite teenage hangout; a few scattered clapboard buildings lingered where ore had once been hauled free, washed, and dragged away down a twisting mule-road. The structures along the meadow's edge, well-silvered and providing a rafter-refuge for mourning doves or the occasional owl, were slowly being swallowed by vines and saplings.

Kids swore the biggest shack near the mine's big black yawning cave-mouth had once held dynamite and pickaxes on its rotting shelves, and making out in the demo shed was a time-honored rite of passage. Scattered layers of charcoal in the center of the meadow held memories of many a bonfire ringed by scraps of lumber and deadwood serving as

benches. Every once in a while a keg was bought—or otherwise ac-
quired—over the county line by some brave soul eager for the bragging
rights. Then it was time for all the silly games bored kids play in the dark,
like daring each other to stand on the ghost stump, put their back to that
huge inky cave, and stand motionless while a stopwatch clicked.

In Paul's time, the record was three minutes and fifteen seconds.

Working with the Squad, he'd been shot at, punched, knifed, hung
out the side of a crashing helo—now *that* operation had been a bitch and
a half—and various other things, but nothing approached the sheer brain-
melting teenage terror of standing defenseless and imagining something
slithering out of the mine to grab its next snack.

It was no fun to play the game during daylight, after all.

Under fire, he was too busy to get scared. There was only time to do
what you'd been trained for, and sometimes not even that.

The Jetta rolled to a stop, its temp gauge creeping suspiciously
upward. The car wasn't a spring chicken anymore, especially with almost
perpendicular inclines in the mix, but she was gamely carrying on.

Like Beck, her big green eyes so dark and wounded. Whoever had
shot Sheriff Sommers—Joe, one of Dewey's boys, Dewey, or God
himself—would answer to Paul soon enough. That was what they called
a *secondary objective*.

Hell, maybe good ol' Law-n-Order would even approve of being
avenged. Maybe Paul could even lay the whole thing in front of Beck like
a one-eyed white cat bringing a dead vole to a beloved human. *Take me
back. Please. I never wanted to leave you.*

He cut the engine, and gathering dusk swallowed the hillside. The
mine exhaled, a chill dank breath, as he opened the door and got out.
The urge to seek cover was almost immediate, and he found himself
thinking of his father's old trailer.

That particular red-and-white house of childhood nightmares out
near the river was probably buried under a wall of blackberry vines now,
and he liked the mental image. A lot.

Nobody ever went behind the demo shed unless it was to piss. Paul
gave the bathroom part of the meadow a wide berth, and counted off his
paces. He knew how to move in complete darkness now; he knew how
to give covering fire and how to pop a few mortar rounds into a
developing knot of enemy so they didn't get any bright ideas. He could
disassemble, clean, and reassemble a rifle in the dark; he could rebuild an
engine blindfolded, call in an airstrike, and watch a buddy's back. He
knew how to slide a knife into kidneys, a skill like the right way to pop

the sharp end of a straw into a Capri Sun pouch. He knew exactly how long it took to hold a struggling man almost off his feet with a garrotte until the twitching stopped and the sphincters loosened.

He also knew what it was like to have a ricochet take out a chunk of your leg, to bleed almost all the way out on the floor of a dodging, weaving helicopter, and how the greyish softness of shock and blood loss felt right on the threshold of death.

There were far worse things than dying. Like your father diving into the bottle after your mother's death and becoming a hideous, screaming stranger. Like Connor Sommers saying *she don't want to talk to you, son, good luck in the service* before hanging up, like the beeping on the other end of a blocked phone line. Like waiting for letters that never came, like knowing you hadn't been enough to stop your father's slide downhill, or enough to hold a honey-haired girl's interest.

Like seeing the only woman he'd ever love cower as if she expected Paul to deck her. Like seeing her entire world crumble as she stared at a picture of her dad pasted on the afternoon roundup, with a heartless talking head grinning at something newsworthy coming out of the backwoods for once.

A divot on the edge of the meadow held another, smaller rotting structure, its back to a wall of vines and trashwood creeping out to reclaim this space. It was too far away from the bonfire, too tiny, and too ramshackle to be bothered with, at least by most. But it saw its share of teenage grope-and-kiss sessions, yes indeed.

Our place, Beck always called it, laughing. *Not even a shotgun shack.*

"I'll buy you a house," he murmured. "A real bungalow, on Church Avenue."

That was the beginning of their very last argument, Beck insisting he could get a job at the mill or even do some college applications since his grades—with her help—were okay, Paul trying to make her see that the mill was already on its last leg and he wasn't college material, the Army was his only way out of both Granite River and his father's breathless, hereditary rage, and he was going to take it.

Now he could see how every single word he'd said could make her feel like she was the trap he was trying to avoid.

It had ended up with a hot, marvelous round of more-than-making-out in the back of his old Camaro, and maybe the dampness on Beck's soft, perfect cheek hadn't been sweat but tears that summer night. *Don't go*, she'd said. *Please. Just stay.*

Even in the dusk he could see marks in rain-softened soil. Small feet in battered sneakers, a smudge through tall grass and bracken. She'd hauled something heavy out here, almost like dragging a body.

The doorway was haphazardly boarded, but there was enough space for a teenager or a slim adult to slip through. Paul ripped a few of the boards free, glad he was full-up on his tetanus boosters. His phone's flashlight function worked just fine, though there wasn't any service out here.

Some places, even technology couldn't reach.

All the way in the back, in a crust-stiffened pile of refuse so old it didn't even reek anymore, an army surplus ditty lay like a short, fat snake digesting a tasty meal.

The goddamn thing weighed almost as much as Beck did. He unzipped it enough to see a flood of cash, and the baggies of crystalline drugs glinted. He'd have to shut the phone off and let his eyes adapt before wriggling out through the door again.

You could see even a small light a long way off during a country night.

"All right," he said softly, as if someone was here to hear him—Dez already planning the next eight steps and contingencies because that was a CO's job, or Beck looking anxiously for reassurance, depending on him to do what had to be done.

He didn't bother to hide his own sign; any halfway competent tracker was welcome to read all this until the rains came through again. Hefting the bag into the Jetta's trunk, he closed the car up with a short, sharp noise that echoed all across the clearing. Paul was about to head for the driver's side and get in as well, but instead, he walked away, cutting past the demo shed's front and onto the ruins of what had been a large graveled space before the mine.

The stump—dragged from God only knew where in the woods, unloaded and set here before Paul was even alive—was chest-high to an adult, though you could climb up on its west side if you knew the trick. The top was a good four feet across, almost level, and standing up there, arms spread and back to the mine, nape prickling and every sense straining alert for the monster's first breath. . . .

Every high school class, freshman to seniors, had a reigning stump champion. Usually, thirty seconds was considered pretty goddamn fearless.

Three minutes fifteen had left them all in the dust, though, and it was his own personal record. Maybe some kid after him would best it, but Paul found out he had no desire to defend the title.

He had better things to do. Paul turned on his heel and headed back for the Jetta, glad he was going to point the car downhill.

It was high time to renew his acquaintance with Dewey Johnson.

Good Rules

WHATEVER WAS IN Tax's pills was far nicer than Hel's pain meds. It was the first time in years Beck had no aches, twinges, or deep unsteady anxiety at all.

Tax's car even smelled new, a stew of finishing chemicals not drained away by hard use yet. Leather seats, press a button to warm your tush while driving or watching the scenery, the windows were deeply tinted, and it had built-in GPS too, not to mention a high-end police scanner bolted under the dash. Even that looked like a custom job.

The lean, proud-nosed man drove exactly the speed limit, obeying every single traffic law and safety measure to the letter, including double stops and staying out of the passing lane. The Honda had satellite radio just like Hel's Jeep, and classical piano played softly—something by Brahms, the text scrolling across the display said.

Tax kept an eye on the GPS, and seemed to know exactly where he was going despite being a complete stranger to Granite River.

It must be nice, Beck thought, to be that certain. Maybe she should have joined the Army herself, if this is what it gave you.

Tax didn't speak until they were heading north on the freeway, leaving Sinaida behind. She could have asked why they'd paid good money for perfectly nice rooms they didn't intend to sleep in, but it was obvious.

She just hoped this guy wasn't mad at the loss of cash.

"I'm sorry for all the trouble," Beck said finally. The right tentative tone to placate an angry male had to be calibrated exactly in each separate instance, and getting it wrong carried painful consequences.

Any woman knows that.

"Huh?" A quick, startled glance—his eyes were very dark, and the gleam of his watch-face against the inside of his wrist was just like Paul's. "Oh, this isn't trouble, ma'am. We've seen way worse."

"Oh." That seemed to close all possible conversational avenues, so Beck shut up, sinking into the leather seat. It felt nice, and with the chemical warmth in her bloodstream erasing the pain, she could consider even this latest disaster quasi-calmly.

"I am kind of curious, though." Tax checked his blind spot, swinging out to pass a lumbering semi in the right lane. Judging from the Honda's immediate response to even a touch on the accelerator, the engine was capable of far more than he asked of it. "You being the one that got away and all."

Huh? She hadn't been able to escape much of anything, ever, and this just proved it. "Say what, now?"

"Man, it's like having a unicorn in my car, you know?" A hint of California crept into Tax's crisp diction. "Klemp doesn't talk about you unless he's well and truly lubricated. One time some jarhead at a joint base started mouthing off while Klemp was having one of his moments drinking to your memory and all that sh—uh, all that stuff, and it took both Dez and Jackson to hold him back. I wasn't any help, I was lipwalking by that point." He wore a wry grin, like she should see the humor in the story, and Beck tried a tentative smile.

It made her face feel weird, masklike. "Paul talks about me?" *Don't ask. It's only going to hurt more later.* But she was feeling zero pain at the moment, and it was a nice goddamn change.

"Oh, yeah. Crazy stories about pranks you guys pulled in high school—did you really ride a bicycle down the side of a mountain?"

He talked about that? "It's more of a hill."

"Not to hear him tell it. According to him, you're the bravest person he ever met, and the funniest too. Then he gets all mopey and says, *but I fucked it up, like always.* I know it's none of my business, but. . . ." He shifted, settling himself more comfortably for the drive. "Can't help but wonder, you know?"

"It's complicated." Where on earth would she begin? "My dad never liked him, so when Paul went into the army . . . I thought he'd forgotten all about me. Guys do that."

"I guess," Tax said, thoughtfully. "Most soldiers remember too much, though, even with the sleep deprivation and adrenaline poisoning. Man, this is great. A star-crossed couple, and him riding in on his busted nag with his tin armor to save his old sweetheart. The guys are gonna *love* this."

I don't find this as amusing as you obviously do, sir. "You tease him a lot."

"And he gives it right back. A very funny fellow, our Klemp. And cool under fire, whew. Everyone thought he'd take over if Dez ever retired. Then Dez got taken out on a stress ticket right after Klemp got hit bad and told to take a medical, so the rest of us said *hell no, we're not going in-country with some stranger.* Army figured it was probably best to just let us all go to our rooms and think about things. Most of us will probably end up taking an honorable discharge." Tax was getting comfortable, or maybe talking to keep her awake. "But I always wondered about him carrying a torch for so long. Sure, he R & R's like the rest of us, but nothing serious, you know? You don't have to worry about that."

Oh, my God. Was he talking about what she *thought* he was? "How did he get hurt? His leg, right?"

"Ricochet, probably, or someone got lucky. It was a bad one. Nicked the femoral artery, and he almost bled out in the chopper carrying us home." He was no longer having such a good time. In fact, Tax looked older now.

And just a little bitter, his mouth drawing down a bit.

"I'm sorry." Beck stared out the windshield. "It can't be pleasant to talk about."

"Better than living through it. So, uh, once we get this Joe guy in a box, what are you gonna do with your life?"

"My God." A jolting, hiccupping laugh bolted up from Beck's belly. Maybe it was the meds, but all of a sudden Beck Sommers didn't give a fuck about being polite, even to a strange man who could potentially pull over and leave her on the side of the freeway if she sassed too much. "You think I'm going to survive this. That's adorable."

Tax was silent for a few miles. The hum of tires on damp pavement was soothing, and the piano music accompanied it perfectly. She could get used to a car like this, Beck decided, and the glimmer of a fresh new plan poked its head from under the crushing guilt. It snuggled into the medicated haze, and started to grow.

You know what you have to do. Joe won't stop, and he's hurt Dad now. Who would he go after next? Helena, despite the risk?

Or maybe he'd decide to do something to Paul? *That* was a particularly horrible thought, even if she had no shortage of those at the moment.

"The statistics are bad," Tax finally admitted. "Think of it this way, though. How many times did you try to leave?"

"Twice." *Including this time, which is working out swimmingly, don't you think?*

"The average is seven." He eased up on the accelerator, keeping them just a touch under the speed limit. "But most of them don't have the kind of help you do, ma'am."

She was beginning to wonder just what kind of help these guys were. "How did you know that it's seven?"

"I like numbers. Dosages and absorption rates, for obvious reasons. Ammo counts, exchange rates, miles per gallon, sequences, fractions, integers, imaginary—you know there are imaginary numbers? Crazy. Anyway, math is a language, and it's got good rules. Comforting ones." Tax visibly caught himself, making a restless motion. "You've got two of Dez the Destroyer's wrecking crew on your side, Ms. Sommers. All you have to do is relax and enjoy the ride."

Is he trying to flirt or is he just weird? For once, Beck couldn't tell. "The Destroyer? Do you guys all have nicknames?"

"Kind of?" His tone heavily implied he'd never really thought about it before, and perhaps was undergoing a revelation. "The point is, we're in the mix now. Klemp's going to clear this kingpin guy first—Dewey? Jesus, what a name."

It was exactly what Beck had thought for a long time, and to hear someone else finally say it aloud was absurdly hilarious. It seemed like a day for her thoughts escaping her own skull and running around wild. "You don't even want to know what it's short for."

"Tell me."

"Dewbert." A ghost of a smile touched Beck's lips. It felt good to be amused by something again, no matter how small. "Old Johnson family name. He's actually Dewbert Junior."

"No wonder he's so angry."

That did it. Beck started to laugh, and Tax joined in. It wasn't the screamy, sob-related howling she'd broken down with last night; no, this was good old-fashioned belly chuckles, shaking her into a limp rag.

She couldn't remember the last time she'd laughed like that. As the last cascading giggles died away, she wiped at her cheeks with cold fingertips, and felt the scab-scrape from blackberry thorns on her cheek.

Paul had Dreeson and the entire extended clan behind him. Dewey was local, he knew what that meant. But Joe was Beck's problem, and she was suddenly, absolutely certain he hadn't intended a "hero rescue."

No, he wanted to kill her. He hadn't been able to do it with the Taurus, so he'd make do by hurting anyone she cared about. Or anyone who just plain got in his way, and it would be her fault.

Joe Halston was her problem to fix. Not Paul's.

SHE'D AVOIDED the Motel Six just south of Granite River, but that was apparently where they were supposed to wait. Tax wanted to order room service again, and could barely conceal his disappointment that a motel didn't have that amenity.

If this kept up, Beck could say she'd visited every motel in a certain radius from Granite River.

Wouldn't the gossips in town just love that statement. Beck sat on yet another hotel bed, listening to the sound of running water.

Paul's friend had checked them in and hustled her to a second-floor room with two beds and a kitchenette; a tiny travel coffeepot, sleek and silver and probably expensive, was placed reverently on the counter, ready for morning. He was very organized, not to mention toting a very professional-looking 9mm in a shoulder holster. That was why he and Paul wore that type of jacket, Beck thought.

She felt clear-headed, reasonably pain-free, and utterly lucid for the first time in a long while.

Tax's wallet was in the bathroom with him, but his keys—including the fancy plastic-headed one full of buttons for his Honda—were on the nightstand next to his bed. He was supposed to sleep closer to the door, he said, with a wink like she should know what that meant.

Maybe it was so he could escape if she mutated while in dreamland or something.

It was like reaching for the bag in the closet again. Her body moved before the rest of her was ready, and she found herself on her feet, her fingertips hovering over the keys.

Oh, Jesus, Beck, what are you thinking? Don't do this. You're going to get yourself killed.

"Better me than someone else." There she went, talking to herself again, crazy ol' Becks.

If she was quick, she could be out of the parking lot before he turned the water off. Her criminal career had merely suffered a minor setback, not a complete defeat. She'd done breaking and entering, theft, possession of stolen goods, blackmail—a real cornucopia, but she'd been an overachiever in school and always liked the feeling.

Why not add grand theft auto to the list?

Stage Set

ONLY A LOCAL could understand the directions to the place out past Simmons End, let alone find it. The bar stood on riverfront property, sure, but the swampy shallows wouldn't fire any real estate developer's imagination and indeed, for a business it was situated oddly. It could barely be seen from the road, which had no name though it had once been paved and was only referred to as *that sumbitchin' curve out near old Noah McCoyle's* even though Mr. McCoyle had been dead for nigh on thirty years.

Nevertheless, the place had power, though the windows were kept soaped over so very little light escaped, and on a chilly spring evening bursts of raucous music occasionally bolted through its swinging front door before finding out they had nowhere to go and giving up in the middle of the parking lot. Taking the sharp bend into the stretch of weed-starred gravel used as said parking lot—another trick only locals knew—meant being confronted with neat ranks of ATVs, and the number of vehicles plus the time of day or night could be assessed with a swift glance to determine what reception any visitor might encounter.

It looked like Dewey Johnson had a moderate amount of employees hanging around tonight. The angry hornet-sound of quads often rose and fell in ghostly cadence all through this stretch of unincorporated foothills, each one a drone servicing chemical hives bubbling with a mix of bespoke or corporate production.

The visitor's section of the parking lot was to the right of the front door, and etiquette demanded putting your car's nose almost to the porch railings. The structure might at one time have been a house but had since been turned into a long low barnlike affair with a wraparound skirt. Around the back, a fog of cigarette or vape smoke lingered on heavy nights; on light ones, just a line cook or waitress on break sent up thin tendrils of nicotine vapor.

Klemp didn't back the Jetta in; politeness had to take priority over setting up for a quick escape. He was fairly sure what he was going to find inside a bar with no name tonight.

It was just like every other shady hole he'd ever trawled for intel. It was a distinct letdown to find out they were the same the world over, with only slight variations in the alcohol on offer.

Getting the ditty properly slung on his shoulder was more habit than anything else. The guards posted along the road had reported him by walkie-talkie now, and a few flickers of movement on the far side of the ATVs were an outside crew, hovering protectively. Looked like six, none of them professional or even high-grade amateur.

In other words, easy as kindergarten.

The stairs, covered with faded AstroTurf, creaked alarmingly. The place was solid enough, though the bathroom was probably just two holes hanging right over this finger of the Linlane River.

Yep, there was the bar, with a fly-spotted mirror behind shelves crammed with bottles both empty and full. There was the neon or its approximations, and the sticky residue of cigarette smoke pushed from many a wet, croupy lung. There were the barstools, the two pool tables with anemic green velvet cherished and inviolate even during the chaos of a brawl, a line of booths with cracked red vinyl upholstery, and a jukebox of uncertain pedigree but great volume.

The juke was a local touch.

A collection of sullen faces in varying states of shaven to heavily forested turned to give the guest a gander, all in the local uniform of denim jackets, jeans, the occasional cowboy hat amid a sea of baseball caps, and combat boots.

Though two guys were wearing Crocs, and one a ratty pair of Birkenstocks. With thick, hand-knitted wool socks, no less. Nothing said Oregon like that little detail.

He took this all in, every inch of his skin alive and aware. Standing in the door like this meant anyone could get a shot, but could also mean he didn't want trouble and was giving everyone a chance to absorb the fact.

Half and half. Those guys and the ones by the wall are the actual bouncers. That's Johnson's personal security in the booths on either side, ready to be bottled and cleared because they're rank amateurs. There's more in the back, but the bartender's usual and those guys are actual customers. Or maybe just alcoholics.

He vaguely remembered Dewey from school. The skinny, bookish boy with chunky glasses and a dishwater mullet had bulked up a bit. He was reedy and his haircut was indifferent at best, but his skin was clear, his mouth had all its original parts, and he had a neat dark goatee. Either Dreeson was right and he didn't sample his own wares, or he tolerated the dosage damn well.

The kid—although Klemp shouldn't call him that, he was only two years younger, after all—did have a bottle of Johnny Walker before him, and two glasses, probably the cleanest in a fifteen-mile radius. The semicircular booth was the largest available, and had been recently customized by a couple of very good jackleg carpenters.

Which meant this guy had a sense of theatrics. It was a nice stage set.

Paul kept his pace slow, every movement smooth. Everyone in here was carrying—except him.

He was halfway to the throne-booth when two stocky men stepped forward in unison. Tweedledee and Tweedledum both had black bandannas tied around their left biceps, and Dum was wearing sunglasses.

Inside. At night.

Klemp couldn't help but smile. "I'm unarmed," he said, pleasantly. "And taken, so don't get fresh if you attempt to pat me down."

Dewey laughed; he had surprisingly resonant tenor. "Paul Klemperer," he said, and settled in his seat, not quite lounging as easily as Tax but still giving a good impression. "Son of a bitch. How's your family?"

"You could come on down to the reunion and grab a plate." There was no reason to be impolite. "Uncle Dreeson's gonna be running the barbeque all day tomorrow, and Gloria's potato salad is actually pretty good. How's your mama?"

"She passed two years ago." Dewey waved a lazy hand, and the goons stepped away.

One of them had a nice Heckler & Koch under his arm. If this went south, Klemp had half a mind to take that piece first. Which was part of the reason he was unarmed—why carry the weight, when all the weapons he'd ever need were scattered around him? It was a veritable garden, as Sparky Lee would say.

Wonder how Beck's doing. But Paul couldn't afford distraction right now. "I'm sorry to hear that. I just got back from the service." In other words, *I didn't know, no disrespect.*

"So I'm told." Dewey lifted two fingers, aiming at the ditty over Paul's shoulder. "I presume that's mine?"

Getting right to business. "So I'm told."

The kid smiled. "Drink?"

"If you're offering."

Now it was the card game. Dewey couldn't look weak to his crew.

The raid on Chapwick's would create temporary cohesion in his units, but the flip side of that was the uncommitted getting nervous. If the daytimers bolted, the shrinkage in personnel could be unprofitable indeed.

On the other hand, a Klemperer disappearing under these circumstances would rob Dewey of Uncle Dreeson's neutrality, and that was just as bad for continued business. There was a sweet spot where the kingpin could turn this into a morale booster as well as a lesson in who was top dog, and it looked like he was about to attempt the move.

The kid had moxie.

Sliding into the booth was like putting himself in a bag with an angry wildcat. Klemp's smile widened as he dropped the ditty just in front of the low table, a solid, satisfying sound reverberating through charged stillness. Even the jukebox was holding its breath.

This felt more like home than the rest of the goddamn town put together. The only thing missing was the consciousness of his team somewhere in the area, guardian angels ready to swoop in if things went fubar.

"How's Beck Halston doing these days?" Dewey inquired, damn near solicitously. "I was sorry to hear about her dad."

In other words, the kid wanted to disavow responsibility for the sheriff's recent misfortune. Fine.

"Sommers," Klemp corrected. First, he decided, he'd use the nearest glass tumbler, broken or not, to gouge out one of Dewey's eyes. Then he'd have to go over the back of the booth, but on the way, he could grab the 9mm strapped under the kid's arm. The HK on Tweedledee would have to wait, but not for long. "She's taking back her maiden name." In other words, she wasn't in Joe's corner—and neither was Paul.

"Used to be a divorce was a real scandal in this town."

Klemp refrained from pointing out that this one was causing a fair amount of waves. This was *not* the right audience for that little observation. "Times change."

"Your uncle says the same thing." Dewey shifted. "Listen, you know I respect him, and I respect you. So, in the politest possible way, I'm going to ask if this is *all* my property being returned."

"So far as I know." Now it was time for a good lie, and Paul hoped he was up to the challenge. So far, Dewey was proving to be calm, in control, and frighteningly competent. "If there's anything missing, I'd—politely, of course—tell you to ask Joe Halston."

"Oh, good ol' Joe." The kid stirred again, but only to pour a couple fingers of whiskey into each glass. He pushed one in Paul's direction; this knee-high table was probably the cleanest horizontal surface in the whole damn place. "I think he's changed his number. You wouldn't happen to have his new one, would you?"

"'Fraid not." Klemp had to decide whether he believed Joe was out of Dewey's pocket at the moment; if he was, it meant shooting Beck's dad was personal but the rest of the casualties possibly weren't. Either way, his work wasn't finished even if he burned this place to the ground. "I'd kind of like to talk to him about landing Beck in this mess, though."

"Ah." Dewey nodded, thoughtfully. "You know, I had a crush on her in eighth grade? Nice girl. Never understood why she married *him*, of all people."

"Well, she's fixing that mistake." Paul kept an eye on the most troublesome group of security. Taking them out as soon as he had Dewey disabled was another prerequisite, and he even knew just how it would happen. "I'm going to ask if this concludes any business you have with her, and with me." He paused—theatrics weren't just for the kingpin kid, in this situation. "In the politest possible way."

"You've got manners." Dewey sounded either approving or mildly constipated; it was a tossup. "And some balls, just waltzing in like this. You know you beat up half the guys here, back in school? One or two of them might be holding grudges."

Then line 'em up and let's get it done. "I gotta get back to the reunion, but if they want that sorted out I'll make some time."

"Man, get a load of this guy." Dewey rested his head on the booth's high back, and made a languid movement. "Hey, Benny!"

A steroid-packed bruiser detached himself from the nearest knot of bodyguards and hurried over. Klemp might or might not have time to take out the bruiser's knee before he went over the back; in any case, he could ventilate the dumbass the first time he popped up from cover with Dewey's gun.

Should it become necessary.

Then he recognized the guy. It was Benny Ramirez, and he'd once knocked the kid's front tooth out behind the middle school's gymnasium.

Great.

"Yah, boss?" Benny gave a slight chin-tip; his left eye was bruised and swelling closed. Looked like he'd been in a tussle recently. "Hey, Paulie. Heard you were back."

"Benny." *Am I gonna have to take the rest of your teeth?* "Good to see you, man."

Dewey let them shake hands, and Klemp didn't have to break Benny's arm and use him for cover because the boss took a hit off his whiskey, his smile bearing a disconcerting resemblance to Uncle D's. "Take the bag back for me, Benny. Hey, do any of the guys in here have any business with our old friend Paul?"

Here it comes.

"Nope," Benny said, gravely. "Not unless he's still Joe Halston's friend, I guess."

Well, that answered that. "The man's no friend of mine," Klemp said quietly. "Not anymore."

"Because he married Beck, or . . . ?" Dewey waved Benny away; the big man gave what he probably thought was a salute before picking up the ditty and setting off for the hall to the right of the ramshackle bar.

So that was where the business offices were. Were there more boxes of jump drives, or was Dewey considering shifting to other accounting methods at the moment?

"It's none of my business, of course," Dewey continued. "Sorry."

Oh, what the hell. "The reasons don't matter." Klemp tossed the remainder of his whiskey down the hatch, showed his teeth in part appreciation, part feral warning. "What matters is that you have your shit back, and Beck's clear. I always liked you, Johnson, but I don't want to come back here ever again."

"Fair enough." Dewey was silent for a moment, contemplating his glass. "I'm surprised you remember me. Nobody ever paid attention in school."

"Their loss." Klemp shifted, as if eager to be gone. "We done?"

For a moment he was certain the kid was going to attempt some shit with Paul Klemperer, and he was going to have to first take Dewey's eye, then his gun, then clear this entire fucking place without getting shot more than once, and even that would make Tax endlessly gleeful.

But Dewey just nodded. "We're done. Thanks for coming by. Tell Beck no hard feelings, huh?" A matching tension vibrated all through his lean frame, and his hand tightened on his drink.

He was as ready as Klemp, though not nearly as trained.

You're wasted on backwoods meth running, kid. But telling Johnson so would just scratch his pride, so Klemp pushed his own empty glass along the table with a fingertip, then slid out of the booth. "Will do. No hard feelings on her end, either. She's local."

"So are you. Despite your best efforts." Dewey grinned, but he didn't relax. "I love this town."

You can have it. "See you around, Johnson."

"Yeah. Sure." The kingpin waved him away, and all the way to the door, Klemp expected to hear a whisper of attacking motion or the metallic sound of a gun being cocked.

In his younger days, he might almost have been disappointed to avoid a fight. Now, with his wounded leg giving a warning twitch and his neck tight, the copper of adrenaline flooding his tongue, he was more than happy to have escaped one.

IT WASN'T UNTIL he got back into cell tower range that his jacket pocket started buzzing. Fishing the phone out while he dealt with the curves of a logging road and ATVs buzzed through the woods on either side—an honor guard, or Dewey's boys keeping an eye on a territorial invader—was a chore and a half.

His heart sank. Tax was calling, and the only reason his buddy would be breaking radio silence was something happening to Beck.

A Good Girl

IT WAS A REAL dick move to steal a helpful stranger's car—not the kind of prank she'd ever consider before, because it was mean—but Beck's conscience had so much else to worry about, this new load of guilt barely made a dent.

Driving through Granite River at night was usually peaceful. The Honda took every curve smoothly, and it was nice to be up so high you could see the world. The tank was full and the seat heater was nice and warm, so Beck also swung by Granite River High School. *HAPPY SPRING BREAK*, the sign near the front of the parking lot proclaimed, and the lot itself held great patches of inky dark, every other streetlamp turned off to save on the electric bill.

First Methodist and Light of God Baptist glowered at each other across Church Avenue, both lit up like Christmas, and there was a good deal of coming and going both there and on Main Street's loop, not to mention the rest of downtown. Of course, with a sheriff in the hospital and a *death toll*—what an awful phrase, and now Beck had to wonder if she was responsible for murder by proxy, since she'd taken Dewey's bag—everyone would be a little on edge. People would be checking in, organizing casseroles and childcare for those affected, taking up collections, and exchanging heated whispers behind cupped hands.

Small towns in TV sitcoms or holiday Hallmark movies were a nice warm blanket of mutual cooperation, and there was certainly that neighborly aspect. But it came with the tittle-tattle, the endless chewing over other people's business, and the hypocrisy of pretending not to see the obvious. Maybe you couldn't have the good stuff without the bad—she'd thought, for at least a couple years, that was the way of marriages in particular and the world in general.

It might be the last time she saw Granite River, and Beck was driving a stolen car. She wanted to slip past her father's house, just to see it again—but Joe might be waiting, and he'd be curious about an SUV with California plates.

Ghostly memories stood on every corner, and if she saw a red pickup of any size, or a white car that could conceivably be a deputy's cruiser, her mouth dried and her hands shook despite the comforting warmth of the leather seat and pain pills combined.

Every corner held a memory of Joe, of Paul, and of Beck herself. There was the corner she and Paul had put a Christmas tree one year, a gentle prank that had turned into a tradition. There was the curve where Maxine Gelightly and Harvey Crew had smashed Harv's car one drunken night their junior year, a few plastic flowers and a faded memorial sign still clinging to the fence. That vacant gravel lot was where she'd learned to drive a stick shift, and under the lilacs on Crosway Lane the ghost of Paul's old Camaro lingered, where he'd first learned how to do that amazing trick with his fingers that sent young Beck over the edge. There was the dead end off 49th that they'd all gone past and into the old quarry to plink with .22s on hot summer afternoons, and the county fire station they'd TP'd that one time. . . .

Laughing, angry, sad—a whole collage of memories, from her first kiss with Paul behind the middle school to the first time Joe had turned in the driver's seat to look at her, his burning blue eyes a stranger's, and hissed *you think you're so special, don't you.*

Before that, though, was the parking lot where she'd met Joe one autumn afternoon, sitting in the two-seater red coupe his dad had bought him, and he'd said *I'll never leave you, Beck. Just . . . think about it, will you?*

There was the spot on the shoulder she'd pulled over on her way out of town before heading up to Eugene and the Planned Parenthood, her knuckles white on the Jetta's wheel and the consciousness of an irrevocable step looming before her.

Finally, she drove down the Strip, every business there dark and shuttered, porch lights on the few houses sandwiched between them burning, and turned on 79th for a hot minute before the hard left onto the highway. She drove slowly past the Grange, then did a three-point a mile away and came back. All was deserted, the Grange's gravel lot empty. She parked the SUV around the side of the building, hidden from the road. A small town also meant she could leave the keys on the front seat, and she probably should have ripped a page out of her old address book to leave a note.

But *I'm sorry* wouldn't cover this.

At least it wasn't winter, and she finally had her good hunting coat. With her purse slung underneath and the Thinsulate zipped all the way up, the hood high and her hands tucked into the sleeves, she was just a shadow in the night.

Her sneakers were old, the bottoms worn. She almost slipped and went head-first into a ditch the first time she had to hide from oncoming headlights, and the walk would take even longer because she had to cut across the end of downtown where Main crossed 58th and Peakins Lane peeled off, making it a five-way intersection.

In elementary school, they said that if you stood out there in the middle of the night and called the devil, he'd come. Beck crossed Peakins before crossing Main, attempting to stay off the pavement and on the shoulder as far as possible.

Peakins Park was empty and silent, too. Later in spring there would be cars parked near the maintenance access gate at night, teenage lovers taking advantage of a dark corner.

What would it be like to live somewhere the history didn't rise up and haunt you in every corner? She ducked under the gate's crossbar, listening intently—a great hush pervaded the town, though it was only just before midnight. The grass in the park wasn't dew-wet yet, but the earth underneath was just one short whistle away from mud.

Another hour's silent trudging, one of her sneaker soles shifting—it would disintegrate or come free before too much longer—with each step, and she made it to the west end of Church Avenue.

The actual churches were at the other end of the Avenue since the early sixties, the last time Granite River found itself needing serious religious expansion. The top crust of Granite River aristocracy still lived on the west side, though, and the sidewalks proved it.

Her nose was full; Beck sniffed hard, restraining the urge to wipe with her coatsleeve. God, she felt six years old again, small and terrified after her mother left. Dad had been up with her every night for months because she'd awakened screaming, utterly certain both her parents were gone instead of just one. Maybe Mom had gotten in some kind of trouble and had to leave? But then, why couldn't she just have told Dad? He'd just been made sheriff that year; there was nothing he couldn't have handled.

Like mother, like daughter, Beck thought, and shivered afresh.

The house she wanted was a solid brick affair with a gated circular driveway. A smaller gate set in the fieldstone wall led to the front walk, and well-trimmed box hedges marched on either side of that concrete strip, holding back velvety lawn turned silver-grey at night. The waning moon had risen, a bone-white sliver peeking between clouds.

Nobody in Granite River—nobody on *earth*—would expect her to come here.

She didn't realize Tax's pills were wearing off until she climbed the steps to the big wraparound porch. An antique wooden rocker stood next to a white wicker table; he probably sat out here on warm summer nights if he wasn't in the rose garden out back, trimming and tending.

Beck pressed the doorbell, swallowing hard against the weight in her throat. As long as she was moving she didn't have to think, but now her journey was at an end.

Muffled chimes cascaded away inside the house. She knew he lived alone, and hoped he wasn't a super heavy sleeper. The porch was mostly hidden from the street; maybe she could sit in the rocker and wait for morning.

It was a miserable prospect.

She rang the bell again. *Sorry to disturb you* was a cliché, but sometimes even hoary old chestnuts were appropriate. Should she start with that, or with the classic *Obi Wan, you're my only hope?*

The porch light flicked on, stinging her eyes. Beck flinched. Movement behind the door—if he kept a shotgun handy, she was probably in very real danger of getting a faceful of shot for her pains.

Tiny noises of unlocking. He opened the door a crack, a tall dark shadow with a bird's nest of greying hair and a dark, striped robe over blue cotton pajamas, his feet in comfortably battered leather slippers.

"S-s-s-sorry—" Beck's chattering teeth chopped the words into pieces.

"Good heavens," Judge Nelson said. "Becca? Is that you?" A quick, flickering glance over her shoulder, then he made a short, paternal gesture of welcome, ushering her inside. "You look half frozen. Come on in."

DAWN ROSE, STINGING red and fluffy pink on the eastern horizon. The smell of bacon tiptoed upstairs, through quiet hallways carpeted in cream with multicolored flecks, and mixed with the aroma of fresh coffee to bring Beck out of sludgy deep unconsciousness.

Judge Nelson's spare room—or one of them, the house was certainly big enough to hold a few—was comfortable enough, though the white lace comforter was probably a real bitch to wash, let alone dry. It wasn't Brent's room; the judge's son was on a tour of duty overseas, another boy who had escaped Granite River. This place was cleaned by Molly Mackenberg's crew of housekeepers; they were probably responsible for the decorative soaps in the guest bathroom and the plump, very aesthetic pillows piled on the bed too.

Molly was doing all right. Her own divorce had gone well, town gossip said, and though her kids were probably teased in school about the whole Molly Maid thing the fact remained that their mother had a client list from here to Eugene, plus her own trim, pretty manufactured out on Shaffee Lane. Bud Mackenberg had custody on weekends, and with his job at the Ford dealership in Sinaida, he was doing all right too. There didn't seem to be a lot of acrimony.

But you never could tell, and now Beck wondered.

She brushed her teeth, grateful she had at least that much in the way of personal toiletries left, and attempted to run a comb through her hair. The waves were separating into curls and fighting any attempt at untangling, so she finally gave up. Maybe a roomful of staties wouldn't want to believe her if she looked like a vagrant, but with Judge Nelson on her side, she had a shot.

The judge had merely nodded thoughtfully at her edited version of events—she had to keep Paul's name out of it, saying only that she'd given the items to an anonymous friend for safekeeping—asked a few crisp questions at certain intervals, and kept pouring milk from a glass Everson Creamery bottle while pressing more Pepperidge Farm cookies on her. *These aren't homemade, but they'll do. Netta used to bake a mean chocolate chip.*

The whole town had turned out for Netta Nelson's funeral. Bone cancer was awful, and it had been swift.

Judge Nelson was at the stove in his kitchen, his grey mane well-combed and his subdued maroon tie thrown back over the shoulder of a crisply ironed white button-down. His dark suit jacket hung neatly on a hook near the door to the patio; the kitchen was just as clean and neat as Helena's but with significantly more expensive appliances. "There you are," he greeted, companionably. "Sleep well?"

"Better than I have in a while." Beck felt faintly ridiculous with her coat and purse both on as if she intended to run out the door after a one-night stand. "I can't thank you enough for this, sir."

"Nonsense." His smile was warm and thoughtful, slightly distracted as he attended to the sizzling pan. "I'm very grateful you came to me, young lady. The entire town has been buzzing. Granite River is a little darker with you absent, you know."

I didn't think anyone would notice. Beck pulled out a chrome stool from the breakfast bar and perched, hoping she wouldn't leave a smear on anything. A faint odor of beeswax polish lived under the heavenly mix of bacon and coffee with a slight tang of woodsmoke—maybe he'd had a fire in the massive living-room hearth last night, to take the chill off. "You're a real charmer, Judge. Thank you."

"Of course. Besides, when a lovely young lady arrives in distress well past midnight, how can a gentleman turn her away?" He turned from the sizzling on the stove to pour coffee into a big blue pottery mug, settling it on the counter before her before returning to his work. "What on earth would I tell your father, if he found out?"

Oh, God. "Have you heard from the hospital?"

"I called Linlane General this morning after I cleared my Monday docket. The sheriff made it through surgery and is resting comfortably. I'm sure he'd be proud of you, Becca. Do you want some milk or sugar with that?"

"Milk, please? But I can get it." She hurried to slide off her perch and do so; his fridge was a big stainless-steel number. The Nelsons used to throw dinner parties; Beck heard they'd even had separate courses. "What about the staties? I'm sorry, I shouldn't be pestering you first thing in the morning, but—"

"I would be very surprised if you weren't anxious at this point. I'm expecting some backup any time now, and once we've finished breakfast we'll be on our way. Don't worry, everything will be handled." Judge Nelson paused, removing the skillet from the gas range. He fished the bacon out of its swimming pool of grease with stainless steel tongs, laying each stripe neatly on a rosebud-painted plate covered with a precisely folded paper towel. "You're quite a brave young lady, you know."

It doesn't feel that way. "I've been scared stiff since this whole thing started," Beck admitted. "And . . . and my ex-husband. . . ."

"Well, in a little while you won't have to worry about him." Nelson's smile widened.

Beck might have tried to articulate her relief, but the doorbell's chimes cascaded through a warm morning and she started, almost slopping coffee out of her cup and closing the fridge door a little too hard. She hadn't even retrieved the milk yet.

"Ah. Backup." The judge patted her shoulder as he eased past, a light dry-leaf brushing. "It's all right, young lady. Why don't you make the eggs? I'll take two, fried hard. The toaster is a bit finicky, you'll have to watch it."

"Yes, sir." Beck swallowed hard and hurried to obey. "Thank you again. And your backup."

"Oh, it's no trouble at all. Be right back."

Whole-wheat bread, thickly sliced; maybe the judge was a health nut, but the amount of bacon he'd cooked kind of argued against it. Beck heard the front door open and a mutter of male voices; for a moment it sounded like Paul and his friend.

Hopefully by now they'd found Tax's car. She'd only borrowed it for a while, so maybe she wouldn't get charges. The judge seemed to think she could plead for immunity, considering the circumstances, and maybe she wouldn't even have to tell the staties about Paul and Tax helping her.

She'd caused them enough trouble.

Beck found more rosebud plates and another coffee mug in the cabinets. She could help make this backup feel at home; maybe it was one of her father's deputies. Probably Gus Jencklin; he never seemed to like Joe much, though he was perfectly polite. Then again, Gus had moved into town their senior year of high school, so he wasn't local.

Not like Joe was.

Beck was at the toaster, watching it like a hawk while butter melted in the small egg pan Nelson had set out, when the men arrived.

Beck turned, ready to give a polite, if not downright chirpy, greeting to her saviors.

Her heart slammed so hard in her chest she swayed, her hip hitting one of the nice matching chrome drawer-pulls. Her skin crawled, every hair trying to stand straight up, and sheer terror nailed her in place.

"Hello, Becks," Joe said softly. He wasn't in uniform, just an Oakland Raiders T-shirt and jeans. He hadn't shaved, and his blue eyes were bloodshot. His service sidearm rode his belt, and one half of his mouth curled up in a facsimile of a smile. "It's nice to see you."

Judge Nelson followed him into the kitchen. "And you've already started on the eggs. My, what a good girl you are, Miss Sommers." He bustled to the stove, and Beck couldn't breathe, couldn't move, couldn't *think*. "Oh, I'm sorry, it's Mrs. Halston, isn't it. You two *are* still married, after all."

Mutual Destruction

HELENA SET THE plate down in front of Tax. "Eat up, young man."

"Thank you, ma'am." Tax had his manners on, but he was looking a bit hangdog, not to mention bloodshot. "I'm really sorry about all this. Klemp didn't tell me she was a flight risk."

"I wish I knew why she's. . . ." Helena cast a nervous glance in her nephew's direction, and *he* wished she wouldn't.

He kept his mouth shut, because there was no telling just what he'd say, even to his buddy.

Normally, Paul would find a great deal of humor in a girl stealing Tax's car. But that girl was Beck, she was out in the open again for God only knew what reason, and two of Dewey's boys had walked into flying bullets last night. Sommers had pulled through surgery, but another one of his deputies—Sam Neesdale—had his cruiser shot up out on Marckola by a group of bandanna-masked shitheads on ATVs who disappeared into the woods after turning the car into a cheese grater.

It was fast beginning to look like a war, and the staties were nervous. Troopers were coming from Eugene *and* Medford to patrol today; Dreeson thought it likely there would be another raid in Dewey's direction fairly soon.

And Beck was gone. Vanished into thin air.

We should put this girl on the Squad, Tax had snarled last night. *So far she's doing better than anyone else here.*

Paul begged to differ, but only because his entire body still vibrated with the feel of her shaking in his lap, like a bell after a good hard strike. Some of Dreeson's boys were watching the hospital in case she'd gotten a wild hare about visiting her father, but that didn't feel right either.

He hoped she was driving to Eugene, or even Salem to make contact with higher-grade law enforcement. It would bring the entire house of cards crashing down, especially for her dad, but it might also conceivably end with her alive.

Tax was also giving him some nervous sideways glances just like Hel. Probably because Klemp couldn't find a single fucking thing to joke about right now. Instead, he applied himself to his own breakfast—barely tasting a single mouthful—gulped the requisite amount of java to get him jump-started, and cleaned up his place at the table at high speed before stalking out to the porch.

Little Nat Barranie was hunched in Helena's smoking chair, bundled up in red plaid, wearing a hunting cap with fluffy fake fur earflaps, and cradling a shotgun. If someone decided to come for Hel, he'd at least raise the alarm; Dreeson thought the kid was capable enough, even if Paul remembered him in diapers.

He gave a brief nod and Cousin Nat paled, hunching even further. Everyone was treating Klemp as if he was his father, liable to snap at any moment.

Times like this, he wished he was a smoker despite the impairment to lung function and the risk of some asshole smelling it on you in-country where no tobacco should be. It was a dead giveaway, especially as the tars and nicotine leaked out through the pores.

What the fuck, Beck? Don't you trust me?

Of course, she probably didn't trust anybody at this point. All he could think was that he'd fucked up somehow, *again*, and she was out there somewhere trying to "protect" everyone else from Joe. God knew she was fucking terrified of the man, and with good reason.

At this point it was in Halston's best interests to make sure her body was never found. The image of Beck lying amid dead leaves and dirt was back in Klemp's head, interfering with rational thought.

No. She's alive, she has to be alive.

He didn't want to think about the alternative, but he had to. If the worst happened, Tax was going to help him hunt down Joe Halston, not to mention anyone else involved.

Including Dewey Johnson, who would find his career cut short in a helluva hurry.

His phone vibrated; he wrestled it free of a pocket and glanced at the face. Then he punched the screen over the "pick up" button so hard he was afraid it might shatter.

"Beck?" *I sound like I've been hit.* "Beck, where the fuck are you?" *You put the SIM card back in. Is it a signal? Are you wanting to get caught?*

"Hey, Paulie." It wasn't Beck's voice. Instead, it was the very last person on earth he wanted to hear from, and Paul stopped on the bottom of the porch steps, closing his eyes. "My wife let me use her phone. How you doin'?"

Yes, I'm going to kill him. Everything else in the world fell away, leaving only cold certainty. "Gettin' by. Dewey's looking for you, by the way. He sends his love."

"That little pissant." Joe's laugh wasn't quite as easy as usual. "I hope you didn't give him what he wanted, or Beck's going to have a very bad day."

She's still alive. But it could be a lie. His free hand curled into a fist. Nat had heard his greeting and was at Hel's front door, calling into the house; if Paul had to deal with a babble of background noise right now he might miss a clue.

So he took another few steps, gravel sliding like tiny bone chips under his soles. "Now why would I give him anything other than a good swift kick in the ass, Joe? Someone burned down Helena's sheds in the junkyard last night, and you know what that means."

That part was a lie, but Paul's instincts told him it was a good one, and had a chance of being believed. If Joe thought he had the Klemperers and Dewey's boys at each other's throats, he might get sloppy and make a mistake.

"Sorry to hear that." Halston didn't sound sorry at all. "Listen, Beck says she gave the bag to you."

Good job, sweetheart. Years ago they'd been able to make whole, complex, and completely hilarious plans just by glancing at each other across a classroom; he hoped some of that old magic still lingered. "Let me talk to her."

"No." But Halston didn't hang up, which was another indication Beck could still be alive.

If she was, he had to play this very, very carefully. "All I have to do is wait for Dewey to find you, Joe."

"Beck doesn't have that kind of time. Which means, neither do you. Here's the deal, *Paulie.*" Joe's breathing was a little ragged. Was Beck struggling? Had he just now caught her, or was he simply excited? "You hand over the bag, I hand over Beck. You can have the bitch, I'm done with her."

If you have hurt her, I will end you. And I will make it slow. He'd heard that kind of threat before, uttered by assets or hostiles hopeless with fury, so he buried it in his chest. It wasn't productive, even if it was completely true. "The whole bag, or just the jump drives?"

Never accept the first offer was standard in negotiations—hostage or otherwise—for a good reason. Besides, Joe's answer would tell Paul if there was another player on the board.

"All of it, Paulie. Don't tell me you've gone on a shopping spree."

Yep. Another player. The drives were useless to Joe, and at this point the deputy had to get out of town, not to mention stay gone as long as Dewey was still a viable force in the area.

Paul forced himself to *think*; God, what he wouldn't give to have Dez here. The man was always six steps ahead of Sunday, as Herrold used to say. "Let me talk to Beck."

"Don't tell me you're still in love with her after all these years."

"If she's dead, you have no leverage, Joe." Patiently, as if talking to a six-year-old, knowing the condescension would provoke. Not too much or the bastard might take it out on his helpless hostage, but enough to raise the chances of Joe making a mistake that could be grabbed, turned, *used*. "Nothing's stopping me from picking up the goods and taking the whole thing to the staties. Uncle D still has a few friends out that way."

"Picking up the goods?" Now Joe sounded baffled.

Which was great. Off-balance was right where Paul wanted him. "You think I'm going to keep that shit at Hel's house? You know how she feels about crank."

"Where is it?"

"Put Beck on." There was motion behind Paul, Tax shushing an excited Nat. Klemp took another few steps away from the noise, grateful the cell coverage was good out here.

It would be a bitch of a time for dropped calls.

"I'll put you on speaker." Shifting material, a slight click as the phone was set down. More small noises—*give me something to work with*, Paul pleaded silently. *Just one little tiny detail.*

A shaken, sobbing inhale. They were inside; the peculiar echo of speakerphone had the dead sound of being in a weatherproof enclosure instead of the faint static of fresh air. A small, maybe useless detail, but it could lead to another. Would Joe have her at the house on Passacola? Somewhere else? He had to have a backup hide.

"Paul?" A tiny, forlorn whisper. At least she was well enough to talk, but she sounded hopeless.

Just hold on, baby. Just take a deep breath and hold on for me. "Hey, Beck." Nice and smooth, as if ordering a pizza. "How you doing?"

"F-fine." A sobbing inhale. "I'm sorry, I told him you had it, I'm so—" The words cut off with a sharp gasp, and Paul's skin was two sizes too small for the clinical, unholy rage buzzing out from his bones.

Joe got off speaker in a hurry. "There. You heard her. Now tell me where."

Think, goddamn you. He had to make a thousand decisions at once, and all of them had to be the right ones. "That's not how this works. You know the Greyhound station on the west side of Eugene? Not the northern one, the one out on Klatsanie Boulevard?"

"I do," Joe said, cautious and businesslike.

"Be there at noon. The lunchtime crowd will give us both cover." Paul plunged onward; if he paused for even a moment Joe might make a counteroffer, and he didn't want that. "You bring Beck, I'll bring Dewey's goddamn bag. When you get there, call this number from her phone. We'll meet, I'll give you the key to a locker, you take your shit and can climb on a bus to Mexico or wherever the hell you're going. At least, that's what I'd recommend, because Dewey's convinced the world would be better off without you and I can't say my Uncle D's far behind."

A short silence while Joe thought it over filled Paul's ear with phantom noise. *Don't hang up. You want this, don't hang up.*

He had an indifferent relationship with Helena's beloved Jesus, and a live-and-let-live one with the dude's father. Oh, there were no atheists in foxholes, but there wasn't any help either; prayers didn't stop the bleeding or give you fire superiority.

But he was praying now. *God, keep her safe. I know I'm a bastard you'd rather not hear from, but she's one of your son's special ones, so just keep her safe this once and I'll take over the job for the rest of her life, I promise.*

"How do I know you won't . . ." Joe was still on the fence, or he was trawling to see what else Paul could be induced to offer.

"Because I don't give a shit about Dewey's meth empire or how dirty you are, Joe, but if Helena doesn't see Beck again soon I'm gonna get it from *her.*" It wasn't what he wanted to say—he wanted to inform Joe that no hole would be deep enough to hide in if anything happened to Beck Sommers—but it had the advantage of being absolutely honest. "And that, plus the fact that I'm related to Dreeson, is how you know I'll come without cop backup. Mutually assured destruction."

"Is that what they call it?" Joe still sounded dubious. "Hold on."

The line went silent, and it took all Paul's self-control not to yell. He was only on mute, the call was still live. It was a dead certainty there was another player—someone bigger, no doubt, someone just as filthy as Joe.

Someone who was calling the shots, who had a lot to lose if Dewey Johnson's jump drives were turned over to the staties. There had to be financial information on the little plastic bastards, and that almost certainly involved payoffs.

Oh yeah, Paul had a pretty clear picture of what was going down now, and everyone involved could shoot each other in a giant circle jerk while singing Kumbaya as far as he was concerned. As long as he had Beck clear, he didn't give a single flying fuck.

Joe unmuted. "All right," he said. "Noon at the west side Amtrak station, on Klatsanie. But if you try to fuck with me, Paulie. . . ."

"We used to be friends, Joe." It didn't matter that their teenage bond had been merely a case of no other options. *Give me something else. Anything, you bastard.* "Where's the trust, huh?"

"Were we friends? Really?" Joe's laugh was a carbon copy of his father's; he despised his old man, but probably still went cringing to him for approval. "Because as long as I can remember, I've hated your guts."

Paul had probably known and returned the favor on some subconscious level, no matter how many drives they went on or beers they sneaked together. "We don't have to be friendly to get this done, then."

"Don't fuck with me, Paulie. Noon. See you there."

Paul waited until the line went dead, then checked the time both on the phone face and his watch for good measure. Then he stood, eyes still closed, breathing in a cool, damp spring morning with the promise of sun later when the marine layer burned off. Birdsong twittered and chattered in the firs, the bushes, the blackberry tangles between junkyard rows.

The foliage meant cover, and that meant good eating.

Joe had a reason to keep Beck alive at this point, which was all to the good. The mystery player was smarter than a dirty, wife-beating deputy, which could be bad.

Either way, Paul had to plan, to account for contingencies, and good *Christ* he wished Dez was here.

"Paul?" Helena, behind him. She sounded oddly breathless.

"It's all right, ma'am." Tax, low and soft, as if they were in the bush. You didn't want sound to carry when you were outside a base's relative safety. "He's thinking."

It was what Klemp told the rest of the squad when Dez got that faraway look and tilted his head a little. *Cut the chatter, Loot's thinkin'.*

And his head hurts, Jackson might add in a mutter, but not very often.

He had to hand it to Joe. Popping a few rounds into Beck's dad not only served as revenge and a way to draw her out but also tied up a loose end; did Halston know the old man was still alive? Anyone could call the hospital and check, so he had to assume either Halston or the mystery player had done so. Which meant Joe was looking to jump ship, probably with the cash; the mystery man, if he wasn't also after the greenbacks as well as the drives, was probably looking for cover.

A smart mystery player would be heading out of town anyway, or maybe even sending someone to take care of Sommers in the hospital just to be sure.

Something deeply incriminating was hiding in those tiny pieces of circuitry and plastic. Beck had told him, haltingly, where she'd hidden the jump drives, separate from the cash and drugs because she had more raw intelligence, not to mention moxie, than anyone in Granite River could ever dream.

If Halston had any brains, he'd've hidden the drives separately in the first place. Still, the kingpin kid and Joe were definitely not on speaking terms anymore. Johnson had to have opened the bag and found the drives missing; the fact that he wasn't gunning for Paul or Uncle D was proof positive he was willing to believe a Klemperer hadn't double-crossed him.

For now.

Paul's eyes snapped open, cold grey sunlight pouring through him since his head was tilted back. He stared into the cloud cover, and all he could think of was Beck's *it's okay, I'm fine*, repeated over and over like a talisman.

Alone, terrified, under pressure that would crack even a seasoned operator, Beck still had the presence of mind to insist she'd given the entire bag, drives included, to Paul. And apparently that had held up.

She'd given him some room. Now he had to work an op with a mystery player, a civilian hostage, a fucking amateur waving a gun around—because Joe would certainly come armed, and might just decide to shoot his soon-to-be ex-wife just to keep anyone else from having her—and whatever lunchtime crowd was in the bus station on a Spring Break Monday.

The Squad had dealt with a lot worse, and he had a buddy backing him up. Beck had put him back on the board, and that was the important thing. She certainly trusted him more than Joe, a good first step. Better than he deserved, really.

He'd left her behind once. It was a mistake he'd spend the rest of his life atoning for, if he could just get her through this alive.

His phone buzzed again, and he would have hurled the goddamn thing toward the shop if there hadn't been a slim chance it was Joe calling back.

It wasn't, it was Dreeson.

They'd found Tax's car. Beck had, very politely, parked it at the Grange, unlocked, with the keys on the front seat.

Not Wise at All

HER WRISTS HURT. Tax's pain pills were a distant memory, and every muscle Beck owned was as stiff as a board. All things considered, though, she'd gotten off lightly—Joe had only slapped her twice and driven a casual punch into her gut before Judge Nelson stopped him with a direct stare and a quiet, avuncular *do you mind, this is a civilized household*.

Nelson had also put the zip ties on her wrists, solicitously asking whether they were too tight. Now the judge hummed softly as he piloted his black BMW sedan through a bright spring morning, settling into freeway speed.

At least she wasn't still tied to a dining-room chair while Joe held her hair, tipping her head painfully back, and shouted questions in her face. Beck's ears still rang; a headache throbbed savagely between her temples.

She'd just been on this stretch of freeway recently; it was still a good forty minutes to Eugene if weather and traffic both cooperated to perfection. They had plenty of time, and Nelson had also made Joe take the gag—a simple red cotton bandanna—out before they put her in the car. The corners of her lips hurt and there was crackle-dried saliva on her chin, but she didn't move to wipe it away.

Because Joe was in the back seat too, and though he kept his index finger locked outside the trigger guard of his familiar police-issue Glock, she didn't think he had much impulse control left at this point.

Beck watched him, barely glancing outside to check for landmarks. To any other car on the highway the trio in the sedan probably looked like a family outing, or coworkers carpooling.

At least Paul had played along during the phone call. Was he furious at her? Probably. She'd done *exactly* what he told her not to, stolen Tax's car as well, and now. . . .

"How long you been talking to him?" Joe asked again.

He wouldn't believe the truth, even if she had the energy to repeat herself. No, her ex-husband—even if the paperwork wasn't done, Beck was going to consider herself divorced in every single blessed sense of the word from this very moment on—was convinced she'd been somehow seeing Hel's nephew for months.

"Joseph." Judge Nelson's patience was growing thin. A lawyer hearing that tone from the bench might well quail and redirect. "I'm not interested in hearing your marital squabbles." He checked the rearview, and his gaze lingered on Beck for a moment.

I might as well ask. Beck wet her lips and wished she hadn't, because Joe stared at her mouth. A long time ago she might have felt flattered, but now there was only weary revulsion. "Why did you shoot my father?"

"Cleanup." Joe didn't even bother to look ashamed. "Everything nice and tidy."

At least he admitted it. And her father had pulled through surgery. Or had Nelson lied?

The judge piped up. "He knew too much." How did he sound just the same—precise, a little amused, full of casual authority? "Your father and I have been business partners for a long time. Mr. Johnson is a junior member of a very large enterprise; when certain others in town went legal, a vacuum was created and he moved in like the parasite he is."

Of all the insanities of the past few days, this was the one she had the most trouble wrapping her tired brain around. *You're lying*, she wanted to scream.

But it all made sense now. Had Dad pushed her to reconcile with Joe because of all this? It was like dusk with heavy fog in the hills above the river—a soft, sticky cloud of lies all around her, and she kept running into things because she couldn't *see*. But it was all she'd ever known, and how on earth could she suspect her own *father?*

He had raised her, fed her, tucked her in at night, come to every choir recital and parent conference, brushed her hair, listened to her every day at dinner, put aside money for college that ended up going for the down payment on the Passacola house—she didn't know how much of that fund was drug cash, now—and a million other things.

Her father loved her.

Yet he had lied, not once but over and over again. Her big, strong, upright Dad, unbending and proud, the man who always said *you gotta have a clean conscience, pumpkin*, had lied about Paul, about Joe, about right and wrong itself. He was a *sheriff*, for God's sake.

And Joe was a deputy.

"I don't think it's wise to ask many more questions," the judge continued. How many others in Granite River or Linlane County were implicated? No wonder the staties were raiding Dewey's operations; they were the only ones who could.

Except some of them were probably paid off too. Beck should have driven Tax's car right up to Salem and screamed her head off on the Capitol steps.

Nelson had apparently spent some of last night packing; he had four suitcases in the back of the BMW. Joe had gotten the memo too because he had a new black Eastpak, beloved of schoolkids, college students, and the houseless. The two men intended to go their separate ways after this, and Beck didn't like them discussing it so openly in front of her.

Either they were very sure they'd escape and never be caught, or they were going to silence her permanently. She had one slim chance of survival left, and she'd probably destroyed every single glimmer of even a bare minimum of friendship with anyone in Granite River after this. Not to mention ruining the reunion and causing Helena grief—Paul would do his best to make sure Beck was safe, because that was just how he *was*.

But then he'd walk out of her life again, this time for good. She'd be right back where she started—or maybe in prison, since she'd spent the last few days breaking every goddamn law in the book. She'd have to live with disappointing Helena, too. Not to mention the knowledge that her father was a liar.

At least in prison she'd be fed, and maybe left alone if she was quiet enough.

"No," she said, softly. "Not wise at all."

Joe moved restlessly, as if he was about to thump her on the leg, leaving a big dark bruise among all the others from the not-accident. At least now she could be a hundred percent sure he'd meant to kill her.

He'd been working up to it for a long time, like any abusive dickwad, and he might well succeed. If Paul couldn't get to Eugene, or was late, or if Joe decided to just start shooting . . . there were a hundred ways Beck could die today. All she could think about was whether or not it would hurt, and how it might actually be a relief.

Nelson began to hum again. After a few minutes, Beck identified the tune.

The asshole was singing a medley from *Oklahoma!*, for God's sake.

Seen the Statistics

PAUL DROVE, BECAUSE he was better at it and Tax was busy study-ing the layout of the bus station from images online, comparing it to a rough sketch of entrances, exits, and blind spots Paul had made from memory on a piece of Aunt Hel's scratch paper.

Beck had the presence of mind to convince Joe that Paul had the entire bag; Tax was a wildcard on their side. On the other hand, she might well break and tell them all about Paul's buddy if they hurt her badly enough, which would mean an ambush.

Or, worse, she might break and confess from soup to nuts, then Joe would go radio silent because he'd have everything he wanted. She'd been smart to split the haul; Paul had been so busy getting Dewey off the board he hadn't had time to pick up the goddamn jump drives yet.

And they might never find her body once Joe finished with her.

The image of Beck lying dead on the forest floor was back again. Sometimes there was a trickle of blood coming from her pretty mouth, other times her eyes were wide open, filmy and terribly accusing. God, like a sadistic drill instructor, obviously thought Klemp was a stupid stu-dent needing the lesson applied over and over, just so it sank in.

Tax reached for his stainless-steel travel mug, full of Helena's piping-hot coffee. "Walking distance," he said, meditatively. "At a brisk pace for an adult in good shape, let's say three miles an hour. I'm surprised she was conscious enough to drive, she must've been in some pain—but she can't have gotten far from that barn." He meant the Grange; he was still a city boy, for all he could survive in the bush as well as any member of the Squad.

"Stubborn girl." Paul wished he could jam the accelerator down, derby around these fucking civilians all over the road. Most people didn't *drive*, they just *steered*, and the difference was acute.

The sheer will keeping Beck on her feet and functioning was impressive. He'd seen men walking with the grey ropes of intestines slithering out of their violated bellies, shock and determination forcing them along until dumb meat simply caved in. She was doing the same, and without the benefit of even cursory training.

"Plus it was the middle of the night." Tax couldn't let it go, or he thought focusing on where Beck had gone last night would help Klemp keep on the rails. "All she had was that jacket but she didn't get hypothermic. Her shoes were in bad shape, too. So unless she had someone come out and pick her up. . . ."

Paul thought about it, and arrived at the same place he had the other however-many times they'd kicked this conversation around. "Possible but unlikely."

"You sure?" It had to be asked, and Tax's tone suggested he was wary of Klemp taking offense.

"Pretty sure. Her dad's ruled out, the other deputies are Joe's friends and it stands to reason one or two of them might be dirty." She had to have gone to someone she trusted, someone she felt was above corruption. And that someone had betrayed her, but *who*? "But I'd guess Joe's been isolating her for years. Hel says she doesn't have close friends anymore, other than Mary out at the coffee stand." Ms. Parrack had been at work this morning, with her cousin Gina in the espresso shack next to her. If the out-of-towner was the secret player, she'd have to be able to clone herself to pull off *that* trick. "And Beck isn't going to risk someone else getting hurt if she can help it."

"Oh, she'll just call *us* to get our asses shot off." Tax sighed, but hurried to clarify. "I'm not mad. You should have told me to tie her up or something."

You're right. Paul hit the blinker, swinging out into the left lane to pass a lumbering semi. "Yeah, that would have gone over real well."

"It would have saved us from this." Tax worked on his coffee for a few seconds, put the cup back. "She said something last night, while we were driving."

Paul let the silence do the talking. He wasn't in a joking mood, and if this was a one-liner he was going to pull over and get a couple things straight with his good buddy.

"She said, *you think I'm going to survive this, that's adorable*." Tax's impression of Beck needed work, but Paul could still hear her behind the words. "I tried to reassure her. But, uh, have you considered your girl might have a death wish?"

"You mean like Jackson?" A short, deep sigh took Paul by surprise; he checked the blind spot and returned to the right lane, comfortably past the blockage. "Or any of us, really?"

"Like a serious case of PTSD. Just how long was that guy working on her?"

"Too long." *And that's my fault, too.* "She could get to her old house from the Grange, but I don't think she'd want to go back there. I don't think she'd try to thumb a ride either." Beck's father had sternly impressed the dangers of hitchhiking on his precious baby girl.

"I hope not. That shit's dangerous."

"Here we are," Paul addressed the windshield, "a couple of highly trained killers—courtesy of Uncle Sam—and this asshole thinks *hitchhiking* is dangerous."

"I've seen the statistics," his buddy said primly, and even in this situation Paul had to laugh.

Still, the chuckles bore an uncomfortable similarity to pre-operation nerves. This could go very, very sideways indeed.

And if it did, Beck would pay a terrible price.

THEY ARRIVED almost an hour early; Tax baled out a few blocks away from the station and vanished while Paul set himself to finding a parking spot in the pickup area. They could have used earpieces to stay in touch, but Joe might spot that and get nervous. So it was good old-fashioned "get in position before playing it loose." At least both of them could ID Beck on sight; Paul might recognize the mystery player on the other side if it was a local.

This wasn't the station closest to Granite River, but it *was* the station he'd left for basic from; four other recruits in the area had gotten on the bus too, the Army already beginning the "don't ask questions, just get in the damn transport" training. If he'd ever bothered to come back on leave, this would've been where Hel picked him up.

He should've come home earlier. But each time he had the chance, he'd punked, leaving Beck in the trenches with no backup. No wonder he'd gotten shot to shit—it was probably the only way Hel's beloved Jesus could get a stubborn, stupid sonofabitch to come back and rescue his first and only love.

Well, he was on the job now, and he would make up for lost time as best he could.

Paul drifted with the crowd. Monday of Spring Break was busier than chickens with scratch to go after. The mystery player could already be here if he knew where to get off the freeway and slip past bottlenecks like Paul did.

Beck. Where are you? His pulse kept trying to pick up the pace, and that damn taste of copper wouldn't leave his mouth. He was too keyed-up, just a hair away from sweating, and that was bad.

She needed him cold and efficient right now. Beck had finally, *finally* outright asked for help, no matter that she'd probably had a gun to her head while doing so, and Paul Klemperer intended to deliver. At this point it didn't matter who the mystery player was.

They just had to wait and see.

Ten minutes after he entered the station, he headed for the rest-rooms on the east side. The men's room was only moderately crowded, and just as Paul was washing his hands with harsh pink powdered soap Tax appeared from a stall and used the sink next to his. He was even wearing a pair of reading glasses with stainless-steel frames, and with the suit and tie from his luggage he looked like a young professional heading up to Salem for the day.

There was a quick tug at Paul's jacket pocket—completely intentional, a friendly reminder he wasn't alone. Grey was the best pickpocket on the Squad; the damn magic tricks were probably practice. The rest of them weren't bad at it either, except Dez, who didn't have or want the subtlety, and Boom, who could manage half the time only with enough luck and if his target was blind drunk.

Now a key from a large, empty coin-op locker would be in Paul's pocket. Even if Beck had been induced to give a description of Tax, this would pass unnoticed unless the mystery player was in the bathroom with them and had eagle eyes, not to mention a dose of telepathy. But everyone else in the bathroom was minding their own business, their backs to the mirror, and they were all strangers.

Joe might trust a non-local, but Beck? Not likely, not with this. Paul kept a lookout for familiar faces, saw none. Tax was moving with the crowd, playing his part and keeping loose watch, but he wouldn't move in until go-time.

It was so goddamn good to have backup. Hopefully Beck was feeling the same relief, knowing he'd be on his way to take care of this.

But Paul didn't think that was likely. She thought she was all alone, and he was her last desperate ploy. Maybe she even thought he wouldn't show at all; Christ knew he'd left her in the lurch before, going off to basic.

Don't think about that.

Time ticked away, arrivals and departures displayed on new digital boards and announced by ghostly voices over a crackling intercom. Tired mothers with toddlers, grandmothers with large bags and rubber-footed canes, a few soldiers coming back after leave or waiting on a layover, and everything in between. People were traveling for work, for family—the reunion Monday was always barbeque day and Paul was sorry to miss that. He'd get a plate later.

With Beck.

Come on, sweetheart. Just stay alive until I can get to you. Stubborn woman, taking the entire weight of the world on her shoulders, trying to protect everyone. The more he thought about it, the more certain he was that Beck had been terrified of Joe coming after Helena next and taken off to draw all the danger away, like Jackson and his fucking "diversions."

Dez hated that. Every time Jackson pulled one of those stunts he was in for a bulling from their leader later, and took it cheerfully. *It worked, right? We all made it, didn't we? Good.*

And Dez would fix the wildcard of the Ghost Squad with a beady glare. *It could have been otherwise, soldier. Get the fuck out of my face and don't do that shit again.*

Noon ticked by. Paul's nerves stretched tighter and tighter; he worked the crowd, but no woman with blonde highlights was his Beck. No sign of Joe or any other face he recognized.

At ten past, his phone buzzed in his pocket. He dug it out, hoping it wasn't Dreeson calling with bad news.

It was Beck's number. "You're late," Klemp said, pleasantly. Adrenaline caused a snap freeze, turning all his insides to pure, clear ice.

"You know how traffic is in the city." The signal was good and strong; Joe came in clear. And behind his words lingered the ghost of an announcement—*all passengers embarking for Roseburg, Medford, Grant's Pass, and points south*—echoed by the overhead speakers. He was in the bus station. "Walk over to the lockers, Paulie. Keep your hands where I can see them."

Oh, no you don't. "Let me hear Beck." Klemp's nape tingled; it was the same sensation he had when an op really got engaged, between the first mortar pop and the resultant explosion, or when a squadmate whispered *light the bitch up, we're a go, repeat, a go* in his earpiece. "Or no play."

"What, you think I'm a welsher?" The bastard even laughed. "Hold on."

There was a mutter—probably a threat—and then the only voice Paul wanted to hear at that moment came through the phone's tiny speaker.

"Paul?" A jagged gasp. "Be careful, he's got a gun."

And you think I don't? But she was doing good, doing flat-out fantastic, trying to give him every advantage she could. A pleasure to work with the woman, indeed and as always. "I wouldn't want it any other way," he said. "Just try to relax, all right? I've got this."

"Paul—" That was all she got out before Joe came back on the line.

"I've enjoyed having my wife back for a little while." Joe didn't sound winded; if Beck was struggling, he'd at least be breathing a little heavier. So she was compliant for now, or the mystery player had her under physical control. "But I think she's right, it's time to move on. Let's get this done, Paulie."

Oh, I agree. It's high time we put this to bed. "Where in the locker bays? There's a few of them, in case you hadn't noticed."

"You tell me."

Nice try, amateur. None of the Squad would fall for that bullshit, not even before Sparky got his hands on them. "Nope."

"North end," Joe said, finally. "Keep your hands where I can see them. You even *breathe* in a way I don't like, I'll pump a couple bullets into my loving wife and take my chances."

"I'm on my way." This time Paul hung up without waiting for more; he wanted Joe a little more unsettled. He stuffed the phone in a safe pocket and turned the bill of his Granite River Logjammers baseball cap—swiped from Beck's Jetta, looked like the one he'd lost just before he went into the service—to the front.

Tax would now know they were in play. And the cap still fit perfectly.

Klemp turned on his heel and ambled for the north end of the locker bays, keeping his hands clearly visible. He even considered whistling, but that would be a bit much.

Besides, his mouth was too goddamn dry.

I've Had Better

"WAIT UNTIL HE finds out what a whore you are," Joe muttered. He held her right arm in his left hand, his own right hand under his folded jacket and the police-issue Glock hidden under it shoved so far into Beck's side she would probably bruise there too, but what was one more? "I should just shoot you a couple times to save him the trouble."

Judge Nelson was somewhere in the crowd, and it was a safe bet he was armed too. Paul had no idea the judge was involved, and she hoped he'd brought Tax. Of course, Beck had stolen his buddy's car, so Tax was probably furious and on his way to Vegas for that wedding.

Beck wouldn't blame him.

She could drag Joe's arm down, force him to shoot her instead of Paul. That was probably how this was going to end, in fact, and for all her frantic thinking in the car there was no way around it. She didn't know if it hurt to get shot.

Guess I'll find out.

At least if he killed Beck right here in public, he might finally suffer some consequences. Maybe Amy Lorton would visit him in prison.

Judge Nelson had cut the zip ties off her wrists, and her hands throbbed with pain. Wiggling her fingers to get some feeling back was dangerous, but she did it; Joe had enough to worry about at the moment. Every time someone in the crowd got too close, he jammed the gun a little harder against her ribs.

The lights were too bright, and the announcements overhead were like the voice of God in an old movie, thundering through her already-massive headache. She felt greasy all over, hadn't really combed her hair, and one of her sneaker soles was flapping loose.

She wasn't even going to die in clean underwear, like Dad joked about. *Change 'em every day, just in case. You remember that, Becca.*

Joe would seem like a solicitous boyfriend to any observer; maybe she looked sick or just woozy from travel. You saw all sorts in bus or train stations, and ignored it with the strict courtesy the non-rich paid each other when they could. If you had the money, flying was worth enduring the security theater.

Beck had never once been on a plane.

"Keep looking down," Joe hissed in her ear. "Or I swear, Beck. . . ."

Usually, he didn't need to finish the sentence. It was an old threat, but somehow at the moment it didn't have the usual sting. "Or you'll shoot me?" She kept her voice low—but she could start screaming, attract some attention.

She just had no idea what to do *after* that, and suspected it was a good way to get shot sooner rather than later.

"I could always take you with me." His tone said he was wearing a patented Joe Halston grin, the one everyone thought was so charming because they didn't notice the way it never reached his baby-blue eyes. "We've had some good times, haven't we? A nice little place in Mexico where I can teach you how to be a lady."

I would actually rather die, I think. And I'm gonna get my wish. "Maybe you had a good time," she whispered back. Thank God she'd taken her birth control pills religiously, hiding them in a kitchen flour canister where he'd never think to look. "But frankly, I've had better."

His hand clamped on her arm so hard she gasped as they stopped at an entrance to the locker bays. She stared at the floor, at the feet of ordinary people passing by in all sorts of shoes—brogans, boots, heels, sneakers, sandals—and a pair of desert-taupe boots appeared, separating from the stream of travelers.

Beck couldn't help herself. She looked up.

Paul sauntered out of the crowd, in a navy T-shirt, jeans, and that same dark jacket. He had a Logjammers cap on, his hair trying to escape from underneath, and his dark eyes glittered from its shade. He stepped far too lightly for his size, almost prowling, like a cat.

And he was looking directly at her. A jolt spilled down her spine from the contact, and a flood of sudden, irrational hope threatened to collapse her like nothing else to this point had managed to.

Paul. Her lips shaped the word, but she couldn't find her breath.

He came to a halt just outside the bays, cocking his head. "Hey, Becks." As if they were the only two people here, or as if this was a crowded school hall at passing time and they had only a brief moment for a stolen kiss before the bell rang. "How you holding up?"

I don't think I'm dealing with any of this very well. "I'm sorry," she began, desperately. "Paul, there's—"

"Shut the fuck up." Joe jammed the gun into her side again, and Beck flinched.

"You keep acting like this, someone's gonna notice, Joe." Paul's eyes had turned even darker. It was almost eerie, seeing the change—pupil and iris almost the same color now, giving his gaze a depthless piercing. When that happened, he was determined to get into trouble no matter what she said. "It only takes one person to alert a station attendant."

"What are they gonna do, arrest me?" Joe didn't snort, but neither did he jam the gun against her side again. "Where is the fucking bag, Paulie?"

"I keep having to teach you how this works." How did Paul sound so effortlessly cold, so goddamn in-charge? It was a far cry from the anxious, touchy boy she'd known. "You think I want you behind me while I waltz right towards the prize?" *Dumbass*, his tone shouted, and she hoped Joe wouldn't lose his temper.

"Then what?" The ice in her ex-husband's tone told her it was very, very close. If he didn't shoot her, if he managed to drag her out of here, he would make her pay.

I would rather die, she thought again, and knew she was going to get her wish.

"I take the key from my pocket nice and slow, a show of good faith." Paul said it slowly and seriously, a good impression of their high school science teacher Mr. Barkley. Maybe Joe even caught the resemblance. "I'll set the key down, and you let go of Beck. Simple."

Beck tore her gaze away from Paul's. She scanned the crowd, looking for Judge Nelson. Now would be a great time for him to come up and stick a weapon in her rescuer's back, and then she'd have to make some kind of move. Her heart pounded so hard she thought longingly of vomiting, but there was nothing in her stomach. Besides, if she twitched Joe might shoot her just on principle.

"I don't think so." Her ex-husband didn't loosen his hold, but he didn't jab her in the ribs again either. "Hold the key up. We'll go there together. If the bag's there, you and Beck can walk. I see you came packing."

"Did you really expect me not to?" Paul's faint steely smile didn't alter one whit. "Come on, Joey."

Oh, crap. He hates being called that. She kept glancing at the crowd, faces swimming because her vision blurred. She wasn't crying; she was just so tired, and her heart was thundering. The pressure behind her eyeballs mounted another notch. Maybe they'd pop out and go rolling amid all the hurrying feet.

"Fine." Joe shifted his weight, and his bruising grip on her arm stayed nice and strong. "Show me the key. Slowly."

Maybe they looked like strangers having a casual conversation; maybe they looked like friends meeting up. Beck kept scanning for the judge while Paul slowly reached into his jacket pocket and drew out an orange tab.

Where the hell had he gotten a key from?

From one of these lockers, duh. He got here early. Beck's breath came short and high in her chest; her heart was thundering again. *Please don't let me pass out.*

Paul held the key up. "See?"

Joe exhaled harshly. A thin sheen of sweat clung to his forehead. "Which locker?"

Paul consulted the attached tab, again like Mr. Barkley, who had moved out of town four years ago. Up to Portland, she'd heard, to marry his husband. The town gossips were still having a great time with that one.

"1131, section D." Paul lowered his hand. The key itself was flat, with a grey plastic head; you could pop the ring holding the flat orange tab if you had a pocketknife or even just a little determination. Beck wondered how many of those they had to replace per year, and how much it cost.

Her brain kept shivering between one inconsequential and the next. Paul was bluffing. It wasn't the right key, and Beck knew because—

"Let's go." Joe gave her a little shake, as if warning a misbehaving puppy.

"You think I want you behind me?" Paul repeated. "You go first."

"And have you jump me?"

"For Chrissake, you dipshit, I'm not going to risk you shooting Beck." Paul all but rolled his eyes. For a moment he was a teenager again, and this was just a prank or a school play. "Aunt Hel would kill me."

Joe was silent for a long moment. Beck watched the moving passengers, her gaze roving desperately. None of them even looked in her direction, all intent on their own little dramas.

"Fine," her ex-husband said. "Which way?"

"You can read." Paul gave the key a little shake, dangling the orange tab like a tiny matador's cape. "Section D." Maybe he was deliberately trying to provoke.

"Paul. . . ." All she could produce was a dry croak.

"It's all right, Beck." How could he sound so certain? "Everything's under control."

THE BAYS WERE arranged like a ladder, two passages on either side with connecting rungs; the D hall was floored with empty, scuffed linoleum greenish under a sickly wash of fluorescent glow. One of the light tubes was at the end of its life, buzzing like a fly zapper. The announcements sounded a bit underwater here, bad acoustics added to speaker fuzz, and the crowd-sound of the concourse turned into faraway seashore static.

72 HOUR LIMIT, the signs said. Beck tried to think how long it had been since she was last here, and couldn't even remember what day it was.

"1131," Joe said. "What next, genius?"

"I'll give you the key, you give me Beck, and we're done."

"Do you think *I'm* stupid?" Joe gave her a contemptuous little shake, as if Beck was the one running this whole thing. He dragged her few steps closer to the lockers, their blank metal faces watching with very little interest. Maybe they saw this sort of thing all the time. "Open it up. If the bag's in there, you can have the bitch. She never was any good."

"Oh, Joe," Beck said wearily. If she was going to die, she might as well tell the truth. "I faked it every time, and Amy probably does too. You have to know that."

A flicker of amusement crossed Paul's face, like he couldn't believe she'd mouthed off in class. That was, after all, *his* job, and sometimes she'd suspected he did it for no real reason except to make her laugh.

"Let's all stay on target, shall we?" He dangled the key again, and pointed at a spot right next to the locker. "Right there, Joe. You can peek in and nobody will get shot, which should satisfy us both."

"Don't." Beck was helpless to stop herself. "Just let him kill me. Please." *Get out of here, I shouldn't have dragged you into this. The judge is here, and he's going to—*

"Beck, sweetheart." Now Paul regarded Joe steadily. "Let me and Joey sort this out. You just hang tight."

"Fucking women," Joe muttered. "Open it up, Paulie."

"Stand there, and I will."

Joe took a step towards the locker. Beck's entire body was leaden, and her vision wavered. Her pulse trip-hammered, and her knees almost buckled.

Paul's back was to the connecting hall. A shadow swelled, quick light mincing footsteps, and Judge Nelson appeared, taking the corner at a speed that suggested he knew what he wanted and everyone should stay out of his way. A knee-length dark overcoat, a fedora over his grey head—added to his wingtips and perfectly pressed grey trousers—turned him into the very image of a busy businessman. Nobody would even look twice.

But one of his gloved hands rose, and there was an old-fashioned revolver glinting in it.

He stepped right up to Paul's back, and jammed the gun against it. "Please don't make any sudden moves, Mr. Klemperer."

Oh, God. Maybe Paul would think she'd double-crossed him. Beck opened her mouth to plead, to say something, *anything.*

Paul beat her to it. "The mystery man." He raised both hands slowly, still dangling the key. "I was wondering when you'd show up."

The judge was having none of it. "This is taking far too long. Open the locker, please."

"I hope you're not nervous." Paul moved slowly, balanced and easy, rolling through each step. "If you get nervous, I might too."

"I assure you, I am completely calm." Judge Nelson prodded him. "Open it."

"Hey, Beck." If Paul was angry it didn't show; there were only those dark, dark eyes. Yet he smiled, a slow, electric grin. "I got a buddy who does magic tricks. You want to see one?"

"Paul," Joe said, almost wearily, "for Christ's sake, shut the fuck up."

The key slid into the lock. Paul twisted it; the click was very loud.

The world shrank to a still, small point balanced on a knife-edge. The frantic pounding of Beck's pulse fell away, the light was suddenly very bright, and every scuff, scrape, dent, and detail stood out in pitiless clarity. She had no idea what Judge Nelson would see when the locker opened, frankly.

All she knew was that Paul was going to get shot, because he was bluffing.

The door began to open, its metal hinges squeaking, and Beck *moved*, slapping her right hand over Joe's on her arm and going limp.

Smart as a Fox

LIKE ANY OP HITTING the redline, it happened quick.

The mystery player went down with a grunt—he'd been focusing so hard on Paul, he probably never noticed Tax drifting behind him, ready to cover a buddy's back. Paul had Joe placed just right, ready for the door to pop wide and distract, and the critical part was getting close enough to immobilize the dickbag before he could get a shot into Beck.

Who apparently had her own ideas, because she dropped floorward just as the door swung wide, collapsing as if her strings had been cut.

Beck! Paul was already moving, popping a short right jab to Joe's face without any real weight behind it. His left hand was occupied with other things—like getting the 9mm in Joe's right hand deflected enough. He didn't ask for much—just a few degrees, just enough to keep her safe.

Four pounds of pull, or a little less if he's one of those light-trigger bastards, gotta hope his discipline's good. Instead of landing a punch, his thumb brushed Joe's hair because Beck's weight was pulling her ex to the side. Paul grabbed the jacket over Joe's right hand, yanking hard, and his girl was smart as a fox, because she also kicked her ex's shin as hard as she could on her way down.

Connor Sommers's baby was a fighter, and it showed.

But it wasn't enough. Joe staggered but didn't go down, and though Beck's arm was torn free of his grasp . . .

. . . He did manage to squeeze off a shot.

All Over

MUZZLE FLASH, her ears ringing, and Beck hit the ground in a graceless heap.

Right on her ass, in fact, and her teeth clicked together painfully hard. She scrambled away, her palms burning against linoleum, and her left sneaker gave up the ghost, the sole tearing free just before her shoulder hit the bank of metal lockers opposite. She was going so fast her head bounced against metal, too, and she saw stars for a brief endless moment.

Am I dead?

A faint ringing was the only sound; either she was temporarily deaf or her ears had decided they'd had enough of her bullshit for a while. She scooted along crabwise, her shoulder scraping the lockers, as Paul hit Joe. It was a good one, a solid shot to the face, and her ex-husband staggered back. There was another bright flash, a padded-hammer sound, and the shot whined away down the hall, tearing gouges in thin metal doors.

Joe staggered back, reeling, and Beck lunged upright. It took her two tries; she was vaguely aware Tax had appeared out of thin air like some kind of genie and had Judge Nelson in a headlock. The judge's revolver was held neatly away but still in his bony hand, and *it* spoke now, the flash drenching the hallway and leaving ghostly afterimages.

Paul drove another jab to Joe's face, but the two of them had scrapped countless times on the playground or behind a school gym, not to mention in the meadow near the old Clemens mine. Joe avoided the blow, throwing himself backward, and Beck staggered frantically, trying to avoid getting in the way.

If he got hold of her now, it was all over.

Everything was moving too slowly, in swimming nightmare-time, and paradoxically too goddamn fast. She dug in her jeans pocket as she scrambled, body-warmed metal squirting between her fingers.

Joe had given her a cursory patdown and pawed through her purse, but on her first visit to Eugene—not too long ago, in fact—she'd spent a few moments in the Jetta, parked neatly across the street in the pickup area, working the orange tab free of a different locker key. Had it been two days ago, or three?

She couldn't remember, and it didn't matter at the moment. What mattered was getting to the end of the hall, because she'd chosen a smaller locker near the far corner of the D section. It had seemed like a great idea at the time, since she could peer down the connecting hall and see if anyone was nearby.

Now, it looked too far away. But Paul and Tax had chosen this part of the storage section too, which had to be a sign, a bit of good luck for once, and—

Joe spun, attempting to grab her; even now, he wouldn't just let her go.

His fingers curled in her hair, giving a sharp, vicious yank. But Paul grabbed his arm, locking it, and Beck tore free. She bolted, each drunk-weaving step sending a slapping jolt up from her left foot, now with only a sock between it and the worn industrial linoleum.

The key slipped away from her tweezing, sweating fingers once again. Material tore and Beck yanked her entire pocket inside-out, the key now free. Another shot whined down the hall, followed by a skittering metal sound.

Someone's going to notice the guns going off soon.

It didn't matter. All that mattered was reaching the right door.

The orange plastic tab was still in the Jetta, and maybe that's why Paul had picked a locker in this section to bluff with. Either way, she remembered where it was—three from the corner, middle row, a bank of smaller cubbies.

It didn't have to be very big.

Beck scrabbled at the keyhole, casting a short, sharp glance over her shoulder.

Tax had Judge Nelson on the floor now; Tax's chin was up as he scanned the hall, his black hair wildly mussed, and he had a very businesslike black automatic in his own hand. He was taking careful aim at Joe's back, but Paul was in the way. Time had slowed down, and Beck strained against its flow.

The key turned. She wrenched the locker open, plunging her hand inside. Her questing fingers found plastic, but that wasn't what she wanted.

She dragged the .38 from Dewey's bag out of the locker's depths just as Joe reached her. She'd even loaded the gun despite the danger; a few days earlier, having driven all this way to hide a final card that might buy her free of a man who wouldn't see reason, she'd thought it very likely she might have to point the damn thing at Joe while she made her getaway.

Beck Sommers had finally won one. She stepped away from the lockers, almost mincingly, and there was now plenty of time to level the gun, making her triangle just as Dad had taught her—*remember, pumpkin, you squeeze, you don't pull*—and thumb the hammer back.

Her finger closed over the trigger.

Beck squeezed.

No Fury

SOMEONE ON THE concourse had noticed their little party. And if they hadn't heard the first few shots, the one Beck squeezed off, deliberately aimed high—or so Paul hoped—probably did the trick, because there was distant screaming in the crowd-noise and the sound of running feet.

Joe skidded to a stop. Paul had the dirty cop's sidearm, and had also been intending to run the motherfucker down. His bad leg ached but it wasn't buckling, and that was all a man could ask for.

Beck stood, slim and short and impossibly small, her green eyes wide and her hair a curling, gold-kissed cloud. Dark circles stood out under those bright, feverish eyes, and her wrists looked far too thin to handle any recoil. Her T-shirt was torn, half the buttons on her plaid overshirt were missing, one of her shoes had lost its sole, and red spots burned high on her flour-pale cheeks.

She was beautiful.

Joe stood stock-still, his hands dropping to his sides. They flexed and released like he could feel her throat under his palms, and Beck stared at the man she had married.

Oh, baby. Don't do it.

More shouts, more running feet. Nobody out there would have any idea what the fuck was happening, but it was only a matter of time before the cops showed up.

"Beck. . . ." Joe didn't sound quite so britches-big now. In fact, he sounded like a man discovering the truth of an old adage—that hell hath no fury like a woman who is done with your bullshit.

Or something like that.

"You shot my daddy." All things considered, Beck's voice was soft, reasonable, almost kind. But there was an edge to every word, and Paul knew that tone, because he'd heard it from his buddies, or from hostiles brought to bay. Hell, he'd even heard it from his own throat, once or twice.

It was the lunatic calm of someone who was armed and had nothing to lose.

"Rebecca." Joe straightened, and raised his hands a little. Any cop would know how dangerous this shit was—a domestic dispute with live ammo—and he had only himself to blame. "Put the gun down."

"I don't think so." Beck took a single sideways step, moving carefully, her gaze fixed on her ex. "Come towards me, Joe. Walk this way."

"Beck—"

"Shut the fuck up and do what I tell you." Visibly trembling, she still held her triangle—and the gun—rock steady. Of course her daddy had taught her how to shoot, but the hammer was down now since she'd already spent one round. That might buy the blond bastard she'd married some time. "Years, Joe. For *years*."

Paul didn't like the thought that she was working up to something irrevocable. He had his own piece, and could get Joe trussed with little problem.

But she might decide to unload into him, too—and it was pretty much what he deserved. Where had the fucking gun come from?

Dewey's bag. She kept quiet about it, just in case. Christ, she almost had Dez beat for plans and contingencies, Paul couldn't wait to introduce the two of them. The world would tilt on its fucking axis; they'd be running the entire country inside six months if they took a mind to it.

If it meant she was alive to do it, Paul wouldn't mind one iota. "Beck, sweetheart," he said, soft but crisp. "Calm down."

"Oh sure." She sniffed, heavily, and her eyes glimmered. But the words were steady. "That's what men always say. *Calm down, it's just a joke.* Not this time." She thumbed the hammer, and it rose obediently. "No, sir."

"Becca—" Joe was having a little trouble keeping up with how thoroughly the tables had turned.

"Shut the fuck *up*," she snapped. "My God. You are such a piece of shit, Joey. You really are."

"Beck." It was risky to keep talking. If Paul kept her attention, Joe might do something stupid like rush her. "He's unarmed, and I've got zips. Let me just get him tied down and we can wait for the cops to arrive, huh? Don't do this, baby. Don't."

"Why not?" Now she sounded sad, and genuinely curious. Her gaze didn't leave Joe, and there was no pity or desperation in it, just weary knowledge. "He won't stop. He'll never stop."

"You're my *wife*—" Joe started, and Paul could have cheerfully strangled the dumbass. He was almost close enough to take the goddamn deputy down, but if Beck got nervous and squeezed again. . . .

"Let me do it." His own voice startled him, pitched loud enough to carry. There was a feedback squeal over the announcement speakers; Beck flinched.

The gun still held steady, though.

"Let me do it," Paul repeated. "If you honestly want him dead, baby, let *me* kill him." *Because if you do, it will eat you up inside.*

Deep down, she wasn't like him. Maybe that was part of the attraction; Beck Sommers was everything he wasn't, all his sharp broken edges fitting perfectly into her softness, making a complete whole.

He'd been missing his other half for over a decade, because he was just as dumb as Joe-fucking-Halston. If he had any ego left after being a card-carrying member of the Ghost Squad, it might be feeling a little bruised.

Thankfully, he'd always known he wasn't the sharpest knife in the drawer. It didn't matter, not so long as he could get her off the ledge right now.

Beck exhaled, shakily. "He won't stop. Ever."

"Yes, he will." Paul willed her to just hang on a few seconds longer. He was almost, *almost* close enough. "One way or another, baby. But if you really want him dead, let me take care of it. Don't do this." All the words he should have said earlier crowded his throat, jammed against each other hot and sour and rocky. "Don't, baby."

"Behind my back," Joe piped up. "The whole fucking time, you fucking whore. I'm glad I shot your fucking daddy. Do it. *Come on, I want you to*—"

Paul nudged him behind the knee, and big blond Joe went down like a dropped brick. Paul wasn't gentle about getting the deputy's gym-muscled arms under control and he had to dig for the zips a little longer than he liked, but eventually he got them on Joe's wrists. The entire time, his heart beat thin and sour in his throat, and he expected Beck to pull the trigger at any moment.

Finally, he had a knee in the bastard's back. Joe wasn't quite a trussed turkey, but it was close. "Tax? How we doing?" Paul turned his head slightly, keeping Beck's shoes in his peripheral vision.

She stood utterly still.

"One player under wraps," Tax replied. "Tucked in all nice and warm. But it looks like we're downrange."

You can say that again. Paul's throat was desert-dry. "You nervous?" If

Beck decided to shoot now. . . .

"Not really." The words bounced off metal locker faces; the speakers overhead started jabbering about *exits in an orderly fashion.*

From the noise on the concourse, nobody was listening.

"Good." Paul turned back, nice and slow, and let his gaze rise.

Beck stood, her head tilted slightly as if she'd just had a good idea for a complex, hilarious prank. The gun dangled in her right hand and her finger was now outside the guard, just as she'd been trained by her daddy on the range. She stared at the back of Joe's head; the deputy wasn't struggling now. Maybe he knew it was over, or maybe he was afraid his ex-wife was going to take a little payback.

I could just throttle him for you. I'd actually enjoy that. "Beck?" Nice and soft, that was the way to play it. "Baby, how are you doing?" If he didn't have two-hundred-plus pounds of dirty cop to hold down, he probably could have approached her, but maybe it was a blessing.

She still might take it into her pretty head to shoot *him*, and Tax would never let him live it down.

Her ribs heaved, deep jagged breaths. She gazed steadily at him then, instead of Joe, and she looked so lost and hopeless his entire chest squeezed in on itself.

Hard.

"I. . ." Beck swallowed, hard. "I think . . . I think I've had better weeks."

She folded down, slow and stiff, and laid the gun carefully on blue-flecked linoleum polished by thousands of hurrying footsteps. She winced as she straightened—it was a wonder she was still upright.

"Yeah." Paul held her gaze, willing her to stay with him. "The cops are gonna cuff us all until they sort this out. Just keep repeating you want a lawyer, okay?"

"Cops?" Her shoulders hunched, and she took two blundering steps backward. Maybe she had some idea of disappearing again, and if she bolted he was going to have to leave Joe to Tax's not-so-tender mercies and chase her down.

Instead, Beck backed across the connecting hall until she met the blank concrete face opposite the lockers. She stood, leaning hard and breathing heavily for a few moments, before sliding down to sit, drawing her knees up.

Beck hugged her legs, put her face against her knees, and began to weep in shuddering, soundless gasps.

Better, Easier

PAUL WAS RIGHT; they cuffed everyone. Dad had taught her how to get out of bracelets, of course, but there didn't seem any point. The thought that her father would be so ashamed of his daughter getting arrested kept circling her head, and each time, she flinched.

The worst of the sobbing had mostly finished by the time the cops found them. Her purse was taken away, so was her jacket, and the EMTs tried asking her questions. Beck just shook her head or stared into the distance, unfocusing the way she'd learned to when Joe was on a rampage and nothing she said or did would make any difference.

It seemed . . . better, that way. Easier.

The forums called it *disassociation*, which was a three-dollar word if she'd ever heard one. Eventually she was uncuffed and bustled onto a stretcher, then they put her in the back of an ambulance. Last of all there was a needle-sting on the inside of her arm, and she was lost in waves of deep sedative warmth even better than Tax's pain pills.

SHE SURFACED briefly in a deep hush broken only by a steady soft beeping paralleling her heartbeat. It was a heart monitor next to a hospital bed; Beck was on her back, staring at a ceiling made of acoustic tiles. Her left arm was cold, a saline drip on a tall silver pole feeding through a taped-down needle into her veins.

Why am I here? Of course, she'd been in a car accident, committed some breaking and entering, stolen another car, walked across town, and ended up discharging a weapon in a public place. It was a wonder she wasn't handcuffed to the bed. She'd deliberately aimed high, but the thought that the bullet could have ricocheted and hurt an innocent by-stander was a torment all its own.

Someone was humming, a soft wandering melody, and for a moment Beck was afraid it was Judge Nelson in the driver's seat. She shuddered, and the humming stopped.

"Beck?" It wasn't a man's voice, thank God.

Helena's face swam into focus above her. Greying hair pulled back, the cords on her neck standing out because she was bird-thin, the old woman smiled. Her dark eyes were deep and velvety.

"There you are." It wasn't Aunt Hel's usual brisk, authoritative tone. "You were in shock and they want to make sure you don't have a concussion. The doctor says you'll be confused and I should orient you. It's Tuesday—or Tuesday night, I guess. It's fine, it's all over. You're safe."

Beck's lips were chapped and cracked. It hurt to whisper, in her dry throat as well. "Hel?"

"Nope, Linlane General." Deep crow's-feet crinkled at the corners of Helena's eyes. "Though I'm told the food is even worse. Your father's stable, he woke up earlier today." The old lady's smile faded. "He's . . . honey, he gave a full confession. As soon as he's well enough, they're moving him to jail. He might be able to get a plea, Dreeson says."

It was ridiculous. Her father belonged in his cruiser or his office, not in *prison*. Then she remembered, and she wished the sedative heat would come back and drown her.

"Joe." Her voice cracked, just like her lips.

"Oh, he's not getting out of hock for a long damn time." Hel nodded for emphasis, and her eyes lit with a spark very like her nephew's—or Dreeson's, come to think of it. "You can rest easy on *that* account, honey. They picked up Dewey Johnson yesterday evening, too. Both of them held without bail, just like Bugs Nelson. Known that man most of my life; it just goes to show you never can tell."

Oh, God. Was there anything else she should ask about? Beck tried to think, but it was like swimming through hardening concrete. "Did . . . did anyone get . . . ?"

"Nobody was hurt, honey. Well, nobody but you." Helena's mouth tightened a little, and her dry, frail fingers patted the back of Beck's hand, cautiously avoiding the hep lock. "They say it's a wonder you were up and moving around."

So nobody got shot. Good. The relief was hot, instant, and scarily deep, but a fresh worry crowded behind it. "I'm so sorry," Beck whispered. "The reunion."

"What about it?" Now Hel looked baffled, and she switched to stroking the cotton shoulder of Beck's hospital johnnie as if soothing an anxious cat. Every stray feline for miles around knew the house near the H & H junkyard was good for a meal or two. "Jeannie and Mabel took over. Cousin Pep did the barbeque on Dreeson's grill, Gloria's so proud she could burst. Amalie Siddons is doing the cleanup and closing up the

Grange; the Barkers are having their reunion later this week and we'll never hear the end of it if she leaves so much as a dirty spoon."

"I ruined it." Beck could barely push the words out. "I thought nobody would notice. . . I'm sorry, Hel."

"We'll have a talk once you're better, Beck." Hel even managed to say it like she wasn't pronouncing sentence. "You're not in trouble. Bobby Barranie—remember him, Sal's son? Well, he's representing you free of charge, and he's pretty sure you might not even have to testify. But if you do, I'll be right there in that courtroom with you. You just rest easy."

How can I not be in trouble? The most important question trembled in her throat. "Paul."

"Probably asleep out in the waiting room; it took some doing for them to let *me* stay in here." Hel's mouth turned down, a brief rueful movement. "But he's all right, honey, and so is his friend. Don't you worry."

"Why did . . ." Her eyelids had decided that was enough, and were drifting back down. Maybe she was still medicated, after all.

"Just rest." Hel leaned over, and for the first time in a long time, someone pulled a blanket up a little higher, tucking Beck in. It reminded her of Dad, and a hot touch on her temple was a tear trickling on an unaccustomed path since she was propped on her back. "I'll be over here knitting. Go to sleep, Becca."

There was nothing else to do, so Beck obeyed.

A Little More Secure

"I AM *NOT ANGRY*," Helena repeated, holding up the hospital johnnie. She folded the blue-flowered fabric with swift efficiency; the resultant square package went on the foot of the bed. "I'm just telling you, young lady, that if you take off without telling anyone again, I might *get* that way."

Paul leaned against the wall near the door, his arms crossed. Tax was out in the waiting room, standing guard; there wasn't much danger now that everything was tied off but he was probably trying to make up for losing track of a green civilian.

Nobody else in the Squad knew he'd had his car stolen yet, and contemplating just who to tell first was a pleasant way of spending time while Paul waited for Beck to be fully discharged. It was like the Army—hurry up and wait until the paperwork's done.

"I wanted to make sure Joe didn't come after you." Beck's legs were still a little shaky, judging from the way she sank onto the chair near the window. The doctors had finally given the okay for her to go home, and she'd worried about the cost of the hospital stay aloud.

Hel had an answer for that one, bless her. Since the divorce hadn't been finalized Beck was still on Joe's police-union insurance, and it was a good plan. That was one worry shelved, but she obviously had masses of them waiting. Paul was looking forward to reassuring every single one of them away.

If she'd let him.

Helena had brought clothes for her, including a new pair of sneakers in her size—Tax's contribution, a peace offering or maybe a bribe to keep his buddy from spilling to the entire squad.

He had to know it was only a matter of time.

"I wish he would have," Hel grumbled. "I have a shotgun, you know."

Beck cast Paul an imploring glance. It was the first time she'd looked at him. Sunshine striped the bed; it was a nice bright spring morning, though rain hovered dark to the southwest.

He seized his chance. "Hel, you want to go ask the nurse about her meds?" They'd given Beck a full checkup and workout, including X-rays; no sign of concussion but it was best to be sure. "They said she can take some home."

Dehydration and contusions, they said, leaving out emotional trauma. *She's very lucky.*

"Oh, that's a good idea. I'll go do that." Hel bustled for her old leather purse, set on the counter. With it over her shoulder she was prepared for battle, and any nurse who got in her way could expect no mercy. "You stay right here with Paulie, Beck. I mean it, *right* where he can see you."

"I'm not a dog," Beck muttered, and it was glorious to hear the faint note of sarcasm. "Yes, Aunt Hel," she added hurriedly. "I promise."

"You keep her in sight." Hel's parting shot was directed at him, and it hit a bull's eye. She swept out the door, leaving them alone together.

It was about damn time.

The cops had released her embroidered bag; it sat on Beck's lap like an obedient terrier. She regarded him steadily, and finally, *finally* he had her to himself.

He just couldn't figure out where to start. "Uh." He cleared his throat. "Your dad's still in and out of consciousness, but I talked to the guards and to Bobby." Now *there* was a weird change in the fabric of Granite River—Bobby Barranie, all grown up in a suit and tie. "They'll let you in to see him."

Little snotnosed Cousin Bobby had made it through law school, and was representing Beck. She'd already given two taped depositions from the hospital bed, and Bobby was thinking he could keep her out of the courtroom even if the powers that be wanted to go over it again in an interrogation room.

Hearing the whole story almost made him sick. Even the bigger news outlets in the state were circling like hyenas; the cops were digging in Dewey's jump drives and having a field day, releasing little tidbits to make themselves look good. A hush-hush statie task force had been working from the other end for at least two years, stonewalled by Sheriff Sommers and his department as well as Granite River's natural inclination to keep town business quiet.

Whatever pull Uncle Dreeson had, it was keeping him and his nephew out of the papers. The staties would have probably liked to sweep Dreeson up for past offenses, but he'd gone legal years ago and also brought them a big fat payday in the form of Beck's cooperation, not to mention said nephew's as well.

The old man was more upset about missing his reunion barbeque than anything else, but Gloria's oldest had done a good job. Half the family had complained about his sauce, the other half vociferously defended his efforts, and it was a good thing the reunion was over, Spring Break nearly done, and extended clan members had gone home or were back at work.

"Oh." Beck nodded. "That's . . . that's good. Thank you." She took a deep breath. "We need to talk."

We sure as hell do. "Yeah. Look, Beck, I don't know how to—"

"Please." She held up a hand; a gauze bandage flashed white on her palm. Battered, bruised, and absolutely beautiful, she indicated the bed. "Can I go first?"

"Yeah. Of course." He hurried to perch gingerly, right where she'd pointed. Whatever she had to say, he had his own speech ready. He'd been practicing it in the waiting room—silently, of course.

No use in giving Tax any ammunition.

I don't know how to tell you this, so I'm just gonna say it. You're going to stay with Hel, and when I go back to New Mexico you're going with me. Or Dez will get my place packed and ship it up here. I'm not asking for anything—you just got out of something awful and you need time. So I'll wait as long as it takes, and if that's forever, then it's forever. But I am not leaving you, and by God, if you have any problem from here on out, I expect to be the first to know so I can fucking fix it.

The whole spiel needed work, but maybe he could get the gist across.

Beck hugged her purse, regarding him mournfully. "First of all, thank you. You could have gotten hurt. I'm sorry I didn't do what you told me to, and I'm so sorry I took Tax's car."

"Yeah, well, he says it's the most fun he's had in months. He likes to stay busy." Paul tried a grin, and was gratified when a slight smile crossed Beck's face.

It died almost instantly, though. "He's a good guy." She was pale again. "But really, Paul . . . I put both of you in danger. I'm so sorry."

"Uh, what exactly do you think I've been doing for years? This was—"

She hunched in the chair, and he shut up. Maybe once enough time had passed she'd lose that hunted, haunted look.

He wanted to be around when it left, and he'd stand guard to keep it away. For as long as it took.

"I also . . . Paul, I have to tell you something." She was pale again, and though the bruise on her cheek was yellowgreen now, the thorn-scrapes healing nicely, and the huge circles under her eyes had faded a little, she wasn't even close to out of the woods yet. "When you left—"

Don't. Please. That's history, we don't need it. "We already went over that, Beck. It wasn't your fault."

"Will you let me finish?" She didn't quite flinch after saying it, but she did tense, and he was suddenly sure challenging any interruption in Joe Halston's house had garnered swift punishment.

It was a good thing the asshole wasn't going to walk free. They had him tied to at least two murders—Dewey's boys—not to mention corruption and drug trafficking. When cop cars were doing the hauling, the meth got to where it needed to in a hurry. Plus there was the little matter of him shooting Sheriff Sommers, and a host of other things, including but not limited to a few counts of assault, battery, and attempted murder on Beck herself.

If Joe ever made parole Dreeson would let Paul know, and something a little more secure could be arranged. A nice hole, six feet deep.

Of course, Dewey had friends in prison, too, and cops had notoriously short life expectancies behind bars.

Finally, Beck spoke again. "I promised myself that I'd tell you, if I survived."

"You didn't think you would." He knew as much from Tax, of course, but hearing it from Beck herself was . . . well, he could tell the unsteady rage in his bones to back off a bit.

She was safe now. That was what mattered.

"No. But here we are." She took a deep breath. Sunlight glowed in her hair, and the bruises just highlighted how fine and soft her skin was. "The day you left for the Army, I was late."

For what? "Late?"

"You know." She shrugged, her eyebrows lifting significantly. "A whole month late. I looked at my calendar that morning and . . . well."

"Oh." *Oh, Jesus.* "Beck—"

"I didn't say anything because I didn't want it to seem like I was trapping you." All in a rush, and if she had been pale before she was nearly transparent now. "And then you were gone and you didn't call, didn't write . . . I had to, Paul."

"You had to what?" *Jesus in a sidecar, Beck.* He'd left her there to deal with it alone. It was a wonder she was even *speaking* to him now. He was goddamn lucky she hadn't turned around and fled screaming at the airport.

"I wasn't going to be a single mother in Granite River. I just wasn't." Now her words tumbled over each other, forestalling any interruption. "So I borrowed every cent I could and made an appointment. I told my dad I was going to Jenna Blackminton's overnight, and I drove up here to Eugene. I went to the Planned Parenthood and. . . ." She dropped her gaze, staring at her the bag in her lap, but something in the set of her shoulders told Paul she was painfully alert.

Ready to escape, if he so much as twitched wrong.

Say the right thing, Paul. For once in your fucking life, use that mouth of yours for something good, and do not *fuck this up.* "Oh, baby." He unfolded from the bed slowly, and it took way longer than he liked to step across the space between them.

He sank to his knees, and gathered her hands in his. Her fingers were icy; he rubbed a little, hoping to warm her up.

"I tried to sleep in my car, but . . . it's a little messy, afterward. I had to keep going into a Denny's restroom, because they're open all night, and I. . . ." She was shaking, again.

And I wasn't there. "I'm sorry. I should've come home and made. . . ." *Shut up. This isn't about you, dipshit.* "Must've scared the hell out of you. And you never told anyone."

Of course not. The girl knew how to keep a secret. It was a rare fucking talent, but then again, his Beck was one in a million. And of course, they both knew what being a single teen mother in Granite River would have been like, even for the sheriff's cherished daughter.

Beck shook her head. Tendrils of honey-highlighted hair fell in her face, but he didn't want to let go to brush them away. He held on, waiting while she searched his face.

Whatever she was looking for, he hoped like hell she'd find it.

"I can understand," she whispered. "If you don't . . . I mean, of course you're angry, and—"

"At myself. At your dad, too. Not you, for God's sake." Just thinking of how terrified and isolated she must have been made him want to go looking for a bareknuckle match or hell, maybe even going back to Dewey's no-name bar and burning the fucking place down just to destroy something.

Maybe he could even find out where Joe was at the moment. It wouldn't be the hardest op he'd ever pulled, and he suspected he'd have Tax's help.

"Are you sure?" Her hands were tense, curled tight. "I know how . . . how men get, with something like this."

If you only knew how sure I am. "If you're expecting me to get shitty with you over this, it's not going to happen. You did what you had to, end of story. I'm just angry you had to deal with any of it alone. I let you down, Beck, and I'm not going to do that ever again. But I am going to insist you stop with the vanishing acts, all right?" Christ, he wanted to grab her, kiss her breathless, and hold her for about the next thousand years.

Maybe a little longer. Like, a double K, or triple.

"I thought I could fix everything." Now she sounded mournful, but some warmth invaded her fingers, and they uncurled just a little. "But it's all just a mess."

"Yeah, well, I've seen worse." It was half a lie; even getting shot and put out to pasture was a cakewalk compared to that look on her face and how it turned him inside out. "But I'm here." *Years too late, and we'll never get that back. But oh well.*

It just meant he had to make the next decade as good as it could be, for her. And the one after that, and so on, until she was called to glory and he went wherever they stashed assholes like him after the final chow-bell. Maybe, if he did his best, Hel's blessed Jesus would throw him a bone and let him rest somewhere heaven-adjacent so Beck could visit every once in a while.

"Yeah." Her fingers loosened even more. "I'm sorry, Paul."

"For what? There's nothing to be sorry about." He searched for something, anything that might comfort her. "Actually, you did me a huge favor, stealing Tax's car. Now I have *great* blackmail material on him. I'm gonna need it."

Beck actually laughed. It was a short, forlorn sound, and died almost immediately.

Still, it was there, and Paul lifted her hands, pressing a kiss along her knuckles. It wasn't all he wanted, sure.

But it was a start.

Clean Conscience

NOT ONLY WERE there two staties guarding the door, but another trooper was inside her father's hospital room, a beefy dark-haired man with florid cheeks sitting in the single chair and paging through a brightly colored magazine. He glanced up sharply when Beck appeared, then rose in a hurry.

"His daughter," Paul said, quietly, his arm over Beck's shoulders. "Give them a few minutes?"

The trooper nodded and hurried out; Paul looked down at her. "I'll be right outside the door. Do *not* vanish."

"I solemnly swear not to Houdini," she replied. It was the sort of thing she might have said back in high school, and probably deeply inappropriate in a hospital room.

He grinned, kissed her lightly on the forehead, and retreated, pulling the door mostly closed. All without even looking at her father.

It was probably for the best.

Connor Sommers had shrunk. Her daddy, big as the pillars of the world, was now just an old man on a bleached bed, clear oxygen tubing under his nose, his stubble even more ferocious than during a camping trip. Other tubes carrying various liquids and medications hung from bags on shining metal poles. The side of his face was puffy and bruised—Hel said he'd hit the front walk pretty hard, gunned down by his own deputy right outside Beck's childhood home—and an edge of white gauze poked above the neckline of his hospital johnnie.

His eyes were open, and bloodshot. He regarded her warily.

It wasn't right for her father to look like this. Hel had brought Beck clean clothes, thank God, but by everything holy she and Dad both needed a real shower. The very idea sounded like heaven.

"Hi, Daddy." Beck's elbows trembled, cupped in her palms; she edged toward the bed. "Joe's in prison. They probably told you, though." She swallowed the urge to say *don't worry, he won't hurt you again.*

Dad's head moved, his greying hair scratching the pillow. The small sound was very loud, even with the heart monitor beeping steadily. The pulse was going strong, his heart ticking like a Timex.

"Becca." A hoarse, husky word. "You all right?"

I don't know. "I'm fine." How many times had she said that? "I'm discharged. Clean bill of health."

"That's good." A dry cricket-whisper. "Becca . . . honey, I'm sorry. I never meant you to find out."

I'm sorry too, Dad. "Is this why you wanted me to stay with Joe?" She'd told herself she wouldn't ask, she would just be calm and quiet, because he was her father and he had been *shot*, for God's sake.

But she couldn't help it. She had to know.

"Oh, pumpkin. No." He lifted his right hand, slowly; the left had a hep lock embedded, a plastic mosquito with a buried proboscis. It took him a while to scratch his cheek; the big strong hands that had taught her so much—how to shoot, how to cast a line, how to change an oil filter—were brittle, trembling claws now. "I just thought . . . you'd been together so long, I thought you'd regret. Throwing it away."

"I tried, Dad." *If you only knew how I tried.* "Really hard. It didn't make any difference."

"Yeah." His hand dropped back to the pale blue coverlet. "Sometimes life is like that."

"Is it because Mom left, and you didn't want me to . . ." *Why am I even asking?*

"Your mama missed out, Becca." His mouth drew down bitterly, but he didn't sound angry. Just tired. "Every day I woke up and was thankful to God she didn't take you with her." A little more of her father crept back into the tired shell lying on the bed. "But I'm not a good man. I never was, I suppose."

But you're my dad. You raised me. "You gotta have a clean conscience," she quoted.

It wasn't fair, and it seemed to hit Dad almost physically. "Do as I say. Not as I do." His eyes glittered, their lashes dark as hers. She had his cheekbones, and his feet, the second toe as long as the first. *Used to put it in statues,* he always said when they were barefoot. *Greeks thought it was real pretty.*

He shifted uncomfortably, and Beck found herself at the bedside. She slid her arm behind his shoulders, got the pillow situated just right, like when he had the liver trouble and couldn't sleep unless he was propped up.

"Pumpkin." Her father caught at her hand when she straightened. It was a feeble touch, and she could have shaken it away. "I knew you always wanted to get out of this goddamn town. I just . . . I couldn't. You married Joe and I thought you were home for good, so I . . . I never meant for any of this. I never, ever meant you to find out."

That was probably plain, unvarnished truth. Beck sniffed, heavily. *Don't cry, dammit. Not again.* "Would you ever have told me?"

"Honestly. . ." Dad sighed. "No, pumpkin. I don't think I would. Couldn't stand the thought of you lookin' at me like this."

"What about Judge Nelson?" He was in jail too, Hel said. Everyone in town was talking about the judge; Molly Mackenberg had even been heard to bemoan ever cleaning *that man's* house. "Did he get you into it? Did he make you—"

"Becca, sweetheart, I got into it myself. I'm sorry. You don't know how—I just, now I look back, and I see how you were trying to tell me Joe was hurtin' you. But you didn't want to hurt me, you were trying to do right, and I didn't listen. I did alla that, not you, not anyone else. Every single bit of this, I did myself." He sagged against the bed, deflating even further. "Suppose there is a God. I'll probably get religion in jail, Christ knows every sad sack does."

"Yeah, well." It was probably the first time in her life Connor Sommers was talking to his daughter like an adult stranger, and Beck wasn't sure she liked it. "We all do things to ourselves, Dad." *Just look at me.*

"Guess I just hoped I'd keep you from it." He blinked several times, and there was a suspicious gleam lingering on his lashes. "You know, let you learn from my mistakes."

Hard to do if I don't even know about them. There were voices near the door—someone asking a question, Paul replying.

"They say a plea might mean a lighter sentence." Beck patted her father's knuckles. How did his muscled, callused hand feel so breakable now, like the thin porcelain cups in Hel's china hutch? "If you cooperate, and tell them everything. Nobody asked me say anything to you about it, Dad, but. . . ."

"'Course not. They got me dead to rights, I might as well admit it." His face squinched briefly, like he was sucking on a lemon. "Beck, pumpkin . . . will you come visit me? Once in a while?"

I have to get out of this goddamn town. I've wanted out all my life. But maybe she could move to Portland, or Seattle.

Paul said something about his apartment in New Mexico, but she didn't want to think about that just yet. It was enough that he wasn't mad at her, that he seemed disposed to stick around.

Well, *disposed* was a weak way to put it. He seemed downright determined, and even if that was a gift Beck didn't deserve, she'd take it with both hands.

"I will," she said, softly. "And I'll write, and call." *At least there's that.* Cops had a hard time in prison, but maybe they'd take Dad's age into account. That was what plea bargains were for, right? "Just rest, and get better. Okay?"

"Yeah. Better." Dad closed his eyes. "I love you, Becca Jane."

Beck patted his left hand gently, avoiding the needle. "I love you too."

That, at least, was the absolute truth. And it hurt. She waited until his fingers loosened and her father slipped back into the twilight doze of the terribly injured.

Then she headed for the door, rubbing at her cheeks almost angrily until the tears vanished.

Partners In Crime

Three days later

TAX WANTED TO get on the road early; a misty spring dawn was turning the east red-gold and lighting a lowering grey sky.

"I can fill up your travel mug," Helena fussed. "Won't take but a minute, and that way you won't have to stop."

"It's all right, ma'am. I have any more java, I'll take off like a slick and just fly the rest of the way." Tax settled the last suitcase in the SUV's back, and nodded to Paul. In short order the car was closed up, and the black-haired man patted at his pockets. "Jesus, Beck, did you steal my keys again?"

"Leave my girl alone." Paul produced them with a jangle. "You asked me to open up your shiny new bit of conspicuous consumption, ya jerk. You just want to show off the thing."

"I want to see the thing," Beck piped up. A few nights of solid sleep in the guest bedroom had worked wonders, though she was still stiff and twinging in unexpected places; Tax flat-out refused to move from the bed in the annex and Paul settled on the couch in the living room each night.

Beck had the idea they wanted to cover all the exits in case she decided to sleepwalk. Or something.

"You want to see the thing?" Tax's eyebrows raised.

Helena made a small scoffing noise. "If I had a nickel for every time I've heard *that*. . . ."

"*Two* nickels," Paul said, the tagline of an old joke, and Tax looked mystified when all the locals laughed.

"All right, recruits," he said when the chuckles died down. Beck kept a hand over her mouth, hiding the smile; the habit would die hard.

But there was a lot more to feel cheerful about these days. She'd even considered switching salt and sugar before breakfast this morning just to get a rise out of Paul; he'd short-sheeted the bed in the annex yesterday and she'd agreed with Tax that it deserved a little payback.

Apparently the Army was as full of pranks as high school, only some of them weren't so good-natured.

Paul stepped close, the edge of his body heat touching hers. It felt good. Familiar, and . . . well, safe. It wasn't healthy to rush into anything after trauma or after the end of an abusive relationship, all the forums said so. Still, her marriage had been effectively over for a long goddamn time, and at least Paul didn't push. He was just . . . steady.

Like he used to be. It was a start.

"Behold this wonder of modern engineering," Tax intoned, and pressed a button on the chunky plastic head of the Honda's key. Beck hadn't even noticed it, and she'd driven the thing.

The car beeped, the lights flashed, the starter engaged, and the SUV's engine caught. It hummed happily, waking up for a long day of doing what it had been designed for.

"Would you look at that." Helena sounded flat-out impressed, and just the tiniest bit awed. "Shoulda asked for that on the Jeep. Any chance you can wire it in, Paulie?"

"I'll look at what it'll take." He squeezed Beck's shoulders, gently. "Hey, are you coming to Eugene with us today, Hel?"

Us. Each time he said it, Beck relaxed a fractional bit more. But her father was still in the hospital; there were complications. The law might not get its chance with Connor Sommers, and Beck didn't know how she was supposed to feel about that.

"Nah. I have knitting to do, and Gloria is bringing by some cake." Helena waved her burning Virginia Slim for emphasis, somehow expressing resignation and anticipation at once. Dreeson kept bugging her to get a vape. "She wants to gossip; I gather the reunion was unusually exciting this year."

Gloria probably wanted to get the dish on Beck, if there was any left. Mary had called, and studiously not mentioned the gossip or the fact that her cousin was still working at the coffee stall. Beck had let it be known she had no plans to ask for her old job back, though it would probably improve business for a while as everyone came to gawk.

The Klemperer-Siddons-Barranie reunion had been a raging success, even if overshadowed by other excitement. Hel and Uncle Dreeson both brushed aside her apologies.

Dreeson still scared her, though. Just maybe a little less.

"I'm gonna have to come back next year for the barbeque," Tax said. "If I'm invited."

"If you don't show up, I will send Paulie to hunt you down," Hel replied, and looked delighted when he kissed her leathery cheek. She retreated to the porch to crush out her smoke, waved, and disappeared into the house.

"You have my number," Tax said. "I expect you to use it, ma'am."

Beck nodded. She wasn't quite ready to offer a hug, so he gravely shook her hand.

"Not too often," Paul mock-growled. The male ritual of parting was accomplished with a handshake, a thump on the other man's shoulders, and a brief, hard squeeze impersonating a hug. "Tell Boom to expect us next month. We fly in the day before the wedding, already got the tickets."

Tax's laugh was warm, and deep. "He'll be thrilled. I get the idea he's worried his half of the church will be empty."

"A church?" Beck zipped up her hunting jacket; it was still chilly at night. "In Vegas? I mean, why that when you can get married by an Elvis impersonator?"

Both soldiers stared at her with something like horror. "That's. . . ." Paul looked at his friend. "That's actually a really good question, and I'm mad I didn't think of it first."

"And that's my cue to get going, before I hear something I shouldn't." Tax pointed at Paul. "You. Don't get shot. And you." It was Beck's turn next. "No stealing cars."

"No promises," she said, and was rewarded with a smile.

"Get the hell out of here, you miscreant." Paul waved him away. "Be safe."

"You too." Tax marched to his car, the driver's door slammed, and he even signaled the turn at the end of the driveway. The brake lights vanished, and then it was just the two of them.

Paul's arm slid over her shoulders. He didn't pinch or clamp down, just stood quietly, looking at the massive laurel hedge shielding Hel's house from the road.

"Do you really want me to go with you?" Beck finally asked.

"Huh?" He shook his head; the curls were softening now, falling in a messy halo like he was a teenager again. "I don't want to have to tie you up and stash you on a plane, Beck. If you don't want to go, what with your dad and all—"

"I do. I've always wanted to see Vegas." She had a whole month to get nervous about it now, too. Great. "And I've never been on a plane."

"You're gonna love it. Crying babies, someone kicking the back of your seat, airsickness—I'd add complaining about the meals, but they don't feed you on flights anymore." He paused, tucking his chin to gaze down at her. "I didn't know you liked Elvis impersonators."

"Maybe we can hire one. For the reception." Beck tilted her head back, regarding him steadily. "You know, surprise your friend, I'm sure he'll love it. We could even hire *more* than one."

"A gaggle of Elvises." Paul's grin widened. His eyes almost sparkled, and Beck thought it was very likely she wouldn't be able to stop herself from kissing him at some point in the not-too-distant future.

She didn't think he'd mind, either.

"A whole *flock* of Elvises," she agreed. "We could get into a lot of trouble in Vegas, you and me."

"I'm counting on it, babe." He leaned down, a shy sweet peck on her forehead, and Beck was surprised at the urge to grab him and demand a real one. No, it wouldn't be long at all; the long years with Joe felt like a bad dream.

But a vivid one. She shuddered, and his arm tightened—not enough to hurt, though.

Just enough to steady her.

"Come on," Paul continued, and there it was again, that soft, thoughtful voice he used just for her. "We should get on the road too. We can stop at the Pie Palace on the way back, surprise Hel with some banana creme."

"Great idea." Beck let him steer her for the house. Vegas could wait. A month was a long time for her right now; she didn't even know how she was going to handle the afternoon, let alone the next few days.

But she had help.

"Beck?" Paul paused, halfway to the steps. The hushed, dripping morning enfolded them both, a soft blanket. "I'm serious. I'm not leaving you again."

"You keep saying that." *I sound ungrateful.* "I mean—"

"I figure I should remind you. In case you need to hear it out loud."

I will not cry. I will absolutely not cry. "I think I do," she said, around the lump in her throat. "For a while, at least."

"Then I'm your man." He pulled her along, taking small steps so she could keep up, and only let go of her at the porch stairs. "Come on, Hel will yell at me if you catch a cold."

"That's not how colds work." But she climbed the steps anyway, and a bright idea occurred to her halfway to the door. "Hey, Paul. . . ."

He turned from watching the end of the driveway as if he suspected Tax would reappear. "What?"

Beck couldn't help but smile. "How does your good buddy Tax feel about mariachi bands?"

"Jesus, woman." But he was grinning too, and he shook his head like he used to when she suggested a good bit of mischief. "You're ruthless. I love it."

"You and me." Beck held her hand out, as if they were in middle school. "Partners in crime? Again, I mean?"

Paul had turned serious once more. He was doing that a lot lately, and she got a little breathless each time. He lifted her fingers, kissed her knuckles, and good God, the man was dangerous to her pulse.

He always had been.

"As long as you'll have me," he said.

finis

Biography

"LILITH SAINTCROW lives in Vancouver, Washington, with her children, dogs, cat, a library for wayward texts, and assorted other strays."

CPSIA information can be obtained
at www.ICGtesting.com
Printed in the USA
BVHW071730011122
650804BV00002B/137

9 781610 261845